D0457761

MVFOL

DRY BONES

DRY
BONES
PETER QUINN

OVERLOOK DUCKWORTH
NEW YORK • LONDON

This edition first published in hardcover in the United States and the
United Kingdom in 2013 by Overlook Duckworth, Peter Mayer Publishers, Inc.

NEW YORK
141 Wooster Street
New York, NY 10012
www.overlookpress.com
For bulk and special sales, please contact sales@overlookny.com,
or write us at the above address

LONDON
30 Calvin Street
London E1 6NW
info@duckworth-publishers.co.uk
www.ducknet.co.uk
For bulk and special sales, please contact sales@duckworth-publishers.co.uk,
or write to the above address

Cataloging-in-Publication Data is available from the Library of Congress

Book design and typeformatting by Bernard Schleifer

Manufactured in the United States of America
FIRST EDITION
1 3 5 7 9 10 8 6 4 2

ISBN US: 978-1-4683-0736-8
ISBN UK: 978-0-7156-4739-4

For Margaret and Bill

In memory of Michael Hanlon

Part I
Under the Apple Tree

DEM DRY BONES

Ezekiel cried, "Dem dry bones!"
Oh hear the word of the Lord.
Oh those bones, oh those bones,
Oh those skeleton bones!

With the toe bone connected
To the foot bone,
And the foot bone connected
To the anklebone,
And the anklebone connected
To the leg bone!

Ezekiel cried, "Dem dry bones!"
Oh those bones, oh those bones,
Oh those skeleton bones.
Oh those bones, oh those bones,
Oh mercy how they scare!

Ezekiel cried, "Dem dry bones!"
With the leg bone connected
To the knee bone,
And the knee bone connected
To the thigh bone,
And the thigh bone connected
To the hip bone.
Oh mercy how they scare!

Dem bones, dem bones gonna walk aroun'
Dem bones, dem bones gonna walk aroun'
Dem bones, dem bones gonna walk aroun'
Oh hear the word of the Lord!

January 1946

NUREMBERG, GERMANY

THE PLANE IDLED ON THE RUNWAY OUTSIDE LONDON, CO-PILOT IN HIS seat but no pilot. Rain splattered intermittently against the window, droplets sliding into one another, plump, plumper, streaming down the glass, vanishing. They had their own momentum. So did time. Days dragged, drip, drip, gathered speed. Years hurtled past, going, gone.

A year since the first meeting with Dick Van Hull in the Drummond Hotel .

Ten months since V-E Day. *Time, gentlemen. Time.*

Two months since Turlough Bassante's call.

Pieces of the puzzle put together. Revelations and connections. The way they fit: *Toe bone connected to the foot bone, Oh those bones, Oh those bones, Oh mercy how they scare.* Dry bones everywhere. Call it Niskolczi's Law: "This world of ours, seemingly so vast, often turns out to be quite small."

The pilot arrived a few minutes later. Red-white-and-blue eyeballs and a phony grin punctuated his puffy, hungover face. Fintan Dunne thought he recognized him as one of the late arrivals at Bud Mulholland's recent Christmas party. But if the pilot recognized Dunne, his sole passenger, he gave no sign. He slouched into the cockpit. "War's over," he muttered, answering a question that hadn't been asked. "In case you haven't heard."

9

By the time they took off for Prague, the weather had gone from threatening to distressing. Pilot and copilot bantered about their latest sexual escapades and the enthusiastic acrobatics of the limey nurses they'd bedded the last several days. "Rule, Britannia, I love, love ya always," crooned the younger one, the copilot, who sounded New York Italian and looked all of about nineteen. "Britannia is a great, great lay."

The wind tossed and rocked the stripped-down, reconfigured Lockheed Electra. Relegated to taxi flights ordered up on short notice by the military brass, it looked ready to join the military aircraft spewed out by the arsenal of democracy and now destined to be discarded on the waste pile of peacetime, sold for scrap, or resold and reincarnated as a workhorse for some small-time, short-hop, five-and-dime airline.

The pilot laughed. Older than his copilot by at least a decade, he seemed to enjoy the buffeting they'd taken since leaving London, potential payback for the annoying assignment of being roused from bed to ferry a single ground-hugger who, with any luck, would soon be puking his guts out.

"They sent us up with half a tank, and battling these headwinds has eaten up what we had," he shouted. He pointed amid a crescent of fluorescent dials at a red arrow resting on *E.* "No way in hell we're going to make it to Prague. This is as far as we go tonight."

Dunne tapped him on the shoulder. He lifted the radio headset from one ear, turned once more. Dunne put his mouth close to uncovered ear. "Where are we?"

"Nuremberg. Down there somewhere." His face was bathed in the instrument panel's weird emerald glow. "Airport's too crowded. We're being directed to the parade grounds, where Hitler hosted those Nazi shindigs. We'll land on the military road. Been doubling as a runway, what with all the air traffic in and out of Nuremberg. Make sure you're strapped in."

Gray-black clouds churned and swarmed through the shaft of light the plane threw ahead. The interior had the claustrophobic feel of a tank or submarine. It was impossible to see any ground lights or trace of the devastation more than half a decade of war had unloaded on cities and towns, visiting a special fury on the ambitions and inhabitants of the once-invincible Reich.

The copilot eyed the red arrow, now nestled on *E*. "I don't see the road." The jovial edge was gone from his voice.

The plane began its descent. A moment later, the pilot pointed at parallel lines of lights visible on the ground. "I told you we were near."

The plane banked right, nose down, descent steepened. Familiar, unwelcome sinking sensation filled Dunne's stomach. The plane hit the runway hard, *bang*, bounced up, came down, *bang*, skidded side to side, almost out of control, until, an instant later, it steadied itself, rolled ahead, wheels rumbling and thumping over the spaces between the giant granite paving blocks the Nazi architects had intended as a permanent parade route for the Wehrmacht to strut in annual celebration of the Third Reich's final triumph. It slowly taxied to a stop.

Dunne reached down and swiped his sweaty palms on the canvas seat covering.

The pilot switched off the motors and turned unsoured puss to Dunne. "Welcome to Nuremberg, Captain. Or what's left of it. The RAF gave it a proper pasting back in March." He took pipe and tobacco pouch from the pocket of his flight jacket. "Three hundred planes, mostly Lancasters, and an escort of Mosquitos. Leveled it in a night. I've radioed ahead to have a jeep pick you up. Quarters are tight. But they'll find you something. We'll see how things are in the morning."

He scooped tobacco from the pouch with the bowl of the pipe, pressed it with his thumb. "Be careful," he said when the door was opened. "It's wet and slippery out there." Tight, artificial, up-yours grin reiterated the contempt he'd spit into his radio when the flight controller in London had tried to cancel their departure because of the weather.

It was an attitude Dunne found irritating as well as inane, as if mortality itself stopped with the German surrender and death could only be delivered by bombs, bullets, and flak from AA guns. But the pilot's confidence hadn't been misplaced—at least not entirely, they'd made it well more than halfway—and he obviously enjoyed reiterating his disdain for the flight controller's timorous warning.

Dunne ignored the wise-guy intonation. Lesson of two wars: Though death was disquietingly random, unpredictable, unfair, it nursed a special predilection for those who thought themselves immune. Night sky over Germany: Vortex of wind and rain rather than flak. But the flyboys might soon find themselves face-to-face with the infinite incarnations in which death greets and embraces victor and vanquished alike.

"Don't worry about me." Dunne took hold of the railing on the roll-away steps. A lesson learned the hard way. Night. Ice. Tumble down a hillside, not knowing where it would end. He tapped his toe to make sure there was no ice on the stairs. "I'm always careful."

A jeep pulled up at the bottom of the stairs. One hand on the wheel, the driver stretched across the seat. The passenger door swung open.

"Colonel Dunne?"

"Captain."

"Good enough, sir. Get in." Pudgy, just south of fat, the driver had broad shoulders that strained against an overcoat a size too small. There were two stripes on the sleeve. "Captains need to get out of the rain same as colonels. I'm Corporal Mundy. Harry Mundy. My orders are to get you to your quarters."

Dunne got in, removed his cap, shook the water from it.

"Be right back," Corporal Mundy said. "Got to get your gear aboard."

"Just a duffel bag." A droplet struck Dunne's cheek. He put his hat back on, reached up, fingered a small rip in the canvas roof. The jeep's interior reeked with musty mix of wet canvas, tobacco, and motor oil; acrid trace of spent ammunition and explosives. Rear seat was stuffed to the roof with cardboard cartons.

Corporal Mundy pulled open Dunne's door. The lashing, sideways rain was unremitting. Mundy was hunched over. He hugged the duffel bag. "Mind keeping this on your lap, Captain? Only a short ride." He gestured with his head at the rear seat. "Afraid there's no room back there."

"Give it here." Dunne stacked the bag on his lap. His mission to Prague was scheduled to be short. The bag was full but not overstuffed.

Mundy scooted around, hopped in the driver's seat, flipped down the collar of his coat, and sprayed water in every direction. "Sorry about the squeeze." He stepped on the gas pedal. Tires slipped and squealed before getting traction. Dunne was jolted back into his seat. Mundy made a hard right. From the inner pocket of his coat, he plucked a pack of cigarettes, jiggled it so that several stuck out, clasped one in his lips, and extended the pack to Dunne. "Smoke?"

"Thanks." Dunne lifted out a cigarette.

"Daytime, I'd offer a grand tour of the grounds. Krauts laid it out like a regular World's Fair. Over there, when the war started, they built a POW stalag on the grounds of the storm troopers' camp." At the end of the granite road, Mundy made a left. "This you got to see." The headlights played across an empty field. "The Zeppelin Field."

He put the gear in reverse and backed up so the beams fell on an immense stone wall. Craning his neck over the steering wheel, Mundy almost touched the windshield with his face. "That's the marble soapbox where Hitler did his spouting." The wipers barely kept up with the incessant rain. "In daylight you can still see the outline of where the swastika was."

Dunne leaned over the duffel bag, glanced up. The podium loomed above. Behind, two massive flanking colonnades were dimly visible.

"Up top was that fifty-foot brass swastika that the boys of the Seventh Army blew to smithereens soon as they took the city. You must've seen the newsreel." Mundy peered up into the dark. "Can't imagine what this must have been like in person. I mean, with thousands of people packed in, torches, flags, them search-lights surrounding the place like pillars of ice, must've been some-thing." Mundy held out his lighter.

Dunne dragged on the cigarette. Eight summers ago, hot, close day in an apartment in Yorkville, he'd listened on the radio to the speech Hitler delivered here—his last from this podium, as it turned out. It was the height of the crisis that Hitler provoked over Czechoslovakia and the fate of the Sudetenland. Distant, unfamiliar places. How many Americans had even heard of the Sudetenland before the crisis arose?

The ranting, high-pitched, angry voice, reinforced by ocean-like choruses of *sieg heil*, *heil Hitler*, needed no translation. The intent carried clear across the Atlantic.

Seven summers ago and 3,500 miles away.

A distance measured in gutted cities, wounded, crippled lives, soul-scarred survivors, and the dead, the endless piles of dead. Shot, bombarded, stabbed, starved, gassed. The dead you saw and learned to act as if you didn't. Those you tried not to think about, butchered, half-burned, derelict corpses. The dead you watched die, some instantly, others in slow, moaning agony. The dead you knew. Friends. Some buried, parachute for shroud, or pounded into pulp, or blown into a fine crimson grit of flesh and bone, nothing to inter. Ghosts.

Remembered names and faces prompted a short prayer, part mental hiccup, part heartfelt: *Eternal rest grant unto them, O Lord, and let perpetual light shine upon them.*

"I feel bad I missed it." Mundy rested his forearms on the steering wheel.

"The rally?"

"No, Captain. The big show. The war. Seems a waste to go through training and get to Germany the day before the Krauts toss in the towel."

The drip, drip on Dunne's cap turned steady trickle. Peter Bunde's wish, too. Not to miss the big show. *Perpetual light on him, too.*

Mundy reached up and covered the tear in the jeep's canvas top with his hand. "Sorry about that, sir," he said. "I would've stuck some adhesive tape over it if I knew I was going to have a passenger. But I wasn't told till the last minute. Nobody cares about the condition of these motor pool jalopies."

"I'm glad for the ride."

Mundy plucked a crumpled handkerchief from his pocket and tucked it in the leak. "That should do for now, at least till we get where we're going."

"Where's that?"

"The town is filled up, what with the trial and everything. Your lodgings are north of the city. Used to be an SS retreat. Nice digs."

"How far?"

"Depends."

"On what?"

"Which route we take."

"What's the choice?"

"Express or local. Express will get us there in no time."

"And local?"

Mundy jerked his thumb at the pile of boxes in the rear seat. "No telling."

"Hooch, chocolate, cigarettes?"

"Yes, sir. Nylons, too. All on the up-and-up. I'm head driver for the motor pool. Officers, enlisted men, anyone for whatever reason, night or day—they need a lift? Call Harry Mundy. That includes the guys in the PX. For a reasonable fare, I'm your man."

"Business must be good."

"Like being the Good Humor Man in a heat wave. When I got here, Nuremberg seemed nothing but a burned-out shit pile. Except the Krauts are crawling back. Say what you want about them, and I know what they done, there's no keeping them down. Dead as the city seems above, below there are bars, clubs, and the fräuleins. You can't believe the fräuleins. Their men are dead, missing, or POWs, but they feel lucky they got us instead of the Russkies grabbing them by the hair and banging the bejesus out of them whenever they get the urge. Throw in a bottle of scotch, pair of nylons, it's whatever you want."

"I appreciate the offer, Corporal. But it's been a long day."

"Yes, sir. Express it is." Mundy pushed open the side window flap, tossed his cigarette, and put the jeep in gear. This time Dunne was ready, bracing himself against the dashboard as Mundy hit the gas pedal. "I'll have you there in no time, Captain."

As they neared the city, the dull, indistinct, nightmarish landscape of ruined buildings and half-standing structures was occasionally spotlighted by an odd-standing street lamp. Though on a grander scale, the thoroughness of the destruction reminded Dunne of villages in France during the fight before this one, the War to End All Wars, which only prepared the way for round two. Despite all the glamour that surrounded the escapades of commandos and special operations, here's how the contest was finally won: One side bludgeoned the brains out of the other with the biggest cudgel available.

"Guess you seen your fair share," Mundy said.

"Fair share?"

"Of the war."

Dunne tapped his cigarette, dropped ash into palm. Fair or unfair? More than his share? Who could say for sure? "I guess."

"Don't worry about the ashes." Mundy grinned. "Like I said, nobody cares about these jalopies." He pointed at a gigantic mound of bricks, concrete, wire lathe. "Don't let that facade fool you," he explained. The cavernous basement beneath housed an improvised beer hall, long tables, and—*ah, ahh, ahhh* (Mundy did a comic imitation of a man about to climax)—fräuleins, oodles of them, not like those cold-fish British broads (he obviously hadn't met the English nurses the pilots boasted about cavorting with) or skinny-malink Frenchies—but full-bodied women, busty, lusty, and hungry for it.

Behind the beer hall, Mundy explained, was a warren of windowless bedrooms with Oriental rugs, canopied beds, gilt-framed paintings. Impromptu liaisons of occupied and occupiers. Place ran twenty-four hours a day. The same scratched records played over and over on the Victrola, nonpartisan mix of "Lili Marlene" and "Don't Sit Under the Apple Tree." Sometimes, if you were there long enough, it was easy to lose track whether it was night or day.

Before they landed in Germany, they got strict orders about nonfraternization. Most of the Heinies, they were told, were still in the grip of Nazi indoctrination. "But you know what, Captain? That's all malarkey, least as far as the girls go. They got one thing on their mind." Mundy cupped his crotch with one hand, tapped the horn on the steering wheel with the heel of the other. *Honk, honk.* "At one point, the brass got it in their heads the Commies were recruiting a regiment of whores to pump military secrets out of GIs. They made it so you want to bring a girl into a GI club, which is where they all want to go, the local police got to certify she's a regular Rebecca of Sunnybrook Farm. That's great for whoever's doing the certifying. Means they get laid all they want. It also means the illegal joints doing more business than ever."

Two young women, sharing a single umbrella, stood Lili Marlene–like in the piss-yellow light pooled beneath a surviving street lamp. They waved vigorously. "See, what'd I tell you?"

Honk. "When it comes to the fräuleins, it's *Deutschland über alles.* As the Brits are fond of saying, 'It's only fraternization if you stay for breakfast.'"

The rain stopped. Dunne was glad for the enthusiasm and boyish innocence of Mundy's monologue. If this war was like the last, those who'd puked their guts, or pissed their pants at that last minute before they went into action, or turned away from the pulverized carnage a single artillery round left behind, they'd treat their memories like tattered photo albums in attic recesses; throw them out once and for all, if they could.

But they couldn't.

After a few drinks in a crowded, happy bar, the sudden flash of a charred corpse, top of its head blown off, motionless hand protecting absent eyes. Or on a calm summer's afternoon, face of approaching stranger turns into Quentin Osbourne's, Billy Coughlin's, a kaleidoscope of the dead and missing. Or in the middle of the night, palm protecting against the flashlight's beam, the barrel of an MP 40 submachine gun—the German Schmeisser—knocks your hand away. Nozzle to nose. Smell of expended rounds still fresh.

Fin, wake up, you're having a bad dream.

Not really dreaming. Remembering, mostly.

Those who lost all control and ended up with haunted faces were secluded in mental wards of veterans' hospitals, some a short time, a few permanently. Most carried on, did the best they could, moved in sync with the unwounded, unscarred, uninitiated.

Mundy began to hum a tune that Dunne recognized immediately. *Heigh-ho, heigh-ho.* He'd seen the cartoon movie the year before he met Roberta. The woman he was dating at the time dragged him to see it.

First name he remembered: Maria.

Her last: . . . ?

Irish-Italian from the Bronx, she worked at the phone company and was taking courses at Hunter College at night. She brought along

a bag of a half-dozen licorice wheels from Krum's, on the Grand
Concourse. "Walt Disney isn't just a cartoonist," she said. "He's an
artist." When he finished his share of the licorice, he fell asleep and
began to snore. She poked her bony elbow hard into his ribs.

Snow White's gaggle of midgets was in midsong.

Heigh-ho, heigh-ho, it's off to work we go.

The next time she jabbed him awake, the wicked witch or
spiteful stepmother or evil queen—whoever she was—was asking,
"Mirror, mirror on the wall, who's the fairest of them all?" He
managed to keep his eyes open for the rest of the movie, which
didn't placate her. Standing outside the theater, she was awash in
the lights from the marquee. Olive skin aglow. A face he'd never
forget. He kissed her on the cheek.

She shook his hand, hailed a cab, and was gone. *Heigh-ho.*

He never saw her again. Things worked out better for Snow
White and her pint-size fan club. *And they lived happily ever after.*

Corporal Harry Mundy and his fortunate cohort seemed destined to enjoy the same fate: Honor of having gone overseas, good
luck of having arrived as the guns went dumb. A lamb in wolf's
clothing, civilian disguised as soldier, willing to share with an officer he'd never met the details of trafficking in contraband and
German girls—Mundy's war was over, for sure.

Heil Harry Mundy, harbinger of peacetime and its pleasures.

Heil Corporal Mundy, messenger of a world on the mend,
stirring beneath dirt, dust, ashes, like first blades of grass in early
spring.

Heigh-ho, heigh-ho, it's home from war we go.

"Where are you from in the States, Corporal?" Dunne asked.

"Hastings, just above Yonkers. You're from New York, too,
sir, aren't you?"

"Good guess."

"Easy. Been around a lot of Southern crackers. You hear
somebody talk normal, you zero in right away. And you got none

of that snooty attitude like the college types. Picked that up right away, too. You live in the city?"

"With the exception of two all-expenses-paid trips to Europe, compliments of Uncle Sam, lived there all my life."

Mundy chuckled. "'All expenses paid,' that's a good one, Captain. I got to remember it." He drove fast but confidently, speeding through ink-dark streets with apparent certainty about where they were headed. "You were in the first war, too? You must've been a kid when you joined up."

"Close." Sixteen. Lied and said he was eighteen. Didn't know what he was signing up for. What kid did? Thought he was tough, fearless, all grown up, nothing left to learn. Like all those other kids—the ones who survived—he learned differently. All grown up when it was over. And glad to be alive.

The jeep braked to a stop. Chest pressed against the duffel bag, Dunne sat back, cracked the door, dropped cigarette on wet pavement. "What's the problem?"

"Damn streets all look alike. The RAF blew up the signs along with the streets. Hard to know where you are. Sorry, but I think I took a wrong turn back there." He shifted into reverse, made a quick three-point turn, and headed back in the direction they'd come. "Between that war and this, you pretty much seen it all, I guess."

"Enough."

"Wish I could say the same." Mundy steered in a tight half-circle around the ruins of what looked to have been a fountain or a monument. "Don't get me wrong. I've had my jollies here in Nuremberg. Still, I'll be glad to get home. Not to brag, but I got a girl *and* a job waiting for me. Don't know a lot of GIs who can claim that, do you, Major?" He stopped again.

Dunne ignored the promotion Mundy conferred. Another sure sign the war was over when enlisted men were so inattentive to an officer's rank. "Are we lost?"

"No, sir. Should've gone right instead of left." He continued talking as he completed the circle. Theresa, his girl, worked same place he did, Anaconda Wire and Cable. Supplied most of the wire for the Northeast's telephones. Two years ago, the plant won an Army-Navy E pennant for excellence in supplying the military. Steady work, good pay, and as long as civilians and the military needed telephones and communications equipment, there was no need to worry about a job.

"Theresa's last name is Kelly." Mundy glanced over. "Don't get me wrong, I know plenty of Irish who are regular as cornflakes. Theresa's family ain't among them. They know Mundy used to be Mundowski. They go to St. Matthew's. Don't want their daughter marrying a Polack from St. Stanislaus who didn't graduate high school. But she's as stuck on me as me on her. Soon as I get home, I'll go after that diploma, and we'll get hitched."

Mundy hit the gas, then slowed down. A bent but still standing street lamp glistened on rain-glossed cobblestones. "This is the old part of the city. Or was." A truck followed closely behind.

Both sides of the street were lined with ugly heaps of broken, blackened masonry and debris piled atop furniture, lamps, china plates, toys, mementos, souvenirs, porcelain figurines—a graveyard for the thirty thousand people entombed beneath, the innocent with the guilty. Ancient or new, eloquent medieval Gothic or plainspoken military modern, one mute testament to the consequences of the war their führer had insisted on: *Deutschland unter alles.*

"I'll have you where you're supposed to be in a few minutes or so."

"Sure thing," Dunne said. The truck was gone.

Except where he was supposed to be was Prague. A simple mission, at least that's the way Bassante had made it seem. Collect the microfiche that contained Dr. Schaefer's archive. Bring it back to London, and Bassante would take it from there. Now this delay in Nuremberg. Nothing was ever simple, was it? *The best-laid plans gang aft agley.*

Time to go home. File this war with the one before, best you could. Yet he couldn't say no to this final piece of business. An acknowledgment of the debt he owed Dick Van Hull. A way to honor Dr. Niskolczi and those others. A farewell to the now-defunct Office of Strategic Services and its founder and chief, General Donovan, whom President Truman had summarily dismissed when he disbanded the OSS barely a month after Japan's surrender.

On hearing the news, Dunne had felt bad for Donovan. He deserved better than an unceremonious shove out the door. But he wasn't the first and wouldn't be the last. That was how the game would always be played. "You want a true friend in Washington," the new president was reported as saying, "buy a dog."

Mundy talked enthusiastically about his postwar plans. Theresa wanted six kids. Four would be fine by him. And a house, maybe on Long Island, near those leafy, easily traveled parkways where land was cheap. Get one of the new-model cars that would soon be rolling off the assembly lines and filling the showrooms. No more jalopies for Harry.

They entered a narrow street. A heavy truck barreled toward them. "Hey, watch it!" Dunne exclaimed.

"Don't worry, Captain." Mundy hit the accelerator. The two vehicles raced past each other, barely an inch of space between them. "Takes a real asshole to think he's gonna win a game of chicken with Harry Mundy."

Dunne asked: "Are we getting close?" Left unasked: *Who's the asshole when a jeep plays chicken with a truck?*

"Not to worry, Captain. Once we're outta here, it's a straight shot." Mundy went on about the weather, brutally cold until the temperature shot up and the rains came, but it was all temporary. Next week it would be Siberia all over, wind and snow, mercury at zero. "No doubt about it," he said. "Can't have a war like we just had and throw all that crap into the atmosphere and not affect the weather. Simple as two plus two." He turned onto a better-lit but even narrower street. A battered white-on-black sign hung askew on the side of the corner building: *Einbahnstrasse.*

A German phrase Dunne was familiar with: *One-way street.*

What followed was a slow-motion mix of sights (inexorable approach of headlamps, nearer, brighter, larger, blurring into single spotlight), repeated cries (*Oh shit!* Was that Mundy's solo? More likely a spontaneous, desperate duet), sounds (anguished *s-s-s-p-putter* of rubber tires' reluctant slide across wet cobblestones, shatter of glass, *clonk* of metal, hollow *womph* of steering column entering Mundy's chest, his explosive guttural gasp, *gahhh*).

Are you dead?

Only way to know for sure, push upward, out of thoughtless sleep toward wavering, uncertain light.

Look. Listen. Above all, heed Bassante's advice: Pay attention.

Sight: Shadows, Blaue Engel? Blaue Teufel? Smell: Whiff of bay rum? Thought: A single one—tailbone connected to the ankle bone—*comes and goes.*

Is someone there?

Face wavers above, mirage-like, slowly comes into focus, lovely face, hair swept up beneath a white cap shaped like a dove.

Angel or nurse?

"Where am I?" *Hears his own voice: cracked, moistureless croak.*

"In hospital."

Murmured directly in his ear, so close it tickles.

"Captain Dunne, whoever had you hold that duffel bag in your lap did you the biggest favor of your life."

Others did favors of equal magnitude. Dick Van Hull for one.

"How's Mundy?"

"Who?"

"The driver."

The dove-shaped cap wiggles side to side. "Oh, I'm sorry . . ."

Poor Harry.

Darkness again. Victrola-voiced Western Union messenger clears his throat and sings (chants, really, as if intoning the "Lacrimosa" from Mozart's Requiem in D Minor) a telegram for Miss Theresa Kelly:

The War Department and the President
regret to inform ye
Corporal Mundy won't be sitting
under the apple tree with anyone else or thee.
Eternal rest grant unto him, O Lord,
and let perpetual light shine upon Harry.

Part II
Operation Maxwell

FORM A-T 3127. OSS   **DATE:** September 15, 1944

NAME: Bassante, Turlough A.

RANK: Major (R&A)

SERIAL NUMBER: 067812647

REQUEST: Transfer (SO)   **DETERMINATION:** Denied (11/3/44)

BACKGROUND INFORMATION (150 words or less): My mother was an O'Donnell, an Ulster Catholic, from Belfast; my father, a Waldensian—an Italian Protestant from Turin. It was an interesting if not an irenic marriage. (They met in that center of cosmopolitan sophistication, Hoboken, New Jersey.) My father worked as a steward on the old Lloyd Sabaudo shipping line. My mother was a laundress. They had nine children. Six lived into adulthood. One Jesuit and one policeman (the same profession, really, just different uniforms). Two of the daughters are married, with a dozen or so progeny between them. The third, married to a Jew, is a childless school principal in Brooklyn. And then there's *moi*. A conundrum to my parents. Child agnostic. Rejected a scholarship to St. Peter's Prep. Insisted on attending public high school.

EDUCATION: Scholarship to Yale. Majored in German. Minored in history. Tutored in Slavic languages. (Why Slavic languages? I wish I knew. But other than a taste for the exotic, I'm unsure why.) Encouraged by the Depression to seek government work, successfully sought admission to the Foreign Service School.

CAREER: The Foreign Service. Posted at various times to Vienna, Prague, Warsaw, and Moscow. Recalled to London in June 1941, when the

Germans launched Operation Barbarossa against the Soviet Union. Asked for a transfer to the OSS in the summer of 1942. My superiors were unhappy with the request, regarding the OSS as an upstart outlier intent on poaching upon the traditional prerogatives of the Department of State. Their objections were overridden at the insistence of General Donovan, to whom I'd addressed a personal appeal. He insisted the State Department enjoyed a surfeit of linguists (in fact, the opposite was true— the Department's lack of truly capable linguists was shocking) while the OSS was sorely lacking (which was true), especially in the field. With the backing of the Joint Chiefs of Staff, General Donovan got his way, and I set off in the expectation of leaving desk work behind to take personal part in assaulting and subverting the Nazi sway over Europe. Instead, I was assigned to the Research & Analysis (R&A) in Bari, here to toil over briefing materials for presentation to operatives leaving for the field. The frustrations of this work are legion. Greatest of all is the direct contravention of the promise made me upon joining the OSS—i.e., that I would participate in the penetration of Occupied Europe, serving on missions to be undertaken behind enemy lines. I request to be assigned to Special Operations (SO), a position I was assured of upon enlistment into the OSS.

January 1945

THE SUMMONS TO GENERAL DONOVAN'S HEADQUARTERS WAS UNEX-pected. Dunne had suspected—or, more accurately, hoped—that the younger, more gung ho OSS agents were at the head of the list for what were clearly the last clandestine assignments before the war's end. Yet the brevity and bluntness of Donovan's summons conveyed a sense of urgency.

The exuberance engendered by the city's liberation the previous summer was absent from the gloomy, wintry streets. As he passed through the lobby of the Hôtel Ritz, Dunne noticed Donovan's head of press relations, Lieutenant Colonel Carlton Baxter Bartlett, in the bar off to the right. He was holding court amid a semicircle of officers.

A trim, taciturn sergeant escorted Dunne down the heavily carpeted hallway to Donovan's office. He pointed to an elegant, gold-leafed, bowlegged chair pushed against the wall. "Have a seat. The general will see you when he's ready." The sergeant planted himself behind his desk and pecked away with two fingers at an ancient-looking typewriter.

The last time Dunne had seen Donovan was the previous spring in London, several weeks before the invasion. The general had sent a note asking to see him. It turned out to be a casual meeting. Instead of sitting inside, they took a walk and enjoyed the spring weather. Donovan did most of the talking—not about what was ahead but the last war, boys of the 69th, especially those who didn't make it back. "I'm sure we'll be successful," he said, without specifying at what. "The question is what price we'll pay."

Near the Houses of Parliament, he had a car waiting. He had the driver take their picture. It all seemed planned. A few days later, a print was delivered to Dunne, signed, with an inscription: *To Fintan Dunne, My highest regards to a soldier's soldier.*

No doubt intended as a gesture of respect and—even more—encouragement to a brother-in-arms under no illusions about the mayhem and gore ahead, but the effect was to leave Dunne rattled and unsure. He fantasized about sending it back with an inscription of his own: *Thanks, but no thanks. This sounds like an epitaph.* Instead, he stuck it in an envelope and mailed it home to Roberta.

The sergeant kept pecking at the typewriter. Pinned on the wall above his desk was a large Mercator map. The borders of the world's nations, Dunne noticed, didn't register any of the changes imposed since 1938.

The casual observer might find it hard to believe this was the antechamber of the U.S. spymaster in chief. But underselling himself had always been one of Donovan's strengths. Those lulled into thinking him a lightweight who'd be quickly KO'd by the bare-knuckle heavyweights prowling the capital's corridors soon learned otherwise.

Without losing his temper or indulging in verbal fisticuffs, Donovan transformed an innocuous-sounding fact-gathering bureau, the Office of the Coordinator of Information, into the Office of Strategic Services, an audacious, all-purpose agency for intelligence gathering, special operations, psychological warfare, sabotage, espionage, and counterespionage. As well as self-effacing master of the internecine struggle among government departments and military services, he became the first man to wrangle a burgeoning multimillion budget from Congress and not have to account for a single dime.

The red button on the phone beside the typewriter silently pulsed. The sergeant grabbed the receiver. "Yes, sir," he snapped, "right away." He nodded at the door. "The general will see you now." He went back to his tap-tap-tapping.

Dunne knocked and opened the door. The blinds were drawn. A single gooseneck lamp provided the only light. Donovan sat in the darkness beyond, dim but recognizable. Dunne took the seat in front of the desk—a twin to the one he'd sat on in the hallway— and waited to see who was in charge: Wild Bill or Black Will.

With those he wanted to impress or manipulate—celebrities, senators, cabinet secretaries, the president—affable, outgoing Wild Bill never failed to appear. But at one time or another, whether it meant crossing a corridor or continent, his associates scurried to answer the summons from Black Will. They'd wait as he studied a lone paper stranded on his uncluttered desk, or stared out the window, or gazed at the ceiling. Sunk in his own emotional trough, he said nothing. After fifteen or twenty minutes (what felt like an hour to the person sitting there), he'd look across, wide-eyed, to find he had company, fumble with a pen or paperweight, and issue a quick dismissal.

Dunne's fear that this might be a Black Will occasion quickly evaporated. After an awkward silence, Donovan thanked him for coming, as if he'd sent a request rather than an order, and got down to business. A mission was coming up involving the rescue of several OSS teams that had fallen into German hands in a failed attempt to bring downed fliers out of Slovakia.

Given the war's imminent end—Germany's failed offensive in the Ardennes, its cities pulverized from the air, the Russians closing in from the east—it might have seemed unnecessary from a short-term strategic perspective. But in terms of the honor of the OSS and the country's long-term interests, it was vital.

"Slovakia?" Unable to hide his surprise, Dunne blurted out the word. Except for its status as part of the Czechoslovak state

Hitler dismembered in '38 and '39, he thought of Slovakia (when he thought of it at all) as thread in the tapestry of empires unraveled at the end of the last war. In peacetime, it was hard to distinguish between Baltic and Balkans: Slovenia, Serbia, Ruthenia, Estonia, Lusatia, Bukovina, Latvia, Bosnia, all indistinct patches on the shifting fabric of central and eastern Europe, ethnic enclaves and nationalities stitched, unstitched, and restitched, now enmeshed in the titanic struggle between the USSR and Nazi Germany. "The Russians are already in there, aren't they?"

Donovan twisted the lamp toward himself. Dark crescents underlined his eyes. He'd put on weight. "In the eastern part, yes. But the Soviets have had a hell of a time getting across the Carpathians. Up until now, the British have controlled most clandestine operations in the western part. They managed the assassination of SS-Gruppenführer Reinhard Heydrich in '42, the governor of the so-called Protectorate of Bohemia-Moravia. But the altered balance of power in the east means we need to take a more direct role."

His face receded into the shadows. "Dick Van Hull has volunteered to lead the operation. Nobody is better equipped. You know him, don't you?"

"We've met, but I've never served with him. I know he's held in high regard."

"His classmate is among the captured. They crewed on the Harvard rowing team. An experience like that, pulling together on the same team or scull, can bind men together the same way as a battlefield. There's truth to the old saying that 'Waterloo was won on the playing fields of Eton.' There's a danger as well. I'd appreciate you not mentioning this discussion to Van Hull, but in part, that's why I'm sending you along. Make sure he doesn't get distracted by any . . . any"—he seemed to be searching for a word—"sentiment."

"I'll do my best." Given a choice, he might have begged off.

But where was the choice expressed (or even implied) in "I'm sending you along"?

"There's something else." Donovan rose and faced the window. Night had settled over the city. "There's an important contact who's been in touch with us. A German. He's in possession of information that can affect events that will arise when the war ends. It needs to be kept out of the wrong hands. We think the Slovakian partisans know where he is. Major Bassante will be in charge of your briefing. He's very good at his job. He'll spell out the details before you go."

"Is Major Van Hull aware of this?"

"He will be after the briefing. I'm counting on you to keep him on course."

Donovan came from behind the desk and flipped a wall switch. The burst of illumination from the crystal fixture above swallowed the lamplight and revealed a spacious, high-ceilinged suite whose dimensions made Donovan seem shorter than he was.

On the walls flanking the desk hung large paintings of military scenes: To the left, a troop of saber-waving cavalrymen riding frantic, frightened horses thundered into the foreground; to the right, lines of blue-coated grenadiers advanced over the fallen and dying, one of them pulling a wounded comrade to his feet.

"They're by Hippolyte Bellangé. Melodramatic, I know." Donovan shook his head as Dunne examined the painting on the right. "'The Old Guard dies but never surrenders.' The French insisted on putting them there. Once they excelled at war. Now, à la de Gaulle, it's mostly melodrama they're good at." He extended his hand. "Sorry to have to charge you with this. But no combination can come close to Van Hull and you."

They shook hands. It was the general's style to stick with big pictures. Let briefing officers fill in the details. "Fin, how long is it now I've known you?"

"Twenty-eight years, sir. I was eighteen. I had a lot to learn."

"You learned quickly. Not everyone did." Donovan didn't mention that time during the fighting at the Ourcq when he'd been hit in the leg and Dunne had come back for him, lifted him on his back, and carried him away just before a German shell obliterated everything in the vicinity. He didn't have to. The bond between them was unspoken. But unbreakable.

Dunne first met Donovan at Camp Mills, before they shipped overseas. Fit and handsome, Donovan was a man in his prime, now-you-see-it, now-you-don't interval when mental and physical components mesh and purr like a smoothly running motor.

The Methodist chaplain who'd teamed with Father Duffy to bless them as they'd left to join the action on the Western Front spouted the phrase "the quick and the dead." A Protestant formulation that proved truer than Catholic mouthwash about *pax vobiscum*. Over the top, into the maze of rusted wire, fatal monotony of machine guns. If you learned to move quick—duck, zigzag, throw yourself facedown in the mud—you had a chance; either that or *requiescat in pacem*. Amen.

By the time they got home, Donovan was gaunt—one of the few times in his life—a genuine national hero, winner of the Congressional Medal of Honor, AEF's most decorated officer. The day the regiment disbanded after a tumultuous homecoming march down Fifth Avenue, when he said good-bye to his Micks, he had a haunted look.

The image that had stuck with Dunne across the years was of the helmeted, mud-flecked battlefield commander poised atop a trench crammed with frightened doughboys mired up to their ankles in foul-smelling, mustard-colored ooze.

All they could hear above the din of artillery fire intended to soften the enemy lines were snatches of what he said . . . *nobody wants to be the last man to die in this war . . . but we are soldiers . . . our ancestors who fell at Marye's Heights . . . bravery that*

will never be forgotten. The final line sounded like it was lifted
from Shakespeare or some old poet . . . *ours but to do and die* . . .
then shrill whistle, shouted command, momentum of fear, obedi-
ence, and loyalty to their buddies—that above all—moving them
forward.

Lieutenant Quentin Osbourne and Private Bartholomew
Mullen were the first over the top, running blindly ahead in a
straight line when they were stuck by a misplaced American
artillery round, bone and flesh blown to smithereens, bits of cloth
scattered on the bristling metal briar, blood transformed into crimson mist.

They were officially listed as missing in action.

The quick moved on. The dead stayed behind.

The room was warm. Dunne did his best to look alert and
interested. He'd yet to feel the inevitable anticipation and anxiety
of undertaking another mission. For now, he was tired, eager for
sleep.

"I wish I could say our work is done. Or even close."
Donovan spoke with a detached reserve, as though addressing a
large audience. "We've seen how the Soviets behaved in Romania,
crushing the non-Communist resistance and turning the country
into a vassal state. It's clear that's their intent in Poland and right
up to the English Channel—and beyond—if they can get away
with it."

Donovan continued: This war was the second act in a three-
act play; ahead, the most important act of all, twilight struggle
between a single-minded, ruthlessly monolithic movement and a
loose coalition of cynic-ridden, querulous, self-indulgent democra-
cies. He and the organization he'd built—"our own legion of
honor"—were crucial to the outcome. If a part of him recoiled at
what it would involve, a deeper part embraced what lay ahead, the
service of a purpose that dwarfed career, comfort, material success.

"The coming showdown will determine the fate of Western civilization and the world."

Dunne didn't ask any questions. He'd only half listened to Donovan's words about the act after this one. He saluted and left the general to his phantom audience.

He didn't begrudge Donovan his view of himself as indispensable. The general traveled in the realms of diplomacy, political philosophy, economic theory. But he was no mere paper pusher. He'd sucked in the sour, poisoned air of real battlefields as well as glided through the marble corridors of strategists and power brokers.

Maybe the general was right about a "twilight struggle" to come. But until further notice, getting in and out of Slovakia alive was all the play Dunne cared about.

Dunne exited the hotel through the lobby. Lieutenant Colonel Carlton Baxter Bartlett was still entertaining a clutch of officers. Rotund, bottom-heavy head of press relations, he was derisively referred to by some as "the Pear," a play on both his last name and the protruding roundness of his hips and buttocks, which was tamed but not erased by his carefully tailored uniform from Wetzel's in New York, tailors to the General Staff.

Since their encounter in Washington three years before—the same night he was introduced to Dick Van Hull—Dunne had run into Bartlett a few times in London. Their conversations were never long. Bartlett was always on the fly, eyeing the room with periscopic sweep for the highest-ranking or most influential person in reach and then heading as straight as a torpedo toward his target. Dunne was sure that Bartlett never brought up their brief prewar association for the simple reason it wasn't important enough to recall. It involved a routine investigation of the blackmailing mistress of an oil company executive whose public relations were handled by Bartlett & Partners.

After he'd unearthed her record of previous arrests for possession of narcotics, shoplifting, and prostitution—which hadn't exactly required Sherlock Holmes—Dunne had been ushered into Bartlett's office for a few polite words, a handshake, and, most important, a substantial check.

The pictureless walls of his understated office gave no hint of the role genealogy played in Carlton Baxter Bartlett's success. Son of a sales manager at Equitable Life, he had the good fortune to be a nephew of Cornelia Bartlett Lee, wife of Ivy Lee, who in his role as VP of the Pennsylvania Railroad and founder of the firm of Ivy Lee & Associates was given the title (his rivals claimed it was self-conferred) "the father of public relations." Though his campaigns on behalf of questionable practices by clients like Standard Oil, IG Farben, and Bethlehem Steel led some to dub him "Poison Ivy," his list of prestigious clients kept him atop the industry.

Bartlett & Partners had taken up where Ivy left off, becoming, as Alvin Capshaw put it in his column in the *New York Standard*, "a shoot off the old vine." Its clients included the New York Central Railroad, MGM, and Generalissimo Chiang Kai-shek. Bartlett volunteered his talents to the OSS before General Donovan had a chance to ask.

The officers around Bartlett burst into laughter. He was living up to his reputation as a bon vivant and raconteur. He ordered another round of drinks. The buzz from the barroom was raucous and happy. It was as if the war was already over.

Dunne decided against going in. He slipped by the entrance without being noticed.

The raw Parisian night felt refreshing.

Returned from Paris to London, Dunne found a note waiting for him from Major Van Hull requesting he phone his room at the Drummond Hotel to arrange a meeting. As soon as Van Hull answered, Dunne recognized the distinct upper-crust Hudson Valley pitch of his voice, not unlike that of the president. Common enough among the OSS's hoity-toity recruits, it had grated on Dunne that time back in '42, when they'd first met in the bar of Washington's Mayflower Hotel.

In that initial period of the OSS's existence, the Mayflower had been General Donovan's favorite fishbowl for showcasing his most impressive catches to congressional and political bigwigs, encouraging them to feel they had an inside take on the country's hush-hush, cloak-and-dagger military outfit. Fond as he was of his Micks, the remnant from the 69th Regiment he'd brought into the OSS, Donovan made no secret of his desire to recruit from the blue-blooded social elite swaddled in the silken WASP cocoon of Ivy League/Wall Street/white-shoe law firm connections. He'd been so successful some joked OSS stood for "Oh So Social."

As Dunne entered the Mayflower bar, Bud Mulholland had signaled from a booth. He was sitting with another officer. Dunne had brought Mulholland, fellow veteran of the first war and NYPD, into the OSS. If he had spotted anyone else in the room he knew other than Mulholland—a man of dour moods and ulcerated soul—Dunne might have begged off. No such luck. He sat and ordered scotch on the rocks.

Mulholland introduced his companion, who was eagerly surveying the room, as "Carl Bartlett."

Without ceasing his scouting, he offered Dunne his hand. "I'm C. B. Bartlett. It's a pleasure." He obviously had no recollection that they'd met before.

"Well, Wild Bill has landed himself a prize fish this time." Bartlett subtly leaned his head toward where Donovan was standing with a strikingly handsome officer sporting a Clark Gable mustache. "That's Thornton Van Hull. A fine pedigree."

"Horses have pedigrees." Mulholland downed his drink. "And dogs."

"You're wrong there, my friend. Biology is destiny. For beasts *and* men."

"Comes to biology, I'll take a good lay over a fine pedigree."

Turning his back on Mulholland, Bartlett spoke directly to Dunne: "The Van Hulls have been Harvard men for several generations. Thornton Van Hull III was part of the merger of Brown Brothers and Harriman. A Harvard man in a den of Yalies, he's a noted collector of the world's finest automobiles. His son, Major Van Hull IV, heads the English as well as Classics departments at Adams-Thayer Academy in New York. It's the school of choice for Social Register families. Sends more boys to the Ivy League than any other prep school in the country. We're all in favor of democracy. That's what this war is all about. But in the end, breeding will out."

Donovan briefly paused to introduce Van Hull. Before he was whisked away, Bartlett stood and gave him a hearty pat on the back. "Welcome, Major, we're a better organization for having you aboard."

Mulholland ordered another drink. "Looks like Donovan has landed another rookie from the firm of Hooey, Phooey and Kerflooey."

Bartlett excused himself. Mulholland lifted his glass in mock farewell. "The Pear's head is so far up his ass he can see out his mouth."

In those early days, Mulholland hadn't thought much of Van Hull either, dismissing him as a Boy Scout, a put-down reserved for the educated, earnest types whose incurable amateurism posed a clear and present danger to those set on eliminating the enemy with clear-eyed, homicidal efficiency. Before long, however, Mulholland came to see that Van Hull was as good an operative as the OSS possessed, someone even he was eager to serve with.

Raised by his New York banker father in Paris, fluent in German, French, and Italian, sharp and skeptical, and prized by Donovan for his high-level relationships, Major Thornton Richard Van Hull could have attached himself to Carlton Baxter Bartlett's

rapidly expanding Department of Information, Communication &
Policy Analysis. Instead, he joined Special Operations and was
rarely out of action since his first mission in Yugoslavia, in the
spring of 1943. Before long, every team dropped behind enemy
lines shared Mulholland's hope that Major Van Hull be at its head.

Dunne had observed him from a distance as part of the pro-
gram to train the OGs dropped into occupied France to coordinate
operations of the Maquis, the Resistance, in preparation for the
Normandy invasion. Neither loner nor snob, Van Hull impressed
Dunne as being as self-assured and unpretentious as any of
Hollywood's cowboy heroes. (Randolph Scott as Wyatt Earp in
Frontier Marshal came to mind.)

DRUMMOND HOTEL, LONDON

Sitting in the lobby across from clean-shaven Major
Thornton Richard Van Hull, Dunne couldn't help notice that the
tense, thick-as-fog mélange of expectation and uncertainty blan-
keting the city pre-D-Day had dissipated, if not entirely disappeared. The occasional plummet of Hitler's last-gasp terror
weapon, the V-2 rocket—too little, too late to avoid the demise of
his thousand-year Reich—sustained whatever dread and doubt
persisted.

"The General is sending a team to hook up with the Slovak
resistance—what's left of it—for a rescue attempt." Van Hull was
in a chair next to the fireplace, its layer of red coals half smothered
by ash. He was thinner than the first time Dunne met him in
Washington three years ago, but his good looks were intact.
"General Donovan recommended I enlist you."

Dunne's blank expression betrayed no sign of his meeting
with Donovan in Paris.

The waiter hobbled over. Spindly neck, scrawny as a pipe
cleaner, sprouted from his wing collar. The sole server, he was

doing his best to keep up. He hurriedly unfolded a linen cocktail napkin, took the glass of scotch and the side of water from the silver tray, and placed them on it. "Will that be all, sir?"

Van Hull sipped the glass of soda water he'd been drinking when Dunne came in. "For now, yes, thank you."

"What's involved?" Dunne preferred his drink the American way, over ice, a request that usually left the English befuddled or offended. He'd ordered water.

Leaning close, Van Hull described the coming mission in the broadest terms. In August 1944, an uprising by the anti-Fascist Slovak rebels succeeded in liberating a contingent of captured American and British fliers. The agents stayed behind to support the Slovak insurgents and locate other downed fliers. Three other OSS teams followed.

By October, a total of twelve agents and thirty-seven newly rescued airmen were being relentlessly hunted by hard-core SS units and forces loyal to Slovakia's puppet government. Operation Dawson was dropped in to arrange a rescue. Foul weather prevented bringing them out by air. Soon after Christmas, news arrived that the exhausted, half-frozen agents and airmen had been captured.

Latest information from the resistance indicated they were being held in Slovakia. As long as the Germans didn't move them to the Reich, there was a possibility the advancing Russians might liberate them. But the Russians made no secret of their displeasure at having Brits and Yanks mucking around in what they considered their exclusive theater of operations.

Van Hull drew a crude map of Slovakia on a cocktail napkin and indicated where the mission would be directed. General Donovan believed very strongly—and Van Hull concurred—the OSS should take care of its own. The mission's job was to assess the possibilities of a rescue. There'd be a full briefing in Bari before they left. The briefing officer assigned from R&A was

Major Turlough Bassante, a protégé of Louis Pohl, the cigar-smoking, self-effacing, universally respected chief of statistical analysis.

Having spent time with Pohl and Bassante in Washington and then in London, Van Hull rated Bassante as the top briefer in Special Operations: "He's brilliant, opinionated, and bitter as an unpaid whore but extremely knowledgeable." Eager to serve in the field, he'd submitted a strongly worded request for a transfer. General Donovan found it amusing, even circulating it after dismissing it out of hand. Bassante didn't have the temperament, he said, a truth everyone but Bassante seemed to recognize.

"The general ordered we start with a three-man mission," Van Hull said. "I told him I preferred to go alone. He dismissed that idea and brought up your name. He said you were experienced and reliable. Brave but cautious. He stressed that: 'Dunne knows how to deal with trouble and, better yet, how to avoid it. He was a cop, a decorated one.'"

Dunne sipped scotch, swallowed what he thought: Caution grew from fear but wasn't the same as cowardice. If you weren't afraid, you wouldn't be cautious and couldn't be brave. Reckless, impetuous, irrational—sure. But brave? Bravery was the ability to elevate self-sacrifice over self-preservation, discipline over common sense, individual human will over the most basic of animal instincts, to move beyond fear and caution. No matter how much training or experience, no matter how confident, you wouldn't know until the moment arrived.

Those who thought otherwise, cocksure they could draw a bright, immovable line between bravery and cowardice, had never been under fire, never felt the surging, suffocating, animal urge for survival. Alongside the luck/unluck of combat—the maddening unpredictability of die/survive—was the iron law of mathematics: The longer you're in it, the lower the chances of getting out in one piece.

"You mind if I call you Fin?" Van Hull asked.

"I prefer it."

"Good. I prefer you call me Dick."

"Not Thornton? That's the name the general used when he introduced us in D.C."

"He made a habit out of that, even when I asked him not to. Loathed that name since I was a kid. I've always used Dick or Rick. Even Richard is okay. I'd rather be a Richard the First than a Thornton the Fourth."

"Richard the First, a.k.a. 'The Lionheart.'"

"You know your English history."

"I know my Errol Flynn. *The Adventures of Robin Hood.*"

"The general said you'd be blunt. He admires that quality. I do, too, so I'll be up front. At this point, it appears the captured men are still in Slovakia. But it's possible they've been taken back to the Reich. If that's the case, this is a fool's errand."

"It's also possible they've already been shot." Dunne didn't bring up the incident at La Spezia, Italy, the previous March. He didn't have to. It was common knowledge how, in accordance with Hitler's Commando Order, the Wehrmacht summarily executed an OSS mission of fifteen men in uniform captured on a legitimate military mission. No one could say with certainty how many other agents had been caught and killed on the spot.

"But the Wehrmacht knows a final reckoning is near."

"I'm not sure they care about reckonings. The SS doesn't, that's for certain."

Van Hull slumped into the chair.

It struck Dunne that perhaps Van Hull wasn't as much a fan of bluntness as he made. "'Ours but to do or die,' that's a favorite line of the general's."

"From Tennyson's 'The Charge of the Light Brigade.'"

"Another chapter of history I learned from Errol Flynn."

"The poet wrote, 'Theirs but to do *and* die,' a more fatalistic rendering. Truth is, there's a personal angle. Lieutenant Michael Jahn . . . one of the captured . . . he's a friend." Van Hull put the glass to his lips, eyed the room over the rim fleetingly.

"When I was a cop—"

Van Hull interjected, "A decorated one, the general said."

"We had a rule. Never mix the personal with the professional."

"I respect that, Fin. The decision is yours." Van Hull crumpled the paper cocktail napkin-cum-map and tossed it on the coals. It smoldered before bursting into flame.

Per Donovan's instructions, Dunne didn't bring up the order he'd been given. Wasn't this mission, be some other and probably with someone less seasoned than Van Hull. He mouthed what was as close to the truth as he could get: "I'm in."

"We leave for Bari the day after tomorrow, at oh-seven-hundred. Major Bassante likes to talk. Never uses one word when he can use three. But he's the best briefer we have. Too thorough for some—but the way I see it, you can never be too thorough."

"Be prepared."

"Boy Scouts' motto."

"Good motto, good advice."

"You ever a Scout?"

"They don't give merit badges for misdemeanors. I chose reform school instead."

Van Hull lifted his drink. "Here's to a successful mission."

Dunne tapped his glass to Van Hull's: "Here's to staying alive."

As Dunne was getting ready for bed, there was a knock on his door. Bud Mulholland stepped hesitantly into the room. He was recently back from a successful mission in Yugoslavia in which scores of Allied fliers had been rescued, and was quartered on the floor above. He turned down Dunne's offer of a drink. He wasn't sure he should have come, he said, but decided Dunne deserved to hear what he had to say, even though it made him feel like a snitch.

"Are you sure you don't want a drink?" Dunne said.

"Maybe a small one."

Dunne fetched two glasses from the bathroom and poured an inch of scotch in each.

Mulholland perched on the end of the bed and focused on the rug as he spoke. He'd heard about the upcoming mission with Van Hull, and after he'd spotted them earlier in conversation at the Drummond decided to fill in Dunne on what he knew: "This is intended not as an accusation but as a piece of useful information, and the more useful information you have, the better the odds of getting through." He downed the contents of the glass.

Before he'd headed out to Yugoslavia, Mulholland said, he'd met a Dutch cabaret dancer at a hotel near Piccadilly Circus. They were headed to her room when she noticed the door of the adjacent room ajar. A heel protruded. He'd pushed the door open. Van Hull was sprawled unconscious on the floor, an empty whiskey bottle by his side. There were more empties on the bureau. They lifted him onto the bed and closed the door.

Mulholland didn't let on to his escort he knew Van Hull, and didn't say anything to anyone until now. "You know I don't talk out of school, Fin, and you know how I regard the major. But I'll give you a bit of advice. He's got an Achilles' heel, and I'm not trying to play the poet. We know the type. Doesn't get drunk every day, sometimes not for weeks, even months, but once the cork is out, there's no putting it back. Long as you're in the field with Van Hull, everything should be fine—but it's always good to keep every possibility in mind."

BARI, ITALY

Dunne and Van Hull flew from London to Bari. A dozen other OSS operatives were aboard, all bound for Yugoslavia, Greece, "the Balkans." Dunne fell asleep over the angry whitecaps of the English Channel, woke as the plane prepared to land.

"It's not wine-dark." Van Hull stared out the window. He had a movie star's profile. Below, waves rolled south to north, unperplexed, lapping at the Italian shore.

"What's not 'wine-dark'?"

"'The wine-dark sea.' Homer's description of the Mediterranean. What color do you see?"

Dunne gazed out the window. "Blue."

"'Azure' is the word Lord Byron used: 'And now upon the scene I look / The azure grave of many a Roman; / Where stern Ambition once forsook / His wavering crown to follow woman.' Perhaps when mixed with blood the sea takes on the color of wine, the way they say it did at Tarawa. Or Normandy. But I doubt that was Homer's point."

Dunne continued looking out the window. They were about to land. After all the flying, all the jumps, all the missions, he still never felt entirely at ease in an airplane. He gripped the seat. In the spring before the Normandy invasion, he'd worked at an auxiliary airstrip in Sussex, training the all-volunteer Operational Groups, or OGs, that General Donovan created as part of Operation Jedburgh, the joint Allied effort to land clandestine forces across Nazi-occupied Europe.

The job of trainers was to instruct gentlemen in the art of ungentlemanly warfare, turning college grads into killers and saboteurs adept at sowing confusion behind enemy lines, conducting hit-and-run raids, contacting partisans, and waging the small-scale warfare that tied down large numbers of enemy troops.

As the long-awaited assault on occupied France drew near, the OG missions grew in number. The last contingent was the best Dunne had worked with, a quartet of three-man teams already intensively groomed for combat at the OSS camp on what had been the grounds of the Congressional Country Club, outside Washington, D.C. Their enthusiasm matched by appreciation of what they were up against, they emerged from training as skilled paratroopers, versatile with small arms and adept in hand-to-hand combat.

The heightened preparations—hurried, confused, sometimes contradictory—left no doubt the invasion was imminent. A last-minute directive required them to share a borrowed Halifax piloted by a baby-faced Brit with a half-dozen Free French paratroopers. A persnickety RAF lieutenant nursing a widely shared resentment at the Yanks' increasing control over clandestine operations forced Dunne to stay behind and sit inside a Nissen hut to complete the necessary paperwork.

Soon after the plane took off, it was recalled due to high winds. Wheels almost touching the ground, a capricious, ferocious gust of wind jerking up the right wing. In an apparent attempt to abort the landing, the inexperienced pilot gunned the engine. Left wing planted itself in wet, pliant earth; plane pivoted, pinwheeled, crashed, burst apart in a centrifugal circle of orange-yellow fireworks.

A scrum of would-be rescuers—on foot, in ambulances and fire engines—rushed the flaming, upside-down wreck, as if there were anybody to rescue. The fire engines prepared to douse the shattered, belly-up hulk as the intense, fuel-fed fire reduced the recruits from hardened, battle-ready agents into char, suet, cinders, soot.

The pilot announced they were nearing Bari. Everyone should prepare for landing. Dunne silently repeated the Suscipiat, one of the prayers from the Mass he'd memorized as an altar boy at the Catholic Protectory, a single tongue-twisting Latin sentence: *Suscipiat Dominus sacrificium de manibus tuis, ad laudem et gloriam nominis sui, ad utilitatem quoque nostram, totiusque Ecclesiae suae sanctae.*

Why remember almost nothing else of the responses? Why remember the Latin but not the English translation?

Why remember one thing and not another?

Nobody could remember everything, but remembering some things was important, even if it didn't seem so at the time.

Brother Andre weaned them from reading from the cardboard cheat sheets placed on the altar steps. A gentle Frenchman, he never cuffed them the way some of the other brothers did, slapping a boy for the slightest infraction. As well as doing his best to give the boys some French—*au revoir, bon jour, merci*—he conveyed his love of Latin.

When Brother Andre called the attention of the other altar servers to Dunne's mastery of the prayers—"Listen to Fintan, *mes garçons*, he has it down *parfaitement*"—how proud he felt.

"*Totiusque.*" A word you could taste. Like licorice. Who cared what it meant? You could make it mean anything you want: "Good luck," for example.

Dunne went to Mass occasionally, to confession when he felt the need, ditto for praying. Hail Marys and Our Fathers mostly. Prayers he didn't remember learning, with words he didn't think about, just repeated. The one prayer that he carefully articulated, that made him feel as though he was actually praying, was the one whose words he didn't understand: Suscipiat.

It was a smooth landing. As they exited the plane, sunwarmed, flower-scented Italian air jolted Dunne with an instantaneous, involuntary reverie of Cuba, eve of war, honeymoon with Roberta in the Hotel Barcelona, melancholy reminder of a distance greater than miles measured; a distance felt in the heart, the kind he'd experienced the week before, on his final leave in London before leaving for Bari, when he'd gone to see *Cover Girl* at a USO movie night. Gene Kelly and Rita Hayworth crooned the lyrics of "Long Ago (and Far Away)."

A lone soldier started to cry. Before long, muffled sobs filled the hall. Old-timers and newly arrived joined in. Technicolor beauty almost too much to bear, Rita could reduce any GI to tears. This case, the blame belonged to the contagion rampant among pining, lonely men (mostly) and boys (many), civilians at heart (almost all): Not just lust—susceptible to instant relief (self-administered or purchased)—but homesickness, the only permanent cure out of reach and unavailable.

When the lights came up, tears had dried. Men skulked out, avoiding each other's eyes, like college boys leaving a Times Square peep show.

The others from the plane piled on the truck waiting to take them to the base. There was no room left for Dunne and Van Hull. A jeep was ordered. They rode into the green-brown foothills until they reached two landing strips lined with B-17s and their Mustang escorts and a sprawling village of Quonset huts. Unpleasant, pervasive odor of gasoline, latrines, and disinfectant hung in the air.

They were quartered in small rooms in a hut on the far side of the airstrips. Van Hull excused himself and went off to take a nap. Dunne unlocked the door to his room. Atop the dented, chipped olive-green metal desk directly ahead was a manila envelope. Typed on the label was his name, and beneath—in all caps—*CONFIDENTIAL: FOR YOUR EYES ONLY*. Inside was the familiar spiral-bound briefing book. He flipped it open to the title page: *OPERATION MAXWELL*.

Van Hull's snoring wafted through the paper-thin walls. After his sleep on the plane, Dunne didn't feel tired. He stuck the briefing book in the top drawer. On his initial missions, he'd devoured the contents. Experience taught that the briefer would do his best to give a crash course in the complexities they'd encounter, making it easier to sift important stuff from fluff conjured up by an overzealous former academic eager to duplicate his Ph.D. dissertation.

He opened the desk drawer to look for stationery on which to write a letter to Roberta. There were several sheets as well as a well-thumbed book he mistook for the Bible until he picked it up: *How to Win Friends and Influence People*, by Dale Carnegie.

The pages were heavily underlined. The section heads were Carnegie's play on the Ten Commandments—Moses as salesman instead of prophet—"Six Ways to Make People Like You" or "Twelve Ways to Win People to Your Way of Thinking." It must have been left behind by a previous occupant who wisely concluded, whatever its postwar applications, it wasn't going to be of much use behind enemy lines.

He started a letter to Roberta. By now she understood that though it mentioned nothing explicit, a multipage letter meant he was about to leave on a mission. (It would be flown back to London and postmarked from there.) He decided to finish it later, tucked the unfinished pages in the top drawer. He lay down— pillow's soft, clean, scent closer to feminine than anything else on the base. Rita Hayworth came back, chemistry with Gene Kelly, lyrics so resonant of that night at Ben Marden's when he'd fallen in love. *Just one look and then I knew,* so true, *that all I longed for long ago* (how did songwriters get it so right?) *was you! Just you!* His snoring soon joined Van Hull's.

They met up with the other operatives in the officers' mess. There was a well-stocked bar. Dunne had scotch; Van Hull stuck to water. Gathered around a radio, they listened to the nightly news on the BBC. Trademark tone of the announcer—upper class, educated, serious but not somber, crisp yet unhurried—had an authority American broadcasters imitated but only Edward R. Murrow attained.

The news was all good. Soviet offensive under way in western Poland, and Prussia was advancing along a broad front. Warsaw and Kraków had been taken. "With the Allies advancing toward the Rhine and the Soviets storming across the Vistula," the announcer intoned, "it's only a matter of time before Berlin will fall."

Their plates were loaded with mounds of potatoes and over-cooked beef. Positive as it was, the news had dampened rather than lightened the mood.

Only a matter of time: Time enough for Hitler's hard-core fanatics to drag down as many opponents as possible; time enough to meet the unmet bullet, the one with your name on it, fatal acquaintance, all the worse coming at the war's finale.

They went outside. Thick purple twilight poured over the gently sloping hills. Van Hull walked away, stopped, and came back. "You have a cigarette?" Dunne handed him the pack. Van Hull took one and lit it. There was a tiny tremble in his hand. "I'm sorry. I should have taken your advice."

Dunne lit a cigarette for himself. It wasn't unusual to get a case of the jitters on the eve of a drop. Everybody did, especially those who'd been dropped before and knew firsthand how easy it was for a mission to go wrong. Van Hull was usually better than anyone else at not letting it show. "What advice?"

"'Never mix personal with professional.'"

"Lieutenant Michael Jahn?"

Van Hull nodded.

"We've crossed that bridge, Dick."

"I'm lucky you volunteered to come along."

"Glad I did." A lie, but a white one. Given a choice—which admittedly he hadn't been—Dunne was more certain than ever he preferred serving with a seasoned operative like Van Hull than a crew of rookies.

"I'm packing it in." Van Hull strolled away. Dunne thought about joining him but wasn't tired and didn't feel in the mood to dive into the briefing book or lie on the bed and stare at the water stains in the corkboard ceiling. He went back inside for a nightcap with the men who remained behind. They smoked, swapped stories about the missions they'd survived, and heaped dead butts and ashes on the tin tray.

Peter Bunde, the third member of their party, a newly minted, sandy-haired lieutenant from Buffalo, New York, and graduate of Canisius College, arrived from Tripoli that morning. First time out of the States, only son of Slovak immigrants, fluent in their language as well as German, he'd act as radio operator and liaise with the partisans. "I was afraid I'd miss the big show," he said. "That would've killed me."

They moseyed together to a Quonset hut set on the northern fringe of the base where the briefing was scheduled. Bunde walked a step or two ahead, barely able to contain his impatience with their laid-back pace. Without looking up from his comic book, the orderly at the entrance tossed his head toward the rear of the hut.

They sat at a square conference table. Above, a fan rotated in leisurely, feckless circles. A brittle, yellow-brown shade softened the inrush of sunlight through the single window. Turlough Bassante, a tall, thin, balding major with pointed nose, entered. "It might get a little warm, but war is hell, and it won't get that hot."

He pulled a map from his briefing book and pinned it to the cork-lined wall behind. He tapped the pink, peanut-shaped space at the center, which closely resembled the outline Van Hull had drawn on a cocktail napkin, with a rubber-tip pointer. "If you haven't already guessed, this is Slovakia." He sat and slid long, bony fingers into a tight clasp. "Before we start, I ask you not to smoke. I'm allergic."

"I don't smoke. Or drink," Bunde said.

"A regular Boy Scout."

"I was."

"Comes in handy in the field," Van Hull said.

"I suppose. But I'm a briefer, not a trainer, and we have business to attend to." Bassante's mouth was fixed in a disapproving pout. "Weather permitting, you'll fly out two nights from now. You won't be able to see much of Bari. Someday, if you've the time, come back for a tour of the old city, Barivecchia, dirty and dangerous but charming in its own way. Don't miss the Castello Svevo, the twelfth-century fortress of Frederick I, the Holy Roman Emperor. 'Frederick Barbarossa,' the Italians dubbed him for his red beard. According to German folklore, he didn't drown on the Third Crusade but fell into a trance beneath the Kyffhäuser Mountains, in Thuringia, there to wait the hour of the Reich's greatest need, when he'll wake and come to the rescue."

Bunde raised his hand, tentatively, like a pupil in a classroom. "Barbarossa, that's the name Hitler gave the attack on Russia."

"Congratulations. Submit that as a question to *Information Please*. You might win a war bond. As for Frederick, the slumbering emperor of the First Reich apparently either hasn't heard or has decided to ignore the summons from the tottering führer of the Third. A wise emperor, Frederick."

Bassante opened his folder. "I presume you've read the briefing materials, so I'm not going to waste time revisiting the intricacies of the situation. Any questions?"

Dunne thumbed through thirty pages of dense, single-spaced text. This was the first time he'd encountered a briefing officer who didn't begin with a review of the printed materials. But he wasn't about to fess up to not doing his homework.

"I take your silence to mean you've familiarized yourselves with the materials."

"How about putting it in a nutshell?" Van Hull said.

Head jutting forward, nose like the needle of a compass,

Bassante turned to him. "Nutshells are the purview of arborists. I'll clarify what—if anything—is unclear."

Bunde raised his hand. "I think I can help. "

"That's quite all right, Lieutenant." Bassante aimed the needle nose at Bunde. "Though I was never a Boy Scout, I've functioned sans assistance for over a year."

Bunde's reddened face registered embarrassment, ire—unhappy fusion of both.

"You were saying, Major . . ."

"Saying what?" The compass point swiveled again toward Van Hull.

"The situation in Slovakia." Van Hull tossed a pack of cigarettes and a matchbook on the table. "The big picture."

"Light that and the briefing is over. That's a promise, not a threat."

"I'm just going to play with it." He plucked a match from the book and worked the tight creases between his teeth. "Helps kill the craving."

Bassante rested his elbows on the table, refolded his hands, putting them together as if to pray, tips of index fingers touching tip of nose. After a moment of silence, he stood, paced, head down, needle pointing south. The problem with a briefing about a drop outside the perimeter of the war in the west, he said, was that the *ordinary* ignorance of most Americans about European affairs instantly turned *extraordinary*.

"In cases like yours"—he nodded toward Lieutenant Bunde—"those with ethnic connections have some idea of the subtleties involved. Yet, more often than not, those connections encourage rather than constrain a paralyzing parochialism that makes it impossible to make an unbiased analysis."

The flush returned to Bunde's face. He squirmed in his seat but stayed silent.

Bassante looked directly at him. "Though I might disagree

with some of your interpretations, Lieutenant, I'm sure you've a grip on the players in Slovakia. Most Americans, on the other hand, are devoid of any historical perspective or nuanced understanding of the complexities outside their borders. It's part of our national profile and extends to the highest reaches."

Van Hull made no effort to hide his boredom, chewing the paper end of the match and doodling in his briefing book a tight, elaborate weave of spirals and curlicues.

"The Slovaks are Slavs," Bassante said. "Hitler loathes them as a human subspecies. His goal is to annex the lands of the east for settlement by the Aryan race. The fittest among the Slavs will serve as hewers of wood and drawers of water. The unfit will be eliminated. But for strategic reasons, he made an exception of Slovakia, using it as a wedge to pry apart what he called 'the wall of Pan-Slavic solidarity.'"

Oblivious to his insistence a few minutes before that he wouldn't "waste time revisiting the intricacies of the situation in Czechoslovakia," Bassante launched into a monologue about the country's creation after World War I, tensions between Czechs and Slovaks, dubious wisdom of incorporating the heavily German Sudetenland, and formation of a proto-Fascist Slovak independence movement under Father Andrej Hlinka, a Catholic priest, and his successor, Monsignor Jozef Tiso.

Bunde raised his hand. Bassante ignored him and went on with his summary. Bunde blurted out, "Just so it's clear the majority of Slovaks have never been Fascists. The uprising against the Germans has confirmed that."

Van Hull pointed at the desultory spin of the ceiling fan. "Can't that go faster?"

"That's as fast as it goes," Bassante said.

"That's *fast*?"

"In Bari, yes." Bassante continued the lecture where he left off before Bunde interrupted, reviewing the Munich Crisis of '38 and Czechoslovakia's dismemberment.

Dunne struggled to keep his eyes open until another vociferous objection from Bunde jolted him to attention: "You've got the facts twisted. While I'm no fan of Tiso, the truth is, Hitler gave him an ultimatum, not a 'nudge.' Either Slovakia declare independence and ask German protection, or Germany would seize Bohemia and Moravia and let Poland and Hungary divide Slovakia among themselves."

Bassante rapped the table with the pointer. "You're being insubordinate."

"That's enough." Van Hull stood. "We're taking a break. Lieutenant, follow me." He led Bunde out the door. Bassante went directly into his office across the hall.

Dunne knew a college boy's argument when he heard one. Van Hull was a college boy, too, except he'd been in the field. Like Dunne, he'd been to a lot of briefings, some bare-bone, others exhaustive, part history lesson, part operational instruction.

Though he knew 99 percent of this stuff would turn out to be useless, Dunne didn't find Bassante's criticisms unfair. He was only half kidding when he'd told Van Hull he was a pupil of Errol Flynn's. No student of history, he skipped over the unbylined, back-page accounts of squabbles and sideshows outside the heavyweight title fights at Dunkirk, El Alamein, Stalingrad, Normandy, Guadalcanal, Midway—milestones everyone knew—that only muddled the straightforward, go-for-glory narrative of the war.

Bud Mulholland claimed he always took along several pages of the briefing book to use as toilet paper. "The point is," he said, "to learn enough so you kill the right people. But don't be afraid of making a mistake. Shoot the fucker before the fucker shoots you."

When they resumed, there was none of the earlier contentiousness. Although he squirmed in his seat, Bunde had obviously been corralled by Van Hull. Bassante launched into a straightforward account of events since Slovakia participated in the German attack on Poland and joined in Operation Barbarossa, committing a relatively small consignment of conscripts to an invasion force of three million.

Overawed by the early successes of the Germans, the Slovaks proved reliable if restrained allies. However, as the attack faltered and Slovak casualties grew, desertions and defections increased. After the defeat at Stalingrad, everybody but the Nazis seemed to accept they'd lost the war. The Romanians and Hungarians, German allies, looked for the quickest way out. High-ranking officers within the Slovak army followed suit.

The Russians infiltrated Slovak-Soviet teams to disrupt German supply lines and erode their defenses along the Carpathian Mountains. In June '44, soon after the Anglo-American landing at Normandy, the Soviets crushed Army Group Center and sealed Germany's fate. The plotting among the Slovak military command took on a new urgency.

The Germans grew increasingly suspicious, and when an entire military delegation of Wehrmacht officers was forced from a train and executed, they acted with customary efficiency and ruthlessness to get ahead of the uprising.

Bassante returned to the map. "Except in this triangle in the center of the country, from Zvolen in the south to Banská Bystrica in the north to Brezno in the east"—he traced the triangle with his pointer—"the rebels managed to secure a redoubt. In order to relieve the pressure on the rebels, the Soviets launched an offensive here"—he moved the pointer north and east of the rebel-held triangle—"at the Dukla Pass, in the eastern Carpathians. They suffered, it's thought, about one hundred twenty thousand casualties. Having stopped the Soviets, the Germans brought the uprising to a bloody and speedy close."

Pinning a second, smaller recon map to the wall, he said, "Here in detail is the triangle in question." Contour lines and color-coded elevations limned an irregular landscape of rifts and rises.

Van Hull went to the board and stood beside Bassante for a closer look. Bunde joined them.

Dunne excused himself and headed to the latrine. Fueled by five cups of morning java, he pissed a stream in the steel trough. He aimed at the cigarette butt in the drain, steady, explosive rain on the Japanese carrier *Hiryu* at Midway, a turning point. The best way to fight any war: Imaginary aerial bombardment of a make-believe enemy vessel. *We will fight them in our urinals, and on our maps, and in our minds.* The paper hull broke apart and spilled cargo and crew into a yellow sea. *Bull's-eye. Bingo. Banzai. Remember Pearl Harbor. Heigh-ho, it's off to Banská Bystrica we go.*

When Dunne returned, Van Hull was still huddled with Bunde and Bassante around the map. Bassante waved the pointer, wand-like, over the paper landscape. "This is the terrain you must live with. The Tiso regime kept American and British fliers downed during raids on the oil refineries under its own jurisdiction. Nearly twenty were held here."

He rested the rubber tip on Banská Bystrica. "Once the rebels liberated them, Operation Dawson was sent in to bring them out and, simultaneously, land supplies and prepare the way for additional OSS teams to assist the rebels and gather intelligence."

"Which I'm sure the Soviets regarded with suspicion." Bunde retook his seat.

"Yes, Lieutenant, precisely. They regard this theater as theirs alone, and unlike the rebels within the Slovak military, loyal to the government-in-exile in London, the partisans take their orders directly from Moscow. Yet they've proved cooperative, or at least not as paranoid and secretive as the Russians.

"In the middle of October, along with arms and medical supplies, a half-dozen B-17s delivered additional agents led by Lieutenant Michael Jahn. This was Jahn's first mission. His job was to set up a permanent base for American support of the sur-

rounded insurgent Slovak military forces until either the Soviets or
the Allies broke through.

"The rebels' position deteriorated rapidly. It was soon clear
the Germans and their Slovak minions would crush all resistance. The insurgents were told to flee best they could and join
the partisans in the mountains. By then the contingent consisted
of thirty-seven men, twelve OSS agents and the rest newly rescued pilots. They waited on an airfield outside Banská Bystrica.
Dense clouds made it impossible to land or take off. Jahn finally
divided them into six units and sent them on different paths into
the mountains.

"The SS teamed up with the Hlinkla Guard to hunt them
down. Jahn's party reunited with several others. They suffered
frostbite. Nurses who'd served in the Slovak army treated them.
The SS captured the nurses the following day. They raped and
killed them.

"Unfortunately for Jahn and companions, the pursuit was
led by Sturmbrigade Dirlewanger, a collection of multina-
tional thugs and psychopaths whose wanton ferocity has made
it notorious even within the ranks of the Waffen-SS. You can
recognize them by their collar patch." Bassante formed an X
with his forefingers. "Crossed potato-masher grenades on a
black shield."

Dunne looked over at Van Hull. He sat with shoulders
slumped, eyes shut. If Bassante knew of Van Hull's friendship with
Jahn, he didn't bring it up.

"We know from the partisans that Jahn and his men eluded
their pursuers for another week. The day before Christmas, they
stumbled on an abandoned lodge and were able to get out of the
cold. They woke to find themselves surrounded.

"The Slovaks and Czechs in the party were shot. Despite
Hitler's threat to execute enemy troops caught assisting partisans,
the Americans and Brits were spared. Jahn is Jewish, which of

course puts him in special danger. Our contacts report that he and the others were taken back to Banská Bystrica. That's the last report we have of their whereabouts. We're acting on the presumption they're still there."

"Are they still in the hands of the SS?" Van Hull had gone back to doodling.

"That's for you to find out."

"Anyone use Victor?" The circles Van Hull drew folded themselves around lightning-bolt runes, insignia of the SS, and crossed potato-masher grenades.

"Not that we're aware of."

"You've lost me," Bunde said. "Who's Victor?"

Van Hull fished in his pocket. He took out a dime and a plastic-coated lozenge. He put the dime back. *"Ecce Victor."* He laid the lozenge on the table. "Behold the lethal pill—the LP—the 'new and improved' insoluble capsule, not glass like the Brits use, filled with potassium cyanide. Swallowed, it travels through the digestive system harmlessly; chewed, it causes instant death. Operatives behind enemy lines have the option to take Victor along. It's up to them when and if to use it."

Bunde shook his head. "They mentioned it in training, although nobody called it Victor. It isn't something a Catholic can avail himself of."

"There are times merely knowing you have a choice brings comfort of its own." Van Hull returned it to his pocket. "Wouldn't you say so, Fin?"

"The final lesson of war: Never say 'never' because you never know. Billy Coughlin declined to bring Victor along on a drop we made in Croatia. He stepped on a land mine. His testicles and everything below were Mixmastered into mush. We left him with his rosary in one hand. We put Victor in the other."

The blood had drained from Bunde's face. "That's terrible. But I'm not taking it with me. It's out of the question."

Dunne studied the torpid rotation of the fan. The question remained:

Which one did he use?

Maybe both.

Perpetual light, Billy.

Victor was nestled in a small aperture sewn in Dunne's fatigues, option, amulet, proviso.

Never say "never" because you never know.

Bassante referred them to a small, detailed map in their briefing books of the drop zone, a meadow twenty miles north of Banská Bystrica. "The success of last summer with some five hundred downed pilots rescued from Yugoslavia and three times that number from Romania set the bar high. Our goals are no less important. We want to erase the embarrassment of our men falling into German hands, bring them out alive, and make clear our interest in helping shape the future of a restored Czechoslovak state."

He turned his sharp profile to the map and poked it with the pointer. "Before we commit any significant force to a rescue attempt we must know the size, strength, and reliability of the partisan network in this area. The worst possible result would be to end up with the new group of rescuers suffering the same fate as the last.

"You'll have to assess the commitment of the partisans to risking additional losses in carrying out the rescue. This means paying attention to nuances. The partisans loyal to Moscow might be reluctant, believing the best course is to await the arrival of the Red Army. Those loyal to the government-in-exile in London will be eager to demonstrate their commitment to the Anglo-American alliance. The configuration of forces in Czechoslovakia needs to be explored. The information you gather will be helpful."

"You've left out one detail," Dunne said.

"What's that?" Bassante put down the pointer.

"Our exit."

"It depends."

"On whether we're still alive?"

Bassante leveled his sharp, inquisitor's face at Dunne's. "Save the sarcasm for the SS. They might find it a novelty. I don't."

Tired and distracted, conscious of the long list of items to attend to after the briefing—inventory of supplies intended for the partisans, equipment checks, final packing—Dunne hadn't intended his question to sound as sarcastic as Bassante interpreted it. "I didn't mean that the way it came out."

"No need for an apology." Bassante waved his hand dismissively, as if brushing away one of Bari's fat, lethargic flies. "It's a lot to absorb, so let me finish up. The timing of your exit depends on whether there's a rescue operation. If the prisoners have been removed to Germany, which can't be ruled out, your radio operator, Lieutenant Bunde, will let us know and we'll make arrangements to get you out.

"Finally, there's the matter of making contact with Dr. Schaefer. The man is a bit of a mystery. A medical doctor who'd served in the Austrian army in the first war, he founded a highly respected pharmaceutical firm. Its success reflects Schaefer's savvy as a salesman as well as his ability to navigate among the treacherous shoals of national and ideological antagonisms."

In the interwar years, Bassante explained, "Schaefer had traveled extensively. Along with headquarters in his native city of Brünn—Brno to the Czechoslovaks—he had branch offices in Vienna, Prague, and Zurich, and maintained a villa in the Grunewald district of Berlin, where, despite his well-advertised disinterest in politics and failure to join the Nazi Party, he acted as open-handed host to members of the regime's hierarchy.

"Unfortunately, no photographs of him are available. One of the few times he spoke for the record is a short interview he gave the *Pharmaceutical News*—it's in your briefing books—during a visit to the United States. After the outbreak of war, he served as an adviser to the Wehrmacht's medical corps, helping expedite delivery of supplies to frontline units.

"In late 1942, the day after the Allied landing in North Africa led the Germans to occupy all of France, Allen Dulles arrived in Bern, Switzerland, on the last train from Vichy. His mission was to set up an OSS listening post on the Reich's doorstep."

Practically every German industry, Bassante related, had ties with Swiss businesses and maintained offices there. Schaefer made several visits to his company's office in Zurich, which aroused no suspicion. Eventually, he contacted Dulles's office in Bern and began providing information on the Wehrmacht's deteriorating position in the east. He also intimated he was privy to a growing body of information of an "especially alarming nature." When the intelligence Schaefer provided proved useful, Dulles arranged a meeting.

Bassante paused and cleared his throat. "It's been no secret the 'special treatment' the Germans have meted out to the Jews in endless rounds of confiscations, deportations, and pogroms. But Schaefer claimed to have chronicled something on a whole other scale, involving systematic extermination at the hands of special firing squads—Einsatzgruppen—and in a network of camps in occupied Poland whose sole purpose was the liquidation of Jews. *All of them.*

"In the spring of '42, in order to fill the quota of labor conscripts demanded by the Germans, Tiso offered to deliver Slovakia's fifty thousand Jews. He did the added favor of using the Hlinka Guard to round them up. Learning of the Jews' deportation to the sprawling operation under way at Auschwitz, Schaefer used his connections within the regime and his firm's status as subcontractor to chemical giant IG Farben to wheedle the authority to visit its plant there.

"He made it a practice to note the names and ranks of those he encountered, and the roles and assignments of different units.

Friend, confessor, confidant, and patron to police, civil administrators, railway executives, doctors, contractors, regular army staff, and SS men, noncoms and high-ranking officers, he constantly added to his summary of conversations, tearful confessions, drunken rants, boasts, rumors. What he uncovered was nothing less than industrialized murder."

Bassante reached into his briefcase and laid on the table a thin, soft-covered report so that the title was visible: *German Extermination Camps—Auschwitz and Birkenau.* "This was published by the War Refugee Board last November. It's a compilation of several accounts. The Germans have done their best to draw a veil over the effort to exterminate the Jews. But at least among intelligence circles and the Allied leadership, the facts are known. If Schaefer's records are as exhaustive as he makes out, they'll add invaluably to our ability to apprehend the perpetrators and their accomplices."

"Do we know where those records are?" Van Hull tossed the wet, limp match he'd been cleaning his teeth with into the ashtray and pulled a fresh one from a pack.

"They're with Schaefer."

"Where's he?"

"He told Dulles he kept the records in a safe in his villa in Berlin. When he returned there in August, not long after the attempt on Hitler's life, he sensed his lack of political conviction was no longer deemed innocent idiosyncrasy but suspected as a possible cover for treason. That night he began turning his trove of information into microfiche and burning the originals.

"Several days later, he drove to Prague, then Brünn, and lay low in the countryside, where he has numerous friends. He was incommunicado until he appeared in Banská Bystrica, where he joined the Slovak military rebels and the partisans. They in turn put him in touch with Lieutenant Jahn and his party."

"Did he give the microfiche to Jahn?" Van Hull continued to glean between his teeth with the match.

"We don't know. What we do know is by that time the SS was ready to overrun the last rebel strongholds. When it was clear an air rescue wasn't possible, Jahn and his men set off to join the partisans in the mountains. Schaefer didn't have the stamina to keep up with them. Instead, he asked that he be roughed up and thrown in a cell, so that it'd look as if he'd been a prisoner of the partisans."

"Did it work?"

"In the short run, it seems so. He's well practiced bluffing his way. Last report from the underground in Banská Bystrica indicated that he was seen driving away in his Tatra 77 from the headquarters of the Sicherheitsdienst, the SS security police."

"Good taste in cars." Van Hull chewed the paper end of the match. "You think he still has the microfiche?"

"Here's hoping you'll provide the answer. If it's yes, you'll take both Schaefer and the microfiche under your protection. The Soviets and their agents will be competitors in that regard. They've their own reasons for taking control of any materials pertinent to their grand narrative of the 'Great Patriotic War.'"

Bassante went over the details of their drop. The partisans would meet them with a horse-drawn lumber wagon, load the weapons and supplies on it, and then escort them to a safe house, about ten miles outside Banská Bystrica.

"You'll be on foot," Bassante said, "and moving as quickly as possible both to take advantage of the dark and because you'll want to. The average daytime temperature in the area has been twenty-eight degrees; nighttime, zero to minus five."

From the safe house, radio contact would be made with Bari. Anton, the partisan leader, ran a bakery. Given Lieutenant Bunde's proficiency in the language, he'd accompany Anton in his delivery truck for a close look at the Hlinka headquarters where it seemed probable Jahn and his party were being held. Once Bunde felt comfortable with the layout, Anton would bring Van Hull and Dunne to meet with the underground unit in town. By then, the arms and explosives should have been infiltrated.

"You have to establish whether the prisoners are where we think they are and if the partisans can support a rescue attempt. Here again, Bunde's familiarity with the language will be important. Once we have some certainty about the fate of Jahn and his party, we'll make arrangements to get you out."

"Nothing ever goes according to plan." Van Hull discarded the match and worked this teeth with the edge of the matchbook cover."

"You might think about getting a Zippo. They might be useless for purposes of dental hygiene, but they don't get wet and are more reliable than matches."

"They need to be refueled and the flints wear out. Matches are a lot easier to replace. Best of all is to know how to start a fire without either."

"Be prepared. Another Boy Scout skill?"

"The more the merrier."

Bassante ended with a pep talk of the kind prepared and distributed by one of the morale/propaganda committees run by Lieutenant Colonel Carlton Baxter Bartlett. The boilerplate advice was framed around pitching ace Dizzy Dean's assertion that he avoided "the fancy stuff," and stuck to "three simple pitches—curve, fastball, and changeup."

In this instance, the simple pitches, which Bassante read from an index card, varied from the patently untrue ("Every mission counts") to the self-evident ("Success depends on teamwork") to the aspirational ("Keep your wits about you").

He put down the card. "Depend on the fact that little, if anything, will go according to plan. So let me add one imparted to me by Louie Pohl. 'The simplest and most necessary of all' is how Louie describes it: '*Pay attention.*'"

* * *

The next day was taken up with final packing and equipment inspection. In the evening, Dunne had just finished writing to Roberta when Bassante stopped by his room. The door was open. "Sorry for barging in. I know you'd like time to yourself before you leave."

"I never relax the night before a drop." Dunne was lying on the bed.

Bassante sat at the desk. He stroked his nose with thumb and forefinger. "You need to know something. I'm responsible for you going on this mission."

"*You?*" Dunne sat up. "General Donovan said he was the guilty party."

"He decided on the mission. Realist though he is, the general has a romantic streak. He's read *Henry V* one too many times. When he frames a challenge in terms of noblesse-oblige athleticism—teammates, the old college try, rah-rah—he's especially vulnerable. You know that old chestnut attributed to the Duke of Wellington—'The Battle of Waterloo was won on the playing fields of Eton'? Well, it wasn't won by public school brats, but by English slum dwellers, Irish spalpeens, and Scottish ploughboys.

"When the general directed me to work up this mission, I told him I thought it unnecessary. The odds against it are substantial to insurmountable. He overruled me, as I presumed he would. Van Hull immediately volunteered but was adamant he wanted to go alone. He understood the odds and didn't want to risk anybody else's life. I convinced the general it should be a three-man scouting operation and to put off a rescue attempt until we had a better picture of the situation on the ground. I recommended Bunde and you."

"You chose Bunde, too?"

"His fluency in the language is invaluable. For sure, he's swayed by the ancestral attachments to the old country typical of the children of immigrants, but he's no supporter of the Tiso regime. He'll work well, I think. He needs guidance, that's all."

"Why'd you choose me?"

"Word of mouth led me to read your file. In your career, you've been around the block more times than almost anyone else in this organization. It seemed to me you possessed the perfect balance between Van Hull's valor and Bunde's inexperience. When I brought up your name, the general jumped on it. 'Dunne knows how to deal with trouble and how to avoid it, and he can spot what others might miss.'

"I'm not sure about finding Schaefer and his microfiche—it seems about as likely as stumbling across the Abominable Snowman—but if it's to be done, it will take not only luck but also the instincts of a first-class detective. Call it 'street smarts' if you like, the ability to distinguish important from unimportant, even if the difference isn't apparent at the time. You have it, I'm sure of it."

"I'm glad you've dubbed it Maxwell."

"Why?"

"Maxwell House Coffee. 'Good to the last drop.'"

"Ah, yes, that advertising slogan attributed to the first President Roosevelt, who on finishing a cup—or so some huckster claimed—blurted out words to that effect."

"I'm hoping this is my last drop."

Bassante abandoned a tentative attempt at smiling. "Subconsciously, I suppose, I chose the name because I grew up in Hoboken. Maxwell's electric sign watches over the town like the eye of God. But we select code names by going through the alphabet sequentially. This mission landed on *M* and was designated Maxwell. It was luck."

"Luck is fate's knuckleball. It has a will of its own."

"A good team is more important than an occasional knuckleball."

"Then let's call it *totiusque*."

"Say it again."

"*Totiusque*. It's from a prayer."

"The Suscipiat. Bane of every altar boy. I was one, too."

"It stuck with me. '*Totiusque*' always sounded to me like 'good luck.'"

"'Luck' isn't a word used in prayers, not Catholic ones. It means 'and all.' But for tonight we can pretend it does. Luck by any other name is still luck. So *totiusque*, Dunne."

Bassante smiled. This time it stuck.

Part III
The Last Drop

Dr. Gerhard Schaefer is a medical doctor and the chairman and chief executive officer of Aigle, an independent pharmaceutical company headquartered in Brünn, a city of more than 280,000 people. At the end of the Great War, Brünn, formerly a part of the Austro-Hungarian Empire, was incorporated into the newly created state of Czechoslovakia. (The city, referred to as Brno by the Czechs, reverted to German rule with the recent annexation of Bohemia and Moravia.)

Founded by Dr. Schaefer and his former partner, prize-winning chemist Dr. Herschel Cernak, in 1920, Aigle has amassed a record of successful product development and profitability throughout these tumultuous years.

Dr. Schaefer appears to be in his early fifties (he declined to give his age and it does not appear in his official biography). Balding, with a gap-toothed smile redolent of old-fashioned German *gemütlichkeit*, he has a friendly, open manner devoid of the haughty superiority that has become the preferred pose of present-day Germany's self-styled Übermensch. He is widely respected for his scientific knowledge, his business acumen, and his interest in literature and the arts.

Dr. Schaefer attended the Twelfth Annual International Pharmaceutical Convention, which was held in Baltimore, Maryland, from April 12 through 15. An unassuming man who speaks English flawlessly, with little trace of an accent, he graciously consented to a brief interview about the state of the industry and the world with *Pharmaceutical News*.

PN: You named your company Aigle in honor of the goddess of good health, correct?

GS: Yes, Aigle, which means "radiance" in Greek, is the daughter of Asclepius, god of medicine, and Epione, goddess of pain relief. A marriage made in heaven, if you will.

73

PN: What effect did the last war have on our industry?

GS: Major innovations were growing in number well before the turn of the century, but the war added a whole new impetus.

PN: What has been the impact of the world economic depression?

GS: As the breakthroughs made during the war came on the commercial market, they helped boost sales. The economic downturn dampened the appetite for research and development, but didn't reverse it.

PN: Will it take another war to spur a new age of innovation?

GS: I was a doctor in the last war. I would hope—though not presume—our species is smarter than that.

PN: Do you foresee another war in Europe?

GS: If there is a surer way for a man to make a fool of himself than to predict the future, I don't know what it is.

PN: Are you a man of strong political beliefs?

GS: Skepticism is the faith of the wise.

PN: Does that mean you don't share the convictions of your countrymen?

GS: I avoid convictions. I have questions, interests, and inclinations.

PN: Doesn't National Socialism require its citizens to make clear their convictions?

GS: I am a scientist and a businessman, not a preacher, prophet, or politician. In the work I do, convictions are antithetical to success. To paraphrase the Irish poet Yeats, the best resist all convictions, and the worst are filled with them. The most intelligent of my countrymen understand that, I'm sure.

PN: Without playing the prophet, can you offer us your view on the areas of greatest promise for the pharmaceutical industry in both the long and short term?

GS: Near term, I would look to the development of drugs to combat common and fatal infections. Long term, I would hope for new vaccines against acute viral infectious diseases such as infantile paralysis.

The Pharmaceutical News, May 3, 1939

January 1945

"Time set." Van Hull tapped a fingernail against the glass face of his wristwatch. "Oh-one-hundred." Dunne gave thumbs-up. Bunde opened his gloved hand, revealed a gold Miraculous Medal in his shaking palm. Light next to door blushed urgent red. Cargo of weapons and medical supplies went out first, men next, into moonless night—Van Hull, Bunde, Dunne last.

He never got used to the initial shock, sudden absence of saliva in his mouth, willing his sphincter shut, tumble into the void, commotion of plane's engines, and sharp, cold, numbing wind, plummeting free fall until brusque, upward jerk of parachute's deployment, noise and buffeting replaced by soundless tick-tock sway of descent.

The plane was quickly out of view. One chute drifted a hundred yards or so below. Dunne couldn't tell if it was Bunde's or Van Hull's.

He landed nearby in a snow-covered field ringed by firs. No sign of Bunde, his radio, or the crates of small arms and medical supplies. Van Hull sidled up beside him. They hurried into the woods, buried their chutes—working hard to break the frozen ground—huddled against the penetrating chill, and waited.

Mizzling, colorless dawn revealed the trail they'd left moving across the snow into the woods. They couldn't stay where they

75

were. Since they had landed almost directly on their target area, Van Hull said, they were about twenty miles north of Banská Bystrica.

Maybe Bunde had been wafted south or north by a rogue wind. Every drop had its quotient of unpredictability, eccentric wind, dissenting breeze, contrary current. Maybe he'd already hooked up with the underground. They stood motionless amid the expectant quiet. The sun broke through, quickly retreated. The morning grew warm. An otherworldly veil of vapory wisps made the woods seem vague, insubstantial.

Van Hull displayed a dime between thumb and forefinger. "My lucky charm."

"It doesn't seem to be working."

"We'll give it another try." Van Hull laid the dime atop his right thumbnail. "Now for that most time-honored instrument of scientific decision making, the coin toss." He catapulted it into the air, caught it in his palm, and slapped it on the back of his left hand. "Heads, we go north; tails, south."

"Shit." He rushed the dime back in his pocket and pointed over Dunne's shoulder. In the distance, a thin drape of silk hung limply from a tall pine, its train lost in the low-lying mist. Dunne circled left; Van Hull, right. They kept each other in sight, starting and stopping alternately, ready to provide covering fire.

Dunne reached the site first. The top of Bunde's parachute, which had never fully deployed, was snagged on the pine tree. His legs were splayed, arms sprawled open, head twisted backward, eyes wide. There'd be no need for him to fret over whether to use Victor or not.

They cut the chute free and placed Bunde's body on it. Van Hull slipped the dime into the vest pocket of Bunde's jacket. "The Greeks always supplied the dead with a coin to tip Charon for ferrying them across the Styx to the land of the dead."

Dunne spotted the Miraculous Medal several yards away,

bright oval of gold on a patch of ice freckled with pine needles. He put it back in Bunde's palm, closed it, whispered: "Eternal rest grant unto him, O Lord; perpetual light shine upon him."

They folded the chute over Bunde, an impromptu shroud, covered it with snow and pine branches.

They decided that though the main partisan strongholds were farther north, in the mountains, it made more sense to head south, toward Banská Bystrica, and get the mission under way. Whatever the reason that Anton and his men hadn't made contact—a mix-up in signals, German activity in the area—the underground had to be aware of the drop and be on the lookout for the rescue party and the much-needed supplies.

They shouldered packs and submachine guns and set off. They passed several farmhouses, abandoned ruins, walls broken and tumbled, some half razed. The ugly, greasy odor of burned bodies hung around them. Van Hull led the way along a ridge. A paved, two-lane road threaded its way through the narrow, steeply sloped gorge below. It was empty of traffic. He held up his hand. Steady half-grind, half-whine of heavy trucks grew stronger. They lay down and took cover.

Van Hull peered through his binoculars, methodically tightening the screw as he brought them into focus. A file of three slow-moving vehicles approached. In the lead was an armored car. An uncovered truck followed. Two rope-trussed men were bookended by soldiers with their Schmeissers at the ready. A canvas-covered truck filled with troops was behind. He rolled on his back, rested the binoculars on his chest, and crossed forefingers, imitating the stick-grenade insignia of Sturmbrigade Dirlewanger.

The column moved out of view. Van Hull put away the binoculars. "Those prisoners are probably what's left of the partisans sent to meet us. They looked pretty banged up. The SS probably knocked the truth out of them. Once they confirm where we landed, they'll shoot them."

"And then come after us."

Van Hull reshouldered pack and weapon. "Let's move."

They climbed off the ridge and trotted north along the road, breaking the trail of footprints. Smashed and derelict vehicles, sides emblazoned with the double-barred Slovak cross, littered the fringes of the road. A charred corpse—top of its head blown off, right hand frozen in position as if to protect now-vanished eyes— stuck out from the turret of a flame-scorched tank. They reentered the woods. A wet snow began to fall. They took refuge in a cow-shed, devoured a meal of cold rations, and pushed north again.

Van Hull led. He told Dunne to be careful to step in his tracks and leave a single row of footprints. As difficult as it was, Dunne kept up. His breathing grew labored; trickle of sweat ran down his back and made him shiver. He felt as if snow were falling inside his head, fuzzy, cottony, obliterating any thought other than leaden weight of his own legs. More sweat formed on his forehead, dripped into his eyes, blurred his sight.

It was dark when the snow stopped. They paused beneath an outcrop in a shallow, cave-like indentation on the side of a steep hill, took off their packs, and sat on the dry ground. The tempera-ture had sunk noticeably. The cold tightened around them.

"We need a plan," Van Hull said.

"I plan to get warm." Dunne stood. He decided to see if there might be a larger, deeper cave farther along the ledge in which it would be safe to light a fire. He'd gone only a few yards when his feet shot out from under him. His helmet flew off. He crashed hard and slid down the frozen stream he'd inadvertently stepped on. He tried to grab a shrub or tree to stop his descent but tumbled into a ravine.

He lay still. A clamor of falling ice and rocks announced Van Hull's descent. "You okay?"

"Christ, I did something to my back."

"Where?"

Dunne touched the base of his spine. "Here."

"You probably bruised your coccyx."

"My what?"

"Coccyx is Greek for cuckoo—the tailbone is shaped like a cuckoo's beak."

"Thanks for the anatomy lesson."

"See if you can stand." Van Hull extended his hand.

Dunne took it and tried to get on his feet. The surge of pain in his right ankle made his eyes well. "My ankle is screwed up." He fell back down

Van Hull knelt, untied the boot, and felt the ankle and the area around it. "The bone isn't displaced. Probably just a bad sprain."

"Some plan, hey?"

"'The best-laid schemes o' mice an' men gang aft agley.' So wrote the Scottish poet Bobbie Burns. 'The best-laid plans of mice and men oft go astray' is how it's rendered in English."

"Just what the doctor ordered. A poetry lecture." Dunne grasped Van Hull's shoulder, made another attempt to stand, but the pain prevented him.

"You should know better than to travel with a teacher."

"Next trip, I'll sign on with a medical student, or better, a nurse."

"For now, let's concentrate on getting back upstairs." Van Hull looked up. A three-quarter moon had appeared. A scatter of stars slipped from behind the fast-dispersing clouds. "*Ad astra per aspera.*"

"It'll take more than prayers."

"It's the state motto of Kansas. 'To the stars is through hard work.'"

"You know Latin?"

"Yes, I know Latin. And Greek."

"College boys like you and Bassante usually do. But you were never an altar boy. You're a left footer, aren't you?"

79

"A what?"

"Protestant."

"I was raised Episcopalian, high church—ritually closer to Catholic than Protestant. But we don't believe in infallibility, either of the pope or the Bible, and we never let orthodoxy get in the way of sanity. Besides, being Catholic isn't a prerequisite for mastering Latin. Some of the greatest scholars of it are Jews and nonbelievers."

"*Suscipiat?*"

"What?"

"*Suscipiat.* It's a Latin word. What's it mean?"

Van Hull helped Dunne stand on one leg and had him put his arms around his neck. "I know what you're doing, Fin. You're stalling. It's not going to work."

"You don't know, do you?" The intense pain in Dunne's ankle made him wince.

Steep, pine-studded slope loomed above. Van Hull bent, hooked his arms under Dunne's knees, and hoisted him onto his back. "'*Suscipiat*,' third-person singular present active subjunctive of '*suscipio*.' 'May he accept.' A prayer from the Catholic Mass, if I remember correctly. Do you know the words?"

"I memorized them as an altar boy. I remember them in Latin. I'm not sure about the English." The opening phrase suddenly came back to him: "May the Lord accept."

"Repeat it to yourself and hang on tight." Van Hull took hold of a cone-laden branch and began to climb. He pushed ahead with steady, strong strides, grasping one branch, pulling, and grabbing another. Dunne clung to his back, aware—more than he'd been before—of Van Hull's prowess, which wasn't manifest in bulging calves or forearms but coiled inside, taut and compact, like a metal spring.

Van Hull didn't stop until he reached the cleft in the side of the hill. He placed Dunne against the back wall; sat beside him, panting.

"About that plan," Dunne said, "we still need one."

"You were on the right track."

"But landed on the wrong ankle."

"We'll see to that first, then find a proper place for a fire, where it can't be seen." Van Hull culled two rod-like branches from a tree, took an undershirt from his pack, and used his knife to fashion several strips. He bound them around the branches, secured the splint with the straps from Dunne's pack, and immobilized the lower leg.

"That helps," Dunne said. "But I'm certain it's broken."

"Me, too."

"A few minutes ago, you said you thought it was a sprain."

"First rule of doctoring: Say whatever necessary to put the patient at ease."

"The legal term is lying."

"I learned it from my mother's father. He was a doctor."

"Sounds more like a lawyer."

"That was my father's father." Van Hull pulled a sock over Dunne's foot and laid pack and submachine gun by his side. "I'm going to find the best place to dig a fire hole. Stay awake. I don't want you to freeze to death. And stay put."

"Sure, unless a taxi comes along. But given our luck, it'll probably be off-duty."

"I'll blink my flashlight twice—one long, one short—so you know it's me." Van Hull slipped off into the woods.

Dunne lit a cigarette, miniature flare enlarged by encircling night, cupped glowing tip in palm, sucked smoke into lungs, exhaled a spectral, slowly rising string. When the stub was so small another drag would raise a blister on his lip, he flicked it into the dark.

He shivered. He dug at the frozen ground, as if he might find warmth below. Above, the clouds were gone. The night sky was crowded with stars. His chin sank to his chest. He struggled to remember why it was important to stay awake but couldn't.

"*Was haben wir hier?*" Harsh brightness played across his face and eyelids. Unsure where he was, unable to see beyond the encircling glare, he lifted his hand to shield his eyes. The barrel of a submachine gun knocked his hand away. The nozzle rested a few inches from his nose. How long had he been unconscious? He had no idea. He reached for his gun. It wasn't there. He stared into the light.

A second voice chimed in: "*Es ist ein Amerikaner, glauben Sie nicht?*"

"*Es riecht wie ein!*"

The two voices laughed in unison.

The light raced over his chest and legs. He was hauled to his feet, propelled against the wall, and patted down; .45 pistol was jerked from his shoulder holster, knife from its sheath on his belt. The pain in his ankle was excruciating. He fell down, rolled on his side, and slipped hand into pocket, into tiny aperture that held the LP.

The light fixed on his face. "*Sind Sie allein?*"

He tried his best with pidgin German, tried again in English: "I don't speak German." He turned his head. With a rapid, furtive gesture, he slid the capsule into his mouth. *Ecce Victor.*

The quick and the dead all rolled in one.

A boot rested on the leg splint, pressure steadily increased. "*Sind Sie allein?*"

In the face of death, straight line of conscious mind bent, curved, turned circular, round and round, closed in on itself, subconscious grooves embedded in memory, words he'd been trained to hear/heed—and trained others to hear/heed—chorused in his head.

Remember what you were told?

Words easy to say back then, hard to act on now.

Don't let terror take charge of your mind . . .

Terror has a mind of its own.

Focus on where you are . . .

Prone, alone, maneuver lozenge to back teeth.

Concentrate on what's directly in front . . .

Eyes shut, black screen, last image: Roberta across the table from him at Ben Marden's, long ago and far away, so far away, face illumined by a single candle, perpetual light.

He prepared to bite.

The SS trooper removed his foot, took hold of him again, and had him half hauled to his feet when the light from behind went out. Strangled, gurgling sound was followed by the thump of a body hitting the ground. The trooper let go. As he swiveled around and pointed his submachine gun, Dunne grabbed his legs.

The trooper pulled loose, reeled forward, and fell to his knees. A blade slashed across his neck. Blood spurted from his carotid artery. A gun butt whacked him squarely in the face. He tumbled backward.

Dunne snatched the light, flashed it on Van Hull—grim-faced, gun and bloody knife in hand.

"Turn that goddamn thing off. We have to hurry. These can't be the only two." Van Hull swiped the bloody blade across his sleeve and sheathed it.

"Hurry where?" Dunne extinguished the light.

"The road is only a little ways. We'll commandeer the first car that comes along."

"Then what?"

"Then we'll figure out what."

"Leave me." He slipped Victor beneath his tongue. *Be prepared.*

Van Hull bent over one of the dead troopers. He stripped the corpse of helmet and bloodstained coat and put them on; swung the dead trooper's weapon over right shoulder, put Dunne's arm around left. "Let's move."

With Van Hull's support, Dunne hopped a few paces on his good leg. "I can't."

"Sit here." Van Hull lowered him onto a rock. After several minutes, he returned with gnarl-headed tree limb.

"Where's the supply closet?"

Van Hull pointed at the woods. "Trick is to know where to look."

"Nice trick."

"Thank the Boy Scouts." Van Hull fit the limb to Dunne's height and started whittling the gnarl into a T-bar. He helped Dunne up.

"Those troopers thought they were tracking a single operative. Didn't expect someone to sneak up from behind. Scouts teach you that, too?"

"Who else?"

"Maybe the OSS should turn training over to them."

Van Hull draped Dunne's arm over his shoulder. "Unfortunately, they've the same policy on throat slitting as misdemeanors. No merit badges."

Supported by Van Hull and the crutch, he hobbled along, making steady progress. They stopped to rest. Letting go of Van Hull's shoulder, he stumbled, fell, gasped with pain. The capsule popped from beneath his tongue and tumbled down his throat.

"Christ, I just swallowed Victor."

"You bite it?"

"No."

"You should be all right."

"I'll lie here till I'm sure."

"Then it'll be the SS, not Victor, gets you."

Van Hull lifted Dunne to his feet. He lost track of how long they walked. It felt as if Van Hull was carrying him. Sky grew light. The brutal ache in his ankle and the discomfort of the crude T-bar against his armpit made him halt. "I'm done."

Van Hull eased him onto a tree stump. In the east, dull tapestry of morning sky had a rust-colored hem. Directly ahead, beyond the trees, was a two-lane asphalt road.

"You said it was only a little farther."

"We got here, didn't we?"

"Where?"

"Where we need to be."

"Nowhere?"

"The road to Banská Bystrica. It's the only way left." Van Hull opened his coat, pulled out his .45, and passed it to Dunne. "We can't keep moving like this. Your ankle can't take much more." He looked around. "I'm going to stop the first civilian vehicle comes by. Cover me."

"Odds are the only vehicles on the road are full of Germans hunting for us."

Submachine gun over shoulder, Van Hull had already started walking toward the road. He turned. "Victor should exit soon. If you want to use it again, be sure to . . ."

The mechanical rhythm of a fast-approaching, well-tuned engine came from where the road curved south. Silver and stream-lined, the car that came into view had no military markings.

Van Hull walked into the middle of the road.

Dunne dropped behind the stump and took aim.

Perhaps the driver was cruising along, not paying atten-tion, or maybe he was testing Van Hull's resolve, but he braked at the last moment, two or three yards in front of Van Hull, who acted as unperturbed as a cop directing traffic at 57th and Fifth. He walked around the car, opened the door on the pas-senger's side, and leaned in. The driver, in brown fedora and brown woolen overcoat, hands firmly on the wheel, turned toward him.

Right eye sighted on the driver's head, Dunne did his best to ignore the distracting throb in his ankle bone and keep the gun steady. He weighed the necessity to act quickly—take out the driv-er if he reached for a weapon, or hit the gas in an effort to escape, or made a move toward Van Hull—against the need not to mistake an innocent gesture for a threatening one and, above all, to make sure Van Hull was out of the line of fire.

Smoke poured from the tailpipe as the car idled in place. "Get a move on, Dick," Dunne whispered to himself. Listening half expectantly for the sound of another approaching vehicle, he was startled by a growl. After a second or two, he realized it was his own stomach. He felt a loosening in his bowels.

Victor and he were preparing to part company.

Stout and smiling, the driver got out. Dunne couldn't see Van Hull. They'd killed two SS troopers and stripped one of his uniform. If captured, their captors would have their revenge before finishing them off.

The driver started to walk toward him. Dunne gripped right wrist with left hand, aimed, and kept Mulholland's rule in mind: *Be sure to kill the right people, but don't be afraid of making a mistake.* Van Hull's head popped up on the other side of the car. He hurried around its front and trotted toward Dunne, leaving the driver slightly behind.

Dunne raised his head. Perspiration slid down his face, onto neck, into collar. *Shoot the fucker before he shoots you.*

"We're in luck!" Van Hull shouted.

Dunne removed his finger from the trigger and lowered the gun.

Van Hull took off coat and helmet and dumped them behind the stump. "Give me a hand," he said to the man in the brown fedora. They reached down, lifted Dunne to his feet, carried him to the car, and lowered him in the back seat. Van Hull tossed in the impromptu crutch and his submachine gun.

Dunne stretched his legs. The driver took hold of his ankle, gently probed and palpated, the way a doctor would. "The splint is well done. But the ankle must be properly seen to. We must hurry." He climbed in behind the wheel.

Van Hull stood back, admiring the car. When he tapped on

the window, Dunne rolled it down. "Can you believe it, Fin? A Tatra 77, a true classic."

"Tell me about it when we get to the auto show." Dunne rolled the window up.

"Only carmaker in America produced anything comparable was the Auburn Automobile Company. My father is an aficionado. Their Cord 810 sedan . . ."

The driver pleaded, "Please, I implore you, let's go." He revved the motor.

After another admiring once-over, Van Hull hopped in the front. Dunne sank into the softly yielding seat. Gray velour upholstery. The slightly overheated interior was like a warm, muscle-relaxing bath. The car quickly picked up speed. Framed in the car window, the white-dusted trees and snow-covered landscape seemed rustic and serene, a Christmas card scene, *Season's Greetings from Slovakia.*

The driver glanced at Dunne in the rearview mirror. "This is a miracle." His eyes were a neutral blue, unperturbed, unreadable.

"He guessed who we are," Van Hull said. "And I guessed who he is: Gerhard Schaefer."

The smile in the mirror seemed unrehearsed. "After a night of nothing but bad luck, this is almost too good to be true." His English was flawless, accent slight.

"Like stumbling on the Abominable Snowman." Dunne cracked open the window.

The smile in the mirror widened. "We've nothing so exotic in Slovakia."

Dunne breathed the cold air that rushed in. "Where we headed?"

"About six kilometers outside Banská Bystrica is a house in the woods, secluded, secure, where I've been staying."

"Mind if I smoke?" Van Hull asked.

"Not at all." Schaefer pushed in the cylindrical lighter.

"We were told we'd be met by a partisan group led by 'Anton' and taken to a safe house about ten miles outside town."

Schaefer slowed the car, swung right, then left onto a dirt road. "Best to stay off the main roads as much as we can. I wish my vehicle was less conspicuous, but it's all I have." He drove the rutted, uneven road at a slow pace. "It takes longer but is safer." He pulled to the side of the road and parked. He extracted the lighter.

Van Hull leaned down, touched the tip of the cigarette in his lips to the red-hot coil, and puffed; handed the cigarette back to Dunne and lit another for himself.

Schaefer plugged the cylinder back in. He laid his hat beside him. "Yesterday everything went wrong. The SS knew something was up, but wasn't quite sure when or where. They carried out a roundup in Banská Bystrica. Anton and several of his men were caught. By this morning, they knew. Anton has been shot. The others were made to talk." He bowed his head. The bald patch atop was visible in the rearview mirror. "I learned of all this only a few hours ago. I didn't know of your mission. When I found out, I decided to see if by some miracle I could make contact."

"Miracle accomplished."

"So far." Schaefer steered back onto the dirt road, which soon ended. They returned to the highway.

Dunne's cigarette tasted tired and dry, less the fault of the cigarette, more of his own exhaustion. After a puff or two, he flung it out the window; it rose, fell, spun wildly, ricocheted off the asphalt, spraying sparks like one of those German rockets whose guidance mechanisms went kerflooey.

Off to the right were a church and a small cluster of houses and shops, some intact, others wrecked and burned, roofs caved in. Directly across the market square was a train station, four engine-less boxcars parked in front. No one was in sight.

Dunne remembered shelled and empty villages he'd seen in

the first war and the endless procession of half-wrecked and ruined places featured in the newspapers and newsreels of this one. Another winter scene: *Season's Greetings from Wartime Wherever. Be glad you're where you are and not here.* Anonymous victims. Anonymous village. People and places the world had never heard of and never would. The unwritten history of all wars. He took a deep breath and closed the window. "There's the church, and there's the steeple. What about the people?"

Schaefer shrugged. "Winter and war have a way of driving them indoors."

"What's its name?" Van Hull asked.

"I'm not sure. Does it matter?"

Van Hull turned to watch the houses go by. "'Thy sports are fled, and all thy charms withdrawn; / Amidst thy bowers the tyrant's hand is seen / And Desolation saddens all thy green . . .'"

"You sound like an Englishman, Major. They love their tea and poetry, at least the cultured ones."

"Did you like the States?" Dunne sank deeper into the plush upholstery.

"'Like' would be an understatement. I love your country for its bluntness and originality. I was there all too briefly yet felt at home. In a different time, I might have stayed. Been easier than returning to the nightmare here. But I had to come back."

Van Hull stubbed out his cigarette in the tray beneath the dashboard "'Breathes there the man with soul so dead / Who never to himself hath said, / This is my own, my native land! / Whose heart hath ne'er within him burned / As home his footsteps he hath turned / From wandering on a foreign strand!'"

"You are a walking anthology!"

"The peril of traveling with a teacher," Dunne said. "Lots of quotes."

"It's standard stuff, but it gets students interested so they'll tackle the moderns, Auden, Eliot, Yeats, and the like."

Yeats. Dunne put his hand on the leather fold in the breast pocket of his jacket.

Why remember one thing and not another?

"But the sentiment is so true. What kind of man deserts his homeland when its very soul is in danger? I've been able to compile important records—a formidable body of evidence—that will help set the record straight about the enormity of the crimes that have been committed. I don't regret it."

"You talked your way out of an SS interrogation." Van Hull glanced back at the deserted village, but it had vanished behind a phalanx of trees.

"Once they had me, I couldn't vouch for what I'd tell them or not. I had no idea of how much 'treatment' of theirs I could take before I broke. Fortunately, they were convinced by my story. I thought the account of what happened reached Bari."

"No small feat to bluff the SS."

"Perhaps you think I should have gone with Lieutenant Jahn and his men, no? They wanted me to. But I knew I'd slow them down and add to their chances of being captured. I had my detention by the partisans faked. They gave me a good pounding to make it look real. It wasn't just my performance, however, that carried the day. The Soviets were on the move and the partisans growing stronger. The SS was distracted. They let me go for the time being. The partisans secured me a hiding place."

"They've been very concerned in Bari about losing contact with you."

"The messages weren't delivered. The partisans blocked them."

"Why?"

"I'm not sure how exhaustive your briefing was, but those in favor of the government-in-exile in London—and return of independent, democratic Czechoslovakia—they want a strong force landed in support of an immediate rescue of Jahn and his men."

"You've seen them since their capture?" Van Hull didn't hide his excitement.

"Not in person. But I know as fact the Hlinka Guards are holding them in Banská Bystrica. Anton confirmed it. He was hopeful that, with Allied help, he could free them. But the partisans who take their orders from Moscow were against it. Their wish is for the Red Army to take charge as soon as possible, and it's they who hold the stronger hand. They control communications with Bari."

"Do they know about the information you've collected?"

"Yes, they know I have it." Schaefer shook his head. "But not *where*. That is my secret. I'm not idly boasting when I say I've risked my life to gather it, to get it all down, writing furiously at night while it was still fresh, dates, locations, names, ranks, branches of the service, doctors, assistants, advisers. I allowed nothing to escape me.

"Many will think me a traitor when the truth comes out, but it is they who in their complicity have betrayed the fatherland, our noble, decent Germany, which was once the bulwark of European civilization. To all of them, I was a reliable ally, eager to help, always ready with a gift for wives and girlfriends. They confided in me their most intimate and important secrets. Once, as I was just coming to a full appreciation of what was underway, an operative at IG Farben shared his car with me on an inspection of industrial operations at Auschwitz. The car bore the insignia of the Red Cross.

"After we'd driven a while, he added in a bragging way that he'd been entrusted with a 'special mission of a sanitary nature.' He jerked his thumb toward the trunk. 'Back there,' he said, 'I'm carrying Passover presents for the Jews.'

"'What kind of presents?' I asked.

"'Gas canisters—a crate full.'

"'Disinfectant?'

"He winked. 'This gas exterminates vermin and rodents of all types—two-legged as well as four-.'

"I soon learned firsthand what he was hinting at, and believe me, the partisans would love nothing more than to acquire what I've amassed so they can pass it to the Soviets. Think how useful it would be to Moscow to have a detailed list of the major criminals and their accomplices in the treatment of the Jews, and then to decide who to prosecute and liquidate, and who to intimidate and turn to their purposes. As long as I'm in their reach, they are content to wait for me to hand it over."

"Are you holed up alone?" Van Hull asked.

"'Held up alone'? I don't know what you mean."

"*Holed up*. Are you living by yourself?"

"Yes, but as soon as we get to my quarters, I'll alert the underground, and we'll move fast to get this operation under way." Schaefer veered back onto the highway. He drove at an inconspicuous speed, almost as if they were out for a Sunday drive.

An exhaust-spewing civilian truck *whooshed* past in the opposite direction. Dunne sighed loudly and opened his eyes. "How much longer?"

"I thought we'd lost you to the arms of Morpheus." Schaefer peered at Dunne in the mirror with a concerned expression. "No wonder with all you've been through. We're ten minutes away at most. I've plenty of painkillers. I'll see to that ankle myself."

"Afraid I can't wait."

"For what?"

"Victor. He's got to leave and won't take no for an answer."

"Victor?" Schaefer's concern gave way to confusion. "Victor who?"

"You certain you can't wait, Fin?" Van Hull asked.

"Victor is even more certain."

Van Hull pointed at the roadside. "Pull over far as you can."

Schaefer did as told. "Who is this Victor?"

"The LP. *Tödlich pille.* He swallowed one a few hours ago but didn't bite it."

"Ach, that. I'll get him another. If he tries to reuse the one he took, he could die whether he bites it or not. Most of the covering is probably worn away."

Dunne opened the car door. "Do it in here or out there, that's the choice."

"We'll be quick." Van Hull got out, lifted Dunne's makeshift crutch from the back seat and helped him stand. Van Hull at his side, Dunne hobbled into the woods. "Is there anything in the *Boy Scout Handbook* about taking a dump on one leg?"

"Whatever works best is the Boy Scout way."

Dunne undid his belt and dropped his pants and underwear. "That's what I most remember about basic training in the last war."

"What?"

"The instructors never got around to teaching how to take a shit in a rifle pit two feet deep with German snipers ready to blow your head off. Turned out to be among the most valuable lessons there was." Dunne squatted on a large log, rear extending past, and gripped the sapling in front. "Which way with Schaefer?"

Van Hull looked into the distance. "That's the reason you had him stop, isn't it?"

"What?"

"To decide whether we go any farther or not."

"If this is a trap, we're only getting in deeper."

"Maybe it's not."

"Maybe I'm Mrs. Roosevelt."

"You think he's an SS plant?"

"He's as phony as a chocolate cigar."

"Then why'd he tell us where Jahn is?"

"Because he knows desperate men will latch on to anything that gives them hope. Who knows that better than the SS? The whole way he shows up in the one car we've probably heard him connected with. 'This is almost too good to be true'—that's the one truthful thing he said." Dunne grunted. "Here it comes."

"Shit."

"What'd you expect?"

"No, I mean where's that leave us?"

"Don't suppose you brought along any toilet paper?"

"I'll buy you a roll when we get home. That's a promise."

"No need. I've something as good." Dunne lifted the leather fold from the breast pocket of his jump jacket. He extracted the operational map they'd each been given. "I knew it would come in handy."

"For Chrissake, you still might need that."

"This is the best use it's had so far. Besides, you've got a copy, and if I lose you, all I need is Victor." As he unfolded the map, a piece of newspaper fluttered to the ground. "Give me that, will you? That's what I was looking for."

Van Hull picked it up and handed it to Dunne, who began to read. He glanced over Dunne's shoulder at the *Pharmaceutical News* piece Bassante had included in the briefing books. "Come on, Fin, it's a little late to catch up on your homework."

Dunne shrugged. "Maybe not."

"You asked for toilet paper, not reading material."

"Sometimes they're the same thing." Dunne focused on the paper, almost as if he were trying to commit it to memory, then threw it away. He used the map to wipe himself. Van Hull helped him to stand and pull up his pants.

Schaefer motioned for them to hurry.

Van Hull waved back. "If he's who you think he is, why didn't the SS spring the trap when he picked us up? Why don't they do it now? Why this elaborate delay?"

"They'll move at their convenience, not ours. Our ersatz Dr. Schaefer probably thinks he can use us to contact Bari and lure in a far larger party of would-be rescuers." Dunne grasped his crutch, poked at the solid cone of excrement behind the log, uncovered a yellow capsule, and flicked it loose. "Get that for me, will you, Dick?"

"Wish I were as certain as you." Van Hull bent down, pinched the capsule between thumb and forefinger, and dropped it in the pocket of Dunne's jacket. "*Bon appétit.*"

"'Shoot the fucker before the fucker shoots you,' as Yeats put it."

"Yeats?"

"From his early stuff. An unpublished poem, I think." Dunne gave the gun to Van Hull. "If it comes to it, fire."

"How will I know?"

"Remember what Bassante said?"

"He said a lot of things."

"'Simplest and most necessary of all: Pay attention.'"

After helping Dunne settle in his seat, Van Hull got in the front.

"The longer we're on these roads, the more dangerous it is." Schaefer surveyed the highway in the rearview mirror. "Well, for now, at least, it's clear."

"Oh, one thing." Dunne's eyes met Schaefer's in the mirror. "A good friend of yours in Bari said if we made contact, we must say hello."

"Who's that?"

"Epione."

"Epione? I'm not sure I remember such a person. Can you describe him?"

Van Hull bolted to attention in his seat. "Epione's a she."

"And she said she knew me?"

"Very well," Van Hull said. "She's Asclepius's daughter."

"Asclepius's daughter?" The face in the mirror suddenly blossomed with an awkward, open-mouthed smile of perfectly aligned teeth; eyes skittered right to left, back again. "This is a joke, yes?"

"Epione is the goddess of pain relief. You must remember her from when the dentist twisted the wire to close the gap between your front teeth."

"So much has happened, it is hard to remember everything and everybody." The slow, steady tilt of Schaefer's body was subtle but unmistakable. His hand slipped around the Luger hidden in the pouch on the side of his seat.

Dunne was about to lunge forward when Van Hull shot Schaefer through the neck, percussive roar deafening as an artillery round. Exiting bullet shattered the driver's window. Smoke and silence filled the car. A thirteenth way to win people to your way of thinking—more direct than anything Dale Carnegie recommended. And more convincing.

They sat motionless in the postblast silence following Van Hull's shot through the neck of ersatz Dr. Schaefer. His body slumped over the steering wheel. Gun smoke trailed out the window shattered by the same bullet that had splattered blood and spinal fluid across the back of the seat.

Dunne wiped a globule from his lips, licked them clean. Salty, repellent taste slipped down his throat. He lay back. Same gray velour cushioned ceiling as seat. They should be in a hurry. But where? He patted his breast pocket. Here was what was left of luck. He touched Victor's small, reassuring bulge. *Totiusque.*

The sky was as gray as the seat and velour ceiling, gray everywhere, up and down, soft as a blanket, noiseless, restful, full of sleep.

Van Hull reached back, bunched Dunne's collar in his fist, pulled him upright, and struck his cheek, more pat than slap. "Fin, save the nap for later."

He handed Dunne the gun, hopped out of the car, went to the driver's side, opened the door, and laid the dead body on the ground. He removed the overcoat and jacket, took his knife, sliced open the left side of the shirt, and lifted up the arm. "His SS blood group is tattooed right where it should be." He dropped the arm. "We were being set up to get another mission flown in." He picked up the overcoat and put it on.

The interior of the car grew cold. Dunne gulped the freezing air. It didn't diminish the accumulated sense of exhaustion he felt. A clatter from behind startled him. Van Hull had the trunk opened. He held aloft a metal disk and tore off the wires attached. He hurled it toward the road and hurried around to the driver's seat. "They're tracking us. At least they *were*."

He put the car in gear. "They say the Tatra 77 is one of the best cars on the road. Now we'll see how it does *off* the road." He drove into the woods. Branches whipped the windows. They jolted and bounced over uneven terrain, plunged into a shallow ditch, shot up a hillock that lofted them over a rift. The car shuddered violently when it landed. The bolt of pain in Dunne's ankle made him cry out: "Where the hell are you going?"

The car zigzagged around trees, veered and swerved through a clearing, and fishtailed across a patch of ice. It barreled through a narrow defile and sideswiped an outcropping of rock that made the fender grind against the front right tire. Van Hull got out and pried the fender back into position.

Dunne tapped him on the shoulder when he retook the driver's seat. "We've got nowhere to go, but it seems like we're in a hell of a hurry to get there."

"We've got a train to catch."

"A train?"

"That village we passed. There were four boxcars. It's a switching station. North-south tracks cross east-west tracks. We'll drive far as we can and walk if we have to."

"They aren't going anywhere without an engine."

"Sooner or later, one will show."

"How can you be sure?"

"I can't. But it's the only shot we've got." Van Hull drove for several minutes before the thickness of the woods and a steep ridge made it impossible to proceed. "I'm going to do some scouting. You have to try to stay awake." He returned so quickly Dunne didn't have a chance to nod off. "There's no way to drive any farther," he said. "Terrain's too rough. It's back to shank's mare."

Dunne wasn't sure he'd be able to last longer than a few minutes, but exhaustion served as analgesia, numbing counterweight to ache in ankle and discomfort of crutch rubbing against armpit. At times, he wasn't sure he was even awake. Van Hull's support and strength propelled them forward.

They reached an icy, half-frozen but flowing stream. Van Hull carried Dunne on his back across knee-high rapids. They rested on the far bank. Van Hull examined a cluster of birch trees, sliced off several mushroom-like growths, and pocketed them.

Dunne got on his hands and knees, removed his woolen cap, and plunged his head beneath the frigid, crystal-colored rush. He kept it there till he couldn't stand the stinging, unsparing cold. He rolled on his back, gasping.

Supported by his elbows, Van Hull lay back, watching. "I was afraid you were trying to drown yourself."

"I was. But I was afraid I'd freeze to death first. Give me a hand."

"I wanted to go alone. I told the general that."

"We do what we're told, like all soldiers." Dunne dried his head with his jacket and put his cap back on. He felt awake and alert. "We better get someplace warm or we'll both get pneumonia."

"The SS has had Mike Jahn and his men all the time."

"No money-back guarantees. We knew that when we signed on." Dunne slung his arm around Van Hull's shoulder. He wanted to ask about Jahn but didn't. Maybe it was different with other agents. In fact, he knew it was. But he also knew that Van Hull and he operated according to the same unwritten code of conduct: Rely on each other for everything, yet know very little outside the mutual, immediate, primitive dependence required to stay alive. Knowing anything more was unnecessary, could only be confusing. When it was over—if you got out alive—you resume different lives, forever grateful to each other but gone your separate ways.

They reached the village in late afternoon. It was as quiet and unpopulated as when they'd driven past. Maybe all the inhabitants had fled, or maybe the SS or Hlinka Guard was hunkered down waiting to pounce on the partisans. They decided to wait until night and look for lights to appear before they approached any closer.

Night fell, but no lights came on. They skirted the market square. The train station was deserted. Dunne sat on a bench beneath the eave as Van Hull approached the first of the four boxcars. He slid the door open and clambered aboard. He struck a match, held it up, and moved into the car. The match went out. Dunne hobbled to the door and peered into the dark. "Dick," he said in a half-whisper, "you okay?"

Van Hull lit another match. Beneath the prick of vacillating light, the floor was littered with piles of rags. The match went out.

"What's in there?" Dunne asked.

Van Hull climbed down. "Better get in." He used his hands to form a stirrup. "Put your good leg here, take hold of the door latch, and swing yourself up."

With Van Hull's support, Dunne lifted himself to the boxcar floor and stretched out his legs. His left foot hit one of the rag piles. There was a soft moan.

"*Wer sind sie?*" The voice came from the back of the car. Dunne's eyes adjusted to the gloom. He made out a form propped against the rear wall.

Van Hull lit another match. Several of the rag piles stirred. He moved forward, careful not to step on any.

There was another moan, louder than the previous one.

The voice from the back spoke again: "*Sie sind nicht Deutsch, sind sie?*"

"*Nein.*" Van Hull stood in the middle of the car. "*Wir sind Amerikaner.*"

"*Amerikaner! Sie sind ein langer weg von zu hause!*"

The tone sounded to Dunne somewhere between surprise and sarcasm. "What's he saying?" He fingered the pile next to him, took hold of what felt like a stick.

"He says we're a long way from home." Van Hull's match went out.

Dunne ran his hand over a sharp prominence, leaned close, and tried to see what he held. A hollow-eyed, shrunken face—skull-like, fleshless almost—rose from the rag pile. The mouth came so close, the labored, foul breath made him recoil. Tightening his grip, he realized he had hold of a shoulder. He let go, rolled toward the door, and took several deep breaths. The stench lingered in his nose and mouth. "Who are these people?"

Van Hull moved toward him. "You have any cigarettes left?"

Dunne groped in his pocket, retrieved a half-smoked butt and a pack with two bent smokes. He handed the pack to Van Hull.

"This'll do." Van Hull lit a match and cautiously retraced his steps toward the rear of the car. He conversed softly in German with the figure in the back.

Dunne crawled into a corner. Several of the piles stirred. The moans spread and grew louder—a chorus interspersed with coughing—then ebbed into silence. The rags, he realized, were inhabited. He touched what felt like a rolled-up blanket; fingered it gingerly, afraid to wake another skeleton. It turned out to be what it seemed: a blanket.

He wrapped himself in it as tightly as could. A wave of exhaustion swept him into the temporary closure of sleep. A foot pushed against his bruised tailbone. He sat up with a start. He half expected the darkened figure hovering above to be an SS trooper.

"Fin, get up." Van Hull handed Dunne his crutch and helped him out of the boxcar into the stationmaster's office.

Dunne lay facing a cold, unlit potbellied stove. Van Hull went into the back room and returned with an armful of excelsior. He pushed the material into the stove, took the growths he'd cut from the birch trees, and put them on top. He brought over a shuttle filled with coal, stuck the blade of his knife against the iron grate, rubbed it back and forth, sending a sprinkle of sparks that ignited the excelsior.

Dunne raised himself to a sitting position, his back against the wall. "You're not a Boy Scout. You're the Last of the Mohicans."

"I ran out of matches." Van placed a few pieces of coal into the stove. "The fungus from the birch will provide enough heat to get the coal started." He built the coals into a glowing pile.

Groggy, slightly dazed, still wrapped in the blanket, Dunne had no idea how long he'd slept in the boxcar. The molten glow from inside the grate radiated a trembling light on two dozen sleeping bodies spread in a loose circle around it, irregular spokes in a rimless wheel.

Van Hull tossed more coal onto the fire. The heat intensified.

"Did you find out who they are?"

"Jews." Van Hull threaded his way across the floor and sat beside him on the floor.

"Where are they from?"

"They're a remnant of the inmates held at Auschwitz."

"Where's the one you were talking to?"

"Here he is now."

A figure wrapped in a brown greatcoat entered from outside. He opened and closed the door as fast as he could. He removed a large earthen flask from inside his coat. He handed it to Van Hull.

Van Hull took a swig. He shook his head from side to side. "Tastes like gin mixed with airplane fuel." He passed the flask to Dunne.

The liquid burned its way down Dunne's throat, forced tears from his eyes. He gave it back. "Packs a wallop Joe Louis would be proud of."

Van Hull swished the liquid around like mouthwash, swallowed. "Fin, this is Dr. Niskolczi. He speaks English and German equally well. I've told him our story." He offered him the flask.

"Be careful. It's *borovička*. Homemade gin. I found it in the shed beside the tracks. Best taken in small doses." Niskolczi declined the flask, and spread his coat on the floor on the other side of Van Hull, and sat.

Van Hull removed his boots and peeled off his wet socks. "The doctor is from Budapest. He's been telling me how he and the others arrived here."

"Perhaps after all I will have some more of that. Just a bit." Niskolczi put the flask to his lips, sipped. "I don't know how much longer we'd have survived if you hadn't come along." He returned the flask to Van Hull.

"Why don't you start at the beginning, Doctor?"

The steel rims of Niskolczi's eyeglasses glowed red in the firelight as he bent forward and glanced at Dunne. "What you two need now is sleep."

"Not yet." Van Hull drank from the flask. "First the story of how you got here."

"I've already told you some of it."

One of the figures on the floor groaned.

"Start again. I want my companion to hear as well."

Niskolczi spoke in a monotone, giving a matter-of-fact account of his career as a physician in Budapest, which led him to the post of assistant chief pathologist at the National Institute for Surgical Research. He was dismissed in 1939 when the Institute was ordered to rid itself of medical personnel of "Jewish blood."

He and his wife and two young daughters managed to scrape by under the restrictions imposed on Jews until the Germans seized full control of Hungary. In June 1944, as part of the "general reset-tlement of the Jewish population in the East," they were ordered to report to the Keleti railway station.

Instructed to bring one suitcase per person and food supplies for "a journey of several days," they were packed into sealed cattle cars "with barely enough room to sit and no sanitary facilities." During a week's journey across Slovakia into occupied Poland, they were sidetracked for periods ranging from several hours to an entire day. The boxcar was stifling. The supply of water ran out. Several old people and infants died. Their bodies were stacked in a corner until the train reached its destination.

"We learned that our destination was Auschwitz. It was still just a word, a place one old woman remembered by its Polish name: Oświęcim. When we'd entered the gates, the SS guards opened the car doors and barked at us to leave our luggage, which would be returned after being 'sorted and inspected.' We were arranged into two lines and marched past an SS officer wearing the insignia of the medical corps.

"Able-bodied women and men were directed right; the aged, crippled, and women with children under fourteen, left. I attempted to stay close to my wife and daughters, but the SS officer in charge noticed the lapel pin I'd been awarded by the Institute for my twenty years of service.

"He pulled me aside. Annoyed to learn I was a physician—when he'd given specific orders that doctors and pharmacists were to be kept separate from other prisoners—he reprimanded the guards. He introduced himself as SS-Hauptsturmführer Eduard Wirths, the camp's chief doctor, and questioned me about my credentials. He was correct and polite, as if ours were a casual encounter on a village railway platform.

"I inquired about my wife and daughters. He said not to worry. He would see they were taken good care of. Behind him, what looked like a factory chimney stack spewed a thick column of black smoke." Niskolczi drank from the flask. "Wirths said that while there was already an expert pathologist on staff, he had a colleague doing important research in racial biology who could benefit greatly from the assistance of a German-speaking professional. 'You will be my gift to him,' he said."

Dunne resisted sleep by concentrating on Niskolczi's description of his first impressions of the camp's "vastness," a seemingly endless series of enclosures bounded by electrified wire and interspersed with guard towers mounted with searchlights and machine guns; long rows of tar-papered barracks stretching in every direction; hollow-eyed laborers in faded, ragged striped uniforms moving at a half-trot.

After showering and having his head shaved, Niskolczi was disinfected with a "burning solution" of calcium chloride and issued a "clean but worn uniform obviously used to clothe several prisoners before me." He reported to the hospital barracks, where he was met by Menachem Gertner, a Polish Jew assigned to be his assistant.

A former medical student at the University of Kraków, Gertner dispelled any lingering illusions Niskolczi might have had about the nature of the camp: "Unlike the larger Auschwitz *konzentrationslager*," Gertner explained, "which is dedicated to intimidating and enslaving Poles and other *untermenschen*, this camp—Birkenau—is a *vernichtungslager*, an 'extermination camp,' one of several in occupied Poland dedicated exclusively to the eradication of Europe's Jews.

"'For now,' Gertner said to me, 'consider yourself lucky. The man to whom you've been sent is SS-Hauptsturmführer Karsten Heinz, a fellow of the Institute for Racial Biology and Anthropology. As long as Dr. Heinz finds you useful, you'll be allowed to live. But you must be careful. Heinz is crafty, demanding, and at the first provocation—whether real or perceived—he'll dispatch you to the gas chambers.'

"A moment later, I was summoned to meet Heinz. Expecting a tall, blond athlete—the Nordic archetype—I was received by a stout, very short SS officer. He had me stand at attention for several minutes, eyeing me from a distance, as if I were a farm animal. When he came closer, I noticed how the soles and heels of his boots elevated his height.

"Gertner subsequently explained that though Heinz had been too short to serve in the elite SS, his research in racial science so endeared him to SS-Reichsführer Himmler, he was allowed to wear boots that raised him to the minimum requirement of five feet, six inches. Jealous of the favor he enjoyed from the SS hierarchy, his comrades referred to him behind his back as *der Blaue Engel*—the Blue Angel—a scornful allusion to the heels worn by Marlene Dietrich in the movie of the same name.

"When he headed a program at the camp to find the most efficient method of sterilizing Jewish women, the prisoners under his direction, aware of his nickname, altered it to *der Blaue Teufel* —the Blue Devil—a better reflection of his true nature.

"Gertner wouldn't go into what was involved in Heinz's 'research,' other than to say that he was fanatically insistent about keeping it secret, threatening immediate execution of anyone who so much as mentioned the work to another inmate or to Heinz's own medical associates."

Niskolczi paused. The flames in the coal-packed stove emitted a low hum. "I asked Gertner if he could find out what had happened to my wife and daughters. He came back the next day. They were alive, he reported. They'd been put to work. I chose to believe him. What else could I do? Sometimes it seemed as if we'd all been sucked into some mass hallucination, a collective bad dream. But then I'd wake and be instantly confronted with the reality of where I was."

Heinz provided a steady supply of "specimens" for dissection. The bodies were those of captured Soviet political commissars and intelligence officers as well as "randomly selected Jews from a variety of different professions and classes." They were accompanied by questionnaires that required "precise and exhaustive" weighing and measuring of organs and bones.

Niskolczi looked through the files that Heinz—"or, more accurately, his prior assistants, since dispatched to the gas chamber"—had compiled during a similar process of dissection and measurement performed on scores of dwarfs, epileptics, cripples, and hunchbacks. In his notes, he referred to his "menagerie of sub-humans." His intent, he noted, was to find a shared biological basis for "racial deviance."

Heinz complimented Niskolczi's work in the highest terms. "He announced that the purpose of the research was to assist in establishing an 'indisputable biological link between Judaism and Bolshevism.' I looked at him incredulously, thinking perhaps that he was toying with me. But he wasn't. The obvious irony of assigning this task to a 'racially diseased Jew' simply didn't enter his mind."

The cadavers kept coming. Although they had all been killed the same way—"by direct injection of chloroform into the heart" —Niskolczi noticed that the Soviet POWs had been subjected to "extreme physical abuse and torture." He also noted that no matter what anatomical measurements he made, Heinz altered them to support the illusion that he was pursuing a legitimate course of research.

One evening, when Heinz had left for the day, Niskolczi went into Heinz's office to deposit a pile of reports. Opening a cabinet drawer that had inadvertently been left unlocked, he made another discovery: The systematic torture Heinz inflicted on captured Soviet intelligence officers had produced thick files on the spy networks the Soviets had insinuated among the British and Americans. Rather than forwarding them to his superiors, Heinz kept these to himself.

Soon after making this discovery, Niskolczi was summoned by Heinz and given the "ghoulish task of preparing a representative selection of the Jewish-Bolshevik racial type." This involved boiling the bodies so flesh could easily be stripped away, then drying and bleaching the bones in a gasoline bath. As soon as properly prepared, the bones were to be shipped to the Anatomy Institute of the Reich University of Strassburg, professionally mounted, and permanently displayed in a public exhibit.

"I had figured out the game Heinz was playing," Niskolczi said. "Knowing the war was lost, he avoided transfer to a combat unit on the Eastern Front by catering to Himmler's racial fantasies, while at the same time compiling an account of Soviet espionage he could use to ingratiate himself with the Allies when he reached their lines."

Niskolczi got to his feet. "I must step outside to relieve myself." He left his coat on the floor.

Van Hull drank from the flask. "How's the ankle?"

"Not as bad as before." Dunne took his turn with the flask and passed it back.

When Niskolczi returned, a rush of frigid air followed. He resumed his position next to Van Hull, sitting silently. Struggling against sleep, Dunne jerked his head up as it sank onto his chest, causing a sharp crimp in his neck. He took a deep breath. Niskolczi had resumed his story. Dunne was unsure how much, if anything, he'd missed.

". . . *Sonderkommando*." Niskolczi repeated the word: "*Sonderkommando*."

"A special task force?" Van Hull asked.

"Yes, in English that's what it means."

"Did Heinz reassign you?"

"No, he resisted. He claimed 'his contribution to Nazi racial science' was being slighted by his rivals within the SS. In truth, he feared a transfer to the front. But he was overruled. The camp was running at full capacity. All the personnel were stretched, but none more so than the eight hundred and fifty prisoners of the *Sonderkommando*. The nature of their work meant they were in constant need of medical attention for cuts, bruises, burns, and pulled muscles.

"Gertner had a deeper knowledge of the camp than I did. He turned pale when he learned of my reassignment. I was whisked to the *Sonderkommando*'s tightly sequestered quarters on a Sunday night. I was stunned. The men all had their own beds. They were dressed in civilian clothes, quality trousers and shirts taken from the baggage of deceased deportees. Some were drinking beer and smoking cigarettes.

"The head prisoner—the kapo in chief—was a burly Slovakian Jew. He invited me outside for a smoke. 'Tomorrow will be exhausting,' he said. 'So tonight relax and enjoy the privileges of the Twelfth *Sonderkommando*.'

"'You mean there are eleven besides this?' I asked.

"He laughed. 'I mean there were eleven *before* this.'

"I presumed he was joking, but there was no merriment in his eyes—only fear mixed with madness. He took hold of my arm. 'This is hell, Doctor. The *real* hell. The other eleven were all liquidated. The devils in charge will leave no witnesses.'

"I tried to sleep that night but was wide awake when we were roused from our beds. The kapo assigned me to accompany him and the lead squad of two hundred men as they rushed to their posts in what he described as one of the camp's four crematoria.

"A large shipment of several thousand Hungarian Jews had arrived in forty-five boxcars. The first column, mostly women, children, and the aged, was marched to a set of steps that descended to a bunker marked 'Baths and Disinfecting Room.' When they were all inside, the metal door was locked and secured with an iron bar.

"From where I stood, I watched as a car bearing the insignia

of the International Red Cross pulled up. A crisply dressed SS officer stepped out and deposited green metal canisters in pipes atop
the bunker. Nobody spoke. Whatever was happening inside that
bunker was utterly sealed off from the summer's day outside.
Eventually, the order was given to put the exhaust system into
operation.

"After about twenty minutes, the door was opened. The tan-
gled knot of naked limbs reached to the ceiling. Despite the exhaust
fans, a sulfurous stink clouded the air. The *Sonderkommando*
sprang into action, hosed the chamber with jets of water to wash
away the pool of blood, urine, and feces, pulled apart the bodies,
and hauled them to the freight elevators. When they reached the
incineration room, crews removed their hair and extracted their
gold teeth.

"Men sweated and gagged. A skinny young man who looked
to be the youngest of the group dropped to his knees. He appeared
in a state of shock. The kapo kicked him and hauled him to his
feet. He dropped again. An SS guard came over and shot him in
the back of the head. His corpse was stripped and thrown in with
the rest.

"The well-fired ovens allowed for rapid immolation. The
ashes, still warm, were shoveled onto a truck, hauled to the
Vistula, and dumped."

The choking sound that Niskolczi made might have been a
cough or a sob.

"There's no need to go on, Doctor," Van Hull said.

Niskolczi might have misunderstood Van Hull or more likely
he posed the question to himself: "Why did I go on? Why didn't I
kill myself? Was it the instinct for survival? Or perhaps the oath I
took as a doctor to 'do no harm'? Thousands of human beings
overcome that instinct each day, killing themselves or sacrificing
themselves in causes that range from noble to deranged. Doctors
are no exception.

"I think the reason was, first, after a very short while, it's impossible to truly appreciate hell while you're still in it. Despite its horrors, it quickly assumes the aspects of the everyday. You get up and go on with business. This is what makes an eternity in hell tolerable. It's the point that Dante missed, I think. As a tourist, he didn't grasp that to see hell from the outside—or merely to visit—is to miss the numbness it induces.

"Second, I came to feel that perhaps I was fated to survive—that I still had some role to play. I wasn't sure if I was deluding myself, justifying my own existence. How can one be objective in such circumstances? Deluded or not, I decided if I was to die, they'd have to kill me."

The fire had subsided. Van Hull walked barefoot to the stove, rebuilt the pile of coals, and stoked it with the shovel. On the way back, he stumbled over one of the sleeping forms on the floor but did not fall.

Niskolczi recounted that along with the psychic and physical exhaustion that enveloped the *Sonderkommando* came an all-consuming focus on staying alive another day in hopes an unexpected turn of events—sudden arrival of the Red Army, Allied bombing, troopers dropping from the sky, something, *anything*—would end this hell.

After a week, he'd lost all track of time. He was asleep in his bunk when the kapo woke him and told him to report to the SS officer in charge. "I didn't know what infraction I'd committed. It hardly mattered. I was certain I was about to be shot. Instead, he informed me I was being sent back to my work with Heinz. I'm sure this is the only time in the history of Auschwitz such a thing happened."

The urge for sleep had left Dunne. He stared at the small red-and-yellow sun that burned in the belly of the stove, its murmur barely audible.

"I'd been saved by Heinz's cowardice. By convincing Himmler that he needed my expertise to achieve his 'scientific breakthrough,' he ensured he wouldn't be among the myriad Germans killed or captured each day by the Red Army. Unfortunately, my assistant, Gertner, paid the price. Ordered to take my place in the *Sonderkommando*, he killed himself by drinking a beaker of calcium chloride."

Niskolczi was immediately returned to the "repetitious, inane work of autopsying Soviet and Jewish corpses." Yet though Auschwitz functioned as before, there'd been a palpable change in atmosphere. Guards as well as the inmates knew it was now a question of *when*, not *if*, the Soviets would arrive, which raised another question: When and how would Auschwitz and its remaining inmates be liquidated?

Niskolczi spoke in a more animated tone than before: "This was driven home the day the camp was rocked by explosions. At first we almost cheered, thinking the Red Army had arrived. Then it became apparent the *Sonderkommando* had succeeded in staging a revolt. They blew up one of the crematoria and engaged the SS in pitched battle for over an hour before they were annihilated."

Despite what had taken place, the death factory stayed busy. The remnant of 70,000 Jews left alive from the original 500,000 sequestered in the Łódź ghetto arrived by train. Ninety-five percent were immediately gassed.

"It crossed my mind," Niskolczi said, "that the Red Army had already passed us by, that the camp would operate until the last Jew had been delivered into the ovens, that only then would it stop, the buildings razed, the ground covered over, every trace wiped away so that the future would never be troubled by Auschwitz's existence."

Finally Niskolczi was summoned one morning to the infirmary. A shipment of several hundred ill deportees had arrived. He was stunned by the instruction "to help treat them." The gassings had ended. The factory was closed. The dismantling of the crematoria began. The men of the Thirteenth—and last—*Sonderkommando* were taken to the forest and executed by flamethrower.

Heinz ordered Niskolczi to pack the research results for shipment to Mauthausen, "where the work will continue." On New
Year's Day 1945, he ignored Heinz's summons to report to his
office and watched from an adjoining barracks as a "visibly drunk
and frightened Heinz" had two SS orderlies load the files with
intelligence extracted from Soviet POWs into staff cars. They hurriedly drove away.

The remaining SS supervised the destruction of the barracks.
Knowing that Heinz had ordered his execution—that he'd escaped
solely because of Heinz's fear of falling into Soviet hands—
Niskolczi slipped into the prisoners' ranks as they were marched
out of camp. "I glanced back a final time at the Gates of Hell. The
legend atop, *Arbeit Macht Frei—Work Will Make You Free—*
mocked all we had survived. Yet even now, *der Blaue Teufel* and
his brethren hadn't finished their work."

The prisoners were herded through heavy snow and brutal
cold. Those who faltered were beaten; those who lay down, shot.
An SS officer halted the column and shouted Niskolczi's name several times. "I didn't respond. I knew Heinz hoped to correct his
oversight in not having me killed."

They continued until the survivors were loaded on boxcars.
Several prisoners came down with typhus. Learning of the outbreak, the train crew re-routed off the main north-south track onto
a trunk line and fled on foot.

"This is where we were when you found us, gentlemen. Now
please, enough said. It's time you got some sleep." Niskolczi lay
down and drew the overcoat around him.

The undertone of fretful mutterings, snores, hacking coughs
was discordant and constant. Staring at a ceiling smudged by half
a century of dust and smoke, Dunne needed a few minutes to piece
together where he was. He sat up. His dry, rough tongue had the
texture of sandpaper; buzz above his eyes, more annoying than

painful. What part hangover? What part echo of Niskolczi's recounting of his time in Auschwitz? He wasn't sure.

Van Hull was in the same position—staring at the fire—as when Dunne fell asleep.

"That was the worst gin I've had since Prohibition." Dunne rubbed his temples.

Van Hull got up and shoveled coal onto the fire. He turned the large earthen flask upside down. "Worst of all, it's gone." He walked outside.

Niskolczi went to the window. Morning sky was as drab and uninteresting as the station's soot-stained ceiling. "You must let me look at that ankle." He knelt beside Dunne, lifted the leg, and pressed around the ankle with his thumbs. "Any pain?"

"Some. But less than before."

Framed in the thin round rims of his glasses, Niskolczi's blue eyes were sunk deep in their sockets. "You should stay off it as much as possible."

Van Hull came back in and offered Niskolczi the flask. "I filled it with water from the pump. It'll have to do unless you know the secret of turning water into wine."

"That kind of magic belongs to priests, not physicians." Niskolczi swigged the cold, metallic-tasting water.

"When was the last time you had anything to eat?"

"Me?" The oversized coat hung on Dr. Niskolczi limply.

"All of you." Van Hull swept his hand over the sleeping forms on the floor.

Dr. Niskolczi rubbed his glasses on his sleeve. "I . . . I really can't say."

Van Hull disappeared into the back room and returned with two empty burlap sacks. He handed one to Dr. Niskolczi. "We're going on a foraging expedition."

"I'm going, too." Using the wall for support, Dunne got up. "Give me that crutch."

Niskolczi shook his head. "It's better you stay off that ankle."

"Save your breath, Doctor. His is a breed that resists listening to reason." Van Hull retrieved the crutch from beside the door. He pulled the .45 from his belt. "The doctor and I will be the point men. You provide the cover."

Dunne checked the magazine. "Lot of good this will do if the Krauts are around."

"Beats nothing." Van Hull went out the door.

Dunne fumbled in his pocket in hopes of finding the cigarette butt that had been there the night before. The lethal pill spilled on the floor.

Niskolczi picked it up and weighed it in his palm. He seemed about to say something but gave it back to Dunne without uttering a word.

They followed Van Hull into the empty, uneven, half-paved, half-cobblestone street. He looked around. "Where do you suppose everyone went, Doctor?"

"There was no one here when we arrived." Niskolczi buttoned his coat, put on a cap, and pulled down the earflaps. "Or perhaps there was but they were afraid to come near the boxcars because they knew they were filled with the sick."

They stepped through shattered storefronts. The gutted interiors were stripped of anything salvageable. Random machine-gun spray pockmarked the facades of shops next to the square.

"Nobody can accuse the Germans of not being thorough." Van Hull turned right onto a lane with four modest cottages, the first three charred hulks, the fourth intact.

"*If* it was the Germans. It could have been the Hlinka Guard punishing the partisans, or perhaps the partisans teaching Monsignor Tiso's loyalists a lesson. Everyone, it seems, has his motive."

Van Hull kicked open the door of the last cottage. He summoned Dunne and Niskolczi with a wave of his hand. Past the small vestibule, to the right, was a bedroom only large enough to hold a double bed and a bureau. The bed was stripped bare. Van Hull looked inside the bureau drawers: empty except for a homey, warm camphor smell, reminder of a time when moths were deemed the prime menace to domestic order.

They left the bedroom and went into the parlor. A richly colored Oriental rug covered the floor. Opposite a red horsehair sofa was an upright piano. Atop it was a lace runner and framed photographs: old woman with an infant in her lap; ebullient bride and tight-lipped bridegroom; the same couple—the man noticeably stouter—in summer clothes, a snow-tipped mountain behind; in front, three children in descending sizes.

Niskolczi, Van Hull, and Dunne stood mute in the middle of the room, as if they'd stepped into a museum exhibit featuring a re-creation of a vanished planet and the comforts, obligations, duties it once orbited around. Niskolczi picked up the porcelain figurine of a ballerina from the table next to the couch. Poised tiptoe, she had one hand extended, the other raised above her head.

He turned it over. "I thought so." He pointed at the letter D above a crown. "Made in Dresden. A beautiful piece." As he carefully replaced it, his shoulders began to shake and heave with sobs. He wiped eyes and nose with his sleeve. "I wasn't sure a place like this still existed."

Lowering himself onto the piano bench, he caressed the polished ebony surface, the gold phoenix logo and the letters of the manufacturer's name: Schwimmer. He tapped a key with forefinger, spread long, elegant fingers, and began to play a slow, mournful tune. He lowered his head and sang—almost chanted—in a high, tremulous voice:

Lacrimosa dies illa
Qua resurget ex favilla
Judicandus homo reus.

He stopped and wiped his eyes again. Van Hull put his hand

on his shoulder. "The 'Lacrimosa' from Mozart's Requiem in D Minor. It's among my favorite pieces of music:

'Mournful that day / When from the ashes shall rise / A guilty man to be judged.'

"You play beautifully, Doctor. Please, continue."

"Maybe another day, in some other place."

As Dunne turned to leave the room, the bottom of his crutch caught on the rug. He stumbled and knocked into the table. The figurine tumbled to the floor and smashed. "Christ Almighty, I'm sorry."

"Forget it, Fin. We've got more important business to attend to." Van Hull left the parlor and entered the dining room.

Amid the destruction in the surrounding village, itself an insignificant fragment of the ruin that had engulfed countries, peoples, and continents and that had reached some terrible—almost incomprehensible—climax in the process of mass murder outlined by Niskolczi, Dunne knew how preposterous it was to get upset by this inadvertent breakage. But he couldn't stop gazing at the broken figurine, imagining he might find a way to fix it.

Niskolczi pushed the pieces under the sofa with his shoe. "It is a thing, a beautiful thing, but *only* a thing. It can be remade. A human soul cannot. History masks that truth. History is what happens to us collectively, as peoples, states, nations. Tragedy is what happens to us individually as human beings."

"It was an accident."

"Of course. Your intent was not to destroy. But regrets are useless. The only way to repair what is broken is to go on living, to look to the future and see to it that the individual victims are remembered, their tragedies honored, their murderers judged."

In the next room, Van Hull noisily piled plates, cups, and silverware from the sideboard on the dining room table. "We'll come back for these. Let's hope we can find something to use them for." Niskolczi and Dunne trailed him into the kitchen. They searched the cabinets and pantry, but the shelves were bare. Beside the back door, above the broom closet, was a padlocked half-cabinet.

"Fin, hand me the forty-five, will you?" Van Hull blew off the lock with a single shot. "Well, what'd you know? The pot of gold at the end of the rainbow." He handed four large cans of beans and three tins of biscuits to Niskolczi, who put them in his sack.

They continued their search. They took the thick coverlets from the beds in the two adjoining bedrooms and piled them by the door along with some pots and pans from the kitchen. "We'll come back for these, too," Van Hull said.

The remainder of their rummaging through the village turned up half a sack of potatoes, three loaves of stale bread, a bag of salt, and a jar of apple jam. Van Hull found two sets of workmen's overalls and jackets in an abandoned woodshop. They stopped in the church on the way back. The altar was stripped, the tabernacle empty, and the benches pushed against the wall, as though the space had been used as a barracks. Van Hull found a box of votive candles in the basement and a half-dozen linen hand towels.

It took two trips to return all they'd scavenged to the station. The gray day grew bitingly cold. Van Hull rebuilt the fire. The rich, comforting smell of cooking summoned Dunne from his nap. Van Hull had softened potatoes in a pot of boiling water, sliced them into pieces, and dropped them into the pan in which he was frying beans. Working expertly on the small surface atop the stove, he transferred the beans and potatoes back to the pot. He wet the stale bread and fried it in the pan. The windows drooled with moisture.

Except for two women and a man stricken with typhus, who moaned in a semidelirious sleep, even the sickest and most lethargic sat up ready to eat. It turned out that the curled figure closest to the door, head covered by a red-and-white kerchief, belonged not to an old woman, as Dunne had thought, but to a frightfully thin yet exceedingly pretty girl of about sixteen. Her green eyes were alert and purposeful. She took off the kerchief. A crop of tight honey-colored curls had already sprouted on her once-shaved head.

Niskolczi nodded toward her. "Frieda Schwimmer," he whispered to Dunne. "Her family is the famous piano manufacturer. At fifteen she was regarded as a musical prodigy, a female cellist who'd one day play in all the great concert halls of Europe. Her mother, father, and two older sisters perished in Auschwitz. How much music do you think she has left in her now?"

He turned his attention back to the room, sternly warning them all not to eat too much and to eat slowly. When everyone had finished, Dunne washed out the pot. He filled it with water and put it on the stove to boil. He tied up a mound of coffee in a linen hand towel and dipped it in and out repeatedly, like a tea bag, until the brew was dark. He scooped out a cupful to taste.

Van Hull stood ready with a cup of his own. "How is it?"

"It's not Maxwell House, but it's coffee."

A line of people formed, each with a china cup to use as a scooper. They helped themselves to the crackers and apple jam. The coverlets were spread across the floor, around the stove. Before long most of those in the room were asleep.

Niskolczi put his coat on and in a hushed voice asked Dunne and Van Hull to step outside. The frigid night, windless and starless, was momentarily refreshing.

"What is your plan from here?" Niskolczi pulled his coat close around him.

"To get back home," Van Hull said.

"That's an aspiration, not a plan."

"For now, it's both."

"Those inside are too weak to walk anywhere." Niskolczi glanced at the station. Votive candles flickered in the windows, a substitute starlight. "But you've done all you can, and I'm deeply grateful. I'm sure the partisans or Russians will come. It's only a question of when. Your duty as soldiers is to get back to your own lines, is it not?"

Dunne shrugged. "I'm not sure all the services see it that way, but the OSS does."

"The more who survive, the less chance the world can deny or ignore what happened."

"We'll figure out a plan as we go along. That's how we got this far."

"Your ankle will make it all the harder, no?"

"He's been doing fine with the crutch." Van Hull folded his arms and hugged himself, an instinctive but ineffective protection against the cold.

"I can help you get a good start." Niskolczi led them back to the station and handed them each a votive candle. "Follow me." They went out the rear door, to a shack atop the siding beside the main track. He stepped in and held up his candle. "It's an old piece of machinery but still in good working order. It should be most useful."

Candles aloft, Dunne and Van Hull stood on either side of the four-wheeled wooden handcar. Dunne sat on the flatbed. "One time, at the Catholic Protectory in the Bronx, two of my dorm mates jumped the wall, stole one of these in the Tremont train yards, and rode it all the way to Penn Station. They made a clean getaway."

Van Hull gripped one of the handles on the cast-iron seesaw bolted to the flatbed and pulled himself up. "I'm not sure this will get us all the way to Penn Station, but if it were the Golden Chariot of Achilles, it couldn't be more of a godsend."

Before they retired for the night, Niskolczi produced a pint-size glass bottle. "This is what's left of the alcohol. Here's to your journey, gentlemen. *L'chaim.*" He took a swig and passed the bottle to Van Hull. "Do you know what that means?"

"To life." Van Hull enjoyed an equally generous draft.

"I'll drink to that." Dunne matched them.

They finished the bottle on the next round.

The itch on Dunne's scalp made it hard for him to sleep. He sat by the stove, picking through his hair until he felt the squiggle of a fat louse beneath his fingernail. He catapulted each one into the fire, where it made a small *pop*. He kept at it, tweezing lice between thumb and forefinger and tossing them into the fire. Finally, his eyes began to close. He got beneath a blanket on the floor and fell instantly asleep.

In the morning, they pored over railroad maps from the stationmaster's desk. There weren't a lot of choices about which route to take. In a few spots a trunk line was available. Mostly they'd have to travel west and south on the main track. The handcar wasn't exceedingly heavy—four men could lift it off the track so it wouldn't delay oncoming trains—but with only two, one with a bum ankle, it would be problematic.

One way or another, they'd ride the handcar as near as they could get to Bratislava—Van Hull fingered it on the map—stopping before the concentration of military traffic would make it almost certain they'd be detained and discovered. From there on, they'd revert to the roads, doing their best to blend in with the swelling flow of those uprooted by the unfolding doom of Germany's eastern empire.

Dunne and Van Hull donned the jackets and overalls rescued from the woodshed. Niskolczi presented them with two workers' caps he'd found in an abandoned locker, the railway metal identity badges still attached. He also pointed out that they needed to do something about the American army boots they were wearing, which would give them away immediately. They substituted string for the shoelaces and pared off the leather high-tops, which gave them a suitably derelict look. They packed a portion of fried bread, crackers, and apple jam in a burlap bag.

After Van Hull went ahead, Niskolczi handed Dunne "a final parting gift": a knob-headed wooden cane. "This will serve you better than that homemade crutch. I took it from that cottage and saved it for this moment. It's hawthorn, an ancient emblem of hope. The Greeks used it to decorate the altar of Hymen, the god of wedding feasts."

"My grandfather had a cane like this. He called it a shillelagh. The Irish carried them to fights and weddings, not that there was always a difference."

"I've something else as well. I took it from you last night after you fell asleep." Niskolczi cradled two pills in his palm. "I did the same with your companion's. I was sure what it was when it spilled from your pocket. It was terribly presumptuous of me. I realize that. You may have them back if you wish."

"It's always nice to have options."

"Yes, but the best option is to survive, don't you think?"

"There are no guarantees. You know that better than anyone."

"I doubt such a thing as Providence exists. If it did, how could what has happened have happened? Still, I believe these people in my care—this remnant—have been entrusted to me so they might survive. The two of you, the way you appeared out of nowhere, have reinforced that belief. Until we are safe and their story told, my work is unfinished. It is necessary for us—for you—to survive this war. It is required of us. After that, who knows?"

"I've always thought of Providence as nothing more than a third-rate city in a third-rate state. But maybe you're right. Maybe there's more to it. Keep the pills."

"What about your friend? Do you think he wants his back?"

"He's not the type to use it. Never was."

Niskolczi folded his hand around the pills and put them in his pocket.

Van Hull helped Dunne onto the flatbed. Niskolczi and a few others from inside the station saw them off. He reached up to shake their hands. "This world of ours, seemingly so vast, often turns out to be quite small. We'll meet in a better place and in a better time—that is my hope."

The day was clear and crisp. Van Hull removed his jacket and draped it over the seesaw pump. "We'll be sweating before long." He depressed and lifted the bar on his side. Dunne held it for support, using it to take the weight off his ankle and pumped. The handcar began to move and quickly gathered speed.

Dunne glanced back. Among those with Niskolczi was the girl with the distinctive green eyes whom he'd noticed the night before—he struggled to remember her name—anonymous Jewish survivor in a place whose name he hadn't bothered to learn, a fragment in a vast shattering of lives, families, communities. She took off her red-and-white kerchief, held it above her head, waved it, a cryptic semaphore—hello, good-bye? Farewell to tragedy and history, to accumulated, systemized hatred? Welcome to what lay ahead, justice done, a new beginning for the survivors, a wedding feast? Who could say for sure?

Dunne stopped pumping, picked up his cane/shillelagh/bridal bough, and waved back. Who knew for certain whether or not Providence existed? Her name came back to him: Frieda. Yes. Her last name the same as on that piano: Schwimmer.

They moved rapidly through tranquil, snow-dusted countryside. An occasional spire jutted in the distance. Dunne removed his jacket. Van Hull had been right about the sweat their pumping would produce. They reached a station. Carbines strung over their shoulders, a trio in the black uniforms of the Hlinka Guard patrolled the platform. As the handcar drew near, Van Hull discreetly switched the .45 from his belt to coat pocket. The guardsmen smoked and conversed, and barely noticed as they passed.

In several places, where the ground was badly cratered, the track had been hastily repaired. Along with on-the-ground sabotage by partisans, Van Hull remarked, Allied planes were undoubtedly attacking trains that moved by day, which explained the lack of traffic. It also boded well for their journey.

They pulled over on a siding and ate lunch. "Maybe we've stumbled on a new form of tourism." Van Hull handed Dunne the flask of water. "After the war, we can create a franchise and rent handcars. We'll call it Maxwell Tours—'Enjoy the sights and stay fit at the same time.'" Van Hull laughed.

Afternoon was as uneventful as morning. They rode the empty track, making rapid progress, traveling as soldiers rather than tourists, uninterested in the sights—rivers, mountains, churches, villages—attention focused on moving fast and surviving.

At sunset, they came to another siding and pulled over. The sky was a Technicolor spread of blue and purple hues, wide and unbounded, a backdrop for Gene Kelly and Rita Hayworth to dance against. "God, Fin, it reminds me of home, like in the song." Dunne lay down: familiar lyrics, sentimental but moving, *for spacious skies, purple mountain majesties, fruited plain.* Hopeful but sad. *Long ago and far away.*

The second day proceeded much like the first. At noon, a German armored car pulled parallel to them on the road next to the tracks. Van Hull gave a casual wave. The driver waved back, offhandedly. They ate the last of their food for dinner.

Near evening on the third day, as they pumped to the top of a steep hill and began a long glide down the opposite slope, they heard the shriek of a train whistle. A moment later, it sounded again, closer. The handcar shot down the incline. When it neared the bottom, they resumed pumping. Behind them, the enormous black bulk of a locomotive crested the hill. The steam-spewing iron mammoth bore down on them with mounting, remorseless momentum, high-pitched cry imminent and earsplitting.

"Let's go!" Van Hull jumped to the ground. He stumbled and fell. Dunne sat on the side of the platform, hesitating to jump and reinjure his ankle. Back on his feet, Van Hull raced to catch up. He drew next to the handcar. "Get on my back!" he yelled. The handcar shook with the vibration of the looming engine. Dunne crouched and jumped on Van Hull's back.

Van Hull staggered but stayed on his feet. The engine plowed into the handcar, scattering the splintered carcass on either side of the tracks. A clattering procession of eight flatcars followed, each loaded with two Panzer tanks secured by iron chains. Lowering Dunne to the ground, Van Hull pulled out the .45 and fired wildly, with spontaneous, irrational fury. The train sped away, oblivious. A hollow click indicated the magazine was exhausted. He hurled the gun in the direction of the fast-receding train and plopped dejectedly by the side of the track, head in his hands.

Dunne lay where he was. Feverish, tired, he felt ready to go to sleep.

As if hearing a sudden summons, Van Hull snapped to. He retrieved their possessions and presented Dunne the still-intact hawthorn cane. Neither spoke. It began to sleet. They found shelter in a culvert and burrowed beneath their blankets.

Dunne slept fitfully. He woke in the dark. His head throbbed. When day broke, they left the culvert. The morning was bright and dry. The sunlight made his eyes ache. He went back inside, lay down, and draped his forearm over his face.

Van Hull felt his head. "You have a fever." He rolled Dunne on his back and lifted his shirt, exposing the dull red rash that covered his chest.

"It's typhus, isn't it?"

Van Hull wrapped him in both blankets. "Get some sleep."

Dunne didn't bother in indulging in the useless exercise of telling him to go on by himself. "I did something stupid. I let Dr. Niskolczi have Victor, yours and mine."

"You won't need it. We got this far, and we're going to get the rest of the way."

"Unless you get sick, too."

"I won't."

"How do you know?"

"I won't let myself. Now close your eyes and get some rest."

Voices drone in his ear, Bassante's, Roberta's, General Donovan's, jabbering together, cacophony of competing words, tones, disjointed syllables. *Brother Andre wants to know: Why is the tailbone shaped like a cuckoo? Or is it the cuckoo that's shaped like the tailbone?* A steeple clock strikes three. They join together in chorus and sing: *Cuckoo, cuckoo, cuckoo.* He shouts, shakes his fist, hears himself spout a Latin phrase ("*ad utilitatem quoque nostrum*"), asks in a loud voice, "Providence? Are we near Providence?"

Van Hull's hand rested on his shoulder, reassuring. "Fin, it's all right. You need to eat something." It was dark again. There was a small fire at the mouth of the culvert. Using a tin can as a pot, Van Hull boiled eggs that he had foraged.

Night twitched into day. Figures flitted past, vague shapes filtered through a stop-and-go reel of shadow and light. Dunne lay, sat, stood, aware of Van Hull's voice, reassuring thread that ran through feverish jumble, knock and rock of boxcar wheels on rails, baritone of tires over concrete, bump and creak of horse-drawn cart, tones plaintive, insistent, wheedling—Czech? Polish? Russian? —Van Hull's fluent and consistent German.

He watched through feverish, red-rimmed eyes: Sodden wooden roof. Cracked plaster ceiling. Single electric bulb dangling lonely and bright. Night sky and its vast spool of stars. Figures in and out of focus. He burned with inner, furnace-like heat; throat so parched dry, he couldn't speak. Van Hull raised his head, poured water in his mouth. He trembled with arctic cold. Van Hull covered him with a woolen blanket.

Van Hull varied their movements, often traveling by day when anyone clearly ill was likely to go unbothered by soldiers or the police. At night, they slipped into the shadowy ring around a bonfire. The ragged circle of several dozen people—civilians, soldiers, women, children—was silent. There was no interaction beyond the sporadic hurling of logs and broken furniture on the blaze. When dawn came and the fire was expired, everyone dispersed.

They stumbled into a half-derelict farmhouse that they thought was deserted but discovered an aged couple living in a back room. Their faces, parched and trenched with wrinkles, reflected their fear. Van Hull did his best to calm them. Although it turned out they were deaf mutes, somehow he got through.

The couple hid them in a potato cellar. Each day, the old woman brought them watery soup made from cabbage and potatoes. When she stopped coming, Van Hull went to the farmhouse. The couple lay in the backyard. The woman had been raped, the old man stripped of his boots. They'd both been shot in the back of the head.

How long did they travel? And where? Dunne had no idea.

The chaos that swelled across the fast-disintegrating eastern frontier of the Third Reich was the fog shrouding them by day, cloud sheltering them by night. On they went through gray-brown, wind-ridden, barren interval between blur of snow and sprout of spring. Gray roads. Gray sky. Gray faces. Gray uniforms. Brown earth. Brown coats, dresses, caps, teeth, boots. Same tired, resigned expression stamped on every face, no matter age or sex or nationality.

Long columns of prisoners from the east straggled along the roadside. SS guards in black greatcoats hovered around them like crows, pushed and kicked them, shot the ones who wouldn't or couldn't get up. People scattered at their approach, frightened as much by the contagion of fever and typhus that traveled with the prisoners as by the SS.

German settlers—some recent, others descendants of *volksdeutsch* rooted in the same spot for hundreds of years—fled west. Their carts were top-heavy with cradles and clocks and bedding.

Foreign laborers and POWs, some of the millions conscripted into the Nazi war effort, deserted camps and factories, hiding by day, scrounging by night, doing their best to stay alive until the Germans were gone.

A woman lay propped against a fence post. Her blouse was open to suckle the child in her lap. They were both dead. The stench of putrefaction hovered around them.

Military units shuffled by, heads down, seemingly indifferent to direction or destination. Their worn, ragged uniforms and cloth caps sometimes made it hard to tell what force or faction they represented. Deserters and partisans hung limp and lifeless from freshly blossomed branches, placards around their necks headlined: *ACHTUNG!* Staff cars roared by. Corpses littered the roadside.

Newly risen blades of grass turned the brown earth green. Heavy rains churned roads into swamps. They took refuge in an abandoned hayloft. In the late afternoon, a column of sodden, slump-shouldered troopers trudged on the road beneath. When they'd passed, Van Hull left without a word.

Dawn sun woke him. Van Hull hadn't returned. Maybe he'd finally decided to go it alone—a thought Dunne entertained, though he knew it wasn't true. Van Hull had either been captured, in which case there was nothing left for Dunne to do but await whatever came, or he'd be back, prodding and coaxing, perhaps attempting another Boy Scout trick, insisting they stay on the move another day.

Head resting on a pillow of hay, Dunne rehearsed his answer. He'd been exhausted before. But this went deeper than muscle or bone, beyond the physical toll required to endure and survive a siege of typhus. This weariness was in his soul. He wouldn't—couldn't—get up. He'd had enough, endured enough. Heroes like Van Hull always seemed to have more to give. But sometimes, instead of death or surrender, the old guard simply wanted to be left alone, to lie undisturbed, to sink unnoticed into abiding sleep.

Victor or no Victor, he was through. Enough. For good. Once and for all. *Au revoir, la guerre.*

Two figures in civilian clothes zigzagged across the yard, rusted hinges groaning a metal complaint as the door was pushed open. They scampered up the ladder, one behind the other, skittish teenagers who couldn't hide their fear. They rushed Dunne to his feet, down the ladder, to a horse-drawn wagon half filled with empty crates. They indicated to Dunne to crawl between the crates. They covered the pile with a tarp and tied it to the sides of the wagon.

The wagon jostled over cobblestones and made several sharp turns before speeding along a smooth road. It came to a halt. The boys who'd put Dunne in the wagon carried him out. The wagon was parked in a capacious brick hall with vaulted ceilings. Barrels were stacked high on either side. The odor of sour hops—similar to stale beer—filled the space. They put him down on a cot hidden behind the barrels.

"Where am I?" He smiled at the boys. Though he wasn't sure by whom, he knew he'd been rescued.

The younger of the two smiled back. "*Nemluvím anglicky.*" He held up one finger. "*Jedna minuta.*" They hurried off. The damp, chilly hall was obviously part of a brewery.

A tall, haggard, gray-haired man with a goatee came from around the stack of barrels. "Please, stay seated." Left hand behind his back, as if hiding something, he offered Dunne a weak hand-shake with his right. "Forgive me, we've no time for niceties. I spent several years in your country, in Pittsburgh, but there's no need for you to know my name or where you are. If you fell into German hands, they'd get it out of you one way or another. You've already had quite an ordeal. You must have a strong constitution to have pulled through."

"It's been mostly thanks to my buddy."

"Yes, your 'buddy,' Major Van Hull, he's the one who told us where to find you."

"He's here?"

"Nearby—in surgery."

"Surgery?"

"A shoulder wound, painful but not fatal, it must be attended to. He's a brave man, or foolish, or reckless. Perhaps all three. None of us in the resistance had any idea you were in the area until a German sentry stopped your comrade. The major struck him with a cane and tried to grab his rifle. The German got off a shot and hit him, but the major beat him well beyond what was necessary to kill. He was fortunate our men were nearby when it happened. They had to pry this from his grip." He brought his left hand forward. In it was the broken half of the hawthorn cane.

"The war is almost over. But the Germans still threaten to drown any resistance 'in a sea of blood.' Our people will pay the price for the murder of that soldier. That's the way it's been from the start—since the British and French sold us out at Munich. I was with the Czech Brigade in the Red Army until I was sent back to help organize the resistance. You've had your play-by-the-rules war in the west, but in the east, there've been no rules. The Germans sowed the wind, and now they reap the whirlwind."

"Can I see Major Van Hull?" Dunne got to his feet.

"Tomorrow. We're sending you both to Prague. It will be easier to hide you there, and we have word fellow agents of yours are working there." He handed Dunne the remnant of the cane. "The major told me a little of your—how shall I put it?—your 'adventures.' I thought you might like this as a souvenir of Czechoslovakia."

"Thanks. It might be a nice place to live, but it's been a tough place to visit."

"Soon it will be once again a good place to live *and* visit, free and independent, rid of Germans. Perhaps you'll return as tourist instead of soldier. Meantime, we'll see to it you're fed and get some rest. You'll also be able to have a hot bath and get cleaned up. Pardon me, I don't mean to be insulting, but you don't look like the Americans we remember from the movies—groomed, well-fed, confident. You look as if you've spent the war in Poland or the Ukraine. As they say in Pittsburgh, you look like shit."

Dunne fingered the piece of hawthorn: more shillelagh than wedding bough, as it turned out. "A bath would help change that."

When it was dark, Dunne was loaded aboard an ingeniously designed transport. The bottom layer of hollow, permanently attached barrels formed a compartment able to hide several men. Atop were layers of barrels filled with beer. He was driven to a windowless basement. Behind a false wall was an apartment that contained a small sleeping area and a spotless tiled bathroom with porcelain sink, toilet, and tub.

A shy girl with blonde braids provided him a Swedish hollow-ground safety razor and Sheffield scissors. Dunne stood before the sink. *Mirror, mirror on the wall.* Thin, bearded, wary, worn-down visage stared back, distant descendant of the face he'd last seen in a mirror in Bari, twin to the myriad faces he'd passed on the road.

He lathered cheeks and neck, reaped his beard with the razor, cropped his hair with the scissors, and shaved what remained. He filled the tub with water so hot he had to gradually lower himself in. He fell asleep. The water was tepid when he woke. He emptied the tub and refilled it.

Clean clothes and underwear were laid out on the bed. The girl returned and hurriedly delivered a plate of sausage and potatoes and a tin container filled with beer. He wolfed the food and drink, lay down on soft, yielding mattress, pulled the down coverlet over his head, last conscious thought before sleep a memory: Niskolczi weeping. *I wasn't sure a place like this still existed.*

The same transport came for him in the morning. He climbed behind the faux barrels. Van Hull was already inside. He was obviously groggy from the painkillers he'd been given. He stared blankly at Dunne for several seconds. "Fin, is that you?"

"The new and improved me."

"You look like death."

"Yesterday, I looked like shit. I'm not sure death is an improvement."

"It's the shaved head."

"You don't look so hot yourself, Dick."

"I guess we're the sad-ass version of the Bobbsey Twins, Rack and Ruin instead of Flossie and Fred."

The driver slammed the panel behind them. They lay in the darkness. Van Hull gently snored. Dunne slept fitfully, unsure how long they had traveled before the transport stopped and the motor was turned off.

A single escort in mechanic's overalls led them out of their hiding place. It was night. He whisked them into the side entrance of a sprawling, multitiered structure with an imposing steeple-like dome. He used a flashlight to lead them through a series of marble hallways that echoed with their footsteps and down several flights of stairs. He extinguished the beam. A bare bulb hanging from the ceiling illumined a windowless basement room packed with empty desks and display cases.

Van Hull, weak and unsteady on his feet, sat on a desk. He gazed at the floor.

"You speak English?" Dunne asked.

Their short, muscular, expressionless escort didn't answer.

Van Hull lifted his head. "*Sprechen sie Deutsch?*"

"*Ja, ich spreche Deutsch.*"

"*Gut.*" Van Hull nodded appreciatively. "*Wie heissen Sie?*"

"Jan Horak." His stoic mien gave way to a torrent of words, accompanied by animated hand gestures.

Van Hull stopped him to translate. "Jan Horak welcomes us to the National Museum. We're in the heart of Prague, just off Wenceslas Square. The building is mostly empty for now. The collections were moved to storage to ensure they survive the war. It's the very last place the Germans would look. But the situation outside is volatile. The Russians are closing in, and the resistance is preparing to take on the Germans and liberate the city on their own. We are to remain here until our American comrades make contact."

"Which American comrades?" Dunne sat beside Van Hull.

Without waiting for Van Hull to translate, Horak fished in the pocket of his overalls. "*Dies ist von der kameraden.*" He tossed a pack of cigarettes to Dunne.

Dunne studied the virgin cellophane. American smokes. *God shed his grace on thee*: Lucky Strikes. Horak handed Van Hull what looked like a calling card. "*Und so.*"

Carefully peeling away cellophane and tinfoil top, Dunne extracted three Luckies; handed one to Van Hull, one to Horak. They lit their cigarettes in the flame of Horak's brass lighter. Van Hull examined both sides of the card Horak had given him. "It's from the '*kameraden*' who sent the Luckies." On the front, beneath the gold embossed seal of the United States, was printed:

LT. COL. CARLTON BAXTER BARTLETT
DIRECTOR OF THE DEPARTMENT OF INFORMATION,
COMMUNICATION & POLICY ANALYSIS
OFFICE OF STRATEGIC SERVICES

On the back was a brief handwritten message: *The age of miracles has not passed! We'd given you two up for dead! Will make contact soon. Stay where you are for now.*

"How did Bartlett get to Prague? I figured the Pear would fight the entire war from the bar at the Ritz, in Paris."

Dunne returned the card. "Where the hell does he think we're going to go?"

"Maybe I should ask Jan if we could borrow golf clubs and play a round at the local country club. But orders are orders. We'll do as the Pear directs and stay here."

Van Hull had another extended conversation with Horak that he summarized for Dunne as soon as the Czech had left. Berlin had fallen. Hitler was dead. The Red Army was at the gates of Prague, and coming from the west, General Patton was in striking distance. The Czech resistance was poised to take matters into its own hands and pay the Germans back for seven years of occupation and humiliation.

An hour later, Horak reappeared with a crew in tow. They brought two cots, bedding, and a supply of dried foodstuffs. He left them his flashlight and told them to stay where they were. When it was safe, he would come and get them.

They lay down on the cots. The silence had the morbid pervasiveness of a mausoleum. It was impossible to tell if it was day or night. They sat up with a start when the building shook as if hit by a bomb. Dunne used the flashlight. Dust from the ceiling circled in its beam like a flurry of snow. They made their way upstairs to an office on the first floor. Gunfire rang out. A tank rumbled by, rattling the window. There was a radio on the stand next to it. Van Hull turned it on and fiddled with the dial. The announcer spoke in rapid-fire style.

"What's he saying?" Dunne asked.

"He's speaking in Czech. 'It's over'—I think that's what he's saying.

"What's over?"

"Wait. Now it's in German" Van Hull translated: "'The nightmare is over. Today, May sixth, Prague strikes for her liberation. Let freedom and justice prevail!'"

Part IV
Hidden Heroes

File 6704-A: Document Declassified and Released by Central Intelligence Agency, Sources/Methods Exemption 3B2B, Nazi War Crimes Disclosure Act, Date: 12/06/2000

***CLASSIFIED: SECRET. Folder 6704-A: DR. KARSTEN HEINZ IS HEREBY SEVERED FROM U.S. v. DR. KARL BRANDT et al. Custody is transferred to Central Intelligence Group, Division Headquarters, Berlin. Information herein not to be shared with unauthorized persons. 2/4/46.

Military Tribunal, Case 1, United States v. Dr. Karl Brandt et al., Folder 6704-A: Document No. 6, Background Notes and Preliminary Interrogation: SS-Hauptsturmführer Karsten Heinz (KH). Submitted by Col. Winfield Scott Thomas, M.D., U.S. Army, Medical Corps, Dept. of Psychiatry. Also present, Maj. Turlough Bassante, Special Agent, Counter Intelligence Corps. Nuremberg. 12/27/45.

COMMENTS: I have been directed to undertake a preliminary interrogation and psychological assessment of Karsten Heinz, in preparation for his formal indictment as a defendant in the trial of German medical personnel, civilian as well as military, for crimes committed in the name of "scientific research" and "medical advancement."

In Heinz's case, the paper trail is extensive and damning. We are in possession, for example, of direct correspondence dated 2/12/44 from SS-Standartenführer Wolfram Sievers of the Forschungs-und-Lehrgemeinshaft das Ahnererbe to Himmler that states: "The war in the east makes it imperative we proceed expeditiously with the study of the Jewish race. By procuring the skulls of Jewish-Bolshevik Commissars, who represent the prototype of this devious and degenerate subspecies, we have the opportunity to produce a definitive document as well as mount a convincing scientific exhibit that will stand the test of time. I have already been in discussions with Dr. Karsten Heinz, an eminent racial researcher on staff at Auschwitz, who is convinced that he now has the materials at hand to establish an organic link between Judaism and Bolshevism."

The interview was conducted in Heinz's prison cell, a spare space that he keeps fastidiously neat. It contains a bed, desk, and two chairs. He was dressed in gray military jodhpurs, heavy gray woolen socks that reached up to his knees, black leather slippers, and a long-sleeved quilted undershirt.

Of stocky build and no more than five feet and three or four inches in height, Heinz is in full possession of his mental faculties. He displays a self-confidence that quickly shades into arrogance, a pronounced indication of the melding of his superego with that of the Third Reich. It is clear the operation of the superego supports rather than opposes the id's desire for self-aggrandizement. A sadistic opportunist who is devoid of sympathy for his victims and dedicated to his own survival, he clothes his actions in terms of scientific idealism and admits no direct role in mass murder. His capacity for narcissistic rationalization in support of justifying his actions is limitless.

INTERVIEW: When Maj. Bassante and I entered with a stenographer, the prisoner remained seated at the desk. I informed him both the Major and I spoke fluent German, but he indicated his preference for speaking with us in English. I told him that since the stenographer needed to be seated and I would be taking notes, I required his seat at the desk. (Maj. Bassante indicated his preference for standing.)

He quickly transferred himself to the bed. The smirk he had been wearing since we entered briefly gave way to a hurt look, which I surmised was less from my insistence on taking his seat than my failure to preface his last name with his rank (SS-Hauptsturmführer) or the honorific of "Herr Doktor."

KH: If that is your wish, Colonel Thomas.

WT: It's an order.

KH: I'm a soldier who has always followed orders. That is the nature of our profession, is it not?

WT: You are also a doctor who took an oath "to do no harm."

KH: As well as a soldier, I'm a scientist. The ethics of the scientist are not the ethics of the layman. Our work involves enlightenment, not sentiment. It is sometimes our duty to experiment on the few in order to serve the health and well-being of the many.

WT: You were an early member of the Nazi Physicians League, were you not?

KH: I joined in 1934 when it was clear the Party had taken full control of the government. The older members—*der alte kämpfer*— resented us newcomers, but I realized no significant research could be done except under the auspices of the Party. Most of my colleagues reached the same conclusion, as did most engineers and scientists interested in aeroplanes and rocketry.

WT: Was it for scientific reasons you joined the SS?

KH: More than any other institution, the SS recognized the medico-biological basis of the state. I felt it was our best hope for building an enduring bulwark against Bolshevism and a despotism of *untermenschen*.

WT: As a member of the SS, you participated in the T4 Program, did you not?

KH: Could you be more specific?

WT: The Reich Work Group of Sanatoriums and Nursing Homes, which operated out of the Chancellery at Tiergarten 4—the T4 Program authorized by Hitler at the start of the war to carry out the mass murder of the chronically mentally ill.

KH: Oh, *gnadentod*—the business of mercy death—was widely discussed. The eminent American physician Foster Kennedy proposed a similar idea.

WT: But it was carried out in Germany.

KH: I have no knowledge of that.

WT: Your signature has been identified on more than 2,000 evaluations as *obergutachter* [senior expert] at the psychiatric institution at Hadamar. In every case you recommended death.

KH: I recommended nothing. I certified evaluations made by subordinates.

WT: There are witnesses who place you at the ceremony at Hadamar, in late 1941, marking the cremation of the 10,000th victim of *gnadentod*.

KH: My interest was in research, not injections.

WT: But you knew about fatal morphine-scopolamine injections?

KH: The theoretical possibility was discussed as a humane method of ending the misery and suffering of the terminally ill. I never injected anyone.

WT: What about the gassings?

KH: At Hadamar?

WT: Yes.

KH: This is the first I've heard of such a thing.

WT: What about your role at Auschwitz?

KH: I obeyed the orders I was given.

WT: Were you aware it was a *vernichtungslager*—an "extermination camp"?

KH: Auschwitz was the size of a city. It encompassed several camps. I was aware of the terrible conditions, but given the wartime conditions and food shortages on the Eastern Front, along with the well-known proclivities of Poles and Jews for the unsanitary, a high mortality rate from disease was inevitable.

WT: Did you participate in ramp duty?

KH: What do you mean by "ramp duty"?

WT: The selection process carried out by camp doctors among Jewish arrivals.

KH: No, I never participated in any alleged selections of Jewish arrivals.

WT: Were you aware of such a process?

KH: I concentrated on my assignment in racial science, an area of inquiry shared by British and American scientists going back to Francis Galton, Richard Dugdale, Madison Grant, and many others. I was ordered by SS-Reichsführer Himmler and Wolfram Sievers to prepare a collection of specimens that might support—or at least suggest—an organic basis for the relationship between Jews and Bolshevism. I carried out the legally authorized orders of my superiors. It was not my place to refuse.

WT: By "specimens," you mean Jewish inmates and Russian POWs?

KH: Spies, traitors, saboteurs, or common criminals—murderers, rapists, and the like—selected for *sonderbehandlung* [special treatment] in view of their crimes.

WT: Did you participate in their demise?

KH: Their bodies were delivered to me after trial and execution.

WT: How were they executed?

KH: In order to ensure their integrity as research specimens, they were given phenol injections directly into the heart

WT: You knew nothing of mass gassings?

KH: I kept to my business. I never witnessed any alleged gassings.

WT: You were resident in the camp during May and June of 1944, were you not?

KH: I was, yes.

WT: You had no idea that Jewish deportees from Hungary were being gassed at the rate of up to 12,000 a day or that the crematoria at Birkenau were working overtime, spewing ash over the entire camp?

KH: As I said, Auschwitz covered a vast area. It was not uncommon for people in one area of the camp to be unaware what was taking place in another. I know nothing of these supposed excesses allegedly visited on the Jews by elements within the SS.

WT: There are witnesses who say you systematically tortured prisoners in pursuit of Soviet military intelligence.

KH: What witnesses?

WT: Subordinates.

KH: Inmates?

WT: Yes.

KH: It's all self-serving drivel! Many inmates were eager to cooperate. They couldn't do enough to ingratiate themselves. Indeed, if Auschwitz was the so-called death camp some allege, it sounds to me as if they should be indebted to me for their survival.

WT: After Auschwitz was evacuated, you were transferred to Mauthausen, were you not?

KH: Oh, yes, but only for a very brief time.

WT: Were you aware of the interrogation and torture of American POWs undertaken by Commandant Franz Ziereis?

KH: I was assigned to treat those infected with typhus—inmates as well as guards. An epidemic was raging in the camp. I never came across any Americans.

WT: Did you assist in the torture and execution of Dr. Gerhard Schaefer?

KH: I never heard of such a person. I'm a physician, not an executioner. If I might add, I answered these same questions this very morning during an extensive interview with an American intelligence officer.

WT: Who was that?

KH: Someone I presume you know: Lieutenant Colonel Bartlett.

WT: Did he identify his unit?

KH: The Strategic Services Unit.

WT: I'm unfamiliar with it.

KH: Well, it's being reorganized into the Central Intelligence Group, with a mandate to counter Soviet operations.

WT: I'll make it a point to contact him.

KH: If you'll permit me to say so, when it comes to intelligence operations, Americans seem not to let their right hand know what the left is doing.

WT: You'd be well advised to focus on your upcoming trial and leave such matters to the experts.

Signed: Col. Winston Thomas, M.D.
Witnessed: Maj. Turlough Bassante
Date: September 27, 1945

November 1945

COLUMBIA CASUALTY & LIFE, LONDON

DUNNE CHECKED HIS MAIL CUBBY HOPING TO FIND ORDERS TO RETURN to the States. Instead, there was a plain envelope of a type he recognized. On the card inside was the single code word used before D-Day to send operatives to a nondescript insurance office above a tailor shop near the American embassy: *BESPOKE.* The office housed a transatlantic line to OSS headquarters in Washington supposedly safe from prying by British and Russian allies, Axis enemies, and rivals in Military Intelligence and the Office of Naval Intelligence. Date and time were the only other information included on the card.

Dunne presumed the office had been closed by war's end and, if not by then, certainly in wake of President Truman's order relieving General Donovan of command and directing that the OSS cease operation.

Word was, Donovan was taken unawares. He shouldn't have been. At home, his legion of enemies—including all the savagely protective, turf-conscious bureaucracies dedicated to preserving their prerogatives, FBI, State Department, War and Navy Departments, as well as the chorus of Roosevelt-haters led by the McCormick-Patterson press empire—had been hunting for his scalp.

The *Chicago Tribune*, which had leaked the top-secret memo Donovan sent to FDR proposing creation of a permanent central intelligence service, ran fire-breathing editorials denouncing Donovan for abetting the establishment of an "American Gestapo" designed to enforce completion of the New Deal's blueprint for the collectivization of the nation's economy.

Most people suspected J. Edgar Hoover as the leaker. Inside the OSS, it was speculated FDR ordered it done to test public reaction to Donovan's proposal. Rumors flew. Then–Vice President Truman resented that the president barely took note of his existence while treating Donovan as a confidant. The brouhaha made Dunne glad he'd got out of Washington and into the action. The odds of being knifed in the back were substantially less than in the capital.

Despite the cachet bestowed on the OSS by the press, everyone inside knew to one degree or another the extent of its mistakes, fiascos, bungling, and outright disasters, like the German penetration of Cassia, the code name for the intelligence network in Eastern and Central Europe wiped out in a single stroke. Yet say what you like about the OSS, unlike the Brits or Germans, who had long-established intelligence and espionage operations, or the Soviets, who built theirs without regard for human or financial costs during the Great Terror, Donovan constructed his organization in the middle of a war, surrounded by civilian and military rivals. The wonder was not just that it made a contribution to defeating the Axis but also—more wondrous still—that it got built at all.

Dunne concluded that the card was probably a practical joke (a lame one at that) on the part of some bored officer in Naval Intelligence with nothing better to do than tweak a friendly (at least most of the time) and now-former competitor. More annoyed than amused, Dunne burned it in an ashtray.

Two days later a similar envelope with the same message was back in his cubby: *BESPOKE*. New time and date. He decided to see what it was about. If the message was for real, it must involve wrapping up bureaucratic details. Government organizations and departments came and went, but the paper shuffling never ceased.

The next afternoon, enjoying the absence of pain in his right ankle—the happy consequence of orthopedic surgery to reset and repair the damage done in Slovakia—he strolled leisurely to the office. The convalescence had laid him up for what seemed an interminable time and delayed his going home, but had proved worth it. He was all healed and awaiting his orders to ship back to the States.

Nearing the shop, he recalled his last visit, rainy Friday afternoon, June 1944. No doubt about the reason for that summons: The invasion was imminent. That day, he'd arrived twenty minutes early. The slight hesitation in the voice he heard on the other side of the wire might have been caused by a transatlantic technical glitch. It was more likely a sign of the apprehension even the most tested, self-contained soldiers felt now that the long-awaited hour had arrived: "You're aware of the confidence General Donovan has placed in you. As of tonight, all leaves are canceled. That means *everyone* . . . Follow the previous instructions . . . for . . . rendezvous . . . Everyone, Dunne . . . Is that clear?"

He'd stopped at a pub. The room was crowded and noisy. Several patrons tried to buy him a drink. He'd put them off as politely as he could and sat alone in a cozy. He'd picked up his drink. The tremor in his hand was barely noticeable. He'd limited himself to two, nursed them slowly, enough to take the edge off, not send him over.

At closing time, the barman rang the bell and shouted, "Time, gentlemen. Time."

The legend stenciled on the door—an inside nod to General Donovan's alma mater, where he'd made his name as a football star—was the same as on Dunne's last visit:

Columbia Casualty & Life

You Can Rely On Us

London Bureau Est. 1910

Though her hair was auburn instead of blonde and cut shorter than that of the woman who'd answered the door on his previous visit, and her lipstick was a deeper, harder shade of red, she
could have been the same woman. But if she wasn't the same person, she was the same type, attractive, early thirties, ready smile,
in-charge, friendly without being flirty. Dressed in black skirt and
purple silk blouse, she was a welcome change from the prissy
British types in buttoned-up, semimilitary tweed suits that made
even the young and pretty seem frosty and unapproachable.

She concentrated on the card he handed her a moment longer
than necessary to digest so short a message. "Why, yes, Mr. Dunne,
I was expecting you. It'll take a few minutes to put your call
through to Washington." She handed it back and took his hat. He
was in civilian clothes, one of the suits he'd had hand-tailored at
Crosby & Lord, not a Savile Row shop but close enough and half
the price. Whatever else the OSS had achieved, it would send home
a cadre of veterans in well-tailored suits.

"Can I get you a cup of coffee?" A question he hadn't been
asked on his last visit.

"I was afraid you'd say tea."

"We're an American company." She smiled. Teeth straight
and white. "I can offer you good strong American coffee."

"Maxwell House?"

She cocked her head with a quizzical tilt. "Is that the only
kind you like?"

"A sentimental favorite. I'll drink whatever you've got."

"We keep a special supply of Horn and Hardart's."

"I like it black."

"That's how you'll have it." Her accent was American but
without any discernible regional twang or accent, a radio voice,
generic like her smile, the kind that could sell coffee or insurance
or toothpaste.

She sashayed ahead on a nice set of gams accented by open-toed high heels with ankle straps, Joan Crawford–style. The office was how he remembered it: file cabinets against the far wall; main space occupied by two rows of sturdy, identical desks, three to a row, each with an Underwood, a silent telephone, and its own pile of papers.

"You came at a good time. The staff will be at a conference all morning. Now if you follow me, I'll get you set up." He resisted pointing out that, coincidentally, the staff had been away at a conference during his visit just prior to D-Day. A newspaper was opened on the desk nearest the door, as it had been, he recalled, on his last visit. He glanced down. It was the previous day's *New York Standard*.

She led him to the same small office as on his last visit. On the table against the wall were a telephone and electric teakettle. "No need for this." She removed the teakettle. "I'll be back in a flash."

He sat at the table. He lit a cigarette and rested it on a black ceramic ashtray with white lettering: *THE STORK CLUB.*

On the wall above was a calendar with the logo of Columbia Casualty & Life, woman holding aloft a torch, an obvious imitation of the figure used by the Columbia film studio, probably borrowed by whoever created this set. Next to it was a picture of the late President Roosevelt, black ribbon draped across the top. Been dead six months. In view of General Donovan's summary dismissal by President Truman and his disbanding of the OSS, it wasn't likely the new president's picture would replace the old.

The presidential face wore a wan smile that couldn't hide its weariness. Anybody earned the right to look that way, FDR had. *Nothing to fear but fear itself.* His most-remembered line. But he'd learned differently. Long list of things to fear. Enemies foreign and domestic. Slander. Betrayal. Cerebral hemorrhage. He gave as good as he got. And wore out in the process. His death came as a surprise, but shouldn't have. Those sad, sagging, tired eyes: dead tired.

"Black, Captain, as you requested." She returned with a mug of steaming coffee.

He took a sip. A taste of New York. "Perfect. Like it's fresh from the Automat."

"That's Columbia Casualty & Life: 'You can rely on us.'" She flashed another all-American smile. "Another minute, I'll have your party on the line." She closed the door softly behind her.

He lit a second cigarette from the first, rubbed the butt in the ashtray, and picked up the phone on the first ring.

"Captain Dunne, I have you connected."

He vainly searched for her name—Rita, Eleanor, Marge. Of course, she'd never given it. Peace might have arrived, but this was one of those corners where wartime protocols survived. "Thank you, Miss," he said.

"Go ahead, gentlemen."

"Fin?"

"Yes."

"It's Turlough Bassante. I'm glad you made it through."

Dunne held the phone away from his ear and looked at the receiver. Maybe the only other name that would have surprised him more was if the speaker had identified himself as President Roosevelt.

"Fin, you there?"

"Yeah."

"I said I'm glad you made it through."

He hesitated, unsure how to answer. "Bunde didn't."

"I know. But he was lucky. It was quick."

"Quick and dead, if you call that luck."

"What was your name for luck? '*Totiusque*,' wasn't it?"

"You've got a good memory."

"Van Hull and you made it through. The odds were stacked against you. Operation Maxwell may not rank among the most famous of OSS exploits, but your determination to avoid capture was remarkable. Among connoisseurs of clandestine operations it's, as the French say, a *succès d'estime*."

"Not so much luck as Van Hull. He's the reason we survived. Either way, it's over and done." Dunne didn't say what he felt: *Who cares about one small, stupid, unsuccessful mission in a war that had been filled with them? What comfort would Bunde's parents get from the details of their son's broken neck?*

Bassante didn't push the discussion of Operation Maxwell any further. "I hope I'm not interfering with your schedule." He sounded as if he were on the other side of the wall, not the Atlantic.

"I don't have a schedule. I'm treading water till we're ordered home."

"It's disintegration, pure and simple. Disgraceful. There are aspects that are disturbing." Bassante talked as though it were only a few hours and not ten months between this conversation and their last. He reported that General Donovan had recalled him to the States right after the German surrender in hopes of him helping put together a proposal for a peacetime version of the OSS acceptable to the new president.

The best-laid schemes o' mice an' men gang aft agley. Dunne was tempted to quote it. Just a college-educated version of Murphy's Law. True yesterday, today, tomorrow. But he listened in silence as Bassante went off on a monologue about the confusion and disarray that followed the new president's order to disband the OSS.

A skeleton staff at the newly formed Strategic Services Unit—the rump of the OSS, Bassante related—was doing its best to maintain a semblance of order and see to basic intelligence gathering but records were being lost. Nobody seemed in control. The skulduggery in Washington seemed endless.

Dunne lit a third cigarette from the second. Bassante's blather was a red light. He was coming at it sideways, with a crab's indirection. But you played the game long enough, you knew what's next: simple, subtle pitches delivered with Dizzy Dean's finesse. He was being set up for another mission.

Bassante seemed to intuit what he was thinking. "In short, it's a mess."

"Sounds it."

"I thought perhaps I could call on you for help."

"In *Washington*?" Dunne lifted the cigarette from the ashtray, exhaled at the calendar's horizontal rows, each beginning with a Sunday. The closest one was three days from now. A pitch worth swinging at: "Count me in. I can be there by Monday. Easy."

"No. Over there. I'm coming back at the end of the week."

"To London?"

"Nuremberg. The war crimes tribunal is set to open on the twentieth. I'll be in London for two days."

"Nuremberg?" He'd made known his availability. Swung and missed at a fastball down the middle. *Strike one.*

"Technically, I wear two hats. In addition to my work with Strategic Services, I'm assisting with the prosecution at the International Military Tribunal. General Donovan arranged it. After he was invited aboard by Justice Jackson, he had me transferred to the Counterintelligence Corps and took me with him."

The combination of the two men—both former U.S. attorneys general, Jackson, an associate justice of the Supreme Court, and Donovan, wartime head of the OSS—generated a good deal of publicity. But as far as Bassante was concerned, it was a star-crossed arrangement. Jackson wanted a knowledgeable, pliable assistant. The general was looking to lead the prosecution. Jackson envisioned a trial based on documentation so exhaustive and specific it would be irrefutable. Donovan wanted a Tom Dewey–type assault on Luciano and the mob, shredding low-life thugs to pieces on the witness stand, cutting deals with one to get him to rat on another.

"I was there when they tried to work out their differences,"

Bassante remembered. "'This isn't the Supreme Court,' the general said. 'This is about drama, not decorum.'

"Jackson wouldn't be moved. 'Maybe so,' he said, 'but I'm running the show, and I'm going to try the case by indisputable documentary evidence.'

"It came out that the general was also against indicting the German General Staff. Jackson cut off the conversation. He fired the general. Poor Donovan sputtered with rage, but next day, ashen and crestfallen, he seemed a spent volcano. He thought I'd leave with him. I told him I felt a duty to the International Military Tribunal. He said he understood. But we never understand when someone we trust lets us down."

Dunne sympathized with Donovan's wounded pride and personal disappointment, even betrayal, as well as Bassante's sense of duty. Everyone has his motive. "That's an uncomfortable situation to be in."

"Dick Van Hull is part of this, too."

"Van Hull?" His name hung in the air like a big, fat Dizzy Dean changeup.

"He's in an uncomfortable situation of his own."

Expect a fastball and a slow ball floats by. *Strike two.*

"If you're willing, Ginny has an envelope. The details are spelled out inside."

"Ginny who?"

"Miss Thompson, the office manager."

Not Rita, Eleanor, Marge, after all. But Ginny. Ginny Thompson, Miss American Efficiency, 1945. With the war over, her name was apparently no longer a secret.

"Don't feel obligated, Fin."

Don't feel obligated. Van Hull carried them through their mission in Slovakia. How could he be anything but obligated?

"Read it over and let Miss Thompson know. If you can't, I'll understand."

A knuckleball. Swing or let it pass: *Strike three.* Dunne ground the stub in the ashtray. Bassante wouldn't understand anymore than Donovan.

On the calendar, above the muster of days, the exhausted (now deceased) president made a final attempt at a smile.

Nothing left to fear.

Nice try.

If only.

After he left, Dunne stopped at the same pub as he had in June '44. This time, midday, the clientele was sparse. He ordered a pint. Two ex-Tommies (woolen khaki trousers gave away their former status) peeked over their shoulders. As ready for the Yanks to go home as the Yanks were eager to go, they attempted none of the friendly banter as when Americans were a much-welcomed novelty. The barman drew the pint without saying a word.

He sat by himself and sipped the beer. Warm as piss. The way the Brits liked it. Never got used to it. What American did? Instead of placing the manila envelope Miss Thompson had given him on the wet, unwiped bar, he rested it on his lap.

She'd clasped it against her purple blouse and thrust it forward with both hands, as though proffering a gift. "Take it with you. But it would be most appreciated if you got back with an answer by tomorrow."

Annoyed at the skill with which Bassante had drawn him in, and already resentful at the idea of delaying his return home, Dunne intended the sharpness of his reply: "I can't give an answer till I know the question."

"I'm just relaying what I was told." She advanced toward the door with a confident, purposeful sway, toenail polish visible through her open-toed shoes same shade as fingernails and blouse. *Purple majesty.* If coast-to-coast television ever became commonplace in U.S. living rooms, as the newspapers promised it would, she'd be the country's perfect hostess. *Miss America the Beautiful.*

He went back to the bar, fetched a scotch, played with returning to the office of Columbia Casualty & Life, handing the unopened envelope to Miss Thompson, making his own declaration of independence: *I've served my time, done my duty, had enough of warm beer, cold rooms, dreary streets, the dead and the damaged, this ruined, grudge-ridden, self-destructive continent. Two wars' worth, Miss Thompson. More than enough.*

Dunne ripped it open. The handwriting was clear, neat, parochial-grammar-school precise, a style uniformly enforced in institutions of every size as though a tenet of the One True Church. Hail, holy penmanship.

He presumed Bassante had written it himself:

Dear Fin,
Sorry to be so careful in communicating with you. The times, I'm afraid, require such caution. The war is over. It remains to be seen what peace, if any, we'll have.

I spend most of my time with the Counterintelligence Corps. The focus is on identifying those within the National Socialist regime—the Wehrmacht, SS, corporations, the scientific and medical communities—whose conduct exposes them to prosecution as war criminals. Given the scope of the crimes, it would be an immense challenge under the best of circumstances. But the CIC is seriously understaffed and/or staffed by wet-behind-the-ears recruits with absolutely no familiarity with the matters at hand.

Worse, it too often seems that among the more knowledgeable within the CIC, not only does one hand not know what the other is doing, but the other doesn't <u>want</u> it to know.

Dick Van Hull has become a victim of this squeeze. He volunteered early on for the CIC. His linguistic skills and field experience were considered invaluable. His enthusiasm for the work was unbounded. Now, however, certain rumors are being spread about

him. He's being pressured to resign. He says he will face court-mar-
tial rather than do so.

I would appreciate your help in this matter. I realize you're
probably scheduled to return stateside very soon, and while I hesi-
tate to delay your departure, I can't think of anyone more qualified
or more appreciative of Dick's qualities as a man and as a soldier.

Please let Miss Thompson know your answer as soon as you
decide. I'll be in London the day after tomorrow.
Turlough

Dunne tucked it back into the envelope. The phone connection to the office of Columbia Causality & Life was supposedly
secure—but not secure enough that Bassante felt comfortable using
it to convey the information in the letter.

He finished the whiskey and ordered another. Two Brits at the
bar played a game of darts. The casual precision of their throws—
feathered tails crowded around the bull's eye—was impressive.
They went back to their drinks. That moment of triumph at war's
end had been just that: a *moment*, sweet and short. What followed
was a collective letdown. Goods still rationed. Streets and people
had a shabby, secondhand feel.

He'd have to write Roberta immediately and let her know his
return to the States was delayed. She'd be as much angered as disappointed, especially since he'd have to leave the reason vague. He
couldn't mention Van Hull. Even if he could, she'd have no way to
grasp the size of the debt he owed him.

Dunne hadn't seen Van Hull since return from Prague, the
previous May. He vividlly recalled how eager Van Hull had been
to get into the streets and join the uprising. Their protector, Jan
Horak, insisted they stay hidden. An intelligence officer with the
Red Army, he informed Van Hull, had already grumbled about the
presence of "American spies" with the partisans. "In order to
avoid complications, you must stay where you are. You had your

war. This chapter belongs to us Czechs. We'll celebrate when it's over."

They slept most of the next several days. The silence and darkness of their hideout added to their cumulative weariness and abetted the rest they both needed. They didn't know about V-E Day and the German surrender or the final liberation of Prague until Jan Horak returned with Lieutenant Colonel Carlton Bartlett.

Bartlett was dressed in civilian clothes, brown ulster over brown suit. They didn't recognize him at first, and he didn't hide his surprise at their drawn appearance. "My God, you two look as though you've been washed, wrung, and hung out to dry."

"We've been playing too much golf," Dunne said.

Bartlett pulled a carton of Luckies and two bottles of champagne from inside his coat. He popped the cork on one, jovially apologized for not bringing glasses, and passed the bottle around. After several slugs, Horak left.

"It's stuffy down here." Bartlett removed his suit jacket. Dunne caught the scent of aftershave. Bay rum.

Van Hull and Dunne sat on their cots as Bartlett, unable to stay still, paced back and forth, stopping only when it was his turn for the champagne. "The general will be overjoyed I've found you. He's not the kind to show any emotion—you know that, Dunne, having served under him in the first war—but you also know how deeply he feels the loss of each and every man. He could barely hide his reaction to what happened with Operation Dawson and with your drop."

"What was the outcome with Dawson?" Van Hull wiped his mouth with his sleeve, lit a cigarette, and rested the champagne bottle on his knee.

"Mike Jahn and the others were taken to Mauthausen, as was Doctor Schaefer, who was also in the custody of the SS. There they were interrogated and executed. The sad fact is they'd already been shipped to Mauthausen by the time you were dropped." Van Hull guzzled the remainder of the bottle and dropped in the cigarette. He lay back, head on pillow, forearm covering his eyes.

Bartlett popped the second bottle. He continued his pacing. It seemed to be a habit, but if it was, it had done nothing to slim his pear-shaped, midbody bulk.

Bartlett explained that his mission had been entirely Donovan's idea: "Wild Bill at his wildest and most daring!" Get into Czechoslovakia and rescue Dr. Herschel Cernak, Schaefer's former business partner, prominent scientist, and Jewish layman, from the Nazis. That part of the mission was complete. The Russians would love to take credit for the rescue. They'd also welcome the chance to question some OSS operatives. "Trick is to get out of Prague pronto. Donovan is seeing to that. You two sit tight for now. I'll let you know when it's time."

Dunne gave him back the bottle. He drained it. "It's a sin to gargle such fine champagne, but with victory at hand, we're entitled to certain liberties." He looked down at Van Hull. "You men are the hidden heroes of this war. But now it's the next one we have to prepare for. In war, as in life, intelligence is the ultimate weapon."

He donned his jacket and folded the ulster over his arm. He turned and repeated himself on his way out, this time with a slight slur: "You two s-s-sit tight, and I'll let you know when it's-s-s time to go."

The champagne left Dunne light-headed. The room felt more prison cell than hiding place. The residual discomfort in his ankle made him limp. He turned out the light and lay down on his cot. He woke in a sweat. His mouth was dry. He had an urgent need to pee. He used the flashlight to guide his way to the bathroom. On the way back, the peripheral play of the beam alerted him Van Hull's cot was empty.

"Dick?" Dunne whispered. No answer. He switched on the overhead light. Van Hull was gone. He went into the corridor. "Dick!" His shout echoed through the marble emptiness. He went up the stairs, flashlight puncturing the dark. The clock on the wall in the office in which Van Hull and he had found the radio indicated 4:30.

He wandered more hallways. He called Van Hull's name but knew he was gone. Mulholland's warning resurrected itself, a haunting refrain: *Once the cork is popped, there's no putting it back.* No use going into the street. No way to contact Horak or Bartlett. All he could do was wait until one of them returned.

It was an agonizing several hours before there was a shuffled commotion of voices and footsteps in the hallway. Arms draped over their shoulders, Van Hull was supported by Horak and a companion. Bartlett, red-faced and in full uniform, was behind them.

Horak and his helper lowered Van Hull onto the cot. Pacing beside it, Bartlett ran his hand through his hair. "Jesus H. Christ!" he exploded. "He's supposed to be a professional soldier, the epitome of the American fighting man, and instead he acts like a drunken circus clown! If Horak here hadn't been alerted there was a boozed-up American busting up a tavern, the Russians would have grabbed him, and then we'd be in some fix!"

Van Hull lay unconscious, mouth agape, arms spread like a crucified man. Dunne patted his cheek. "Dick, it's Fin. You all right?"

"All right? Look at him! His pathetic antics came within a hairsbreadth of drawing the Soviets' attention and scotching our chance to get out of Prague."

Without stopping his relentless pacing back and forth, Bartlett let Dunne in on the arrangements General Donovan had made to land a plane full of medical supplies that would whisk them to the west. Tonight, Bartlett would leave his quarters on the pretense of joining the celebration of the reopening of the Prague State Opera House. He would have already sent Dr. Cernak ahead to the plane. His car would swing by the museum. "Horak will have Van Hull and you at the side entrance, and you'll hop in. There better not be any slipups. I'm counting on you, Dunne."

After Bartlett left, Dunne and the two Czechs carried Van Hull to the bathroom, sat him in a chair, put his head in the sink, and ran cold water over him. Horak went upstairs and came back with two sets of fresh clothes, suits, shirts, and shoes. They stripped off Van Hull's old clothes, re-dressed him, and laid him on his cot.

Dunne changed into his new clothes. He gathered his and Van Hull's discarded outfits and checked the pockets before he stuck them in the tall garbage pail. In the pocket of Van Hull's trousers was a badly creased, tattered photo of a handsome, youthful lieutenant with blond wavy hair. His lips were parted as if he were about to speak or sing or ask a question. Van Hull must have had it with him since they left Bari. Dunne strained to make out the faded handwritten inscription on the back: *Dick, One man loved the pilgrim soul in you / And loved the sorrows of your changing face. Mike.*

He lit a cigarette, exhaled through his nose. He should be anxious, worrying whether they'd be intercepted and detained by the Russians. But he wasn't. Operation Maxwell was over. The war with the Japs was still on. But the OSS was undoubtedly readying a new set of field operatives for that mission, highly trained, eager men—crème de la crème—their enthusiasm not yet curdled by experience, memories not yet tainted by the memory of those who never come back.

Van Hull was motionless. Dunne gently lifted Van Hull's hands and folded them on his chest. He'd learned almost nothing about Van Hull in their time together, none of the details of childhood or prewar life and career, yet he knew everything he needed —or wanted—to know, everything important.

Dunne tucked the photo he'd found into the pocket of Van Hull's jacket. His handsome face was relaxed, peaceful. The cold water left it with a rosy glow.

Jan Horak appeared at the door. It was time to rendezvous with Bartlett. They carried Van Hull upstairs into the waiting car, raced to the airport, and boarded the plane, which took off immediately. Once they were aloft, Bartlett broke out a fresh supply of champagne. Van Hull abstained. He sat beside Dr. Herschel Cernak, a frail, shy, white-haired man in his seventies, the horror he'd witnessed imprinted in his wide, anguished eyes. He and Van Hull spent the entire flight to Paris conversing in German.

They landed in Paris and spent the night at the Ritz, a luxurious but very brief interlude for Van Hull and Dunne, who were flown to London the next morning. Dunne expected an intense debriefing. Except for an hour's conversation with one of Bartlett's aides, there was none. A doctor examined Dunne and advised him that unless he wanted to walk with a limp for the rest of his life, he required a corrective operation on his ankle.

Van Hull came to see him while he was recuperating. He was thin but otherwise his old movie-star self. General Donovan had called him back to Washington to help make the case for keeping the OSS in business. He held out a soft, circular package wrapped in plain brown paper.

Dunne tore off the wrapping. Inside was a roll of toilet paper.

"I promised, remember?"

"I'll keep it as a reminder of our vacation in Slovakia with Maxwell Tours."

"Minute I found that photo of Mike Jahn in my pocket, I knew who put it there."

"Figured you went to a lot of trouble to keep it."

"The quote on the back is from Yeats."

"Whaddaya know? My favorite poet."

Van Hull laughed. "Mine, too. 'When You Are Old and Grey' is the title." Van Hull handed Dunne a second package in the same brown wrapping.

"What's this?"

"Open it and see."

Inside was a book. He read the title aloud: "*The Oxford Book of Modern Verse.*"

"A first edition. Yeats edited it. Given your newfound love of poetry, I thought you'd enjoy it."

That was the last Dunne saw of Van Hull. He'd believed their paths had permanently diverged until Bassante's phone call.

The pub had filled up. The crowd made it feel less gloomy. He resisted having another scotch. Didn't see much use in waiting until tomorrow to give his answer.

When she opened the door to Columbia Casualty & Life, Miss Thompson couldn't hide her surprise. "Why, you caught me just in time."

He stepped inside. The office was as empty as it had been earlier. "Everyone has left for the day. I was just closing up."

"The answer is yes."

"I'll convey it right away." Her wide smile gleamed with alabaster teeth.

December 1945

SEVERAL TIMES BASSANTE SCHEDULED MEETINGS AND EACH TIME postponed because of "urgent business." His patience at an end, Dunne was surprised to find Miss Thompson at his door, pert and pretty in fur-collared coat and gray hat, brim turned up, with a bottle wrapped in Christmas gift paper. "'Tis the season. Major Bassante hopes this ration of French bubbly will keep you in the holiday spirit. He also asked I convey his personal regret at the unavoidable nature of these delays."

"Tell him thanks, but I'm on my way home." He forced an unconvincing grin. "Merry Christmas."

At the landing, she wiggled the fingers of her right hand, a nonchalant good-bye. "I trust you've been good so Santa won't feel compelled to shove a lump of coal up your . . . your"—she put forefinger to lips as if searching for the right word—"stocking."

Christmas Eve, he went solo to midnight Mass at the Jesuit church on Farm Street, a long ceremony, three priests, clouds of incense, and a well-trained boys' choir. Before Mass, he'd shared with Bud Mulholland the bottle of Dom Pérignon Bassante had sent via Miss Thompson. He dozed during the sermon. In a suddenly empty church, Miss Thompson did a stripper's strut down the aisle, hips swaying rhythmically, fingers wiggling enticingly. She let her coat drop to the floor. Besides a sparkling, champagne smile all she was wearing were coal-black stockings and black high heels.

He woke with a start. No kind of dream for church. The altar boys repeated the concluding words of the Suscipiat with clarity and emphasis: ". . . *totiusque Ecclesiae suae sanctae.*"

He waited until Christmas morning to open the present Roberta had sent: blue-and-white-striped shirt and tie from Rogers Peet that matched perfectly. The accompanying letter was affectionate and understanding. She knew he wouldn't have put off his return if it hadn't involved business of real consequence. She just hoped it would be over very soon. "It feels like forever, Fin: *Long the skies are overcast / But soon the clouds will pass / You'll be here at last.*"

Rush of homesickness surged from stomach to throat. *Long ago and far away.* Goddamn Bassante and his last-minute pitch.

Dunne wore the shirt and tie to the Christmas dinner Mulholland had booked in the private dining facilities of a high-class hotel. *No greasy, skinny-assed goose, I promise,* Mulholland wrote on the invitation. *This will be an American affair from soup to nuts.* He'd hired his own cook—a colored sergeant who boasted he'd helped run General Eisenhower's kitchen—and had him prepare a Yuletide feast, centerpiece an outsized rib roast liberated from the larder of the General Staff.

The guests comprised a mix of former OSS men, Army Air Corps, and Naval Intelligence, several accompanied by slim, wan, impossibly polite English girls in their late twenties. The girls fussed over the hors d'oeuvres. The men mustered at the bar. Mulholland handed the cook the carving knife and jokingly threatened to use it on him if the roast were overdone. "Better be the American way, medium rare, or else!"

"Don't worry, done it right for Ike, do it right for you." The cook wiped knife on apron, muttered, "Wasn't for my cookin' Ike wouldn't had the swing he needed to roll them Krauts."

Dinner was served. The roast was medium rare and delicious. Mulholland summoned the cook from the kitchen for a round of applause. Everyone ate heartily, especially the girls. After dinner, one of them did an a cappella solo, *a bluebird over white cliffs of Dover, tomorrow, just you wait and see.* Sweet but sad.

They went back to the bar.

"This is beginning to feel like a goddamn wake," Mulholland barked. "War's over, everybody! Get some goddamn music on the radio." The bartender tuned in a tribute to Glenn Miller, who'd gone missing the previous Christmas when the plane carrying him to rejoin his fifty-piece Army Air Force Band in Paris went down over the English Channel.

"Moonlight Serenade" came on. Some of the guests started to dance with their dates. The party finally took off when a late arrival showed up with a portable phonograph and a mixed stack of V-Disc 78s and prewar swing records made by Benny Goodman, Louis Armstrong, and Tommy Dorsey.

"Come on," he roared. "Let's get it shaking!"

Dining room became dance hall. Table and chairs were pushed against the wall. The English girls, previously reserved, revealed themselves expert, uninhibited jitterbuggers. Even Mulholland joined in, doing a passable Lindy. The longer it went on, the more girls and soldiers wandered in—mostly Army Air Corps—spontaneous jumble of jiving, swinging, colliding couples caught up celebrating first postwar Christmas.

Peace on earth—long as it lasts. Goodwill to all—for now.

The cook stood next to Dunne at the bar. "Man, makes you wonder, don't it, the way Mister Charlie can't abide the colored but can't get enough of our music."

Next morning, Dunne received another telegram from Bassante with a New Year's greeting and solemn promise to keep the next appointment, which he scheduled for the following week, at the Drummond Hotel, at one in the afternoon.

January 1946

DUNNE ARRIVED EARLY. THE CLOCK IN THE HOTEL LOBBY WAS FIVE minutes shy of one. The only other guest, a tweedy, professorial type, slouched next to the softly playing radio in the corner. Dunne caught a few lines of a BBC commentary on "the spirituals of the American Negro." Uninterested in the radio as well as the copies of the London *Times* and the *Tribune* splayed on the stub-legged table in front of his chair, Dunne signaled for the waiter.

Black swallowtail coat hanging from curtain-rod shoulders, the waiter turned out to be the same one from a year ago. He approached with a slight limp. His parchment-like skin tautly stretched from crown of head across sharp jut of cheek and awkwardly prominent Adam's apple. He replaced the used napkin with a fresh one and served Dunne's scotch and side of water from a tray the same tarnished silver as his thinning hair. Decidedly less harried than he'd been the year before, he lowered the glasses onto the table with the solemnity of a priest placing a chalice on the altar.

Dunne was resolved not to give vent to his resentment at Bassante's several reschedulings. What good would it do? Bassante would have his excuses—true or false, Dunne didn't give a hoot. All he cared about was finishing this last bit of business and getting home—ASAP.

Bassante arrived punctually at one and checked his coat. His well-tailored blue chalk-stripe suit gave him a passing resemblance to those transatlantic diplomats in the newsreels shuttling in pursuit of a framework for Europe's postwar reconstruction. He leaned over the front desk. His needle nose pointed down at the clerk, who nodded in Dunne's direction.

"Don't get up." Bassante gestured for Dunne to stay where he was. "I owe you a *mea maxima culpa*." He rearranged the adjoining chair so they sat shoulder to shoulder. "I see you've already ordered a drink. It would be rude to make you drink alone. This nation, unlike ours, frowns on bad manners."

The waiter returned. Bassante ordered a glass of sherry. His face had lost none of its fierce angularity, but he seemed more at ease than in Bari. "Let me reiterate my apology for all these delays as well as my great gratitude for your patience."

"Just so you know, I'm over my surgery, my papers are filed, so whatever this involves, it better be quick."

"It will be, I promise." Bassante felt under his chair and did the same to the table.

"Are you doing what I think you're doing?"

"What's that?" Bassante sat back.

"Scouting a mike."

"I suggest you do the same."

"You're serious, aren't you?"

"Did you choose the chair or did someone direct you?"

"Does it matter?"

"Check the chair and we'll know."

Dunne ran his hand across its underside. Nothing.

The waiter returned. A tray with sherry-filled crystal glass was balanced on his right palm. "Will that be all, sir?"

"Fine for now, thank you."

"As you wish, sir." He retreated with studied footsteps that mitigated his lameness.

Bassante raised his glass in a quasi toast. "Here's to Kipling. He had it right. 'Lo, all our pomp of yesterday / Is one with Nineveh and Tyre! / The tumult and the shouting dies / The Captains and the Kings depart.' No empire lasts forever. The best the Brits can do is shuffle off with a modicum of dignity. This is among the truths—"

"Look, Bassante, let's get down to business, *now*! The war's done, and I'm going home." Dunne slammed down his glass. The sound echoed through the room.

The gentleman by the radio gave a daggerlike stare in their direction. Obviously perplexed—if not surprised—by their rude behavior, he fumbled with the dial, momentarily amplifying a snatch of the spiritual he'd been listening to: "Oh those bones, oh those bones, oh those skeleton bones." He flipped the dial in the opposite direction, turned the radio off, and headed to the dining room.

Bassante sighed. "I'm afraid we've put another dent in Anglo-American relations."

"Let's cut to the chase, okay?"

"You're right. I apologize again. It's complicated." Bassante picked up the *Tribune* from the table. He crossed his legs, resting right ankle atop left knee. Toe caps of his narrow, elegant black wing tips were decorated with intersecting circles of subtle perfo-rations. "I don't know if you saw it, but there was an important article in this paper back in October."

"I don't read the papers, *especially* the English ones." A taxi pulled up in front of the window. A bowler-hatted Brit with umbrella hooked on his forearm got out. The taxi idled where it was, awaiting another hire. Dunne felt ready to run out, hop in, get back to his quarters, and start packing.

Bassante folded the newspaper and tapped Dunne's knee. "You should look up this one. Everyone should. 'You and the Atom Bomb,' by Orwell, an English journalist. Bleak but prophetic. What we face, he writes, is not the kind of *drôle de guerre*—the phony war that preceded the German blitzkrieg. This is a struggle neither side can wage outright. It will be fought through subversion and in proxy wars, a *guerre froide*, or cold war, a 'peace that is no peace.' It's already under way. No way to tell when it will end."

"What's any of this got to do with Dick Van Hull?"

"I'm the one who got Dick involved, or at least got him started. Donovan called him back to Washington to help save the OSS. Once Truman pulled the plug, I recruited Dick to the Counterintelligence Corps. The CIC's brief, I explained to him, is ensuring that the prosecution of war criminals doesn't end with the handful of headliners on trial in Nuremberg. The Reich's terror apparatus wasn't limited to the SS, the Gestapo, and the like. The murder of millions wasn't the work of a small gang of fanatics.

"The crimes couldn't have been carried out without the *schreibtischtäter*, the 'desk criminals'—eugenicists, physicians, scientists, industrialists, railroad officials, professors, bureaucrats, and paper pushers who signed the necessary forms and assigned subordinates to do the dirty work. The British War Crimes Group has ten thousand names of those involved in abetting mass murder. The actual number is far beyond that—horrifyingly far."

"How do you try that many?"

"At a bare minimum you put in place a process that establishes the dimensions of the crime, identifies those involved, punishes the worst offenders, and publicly brands and bars their accomplices from government employment."

"Isn't that what's going on in Nuremberg?"

"It's a start. An infinitesimally small start. But more and more, the emphasis is putting the war behind us, wiping the slate clean, and squaring off against the Russians."

"You still haven't explained the fix that Dick Van Hull is in."

"I'm getting there. With his linguistic skills and OSS experience, he was perfect for the job. He was with me at a CIC briefing last summer when it came up that Reinhard Gehlen and several adjutants were in Washington to confer with some of the brass."

"Should I know who Reinhard Gehlen is?"

"Forgive me for taking for granted what I shouldn't. Gehlen was made head of German military intelligence for Eastern Operations when Operation Barbarossa was launched. He amassed a tremendous amount of data on the Red Army. No mere observer, he was intimately familiar with the fact that at least three million Soviet POWs were systematically starved to death, that the interrogation of prisoners routinely included torture and execution, that millions more civilians were murdered throughout the Baltics, Ukraine, Belarus, and Poland, and that the extermination of European Jews had been undertaken by the SS.

"After Hitler fired him in March of '45, Gehlen and a cadre of aides transferred the reams of information they'd gathered on the Red Army to microfiche. The Wehrmacht's surrender was unconditional. Gehlen's was on *his* terms. Although he was far more implicated than Nuremberg defendants like Konstantin von Neurath and Franz von Papen, who were never near a battlefield or concentration camp, Gehlen offered his archives and expertise in exchange for immunity. He counted on present utility trumping unsavory past. He hasn't been disappointed. He's been returned to the American zone in Germany and put to work. Van Hull vociferously opposed Gehlen getting a free pass."

"That got him in Dutch?"

"That was the start. The decision on Gehlen had been made, so I had Dick reassigned to me in the research unit in Nuremberg preparing for the upcoming doctors' trial, which won't get going until the Nazi grandees' has ended."

Finished with his drink, Bassante signaled the waiter. "Another sherry for me and a scotch for my friend."

"No thanks. I'm still working on mine." Dunne rubbed his hands together. Across the room, the fireplace where he'd sat with

Van Hull and discussed Operation Maxwell was out of commission. The wall directly above was scarred by a prominent crack, a consequence of the V-2 rocket that hit farther down the block and reduced a row of stately eighteenth-century town houses and their inhabitants into dust and debris.

A downpour descended on the pedestrians outside, who seemed universally prepared, black umbrellas sprouting the length of the block.

"Someday, I suppose, by dint of natural selection, the Englishman and his umbrella will evolve into a single organism." Bassante tossed the newspaper on the table. "*Homo britannicus*: a subspecies distinguished by umbrella-like appendage, tight ass, and stiff upper lip."

"You were talking about the doctors' trial," Dunne said.

The waiter returned with the glass of sherry.

Bassante watched until he was out of earshot. "An odd affair: Twenty-three defendants are scheduled for indictment, including Karl Brandt, Hitler's personal physician; a twenty-fourth is the subject of a jurisdictional tug-of-war. Van Hull is in the middle."

The various involvements of the defendant in question, SS-Hauptsturmführer Dr. Karsten Heinz, were ticked off by Bassante: participant in the T4 Program, assistant physician at the Auschwitz Concentration Camp, member of the Reich Research Council, fellow of the Berlin-Dahlem Research Institute for Racial Biology and Anthropology, and associate director of the Research and Teaching Community for the Ancestral Heritage, the Forschungs-und-Lehrgemeinshaft das Ahnererbe.

Bassante recounted being present for the interview with Heinz conducted by Colonel Winfield Thomas, former head of psychiatry and neurology at Albany Medical College, at the prison in Nuremberg. Bassante liked Thomas—they were both "devotees of Sigmund Freud"—and agreed that Thomas would do the questioning.

As Bassante told it, Heinz denied any awareness of Auschwitz's role as an extermination camp. He had never participated in any of the "alleged selections of Jewish arrivals," never witnessed any of the "alleged gassings," never encountered American POWs at Mauthausen. He joined the Nazi Party and the SS for practical reasons. He was never a National Socialist fanatic.

"Although it's contradicted by everything we've found in his SS file, that's the line he sticks to. In other words—at very best—he didn't sell his soul; he merely rented it. Now it seems he's looking to change landlords." Instead of sipping his sherry, Bassante downed it in a single swallow. "Son of a bitch smirked the entire time. At the end, he let it slip he'd already had 'extensive conversations with an American intelligence officer.'

"Colonel Thomas asked, 'Who?'

"'Someone I presume you know,' Heinz responded. 'Lieutenant Colonel Bartlett.'

"Thomas looked at me quizzically. He presumed that since I was with the CIC, I'd have an idea who this Bartlett was. I shrugged, thinking to myself that the only Bartlett I knew was Carlton Bartlett, who must have finished up his work with the Strategic Services Unit by now and hurried back to the Stork Club's Cub Room to wine and dine clients and regale them with war stories.

"Heinz picked up on our confusion and savored it, noting with a less-than-subtle tone of glee, 'When it comes to intelligence operations, Americans often seemed not to let the right hand know what the left is doing.' Thomas asked if Bartlett had identified his unit. 'The SSU,' Heinz said, 'which is being reorganized with Bartlett's help into the Central Intelligence Group to counter Soviet espionage.'"

"How would he know that?"

Bassante surveyed the room. "Only one way he could know."

"Bartlett?"

"Bingo, the Pear."

"But why?"

"We know from other sources that under the pretext of establishing a biological link between Judaism and Bolshevism, Heinz made a special practice of extracting information from captured Soviet intelligence officers. Unlike Gehlen, an intelligence gourmand who indiscriminately amassed material—much of it inaccurate, out of date, or deliberately planted by the Soviets—Heinz was an epicure. He focused on quality over quantity, making a painstakingly accurate compilation of dossiers and constantly refining what he got. I've no doubt he's proposing to trade what he has for immunity to prosecution and whatever else he can get."

"Can he pull it off?"

"As well as testimony detailing his work at Auschwitz, we can also place him at Mauthausen. He was present when the commandant, Franz Ziereis, interrogated the prisoners from Operation Dawson. I'm also sure Heinz carried out the order to prepare Michael Jahn's body for inclusion in the SS's collection of Jewish skeletons."

"If that's not enough to hang him, what is?" Dunne finished his scotch. He brought up the account he'd heard from Dr. Niskolczi of his experiences at Auschwitz and the work he'd been forced to do for Heinz. Bassante said Van Hull had already recounted their meeting with Niskolczi.

"Let's hope that if the doctor survived, his testimony has been taken down." But, Bassante added, "Heinz has got another card to play. He undoubtedly regards it as his trump. Although he feigns ignorance, we know that along with being present for the interrogation of the OSS men, he assisted in that of Dr. Gerhard Schaefer. The *real* one." Bassante signaled to the waiter for another round; this time Dunne joined him. "It's like in that old spiritual: 'Toe bone connected to the foot bone, foot bone connected to ankle bone.'"

"Schaefer was brought to Mauthausen?" Dunne asked.

Bassante put an index finger to the tip of his nose. "He was brought there along with Jahn and the others. We know that before murdering Schaefer, Ziereis—with Heinz present—extracted the location of the archive. This means Heinz is able to deliver the all-time double play of the intelligence game, one-of-a-kind Tinkers-to-Evers-to-Chance proposition that can provide a handle on Soviet spying *and* on Nazi war criminals."

"Including himself, no?"

"That's the point. He'll give it up as long as it isn't used against him."

"How do you know what Heinz told Bartlett?"

"The Pear isn't the only who knows how to play this game. He's got his flies on my wall. I've got mine on his."

"Then you know where Heinz claims his materials are stored?"

"That's the sixty-four-dollar question. He's got the Soviet material hidden in the American zone. Only he knows exactly where. The Schaefer material is another matter."

"How so?"

"According to Heinz, Schaefer confessed that after fleeing Berlin, he stopped in Prague and deposited the microfiche in a safe-deposit box he held jointly with his former partner, Dr. Herschel Cernak."

"Herschel Cernak!" Dunne blurted out the name loud enough to draw a disapproving glance from the desk clerk.

Bassante moved forefinger from nose to lips. "Keep it down. Schaefer succeeded in having word slipped to Cernak, who was being held in Theresienstadt."

"Van Hull and I flew out of Prague with Cernak."

"'The ankle bone connected to the leg bone.' That's what's taken me all this time: putting the connections together. Soon as Heinz was taken into custody and was interrogated by Bartlett, he offered to deliver the Schaefer archive. By that time, Van Hull and you had been given up for dead. Heinz described his information about the safe- deposit box as a 'down payment' to be followed by his trove on the Soviets. It was Bartlett's idea to make the dash to Prague, not General Donovan's."

"So Bartlett got Schaefer's material?"

"He got the safe-deposit box, but Schaefer's microfiche was gone."

"Who has it?"

"A member of the non-Communist resistance, Jan Horak."

"He helped Dick and me."

"'The thigh bone connected to the hip bone.' Horak also helped arrange the rescue of Cernak, who alerted him to the contents of the box. He wanted to ensure that Horak's faction, the non-Communist partisans, had possession of it."

"Which means it's still in Prague?"

"For now. Horak conceived an instant dislike for Bartlett. Once Bartlett told him he'd learned about the safe-deposit box from an SS doctor, Horak suspected a deal was in the offing. He decided to take possession of the box's contents. When he did, he got in touch and let Van Hull know. Unfortunately, Dick went to Bartlett and challenged him on his dealings with Heinz and what he intended to do with the information."

"Unfortunately? How could it be otherwise? It's personal. Heinz abetted the murder of Dick's best friend."

"Aye, there's the rub—*personal*." Bassante held the armrests so tightly his knuckles blanched. He sat up, frozen, rigid posture.

"You look as if you were just strapped in the electric chair."

"Dick and Michael Jahn weren't just friends, Fin."

"What were they?"

Bassante cleared his throat. "The ancient Greeks referred to it as *pareunos*, meaning 'lying beside' or 'bedfellows.' But what was once second nature to men like Socrates, Plato, and Alexander the Great has become scandalously unnatural to us."

"What are you getting at?"

"I don't like saying it."

"Saying what?"

Bassante's hushed voice was hum/hiss: "*Homos.*"

"Who?"

"Dick Van Hull *is* and Mike Jahn *was.*"

"Was what?"

"Come on, Fin, now you look like the one in the hot seat. Queer, faggot, fairy, sissy. Impolite words for it galore. Pervert. Sodomite. Homo is about as polite as it gets."

Dunne resisted guzzling his scotch. At the Catholic Protectory, he didn't know at first what the older boys meant when they hurled that word—"fairy"—at Jimmy Kelly, pulled down his pants, whipped him with knotted twine when they saw his erection. *Jimmy the fairy / Cock long and hairy / Got a hard-on for us all.*

Jimmy cried himself to sleep at night. He tried to fight back. One or two friends stood by him. But his persecutors were relentless. Finally, he made a successful escape. The boys joked among themselves, "Jimmy's gone to live with his fairy godfather."

Outside, a hole opened in the low-hanging ceiling of blanket-gray clouds. Sunlight poured through. Wet street glistened. Clouds the color of coal fumes crowded toward the leak. Rain or shine? Dunne pondered the questionable sky:

Who'd have suspected Dick Van Hull?

Suspected what?

Suspected that he was in love with Michael Jahn.

Stack it beside the mountains of bodies, ruined cities, death camps, sewers overflowing with pus and blood and shit of two wars, what difference does it make?

On the NYPD, he knew cops who made a special racket of shaking down speakeasies that catered to queers. They kept up the practice when liquor went legit again and the speaks along Third Avenue in the upper forties and fifties became the "Bird Circuit," a string of bars whose clientele was men seeking the company of other men.

There were vice squad detectives who for the right price ignored whatever went on in cathouses or nightclubs, no matter how low or pornographic, but wouldn't tolerate queers and made a practice of busting them on morals charges any chance they got.

As lead detective on the vice squad, Bud Mulholland took the opposite tack. Despite his rep as a hard-ass, he framed his approach this way: "Seems to me, what queers want most of all is to be left alone, so until someone can explain the harm they do me or anyone else, I'll do just that. Live and let live."

That photo with the Yeats quote, Dunne realized, the one he had returned to Van Hull, should have tipped him off. But it hadn't. Maybe a lot of queers were like Van Hull. You wouldn't know unless they told you.

The clouds pressed forward and plugged the leak. The sky decided on rain.

Dunne sensed what Bassante was thinking: *Does Van Hull being queer make a difference? Would you rather have no part? It's time to make up your mind, Fin.*

Live and let live.

Is that an opinion or a conviction?

Does it matter?

It's easier to change opinions than convictions.

Sometimes opinions become convictions and seep into the marrow.

In this case, which is it?

An opinion that's become a conviction and changed slightly in the process.

Slightly how?

Love and let love.

"I wouldn't be here except for Dick. He's the best soldier I ever met. He should be getting a medal for what he did during Operation Maxwell."

"He lived with Jahn in Greenwich Village before the war. His sole purpose with Operation Maxwell, according to Bartlett, was to rescue his queer lover. That's why he risked your life and got Lieutenant Bunde killed."

"That's a goddamn lie. You and I know it. You're the one who argued for a three-man mission. Dick Van Hull wanted to go alone. General Donovan was behind the drop. He told me so himself. It involved the honor of the OSS, he said."

"The reigning orthodoxy on Donovan is he was a lousy manager who ran a sloppy organization that not only tolerated a high degree of incompetence but was a home for queers and Reds."

"They're claiming Dick is also a Red?"

"Fairy is fatal enough. Bartlett is already a force in shaping whatever new intelligence organization comes into existence, and he's making no secret he's part of a team that isn't going to allow a reconstituted agency to be built on Donovan's lax, slapdash willingness to employ gumshoes, con men, eggheads, queers, radicals, and assorted riffraff. Bartlett and company are determined to root out 'undesirables and unreliables.'"

"Where's Dick now?"

"In Washington. He says he won't resign as long as there's any chance Heinz will escape prosecution."

"He saved my life. I'll do anything I can."

"He doesn't want you involved."

"He's my friend." He repeated the words: "My friend."

"Jan Horak is being watched by the Reds in the Czech security office. But I'm trying to arrange a military flight to Prague—no easy matter—to return a packet of files seized by the Nazis, innocuous stuff dressed up as urgent. When the clearances are in place, it'll be in-and-out, the 'in' part a rendezvous with an associate of Horak to take possession of the Schaefer microfiche. Once we have that, I'm confident we can scuttle Bartlett's scheme to excuse Heinz from prosecution and arrange for Van Hull to leave the service in honorable fashion."

"Will Dick go along? "

"If Schaefer's archive is actively employed in the prosecution of war criminals and Heinz is headed for the gallows, yes, he'll resign. Like you, Dick's had enough."

"And my part?"

"If I went anywhere near a flight to Prague, Bartlett would be tipped off. You, on the other hand . . ."

"When do I leave?"

"Soon as I can arrange it. Lots of moving parts—flight clearances, weather, scarcity of aircraft." Bassante caught the waiter's attention, scribbled in the air, signaling for a bill.

The waiter delivered it facedown, on a small, square filigreed silver tray. "Thank you, gentlemen."

Bassante paid it and left an American-size tip. They paused beneath the hotel's green copper canopy. The doorman offered to call them a cab.

Bassante stepped into the light drizzle. "Thanks, but we could use a bit of exercise." As they strolled toward the corner, he related his Yuletide trip to Bolzano, in the South Tyrol, where his father had been born. Business masked as holiday, he brought relatives coffee, cigarettes, and scotch while investigating rumors of an expanding escape route SS veterans and their henchmen were following from Austria into Italy, with the goal of embarking for South America.

The border, Bassante discovered, was a sieve; smuggling of SS personnel, an open secret. Allied supervision was chaotic at best. Red Cross travel papers as well as assistance from hard-core anti-Communist elements within the Vatican were readily available. He'd dispatched a report to Washington on these routes—British Intelligence dubbed them "ratlines"—but heard nothing back. Drizzle thickened into rain.

Bassante flipped up the collar on his overcoat. "I spent time in Moscow, Fin. I'm not among the 'useful idiots' Lenin scoffed at—self-deluded naïfs like Ambassador Joe Davies or willfully blind journalists such as Duranty of the *Times*. I saw Stalin's terror firsthand. I've no doubt a line must be drawn. But it's equally clear our goal must be to prevent, not provoke, another war. This last one killed sixty million people. Sooner or later—probably sooner—the Russians will have an atom bomb of their own. Another war will spell the end of civilization. Our last hope is to be strong, resolute, and wage a *guerre froide* that prevents further expansion of the Soviet empire and awaits its collapse from the weight of its own contradictions, even if takes an entire decade."

Rain became downpour and splashed about their feet. The musty odor of wet ash from demolished town houses pervaded the street.

"Either we go inside or hail a taxi," Dunne said.

Bassante paid no attention. "From a strategic point of view, relying on the likes of Gehlen and Heinz is unwise. They'll never play down the menace we face. It's not in their interest. They'll always exaggerate to reinforce their own value. Their potential as double agents is rich. The greatest regret among many of them isn't that Hitler waged the war but that he lost it. Yes, they despise the Soviets, and they despise us equally.

"Beyond the practical is the moral. I was there when Van Hull confronted Bartlett. It was after Gehlen's recruitment, when we learned about Operation Overcast, which also brought engineers and scientists from the Nazi rocket program to the U.S. There was no question about the thousands of Jews and inmates from the Dora concentration camp they'd worked to death as slave laborers at the Nordhausen rocket works. The official line was the Nazis were being brought over 'purely for purposes of interrogation.' But it was obvious there was more involved, that these were just the vanguard. This wasn't a postscript to war crimes investigations but a prelude to a new arrangement.

"Bartlett told Van Hull he was acting like a sentimental schoolgirl. Why keep beating the dead horse of Nazism when the Siberian tiger of Communism was poised to sink its fangs into our neck? The simple fact is that the next war has already begun, and if we don't use these Germans, the Soviets will.

"Van Hull didn't back down." Bassante raised his voice to be heard over the rain's pelting racket. Water coursed off the brims of their hats. "The greatest danger we face, he told Bartlett, is in becoming the enemy we oppose—a force that not only absolves and employs murderers and torturers but also emulates them."

Dunne looked up and down the street. No cabs anywhere. He nudged Bassante's elbow. "We'll drown here. Let's go back to the hotel."

Bassante gestured at the ruin-strewn lot. "It wasn't Flash Gordon and his merry band of rocketeers did this. The perpetrators worked at least twenty thousand slave laborers to death in building machinery whose sole purpose was to serve the Third Reich. They fired thirty thousand V-1s and six thousand V-2s that wrecked entire city blocks, killed nearly ten thousand civilians, and wounded fifty thousand more.

"Their thoroughness was Mephistophelean. The hair they shaved from the heads of dead Jews was used as insulation in their rockets and delayed-action bombs. The anarchists of old who hurled a bomb and killed a dozen people were hanged in the name of protecting civilized society. These long-distance bomb throwers —part of an apparatus involving scientists, technicians, and specialists working in the cause of a psychopath dedicated to the production-line homicide of millions—are awarded new careers."

The rushing water seeped into Dunne's socks. In the field, faced with the stark assignment of survival, small annoyances hardly registered. Now the chill wetness was a distracting bother. He'd already signed on to do what he could for Dick and Dr. Niskolczi and the others. *See that the murderers are judged.* He nudged Bassante again.

Bassante still didn't move. "Van Hull didn't dispute that the information they possess is highly valuable. But what lesson do we teach, he asked, if we allow their usefulness to erase their crime?

Wouldn't it be more just, he objected, to try them for their crimes, to set the record straight and arrive at sentences that acknowledged the suffering of their victims? Those sentences might be reduced. For those who admitted what they'd done and offered to make some form of personal reparation, a pardon might be possible. Wouldn't this be far better than pretending that their crimes never occurred, that they didn't work and starve masses of men and women to death, that thanks to them and the services they rendered Adolf Hitler, these houses and their inhabitants—along with countless others on the continent—were wiped off the face of the earth?

"I think if we can force the indictment of Karsten Heinz, we can do more than see that justice is done to a single criminal. I think we can begin to reverse the tide that's permitting the mass absolution of thousands of them. Van Hull shares that hope."

Umbrella bobbing above his head, two more dangling from his forearm, the waiter who'd served their drinks came up beside them. "I've been watching from inside. 'If you Yanks are to carry on a conversation amidst a deluge would do old Noah proud,' I think to myself, 'you each need to 'ave one of these.'" He handed them each an umbrella.

"This is most generous of you." Bassante reached in his breast pocket and took out his billfold.

"Please, sir. The generosity has been on your part. The gratuity you left covers this and far more."

They opened their umbrellas.

The waiter smiled. "Like the song says, keep 'dem dry bones' dry! Keep 'dem dry bones' dry!"

Bassante stopped by two days later. The flight to Prague was scheduled for the next afternoon. A car would take Dunne to the airfield. The arrangements in Prague were all made. As long as the weather cooperated, the mission would be in and out. "This time it really will be your last drop." Bassante gave Dunne his hand. "*Totiusque.*"

Part V
New Trajectories

Fintan Dunne: "A Soldier's Soldier"

BY

ALVIN CAPSHAW

Beginning with this issue, *Modern Detection* is adding a new Profiles column to its roster of articles, feature pieces, and news roundups covering what is among the fastest growing sectors of the service industry. Each month, Profiles will spotlight a leading practitioner currently at work in the profession and offer his insights on what lies ahead for the trade.

The need for such an addition is clear. In the five years since it began publishing, *Modern Detection* has made significant progress in dispelling the demeaning stereotypes and clichés about the private security industry relentlessly popularized by cheap novels, pulp magazines, and B-grade films.

Unfortunately, fiction continues to trump fact. All too often, the mention of "private investigator" conjures up in the mind of John Q. Public a seedy "gumshoe" who operates from a shabby office in a questionable part of town and serves a clientele of lowlifes and outright criminals.

Although it might seem like a case of "preaching to the choir," it is worth reminding ourselves that the immense gulf between this hoary myth and everyday reality cannot be overemphasized. The vast majority of those working in today's private security sector are employed by one of the several corporate entities that account for more than 90 percent of the industry's revenues and profits.

In a growing number of instances, private security operations are part of conglomerates that include unrelated businesses such as auto-parts distribution and resort and hotel properties. (More about that in a minute from the subject of this month's Profile.) Though the products are different, the standards of quality, cost effectiveness, and, most important, customer satisfaction are the same.

No organization better exemplifies the highest standards and practices of the industry than International Services Corporation (ISC), which is headquartered in several sleekly updated floors high up in the Graybar Building, adjacent to New York's Grand Central Terminal. Over the last decade, ISC has consolidated the largest and best-run private investigation agencies across America into a smoothly functioning, highly coordinated operation. While its clientele is confidential, it is no secret that its customers include leading law firms, prominent investment houses, and corporations along with well-known personalities of stage, screen, and "high society."

Together, the leadership of ISC's private security team represents a veritable "Who's Who" of seasoned investigators whose collective qualifications, experience, and achievements are unmatched. Fintan Dunne, a senior partner, is a case in point.

Standing in his outer office, a visitor immediately turns his gaze on a wall covered with framed awards, news clippings, and photos of Dunne with a wide spectrum of civic, military, and business leaders. In one corner is a signed photo of Dunne being given a one-arm hug by former New York mayor William O'Dwyer; in another, he is bookended by smiling star of stage and screen Joan Crawford and husband Alfred Steele, chairman and CEO of Pepsi-Cola.

Most prominent of all is the photo of Dunne with his mentor and former commander, the legendary leader of New York's "Fighting 69th" Regiment in World War I and founder of the Office of Strategic Services (OSS), General William Donovan.

As a lad of eighteen, Dunne enlisted in the 69th and served under Donovan through some of the Yanks' bloodiest engagements. Emerging from that struggle with an array of medals that made him the AEF's most decorated warrior—and that included the Congressional Medal of Honor—Donovan has often insisted that "the true heroes" were the fearless doughboys like Fintan Dunne who served under him.

After the war, Dunne joined the New York City Police Department as a patrolman. Over the next decade he rose to become a lead detective on the homicide squad. He subsequently left the police to start his own investigation agency, quickly earning a reputation for the intensity and discretion with which he handled each and every case.

In the wake of Pearl Harbor and entry of the United States into World War II, William Donovan was charged by President Roosevelt with building the nation's first agency for centralized intelligence gathering, counterespionage, and psychological warfare. Fintan Dunne was among his first recruits.

Dunne served in the OSS for the duration. The majority of his time was spent overseas as both a trainer of the OSS's clandestine operatives and as participant in the thrilling, highly dangerous missions that, in Winston Churchill's words, "set Europe ablaze." As with so many of his fellow colleagues in that highly select and secretive society, Dunne remains mum on the specifics of his activities behind enemy lines.

In the wake of V-J Day, finished with helping wrap up the business of the OSS, Dunne returned to New York and restarted his private investigation business. It quickly flourished. In 1950, he attached his fast-growing business to the multicity affiliation the All-American Detective Agency (AADA), of which he became a partner and principal. AADA was acquired by ISC in 1955 for an undisclosed sum.

Meeting Dunne for the first time, a visitor is immediately struck by how much he has been shaped by his years as soldier, police officer, private investigator, and OSS operative. His waistline is trim, step spritely, and manner crisp. His handsome, impassive features call to mind actor William Holden. He greets his visitor with a mix of quiet intensity and friendly reserve as he takes in everything from cut of hair to strength of handshake and brand of shoes.

As opposed to the walls in the reception room, those in his office are bare. His desktop hosts phone, clock, ashtray, a silver framed photograph of his wife, Roberta, and a single folder. It is immediately apparent that this is a well-organized professional operating by a tight schedule, a fact he makes explicit when he instructs the alert, attractive girl who serves as his assistant "to hold my calls for the next ten minutes."

The window behind him frames an expansive view of the city's

Lower East Side, which is his "hometown." Orphaned at an early age, Dunne is yet another of the myriad disciples of Horatio Alger who by dint of hard work and education—he attended parochial school and Fordham University—has gone and "done likewise," pulling himself up by his own bootstraps (or, in this case, shoelaces) from the city's streets.

Discussion of current client work is obviously off-limits. But Dunne is equally adamant in ruling out any attempt to revisit past cases. "People who enjoy talking about what they do," he observes, "should be in advertising. The business of this business is keeping the business to yourself."

Dunne's status as a partner at ISC permits him to spend several months of the year in Florida, where he and his wife, an interior designer, have a home. He lights a cigarette, swivels in his chair, and looks out the window. "I'll always be a New Yorker," he avers. "But the dark and cold of winter always feels a bit like wartime to me. I prefer the warm embrace of sunshine."

He makes it clear, however, that he is in touch with ISC operatives throughout the year, consulting on cases via telephone and, when necessary, traveling to branch offices throughout the country: "For me and for all of us at ISC, the needs of our clients are always paramount." When it comes to the future of the private security industry, Dunne is forthright in stating how he sees "the shape of things to come." It boils down, he says, to three factors: "education, professionalization, and conglomeration."

Back when he started in the business, Dunne remembers, "with the exception of Pinkerton and a few others, it was largely made up of sole operators who rented an office and hung out a shingle." Today, the situation is quite different. As the consolidation of the industry continues to gather momentum and investigators specialize in specific industries and interests, higher education is a prerequisite.

Dunne points out that experience in the military and/or police will always give an aspirant a leg up. Yet in the final analysis, an ISC private investigator is no different from a professional in its accounting or legal departments: "He's not going anywhere unless he has the requisite level of schooling."

Professionalization, he explains, means more than properly training individual investigators or inculcating in them the highest standards.

Rather, it involves "replacing chance with certainty in everything we do, whether in the field, the lab, or the executive suite." To achieve this, "we must focus on the integration of advances in medical and scientific techniques into every aspect of our organizational framework."

Key to consistency and quality of performance, Dunne adds, is predictability and stability of revenues and profits: "If the till is full one year and empty the next, a firm's ability to invest in expanding and enhancing its operations in any consistent way is undermined." This is where the third factor—conglomeration—comes in: "By bringing together businesses whose revenues grow or dip at different points in the business cycle, income flow is made smooth and such inconsistency is averted."

The buzzer on the intercom sounds. The allotted ten minutes is at an end. Fintan Dunne escorts his visitor to the door.

As the visitor takes his leave, he stops to get a last and closer look at the framed picture of Fintan Dunne and General Donovan. They are both in uniform. The London landmark, Big Ben, looms in the background. Beneath, in a clear, bold hand, is written: *To Fintan Dunne, My highest regards to a soldier's soldier. Bill Donovan, London, May 1944.*

June 1958

Instead of storming into Ken Moss's office, Dunne went straight to his own. Miss Teresa Dolores O'Keefe greeted him with her customary smile—delicate, understated—lifted the eyeglasses roped around her neck, and rested them on the bridge of her nose. Like all ISC executive assistants, she wasn't to be conflated with standard secretaries found at other firms or the denizens of the typing pool parked at desks in the rear of the office.

Miss O'Keefe was a graduate of the College of St. Elizabeth, English major, German minor. Smart and alluring in knees-together, virginal, parochial-school fashion, she was the daughter of a Jersey City cop who was gunned down in a waterfront shoot-out. Her mother was left with five kids and went back to work as a bookkeeper in the Garment District. Miss O'Keefe had four brothers: one older, KIA in Korea; three younger, fireman, cop, student at Manhattan College. It could be, Dunne suspected, that her air of convent-girl innocence was acquired rather than innate.

If she followed the company script, she'd find a husband within ISC in the next year or two, becoming a suitable helpmate as her spouse rose up the ladder, or she'd be promoted to researcher or junior section specialist, the highest station any female employee could reach, there to earn a decent living as she spun her way to spinsterhood or to be whisked away, Prince Charming come at last.

188

Or maybe she'd write her own script. She'd never mentioned she was working on a novel. But one day, while she was at lunch, he sneaked a peek in her bottom drawer. It held half a dozen of the same marbled-covered composition books, each page filled with her work-in-progress, *Springtime of Our Love: A Novel of World War II*, a romance set in occupied France. Boy resistance fighter falls in love with girl resistance fighter.

They struggle against the siren song of lust as well as the serial depredations of the Germans: *The passion they shared was fiery, unquenchable. Yet, they vowed, until the conquest of their motherland, their sweet Marianne, was undone, it must go unconsummated.* Wasn't to his taste, but without letting on he knew what she was up to, he wished her success, best-seller list, screenplay, the works.

She brought him a mug of coffee, laid a file of correspondence on his desk. "Your Monday morning staff meeting is in fifteen minutes. Mr. Billings is scheduled to make a presentation. Partners as well as senior section specialists are expected to attend."

He thanked her and sipped the coffee. He sat at his desk, opened the monogrammed leather attaché case Roberta had bought him at Crouch & Fitzgerald, and took out the lone contents: June issue of *Modern Detection*. He read the article for a third time. It was Ken Moss's handiwork. It had to be. There was no doubt about it.

Dressing down Moss in a reverberant roar sufficient to rattle the thin walls and glass partitions of the newly refurbished ISC executive floor and bring people to their office doors could offer short-term satisfaction. Long term, Dunne realized, along with making Moss into the apparent victim of an ill-advised tirade, he'd be deemed lacking in the cool-headed, logical, problem-solving approach that marked an ISC executive.

Dunne's title of "partner" seemed to elevate him above the rules and expectations governing employees of lesser status. But it wasn't bestowed out of organizational considerations. Thanks to the influence of Louis Pohl—"Pully," as all his friends called him—a buddy from OSS days and a bigwig within the company, the management at the time thought it would appeal to existing and prospective clients, affording the Private Investigation and Security Department the feel of detective agency and law firm wrapped in a well-managed corporation.

The contract he'd signed required his presence in New York headquarters only six months of the year—May 1 through October 31—in order to "provide counsel and support to ISC Private Investigation and Security" as well as assist in "identifying, soliciting and signing new business." It also stipulated that the company provide a sublet "within walking distance" of the office.

In practice, since becoming a publicly traded company, ISC didn't have partners. Whether "associates" or "specialists"—the new designations of choice—all were salaried employees. Dunne's contract would either be renewed (or not) at the end of the year.

Louis Pohl had thrown himself out a window of the adjacent Commodore Hotel the previous February. Though Pully didn't leave a note, it seemed certain he'd suffered a nervous breakdown. He'd called down to the front desk, gibbering about the walls in his room turning into blood and the chairs talking to him. By the time the house detective reached his room to see what was going on, Pully was splattered on the sidewalk below.

Dunne and Roberta were vacationing in Havana when it happened. There was no funeral. He sent a note of condolence to Pully's mother in Forest Hills, and she wrote back an anguished, painful-to-read response that he kept in his desk drawer. She had her son's ashes in an urn on her mantel. She couldn't understand why he'd taken his own life. He'd always been "serious and individualistic," never seemed suicidal. She wished she'd known of his intent. She was sure she could have talked him out of it.

"To lose a child is to have your heart forever broken," she

wrote. "You don't recover. You go on. But to lose an only child and in such a manner—oh, Mr. Dunne, you can't imagine."

She was wrong. Though he could never fully comprehend, he could imagine. Soon after he returned from Europe, he'd visited Peter Bunde's parents in Buffalo, sat with them in their living room for a long winter's afternoon. Grief was lined deep in their faces like the ruts water carves into rock.

On the practical side, Dunne knew that with Pully's demise he no longer had a "rabbi" to watch over him in the inner ranks of management. A new generation of button-down business school graduates in their late twenties and early thirties—one or two who'd served during the Korean conflict but never made it overseas—was surging into leadership positions and pushing to hire consultants to help "identify and implement long-overdue efficiencies" and "reengineer the company's basic business model."

They had already succeeded in a number of cosmetic changes, scrapping "departments" in favor of "sections," which, they maintained, rid ISC of the musty odor of "old-fashioned bureaucracy." (The Private Investigation and Security Section was known in-house by the tongue-in-cheek acronym PISS.) They made no secret they thought "partner" detracted from the image projected by the new corporate motto, *ISC: Where Management Is a Science*—coined by Ken Moss, Junior Associate, the Communications and Public Relations Section (CAPS)—which they applauded.

The part-time arrangement proved more than amenable to Dunne and Roberta. They found they enjoyed the city more than when they'd been full-time residents, going to the theater and trying out new restaurants. Though the city could be a sweatbox in summer—unlike the heat in Florida, a shroud that rarely lifted—it came and went in waves. The apartment and office were air-conditioned. Each July, Roberta got away with her girlfriends (all married to well-to-do husbands) on a month-long vacation, which this year had turned into a two-month cruise to the Orient.

In years past, Roberta and he had taken long weekends on Block Island or Shelter Island, staying at one of the inns. But with her away, Dunne was content to stay in the city and wander around Greenwich Village, where new-style "beatniks" had replaced old-time bohemians, or Little Italy, where you could sit outdoors and linger over a glass of wine for hours at a time.

Once he walked toward Dry Dock Street, thinking he'd visit where he'd lived as a kid. Quickly reminded that everything between Avenue C and the East River Drive had been torn down—or was being torn down—and rebuilt, he turned around and didn't bother.

Now and then, he rode the subway up to the Bronx Zoo. He liked to smoke and watch the animals sleep, especially the polar bears. Ferocious as they were reputed to be, their placidity struck him as profound. He felt it wasn't merely a seasonal torpor or depressive resignation to captivity. They periodically roused themselves for a rowdy splash in the icy-looking pool.

Roberta accompanied him one visit. He shared his observation with her.

"You're indulging in anthropomorphic projection," she said. "The poor animal is bored out of its mind."

Maybe. But they didn't have to hunt their next meal; didn't worry about retirement or medical care; never thought about how their lives would end, regrets they'd carry to the grave, opportunities that had escaped their grasp, about usefulness or relevance. He thought he heard something deeper than resignation or stupor in the sighs they emitted as they slumbered. He was sure he'd never met a human being capable of such contentment.

In the short period of full retirement several years back, Dunne faced up to the fact that although he was financially set after the sale of his agency to ISC, he wasn't ready to let go. The arrangement with ISC was a happy one. At least it had been. He was aware of the change that had taken place since he'd returned the month before. At first he imagined he was reading into things. No longer. The memo from Ken Moss announcing ISC's new motto proclaimed that "we are moving to take hold of the future and position ourselves on new growth trajectories." He wondered if and when those trajectories would rocket him out the door— lately, more when than if.

In hindsight, he recognized that ISC's interest in PISS had been waning for some time. Nobody had been fired (at least not at the upper levels). But after Louis Pohl's suicide and Jeff Wine's retirement, the L.A. office closed and the slots left by other retirees went unfilled. The section was profitable. Whether in its present configuration it exhibited the "dynamic growth characteristics" the annual report touted ISC as demanding from all its sections remained to be seen.

The new emphasis in Private Investigation and Security, it was explained, must be on selling, installing, and servicing electronic security and surveillance systems, a business requiring far fewer employees and in which profit margins were far higher. It also avoided the personal volatility and unpleasantness endemic to private investigations such as occurred the previous year when Pepsi-Cola chairman and CEO Alfred Steele indicated the company had a matter of "utmost delicacy" that needed handling.

Mrs. Steele, formerly Academy Award–winning actress Joan Crawford, had traded in her fast-fading stardom to become his wife and help burnish the image and boost sales of the perennial also-ran to Coca-Cola. Two days before, she'd received a black-mail threat. Postmarked L.A., it claimed to have a copy of a stag film she'd made in the days when she was Lucille LeSueur, a sexy, intensely ambitious Midwesterner clawing her way from chorus line to front and center on the silver screen.

Steele said his wife denied the authenticity of the film yet feared even a coincidental resemblance to one of the performers could be used to embarrass her. Dunne advised Steele his best

193

course was to go to the police because even if he paid what was demanded and got the film, there'd be no way to ensure the blackmailer wouldn't have more copies and keep coming back. Steele listened and said he'd discuss it with his wife.

The next day, Dunne was dictating a letter to his Miss O'Keefe when Joan Crawford, tightly girdled, elegantly decked in pearls, white turban, and black dress, arrived unannounced in his office. She ordered Miss O'Keefe out and closed the door.

She perched on the edge of his desk. He lit her cigarette for her. Sleek and polished as chrome, eyebrows arched and emphatic, she sucked it so hard she squinted.

He'd met her at the Pepsi Christmas party at the Waldorf Astoria. She sat next to him, crossed her legs, shapely ankle brushed his thigh, perhaps accidentally. They exchanged a few pleasantries. Beneath her cosmetic facade and quiet elegance, mink stole, mink hat, mink cuffs, was a wartime urgency, physical, immediate, demanding.

He left the party right after and hadn't seen her since. Until now.

She leaned back and exhaled. "My husband conveyed your advice. You think we should go to the police?"

"From my experience, that's the only way to—"

"That's bullshit, Dunne." Her nostrils flared, voice rose. "Do you think my husband retains mugs like you to sit on your keisters and tell him to fuck off the first time he gives you a real job to do?"

He endured her angry monologue on "the low-life, backstabbing scum" in Hollywood and "the lazy, greedy cocksuckers" who worked for her husband in New York, interrupting at one point to warn that if she didn't want the whole office to know her business, she should lower her voice.

She ignored him, pacing back and forth. If she was putting on an act, playing a fury-fueled Amazon determined to do what had to be done until she got what she wanted, it was an award-winning performance. She left as abruptly as she'd arrived. Her parting words: "I want that film, Dunne. I don't give a rat's ass how you get it."

No need to ask whether she was in the film or merely afraid of a "coincidental resemblance." He had his answer. He made the eight-and-a-half-hour flight to L.A. With Jeff Wine's help, he identified the blackmailer as a broken-down, boozed-up ex-screenwriter living in a dilapidated bungalow in Santa Monica. The rat's ass turned out to be two outstanding warrants against him, one for bigamy, another for embezzlement, which Wine flushed out of the local court files.

They greased the police to pick him up and ransacked the bungalow. They found a single copy of the film stashed in a duffel bag on the top shelf of the bedroom closet. The copy was badly degraded, grainy and faded. The sexual frolics were fuzzy but discernible, yet it was next to impossible to identify the individuals engaged in them.

He delivered the film to Steele, who was satisfied with the results. His wife reappeared in the office soon after. Arctic instead of volcanic, she waited for Miss O'Keefe to escort her from the reception area to his office, shook his hand, and offered a few words of thanks, concluding with a coldly whispered admonition: "If this ever reaches the papers, I'll find who's responsible and have his balls delivered on a platter."

It struck Dunne as less a threat than a promise.

ISC voluntarily surrendered the Pepsi account at the end of that year. Dunne found himself increasingly engaged in a role like that of the oversized cardboard cutout of TV host Garry Moore in the Liggett's across the street set up to plug cigarettes or shampoo or toothpaste (he couldn't remember which).

He accompanied the associates and specialists to the lunches where they pitched clients on the "efficiency and effectiveness of electronic security." He knew the prospects had been told ahead of time about his OSS and NYPD background as well as his acquaintance with "the boys at the top." Following a few words about the "depth of talent at ISC" and the "new science of security management," he stuck to his cardboard cutout role, wordlessly nodding as the sales pitch proceeded.

When the deal was sealed and they came in to sign the papers, the clients were guided past Dunne's office. He told them how much he looked forward to working with them and shook hands as they scanned the wall behind him filled with the photos and news features Ken Moss had taken care to have framed and hung. Their faces registered how impressed they were. (The fact that Joan Crawford was an ex-client and Mayor O'Dwyer and General William Donovan had never been clients went unmentioned.)

The last to arrive at the senior staff meeting, Dunne was surprised to find Ken Moss, junior associate, in attendance. Moss wasn't at the table with the section heads but in a chair against the wall, behind Wynne Billings, senior specialist in the Strategic Planning and Marketing Section (SPAMS). Moss was writing in a notepad and didn't look up.

After a round-the-table summary of present business by the section heads, the meeting was given over to Billings. A graduate of Dartmouth's Tuck School of Business, muscular and athletic, with a blond crew cut and a fresh, alert, narrow face, he resembled the Kansas City A's up-and-coming outfielder Roger Maris. As with Maris, who was rumored to be a potential addition to the Yankee lineup, the scuttlebutt on Billings left no doubt he was headed for big things.

He stood at the end of the table, behind a Kodak projector. Ken Moss turned the lights off and pulled his chair next to him.

"Ken, let's have slide one."

Moss hit the button atop the projector. *Click.* A sleek, propellerless airliner with swept-back wings flashed on the screen. "Take a good look, gentlemen." Billings paused, lit a cigarette. The slight, insect-like whirr from the projector filled the room. He spoke with a slow-paced, deliberate emphasis, spacing the words distinctly: "This . . . is . . . *the future.*" Another pause. *Whirr.* "This . . . is . . . *the Seven-Oh-Seven.*"

In the fall, Billings said, Pan Am would put the 707, the world's first commercial jetliner, into transatlantic service. Home and abroad, fast as they could, all the big carriers would follow suit. The new age heralded by the H-bomb, television, Sputnik— an age in which distance ceased to matter—would take another giant leap forward.

The wisps from Billings's cigarette swirled like cinematic fog in the projector's beam. *Click.* The Mercator map that came up reminded Dunne of the one mounted outside Donovan's office in Paris. On this one, however, parabolic trajectories rose from New York, Los Angeles, London, Chicago, Tokyo, Paris, etc., crisscrossing continents and oceans and weaving a great global web.

Dunne momentarily mistook the arching lines for the ones newspapers used to illustrate articles on the likely delivery paths in an exchange of nuclear-headed missiles between the United States and the USSR; Billings made clear they were the commercial routes that within a few years fleets of jetliners would regularly travel.

"The 707 is the embodiment of the forces that will shape the decade ahead and, in so doing, decide the fate of our country and of the free world. We're facing a sea change, gentlemen. I mean that literally."

Click—the next slide, a single word in capital letters: *SEA.* "The essence is in these three letters: *S . . . E . . . A.*" Billings walked the length of the table and stood next to the screen: "Synthetics, electronics, avionics." The rehearsing he'd obviously done with Moss was paying off. He had everyone's attention. "Let's take them one by one. First, *S.*"

Click. The caption *S IS FOR SYNTHETICS* appeared on the screen. "Chemistry is key, gentlemen. The economy now rests not on rubber or cotton or gold but on polymers, synthetic compounds, the man-made ingredients out of which everything from *A* to *Z*, from acrylic paints to space suits, Christmas trees, and zithers, is being made."

One by one everyone at the table had lit a cigarette. The glowing tips flared like fireflies in summer twilight. They stared in silence at the slide. Smoke and specks of dust churned and swarmed through the shaft of light connecting screen to projector.

Dunne closed his eyes and stopped listening.

Moss shut off the projector and flipped on the lights. Dunne opened his eyes. He wasn't sure how much of Billings's presentation he'd tuned out.

"Aviation plus electronics equals avionics. We all know it: Whoever wins control of space will win the Cold War." Billings tossed his red-and-gold regimental striped tie over his shoulder. He moved in front of the screen, white shirt blending into white background. "The trajectory of change is now clear, constant, and certain. Forget about the doldrums the economy is now experiencing. The country's greatest period of growth is still ahead. These are the industries that will drive it—of that there can be no doubt.

"Domestically, thanks to the Interstate Highway Act passed two years ago, we have in place the largest public works program in . . . the history . . . of . . . the *world*, a *twenty-six-billion-dollar* construction project that will result in forty-one thousand miles of unobstructed roadways. Along with fulfilling its primary purpose of allowing the quick evacuation of our cities in case of atomic attack, the interstate system will have lasting and beneficial effects on commerce and communication.

"The future, however, no longer depends on Bismarck's famous formula of 'blood and iron' or, for that matter, on concrete and steel. They have their place. But it's above, not below, in the celestial rather than terrestrial, where our nation's and the world's destinies intersect, where military and commercial investments merge, and present and future converge. The same ingredients that will decide who controls the skies above and space beyond will distinguish winner from loser.

"What will change, what is changing as I speak, what is being ramped up by the revived economies of Europe and Asia, especially the surging performance of our former enemies in Japan and Germany, is the *velocity . . . of . . . change*.

"The past is past, over and done, good-bye, *sayonara, auf wiedersehen*. The future is on the runway. The choice for us at ISC is clear: stay behind . . . or . . . get . . . *aboard*.

"Which will it be?"

A spontaneous round of applause accompanied Billings as he walked back to his seat. He collected his papers. The section heads crowded around as if greeting a teammate at home plate after he'd scored the winning run.

Ken Moss unplugged the projector and returned it to its plastic case. Dunne avoided the huddle and went over to him.

"Wynne hit it out of the park, don't you think?" Moss's round, beaming face reflected the supporting role he'd just played, moon to Billings's sun.

"Babe Ruth couldn't have done it better."

"The Babe is history. Wynne is the new breed. A regular Mickey Mantle, or Roger Maris, that kid out in Kansas City, the kind destined to topple the old records."

"Or Willie Mays."

Moss's confused expression indicated his uncertain reaction to adding a Negro to the lineup of Mantle, Maris, and Billings.

"Ken, I'd like you in my office at eleven." The more effective way to remind Moss of his lower status in the ISC hierarchy would have been to have Miss O'Keefe summon him. But though it hadn't entirely disappeared, the rage he'd felt toward Moss had dissipated.

"Sure, that shouldn't be a problem."

Miss O'Keefe was at her desk scribbling with a mechanical pencil in a composition book. She closed it as soon as he came in. "There were no calls, Mr. Dunne."

"Ken Moss will be by at eleven. Have him wait five minutes, then send him in."

"Yes, Mr. Dunne." She returned to her composition book.

Ken Moss had pestered him the previous October to sit down with Alvin Capshaw to do an interview for an upcoming issue of some magazine he'd never heard of. He refused. Moss came to his office and handed him several back copies. "It's an industry-sponsored publication. ISC and a consortium of other companies finance it. All the pieces are positive. There are no newsstand sales, but it's sent to all the major corporations, banks, brokerages, and law firms."

"Sounds like malarkey."

"It's public relations."

"Stunt?"

"Tool."

"What's the difference?"

"I wish you'd reconsider."

"The business of this business is keeping the business to yourself."

"Nice line." Moss wrote it down in his notepad. He stayed around, asked a few more questions.

Didn't give it another thought until that morning, parked on a stool at the counter in Chock Full o'Nuts for his regular breakfast of coffee and powdered doughnut, he remembered he'd stuck an envelope from Ken Moss in his case when he'd hurried out of the office the previous Friday.

He snapped open the case, slapped the envelope on the counter, and extracted a copy of *Modern Detection* with paper-clipped note: *Fin, Enjoy! Ken.* He almost spit out a mouthful of coffee and doughnut when he flipped to the table of contents and saw listed, under *Profiles, Fintan Dunne: A Soldier's Soldier.* Shock turned to fury at the photo of General Donovan and himself accompanying the piece—the same one Ken Moss had talked him into hanging outside his office.

He was glad he'd decided against subjecting Moss to a verbal blitz that would have embarrassed them both. Though he was still fuming when he saw Moss in the conference room, Billings's pep talk/lecture/pronouncement had a smothering effect. The hand-writing on the wall, up to now as indistinct as the faces in that Joan Crawford stag film, was now as unmistakable as the gigantic neon Pepsi-Cola sign across the East River.

True, Billings had skated as skillfully as Dick Button across the thin ice of lofty generalities, but it didn't take an Ivy League degree to figure out that ISC's new trajectory meant concentrating on a narrow spectrum of interests and investments.

Maybe, if Louie Pohl were still alive, there'd be a chance of getting a contract renewal for another four years. But Louie's mortal remains were on his mother's mantel in Forest Hills. Dunne had little doubt that when New Year's rolled around, odds were his office would have a new carpet, a fresh coat of paint, and a younger occupant.

Maybe he'd go back to running his own agency. But those days were over and done. Small agencies had gone the way of rumble seats and big bands. Even if he were pigheaded enough to try, it couldn't be done on a part-time basis. Roberta and he would have to spend all year in New York, which neither was pre-pared to do.

He thought back to Billings's phrase, "the velocity of change." Time had its own momentum, backward as well as forward, the present rises, the past sinks, vice versa. The week before, he'd passed the same playground he passed every day on his way to work. A boy and girl rode the seesaw up and down, chorusing, "Seesaw Marjorie Daw." He stopped and watched. Suddenly, he remembered his father watching him and his sister, Maura, on a seesaw in the playground in Tompkins Square Park, the day that Mayor Gaynor cut the ribbon to open it—the only time his father had taken them there.

Seesaw Marjorie Daw
Johnny will have a new master.

The boy was bigger than the girl. Without any warning, he stopped the up-and-down motion, squatted on his end, and left the girl suspended in the air.

"No fair!" she squealed. "Let me down!"

The boy stayed where he was. The girl kept crying, "Let me down!"

Dunne hollered, "You heard her! Play fair! Let her down!"

The identical words his father had used when he played the same trick on Maura.

The boy looked over. His face was red. He pushed off the ground with a frog-like spring of his legs. Up he went, down she came. They resumed their chorus:

Seesaw Marjorie Daw
Johnny will have a new master
He shall earn but a penny a day
Because he can't work any faster

Roberta smiled at him from the silver-framed photo beside the phone. Her hat was shaped like a ball of dandelion florets. Already out of date. She'd be irate to know this was the photo he kept on his desk. But she didn't know, and he didn't care. Her face was radiant and expectant. The Versailles on East 50th Street, his first week home.

She'd met him at the dock as soon as he disembarked. She'd rented a room at the Plaza. A lot of lost time to make up for. *The passion they shared was fiery, unquenchable.*

And consummated.

Over and over.

Ahh.

New York, thirteen years ago, when Ken Moss was twelve, probably, and Billings sixteen, half their lifetimes ago, yesterday for Dunne, ship slips through the Narrows, into embrace of bay and harbor, sun setting behind the Palisades like a red-hot nickel slowly sinking into a slot machine, *whammy*, biggest jackpot of all, home alive and whole, towers of lower Manhattan hived with electric light, buzzing hello, not a bomb-pasted building or bullet-riddled street in sight, no rain, no ruins, no rocket's red glare, booze and gasoline plentiful and free-flowing as the waters of the mighty Hudson.

Eventually, the gravity of memory—of those who didn't make it back, of events better forgotten—would reassert its weight. But those first few days, everything is present tense. Roberta is in the bed at the Plaza. No dream, not this time. Listening to Perry Como in the Versailles. (Dunne palms a five-spot to the photographer to snap a shot when she's not looking.) They are in the cab on the way back to the Plaza. The driver watches in the mirror as they pet like hormone-crazed school kids.

Intense pleasure like intense pain admits only one moment: *Now.*

Seesaw Marjorie Daw.

That was then.

He heard Ken Moss bantering with Miss O'Keefe.

"He's running a little late. Have a seat. He'll be with you in a moment."

"I'm on a pretty tight schedule myself."

"You'll just have to wait."

Dunne pressed the intercom button: "It's all right, Miss O'Keefe. Send him in."

A few seconds of silence told him she was annoyed at being overruled for following instructions given a few minutes before. "As you wish, Mr. Dunne."

Thumbing through the magazine on his desk, Dunne didn't look up.

Moss lurked by the door. "You wanted to see me? Here I am. In the flesh."

"Have a seat."

"Wynne is bringing me along to a meeting at GE. We leave in fifteen minutes."

"This won't take fifteen minutes." Dunne folded the magazine shut, pushed it across the desk, asked, "Alvin Capshaw, I presume?"

"I wrote most of it." Moss grinned and sat. "Capshaw lent his name to it. He doesn't come cheap." He shunted French cuffs above thin wrists covered with honey-colored fuzz, lifted the magazine on left palm, wet right index finger on tip of tongue, and turned the pages. He held up the picture of Dunne and Donovan. "Can't argue with publicity this good."

"It's bullshit."

"Bullshit?" Moss dropped the magazine onto his lap.

"I told you I didn't want any part of this."

"Which is why I didn't bother you."

"So you went ahead and made it up?"

"We'd already paid for the pages."

"You should have asked for your money back."

"I did. It was too late."

"You've made me into a liar."

"A liar? How?"

"I never told you I went to Fordham."

"You told me you went to school in the Bronx."

"The Catholic Protectory was hybrid reformatory and orphanage."

"It was in the Bronx, right?"

"Not near Fordham. The zoo is near Fordham. I wasn't schooled at either."

Moss ran his finger down the page. "Here: It says you 'attended' Fordham. That could mean you went and watched a football game."

"With Horatio Alger and William Holden?"

"Those are allusions, that's all."

"*Delusions*, you mean."

"*Modern Detection* isn't *Time* magazine. It's not all tied up in fact-checking."

"No kidding."

Moss sank down in the chair. "I did my best with what I had."

"Your best is to have me say, 'I prefer the warm embrace of sunshine'?"

"What's wrong with that?"

"I sound like a moony schoolgirl. Then again, it's a cut above drivel like 'education,' 'professionalization,' and, er, what was the last of the trio?"

"Conglomeration."

"That's it. I guess when General Donovan calls to find out how I had the nerve to make commercial use of his photograph, I can tell him I was 'conglomerated.'"

"The picture is on your wall."

"My wall isn't printed and distributed across the country."

"I'm sorry you feel that way. I thought I was doing you a favor." Moss folded his hands together, an almost penitent gesture. "I really did."

Whatever residue of anger Dunne entertained drained away. Moss accepted his offer of a cigarette and pulled out a lighter. His fingers shook as he thumbed the flint wheel. "I know what you're thinking, but it's not that way."

"What way?"

"Wynne and his buddies."

"What about them?"

"Wynne is in a hurry."

"I figured that out on my own."

"But he's not trying to throw you overboard. He wants to bring new ways of thinking to ISC—a strategy in sync with the changes going on all around us. It's dogma with him: 'Change is good.'"

"I don't think the change from Weimar Republic to Third Reich was so hot."

"You know what I mean, Fin." Moss snapped his fingers. "Times change, and we change with them. The velocity of change makes it all the more urgent. Put the right pieces together in the right way, *snap, snap*, each part of the company has got to support the others, *snap*, and if we do it right, *snap*, the way Wynne has laid out, *snap, snap*, we'll achieve amazing synergies."

"Synergies?"

"When the parts work together to achieve what they couldn't on their own. A pile of bones is just a pile of bones. Assemble them correctly, *snap, snap*, you get a Mickey Mantle or Roger Maris. Wynne respects you as a professional—as I do—but also as a vet, somebody who did his fair share—and more—when it really counted.

"As we move into synthetics, electronics, and avionics, the need for investigation and security grows exponentially. Not the old-style grunt work like with Pepsi and Miss Crawford. But on a new, higher level. Wynne didn't mention it at the meeting, but the biggest factor of all is national defense; twenty-six billion dollars for highways is cheap change compared to what it'll take to trump the Reds in Europe, Indo-China, the Americas, and, last but not least, outer space.

"Wynne put it to me this way: 'Change is nothing more than a synonym for opportunity.' He might have borrowed from Dale Carnegie—he does that a lot—but that can't take away from the truth of it."

Moss stood, crushed his cigarette in the ashtray on Dunne's desk. "I have to run or I'm going to be late for that meeting with GE. We'll talk more when I get back."

Miss O'Keefe entered simultaneously with Moss's exit. She placed a sheet of paper on his desk. "Here are your appointments for the rest of the day. You're scheduled for lunch with Mr. Lawson at Longchamps at twelve thirty."

"Lawson?"

"Mr. Brigham Lawson from Pan Am. Mr. Billings arranged it, remember? Unfortunately, he can't join you, so the reservation is just for two."

Lawson, Brigham: Billings brought him by the office several weeks before on the way back from lunch. Lawson was flying on a full tank of martinis or Manhattans. Friendly to the point of blustery, he was very taken with the picture of General Donovan. He'd served with the statistical control unit for Major General Curtis LeMay's Bomber Command during the devastating B-29 raids on Japan.

"All I got to fly was a desk," he joked. "Must have been a thrill to work with Wild Bill. We had a saying in Bomber Command: 'The Marines did the fighting, the Army muddled through, the Navy grabbed the glory, the Air Force won the war, and the OSS had all the fun.' Ha, ha, just kidding." The back pat he landed bordered on painful.

Dunne wasn't looking forward to lunch.

Miss O'Keefe perched her eyeglasses on her nose, picked up the copy of *Modern Detection* Moss had left on the chair.

"Keep it if you'd like. Might be of interest to a novelist."

"A *novelist*?" she asked in the questioning tone of someone unsure whether to feel affronted or appreciated. "What makes you think I'm a novelist?"

He felt a flush of embarrassment. Crassness of peeking in her drawer without permission. He swiveled in his chair and fussed with a stack of papers on the window ledge. "Aren't all English majors would-be novelists? Goes with the territory, no?"

"I suppose."

"Or poets. A buddy of mine in the war majored in English at Harvard. He was mad about poetry."

"Is he the one who gave you *The Oxford Book of Modern Verse*?"

"The what?"

"The book in your bottom drawer."

He slipped open the drawer and lifted some papers. "I forgot it's here."

"I've borrowed it on occasion. I hope you don't mind. I know you don't consider bottom drawers sacrosanct."

Miss O'Keefe showed him a smile he hadn't seen before, slightly askew, street-wise. "Oh, one more thing." She pulled a slip of paper from her jacket pocket. "While you were at the meeting, I was away from my desk and the receptionist took a call for you from"—she looked at the slip—"a Mr. Bassante."

"Bassante?"

"Tourloff Bassante."

"T-u-r-l-o-u-g-h?"

"Yes, that's how it's spelled."

"It's pronounced 'Tur-low.'"

"I'm sorry. I've never heard the name before."

"What was the message?"

"No message, no number. He said he'd call back."

Summer dragged, June wilted into August. If Roberta was around, she'd have them going to clubs, movies, plays, and on weekend jaunts. With her on a cruise, Dunne mostly went to work, came home, made himself a Manhattan and a sandwich, and watched television, which mostly consisted of summer reruns. Three (sometimes four) nights a week he swam a mile worth of laps at the Grand Central Y.

Bassante never called back. Miss O'Keefe checked the phone directories for the five boroughs and surrounding counties, didn't turn up any Turlough Bassante. Dunne assigned Mike Del Giudice, an Iona College graduate fresh out of Naval Intelligence and an eager-beaver recruit in PISS, to see what he could find.

Del Giudice reported what Dunne already knew (Bassante was raised in Hoboken, educated at Yale, joined the Foreign Service, was recruited into the OSS and subsequently into the CIC); he also answered what Dunne didn't know: What happened to Bassante in the wake of the accident in Nuremberg that killed Corporal Mundy?

(Though Del Giudice attached no significance to the name— a passing reference: Harry Mundy—Dunne saw him clearly. Face against the windshield. *That's the marble soapbox where Hitler did his spouting.* Dunne recalled some things clearer than others. No surprise. The surprise was in the swiftness and vividness with which they came back—jolting immediacy triggered by word, sight, smell—like sticking a finger in a light socket.)

Dunne had a hazy recollection of Bassante coming to see him in the hospital, sharp nose pointing down, words repeated softly several times: *Fin, I'm so sorry.*

By the time Dunne felt himself again, he was on a ship home. He wrote both Bassante and Van Hull. Neither responded. Once, on a whim, he called the Adams-Thayer Academy, where Van Hull had taught before the war. The secretary said Van Hull was no longer connected to the school. She had no knowledge of where he currently lived or worked. There was no listing for Thornton or Richard Van Hull in the white pages.

Eventually, once he was settled back with Roberta and felt as though he had his bearings, he looked into the fate of SS-Hauptsturmführer Dr. Karsten Heinz. He'd never been brought to trial. Sent to London for "special interrogation," he escaped hanging but not death, meeting his end when he contracted a fatal case of "bronchopneumonia."

Bassante had stayed with the CIC, Del Giudice reported, until 1947, when he transferred to Research & Analysis at the Pentagon, which was to a large degree a reconstituted version of what had existed in the OSS. From there, he circled back to the Department of State.

The paper trail that Del Giudice turned up on Bassante contained newspaper accounts of testimony he gave in 1952 before a congressional committee investigating Communist infiltration of the State Department. Bassante was closely questioned about his participation during his senior year at Yale in the "Student Congress for Economic Recovery and World Peace," held in New York, in 1931.

Q: Were you aware the Student Congress was a Communist front?

A: No, Congressman, I was not.

Q: How's that possible? Everyone knew.

A: Not everyone.

Q: Who besides you, Mr. Bassante?

A: The Vice President of the United States, Mr. Curtis. He sent a greeting.

Bassante was dismissed from the State Department the following year, 1953, when John Foster Dulles became secretary. He taught a course at Georgetown for a semester, then left Washington.

Where to?

Del Giudice: *I'll keep working on it.*

Dunne: *Don't bother.*

If Bassante wanted to get in touch, Dunne decided, it was up to him. Dunne was content not to get involved in wartime reminiscing, which was why he avoided reunions of the 69th and the OSS. Same diehards attended. Booze flowed, bullshit followed, fraternal invariably degenerated into sentimental.

Dunne took Ken Moss's advice. Instead of accepting the inevitability of being fired, he decided to hang in. While he couldn't pretend to be a true believer, he found himself engaged in redefining the business. At a minimum, he wasn't bored.

A toxic mix of formless smog and smothering heat lay over the city. Exiting the air-cooled marble lobby of the Graybar Building, Dunne was dizzy for an instant. He started to walk the short distance up Lexington Avenue for a swim at the Y when he realized he'd left his earplugs upstairs. Instead of backtracking and dealing with lunchtime elevator traffic, he veered east across the street to Liggett's.

The gray, oppressive air reinforced the everyday uniformity and anonymity of the pedestrian crowd. He didn't home in on furtive moves by any particular person but sensed it: subtle, deliberate, purposeful, a stalker's step.

He was being followed.

In Liggett's, he meandered up and down the aisles, bought cigarettes and shaving cream as well as earplugs, stood by the cutout of Garry Moore by the checkout counter and watched hurried flow in and out of the store. People zeroed in on the items they wanted—pens, prescriptions, shampoo—paid and left. Turnover at the lunch counter was slower, patrons distinctly older, slightly shabby, residents of East Side tenements, there more for air-conditioning than a meal.

He crossed the street, lingered in the entrance of the Y. The tail was gone. Or maybe he was mistaken. Maybe he misread accidental zig for intentional zag. It happened. Radar operator misidentifies flock of birds as fighter plane; blip on sonar turns out to be school of fish instead of submarine. The heat might have played a part; dizziness he'd felt.

After his swim, he walked to the Roosevelt Hotel, through the lobby to the entrance into Grand Central, across the great hall to the Graybar entrance.

He knew for sure he was no longer being tailed. Maybe he never had been.

The rain on Saturday cooled things off. He caught up on paperwork, watched TV. For dinner he had a couple of beers and a corned beef sandwich at the Blarney Stone on Third Avenue. The heat returned on Sunday. He took a long walk through Central Park. He visited the zoo. The monkeys barely moved. The lions slept. The lone polar bear in view was comatose.

Buzz. Monday morning. Miss O'Keefe on the intercom: "Moss is eager to see you. He says it's important. What time shall I tell him?"

Dunne flipped the pages of the newspaper spread on his desk. "Anytime." He went back to the paper. *Cuban government reports rebels routed in Oriente Province. Red China will probably have an atomic bomb within five years. Sale on summer suits at Rogers Peet.*

Buzz. Intercom again.

"What is it now?"

"Mr. Moss is here."

"'Eager' was an understatement."

"Shall I send him in?"

Dunne folded the paper and stuck it in his briefcase. He pulled a file from his desk, opened it, poised pen as if to write. "Fire when ready, Gridley."

Moss's smile resembled that of the cat savoring the taste of swallowed canary.

"Sit, please." Dunne put down the pen. "You've got news I'm told."

"Happy news."

"I can see."

"My ship's come in."

"Staten Island Ferry or Good Ship Lollipop?"

"Best ship afloat."

"Which is that?"

"Bartlett and Partners. I've been hired at twice what I make here. I'll have my own assistant, an office with three windows, and an expense account."

"Congratulations. Did Bartlett do the hiring?"

"The colonel?"

"That's how he liked to be addressed." Dunne resisted mention of "the Pear," the derisory nickname employed when Bartlett wasn't around.

"Of course, I forgot. You were both OSS. I should've known you were buddies."

"'Buddies' is stretching it."

"He hasn't been part of the firm for a while now."

Dunne dusted off a cobwebbed memory: Item in the paper on Bartlett's return to government service. Aglow with praise for his wartime record and role in helping set up the CIA, it read like he wrote it himself, which he probably had. "Sorry to see you go."

"You're not still sore about that piece in *Modern Detection*?"

"I'm grateful. It got me thinking."

"I'm glad because here's the kicker: It got me the job."

"How's that?"

"The crew over at Bartlett's loved it. It's exactly the kind of 'proactive public relations' they want inside their shop. They want to make intraindustry publications the norm for all types of businesses—create the template in-house, tailor the articles to the client, and target a specific audience. When they found out the piece was not only my idea but that I'd written it, I was offered the position of corporate editorial director."

"Nice title."

"Nice job."

"You tell Billings yet?"

"A minute ago."

"How'd he take it?"

"Wynne is thrilled. He said he's been thinking for some time how to build a relationship between ISC and Bartlett and Partners. Louie Pohl was a big stumbling block. He insisted we keep our distance. But with Louie out of the picture and me going over there, Wynne thinks we'll have a real opportunity to work together." Moss gave him a casual imitation salute and was off.

Dunne gazed out the window. He was sorry Moss was departing. He wouldn't have expected to feel that way, particularly after his initial reaction to the article in *Modern Detection*. Although there was no physical resemblance, something about Moss reminded Dunne of Peter Bunde—youthful enthusiasm blended with inexperience, one part optimism, two parts innocence, a desire to do the right thing and the presumption it would all work out in the end.

Take along the Miraculous Medal; leave behind the lethal pill. It had worked out for Bunde, just not the way he expected.

Buzz. Buzz. Buzz. The stabbing persistence of the intercom interrupted his reverie. He glanced at his watch. It was 11:30. He was incredulous at how long he'd been gazing into space.

Time, gentlemen, time.

"Mr. Dunne, I've confirmed your reservation."

214

"What reservation?"

"At Longchamps."

"When?"

"Lunch. Today at twelve forty-five."

"Who with?"

"Mr. Lawson from Pan Am."

"Cancel it."

"*Now?*"

"I got a bad headache."

"When did that happen?

"Just now."

"I'll bring you some aspirin."

"I need fresh air, not aspirin. I'll get it myself."

He slapped on his hat and rushed past her desk. He felt her cold glare without seeing it. She'd a right to be peeved. He knew he should apologize. He didn't have a headache. But the craving for fresh air was immediate. He couldn't wait.

Maybe it was a delayed reaction to the mention of C. B. Bartlett's name, like when you wake in the middle of the night suddenly short of breath, as if someone were sitting on your chest. Bartlett's name brought so much back, memories he was happy to escape. More likely, it was the effect of Moss's news. He'd come to feel that he could work with Moss, that with his help he could cut through Billings's corporate gobbledygook and carve out a position at ISC in which he felt comfortable.

No more.

When the elevator reached the lobby, he realized he was out of cigarettes. He crisscrossed through the traffic inching its way down Lexington Avenue. A cab jerked ahead, cutting toward the curb by Grand Central. The brakes screeched as it stopped just short of slamming into Dunne.

Dunne slapped his palm on the hood. "Watch it!"

The cabbie poked his head out. "You watch it, asshole!"

"Takes one to know one."

"Stick it up your stuck-up ass!"

As he reached the east side of the avenue, Dunne stopped, intending to have the last word, and caught a blurred reflection in the front window of Liggett's. A figure darted behind him—male, tall; hat, straw—and veered to the left.

This time he wasn't dizzy; this time he was sure: a tail.

He entered and exited through the revolving door. He turned left, walked rapidly to the corner of 42nd Street. He passed Grand Central. At the corner of Vanderbilt, he crossed to the south side of the street, ignored the entrance to Rogers Peet at 16 East 42nd Street, and went left at the corner to the store's main entrance at 41st and Fifth.

The store was quiet and cool. A bow-tied clerk with round tortoise-shell glasses and slicked-back hair approached. He had an Ivy League look but none of the trademark hoity-toity reserve of a Brooks Brothers floorwalker. "Hot out there, huh?"

"Lot nicer in here."

The salesman smiled. "Here for the sale?"

"I need a jacket."

"This way." He led the way toward the back of the store. "Smart to come now. Lunchtime, we'll be swamped."

Dunne stopped at the first rack of suits, fingered a blue-striped seersucker.

"Summer clearance. Best bargain in the store." The salesman tapped the rack with his sales book. "Forty-nine dollars reduced to twenty-nine. Let's see if we have your size."

Dunne removed his suit jacket and tried on the one he'd been touching.

The salesman shook his head. "Not even close. The sleeves are too long. Look at the shoulders." He put down the sales book, pinched the fabric, and tugged. "Way too big." He began to search through the rack. "What size you usually take?"

"I'll take this."

"Huh?" Salesman's eyes widened behind tortoise-shell circles.

Dunne took out his billfold. "It's perfect."

"It doesn't fit."

"It's good enough."

"You haven't tried on the pants."

"I don't want the pants. I need a hat."

"The hat department is upstairs."

Dunne went over to a mannequin, took the straw hat, and donned it. It fit.

"That's for display only."

"This should cover the jacket and hat." Dunne peeled two twenties and a ten from the billfold and handed them to the salesman.

"This is too much."

"It includes a tip." He removed the price tag from the jacket.

"T-t-tip?" the salesman stuttered. "I don't get tips."

"There's a first time for everything."

"I have to write up a sales ticket." The salesman trailed behind Dunne.

"Keep it." Dunne started toward the store's 42nd Street entrance.

"And these?" The salesman held up the jacket and hat Dunne had arrived in.

"Send them to the Salvation Army."

Dunne quickly exited and walked west to the corner and joined the current of pedestrians streaming down Fifth. A group of tourists studied the staid and dignified facade of the New York Public Library across the way, clicked cameras at the stone lions flanking the stairs as their guide talked in German.

He turned down the brim of his hat as if to shade his eyes from the sun and followed as the tourists moved south. On the east corner of 41st Street, a man lounged, back against wall, face half hidden behind the newspaper he paged through. He wore a narrow-brimmed straw hat, white straw in the process of turning yellow—last year's merchandise, maybe the year's before. Periodically, he peered over the top of the paper at the store entrance. Taking no notice of Dunne, he lowered the paper and eyed his watch.

His face was clearly visible. Haggard, seeded with two days' worth of stubble and creased by pleats that curved from eyes to chin and accented the sharply pointed nose, a compass needle holding steady north, at the entrance to Rogers Peet—it was unmistakable.

Turlough Bassante.

Dunne walked leisurely halfway to 40th Street before he turned back.

Bassante had tucked the newspaper under his arm and crossed the street. His face was pressed to the front window of Rogers Peet. He used the paper as a visor.

"Who you looking for?" Dunne positioned himself by Bassante's right shoulder.

Bassante stepped back, studied the reflection in the window. "I should've known."

"Known what?"

"Never try to outfox a fox."

"Especially when there's no need. If you left a number, I'd have called you back."

"I wasn't sure about getting you involved. Last time I almost got you killed."

"Let's talk."

"This time might be no different."

"Suppose we go back to my office."

"No." Dark patches underlined the furtive, darting movement of Bassante's eyes. "That wouldn't be wise."

"Where?"

"Over there." He nodded at the library on the other side of

Fifth. "Third floor, a bench opposite the entrance to the Main Reading Room. Tomorrow, at noon."

"This is silly. I'm through playing games."

"I'm not crazy, if that's what you think."

"I said silly, not crazy."

"I'm scared. Nothing wrong with that, is there?"

"Not if there's something worth being scared about."

"I'll let you decide."

"How do I know you'll show?"

"You don't. But I will. You've got my word."

Bassante started to move away but stopped. "Oh, one other thing. Sorry to have put you to the expense of purchasing such an ill-fitting jacket." He pinched the shoulders much as the salesman had. "I trust you can take it back."

"It did its job. I'm going to donate it to the Salvation Army."

"A worthy outfit—the Salvation Army that is, not the jacket." Bassante crossed in the middle of the block. Stroll became sprint as the light changed and the pent-up herd of cars, cabs, and buses let loose and stampeded down Fifth.

Shorty before noon, Dunne sat on the library steps and smoked. He reserved judgment on Bassante's sanity. It was obvious the years since the war hadn't been kind: wrinkled and worn clothes, face, mind.

It crossed Dunne's mind this was a charade on Bassante's part to prepare to put the touch on for whatever he could get; a strung-out song and dance to make it seem he wasn't a beggar but a wartime buddy caught in some mystery-shrouded vise. A man has his pride. Stripped of everything else—money, work, wife, family—that's about all he has.

It was all so unnecessary. Over the years, he'd helped whoever came to him. When they asked for a loan—and money was always what they needed—they got it. No exceptions. He told them not to worry about paying it back. But they'd insist they'd only take it on the understanding they'd pay it back. Which they never did. No exceptions.

Bassante was where he said he'd be, on a marble bench across from the entrance to the Main Reading Room, in the same clothes as yesterday. Hunched over, eagle's beak pointed toward the floor, he held his hat between his legs and worked the brim.

A group of high school students gathered in the middle of the entrance hall around their guide, an attractive redhead in a pink blouse and tight black skirt. She pointed at the trompe l'oeil painted on the ceiling. They craned their necks.

Bassante leaned back. "Recognize it?"

"Sure." Dunne sat beside him. He kept his eyes on the librarian. She moved away, hips swaying rhythmically. A sight that never got old.

"Prometheus stealing fire from the gods."

Dunne looked up. "He gets around. There's a statue of him doing the same thing at the rink in Rockefeller Center."

"Yes, that's quite true."

"Why are you scared?"

Bassante's eyes were fixed on the ceiling. "Prometheus carries the flame in his right hand. You'll also notice his right knee is prudently raised to cover his sexual organs so as not to arouse the prurient interests of the hoi polloi."

"Why don't you try answering my question?"

"I'm afraid . . ." Bassante lowered his head.

"Of what?"

"Of what happened to Louie Pohl happening to me."

"Louie committed suicide."

"He was murdered." Bassante laid his hat on the bench and folded his arms. A steady stream of visitors passed in and out of the reading room.

"By who?"

"Same people who want to kill me."

"Why?"

"Same reason they killed him." Bassante extracted a thick envelope from the breast pocket of his jacket. "I wrote it down last night."

His severe profile reminded Dunne of the pictures on the holy cards they gave out at funerals, virgins and martyrs whose ferocious sanctity seemed to test the bounds of sanity. "Can't you just tell me?"

"I want you to have the facts in writing, as fully as I can lay them out. If parts seem repetitive or verbose, forgive me. You remember, I suppose, what Dick Van Hull used to say about me: 'Bassante never uses one word when he can use three.' Think it over. If you want no part, I understand. You have a good life now. Why plunge back into the past?"

"Why did you?"

"Why did I what?"

"Plunge back into the past?"

"I never left."

Dunne weighed the envelope in his palm. "It feels fairly substantial."

"I wrote it by hand—it took several hours—but I think it'll provide most of what you need to know."

"Where can I reach you?"

"Here, same time, same place, tomorrow."

"What if you don't show?"

"I did today, didn't I?"

"You pitched me like this once before, remember?"

"This is my last pitch, I promise."

Miss O'Keefe was scrawling intently in a marbled-covered composition book. Blushing slightly, she covered it with her forearm. "Mr. Billings said to call soon as you got in. He said it's important."

"I'll call him later." He sat at his desk, sliced open the envelope with the sterling silver letter opener Roberta had given him for Christmas. The pages inside were covered with handwriting he recognized: clear, neat, precise. Hail, holy penmanship.

Part VI
Amid a Crowd of Stars

New York City
August 15, 1958

Dear Fintan,
Please forgive the indirection with which I've gone about contacting you. My hope is that, after reading this, you'll better understand my actions. I've often reflected on and regretted the outcome of the mission you undertook to Prague. I don't know what memory you have—if any—of the several visits I made during your hospitalization. The attending physicians predicted you'd eventually make a full recovery. Thankfully, I take this to be the case.

As you were undoubtedly made aware by the Military Police, the collision was judged accidental. Yet that you were in Nuremberg at all—that you left London without adequate fuel to reach Prague —was never explained to my satisfaction.

I was informed by the MPs that the other vehicle lacked registration papers of any sort. The driver was never apprehended. The MPs presumed he was a German civilian afraid of the consequences of having collided with an American jeep. They laid blame for the crash on your driver, a reckless, inexperienced recruit who raced the wrong way down a one-way street.

Jan Horak's contact in Prague waited for you at the rendezvous point. When you didn't arrive, Horak got word to me, and I used our contacts to assure him I'd make other arrangements. He was arrested two days later by the Communist faction within the Czech intelligence service and charged with having been a Nazi collaborator, which he most certainly had never been.

Despite his arrest, Horak succeeded in smuggling news to London that he'd managed to get Dr. Schaefer's microfiche in "the right hands" and keep it away from the Soviets. I never received it. Perhaps the message wasn't from Horak but a ruse on the part of the Soviets, or perhaps the microfiche did reach those within our own

225

camp who had no wish to share it or risk it being made public.

Horak was never brought to trial. He was still imprisoned at the time of the Communist coup in 1949. His fate remains uncertain.

The case of SS-Hauptsturmführer Dr. Karsten Heinz seemingly resolved itself. Removed from the trial of Nazi doctors, he was brought to London for "special interrogation" about Soviet penetration of Allied intelligence. Shortly after landing in London, Heinz was struck by a virulent strain of "bronchopneumonia," which was rampant that winter, and died. His case was closed and his name removed from the Central Registry of War Criminals and Security Suspects (CROWCASS).

Meanwhile, as a result of my earlier sojourn in the South Tyrol, I stayed in touch with a trustworthy cadre within the CIC who kept me abreast of the swelling number of Nazi fugitives—SS officers, Gestapo agents, security and concentration camp personnel and collaborators—who were making their way over the Alps into Italy and embarking from there to South America.

It didn't take long to come to the conclusion that while one part of the CIC was laboring to identify and detain the escapees, another part was expediting their escape. I presumed at first that a few rogue agents, exploiting a lack of administrative oversight, were responsible. Instead, it became clear there was a deliberate policy at work.

In conjunction with elements in the International Red Cross and the Vatican, American officials were abetting the flight of those deemed useful in a crusade against a single-minded, highly coordinated global campaign of Communist subversion and aggression. The supposed utility of the escapees in this struggle took precedence over all other considerations, including their wartime roles.

From the beginning, a thick cloak of secrecy was in place. The confusion that followed the demise of the OSS added to the opacity. Yet all roads led to Rome and Lt. Col. Carlton Baxter Bartlett. Ensconced in the former office of Count Ciano, Bartlett had positioned himself as the spider at the center of this web, instantly able to detect and react to whatever disturbed his skein of silken wires.

As well as being involved in amassing and distributing the money needed to build and sustain electoral opposition to the hugely popular Italian Communist Party, he acted as liaison among the

War Department's Joint Intelligence Objectives Agency (JIOA), the CIC, and the nascent operations of the Central Intelligence Unit (soon to become the hush-hush Office of Policy Coordination).

There was a degree of irony in this. Over the years, any number of high-ranking officers and would-be successors to General Donovan thought of Bartlett as nothing more than a rotund, soft-centered, sybaritic, self-promoting huckster and manipulator of public opinion who lacked the ambition and ability to have any real role in setting policy and running the nation's intelligence operations.

For my part, from the moment I met him, I detected in Bartlett no mere flatterer or status seeker. Beneath the aromatic whiff of bay rum, I sniffed the spoor of a creature fueled by ambition, cunning, insecurity, ruthlessness, and paranoia, the qualities possessed by skilled and successful bureaucratic infighters in all times and climes.

Names and dates may change—stakes may vary—but the game is played the same, be it in palaces or presidiums, the bedchambers of imperial Rome and Byzantium or the boardrooms of London and New York. (Consult the works of Procopius, Suetonius, Gibbon, et al., to fill in the details.)

It wasn't long before the antagonism between Dick Van Hull and Bartlett came to a head. On learning that Karsten Heinz's prosecution had been postponed, Van Hull used his father's contacts in Washington to bring the matter to the attention of senior members of Congress and point an accusing finger at Bartlett. Before anything could come of it, Heinz "passed away."

The die, however, had been cast. Van Hull's father received an anonymous letter detailing his relationship with Lt. Michael Jahn. The letter predicted a formal inquiry into the circumstances surrounding Operation Maxwell and left no doubt that his son—now regarded as a war hero—would be exposed as a "deviant whose actions had been motivated not by selfless patriotism but by the insatiable demands of his own perverted lusts."

Up until this point, Van Hull had ignored Bartlett's warnings not to interfere in "covert intelligence operations and decisions relating to national security clearly outside your purview." With Heinz dead and the threat hanging over him of a public airing of his homosexuality, which would deeply wound his father, Van Hull *resigned his commission and returned to New York.*

Soon after, my work with the CIC came to an end—thanks to Miss Ginny Thompson. You remember her, I'm sure. She ran the OSS's London communications subsidiary—so sweet, so American, a charming coquette with a frame hard to ignore or forget. One fine summer's night, she disappeared. I presumed she'd eloped. Alone and unwed, she surfaced in Moscow a few weeks later.

Her real name was Anna Nekrasov. She was born to Russian parents who'd emigrated to Paterson, New Jersey. When Anna was 12, as the Depression reached its deepest depths, her parents moved the family back to the USSR. When she came of age and went to university, she was recruited by the NKGB and slipped into England.

The paperwork at the OSS office in London indicated that I had been responsible for her hiring. It was true I'd cosigned the papers but only after Bartlett directed me to. (His infatuation with Miss Thompson/Nekrasov was no secret.)

Bartlett denied having given me such an order. Since it was my word against his, I knew the best course for me was to avoid controversy, resign, and be done with it. I returned to the State Department, where, given my Foreign Service experience and stints in the OSS and CIC, I was made Special Assistant for Intragovernmental Affairs and Public Information.

The general rule at State is the longer the title, the lower the job. That was not quite true in my case. Mine was a narrow but not unimportant portfolio. My primary responsibility was "to coordinate the work of the JIOA and State Department" and "to approve and distribute such information appropriate and necessary for public consumption without in any way endangering or impeding the requirements of national security."

I wasn't long at it when I was informed of an agreement ratified by the State-War-Navy Coordinating Committee to expand a program put in place by the Joint Chiefs that authorized entry into the U.S. of approximately a hundred German scientists. (If my memory is correct—admittedly, an increasingly iffy proposition—I brought up Operation Overcast during our discussion at the Drummond.)

The new project, code-named Operation Paperclip, increased the quota dramatically. It also turned a blind eye to the past, stipulating

*only that those admitted to the U.S. should not include "any person
or persons planning the resurgence of German military potential."*

It quickly became apparent that, as was the case with Overcast,
the bulk of those seeking entry to the U.S. as part of Paperclip had
been active Nazis and enthusiastic participants right up until the
Third Reich's Götterdämmerung. By act of Congress, such individuals, many deserving indictment as war criminals, were to be denied
entry to the U.S. Accordingly, I made sure their applications for
visas were denied.

The JIOA reacted swiftly. Lt. Col. Bartlett was recalled to
Washington, where he supervised "revising" the bios of all those
denied visas. It turned into an exercise in creative writing. All mention of promotions or honors bestowed for their wartime service to
the Reich were excised, as was membership in the SS (in which, for
instance, Wernher von Braun, head of the rocket program, had been
appointed an "honorary" Sturmbannführer).

Aware of the potential for public controversy, Bartlett and the
JIOA went on the offensive. A press release announced that a number of "world-famous and low-paid German technicians" were
coming to the U.S. in order "to share their expertise and experience
with their American counterparts." It was hoped they'd eventually
seek to become American citizens.

The release stipulated that "each of these visa applicants has
been selected after a careful and thorough vetting of his background," which was true, of course. What went unsaid was what
this vetting had uncovered.

The next thing I knew, I was exiled to the Department's ultimate Thule: the Educational and Cultural Division, where I was
tasked with preparing instructional and informational materials for
distribution in the academic community. That's when our mutual
friend Louis Pohl—Pully—got in touch with me.

During the time I'd spent under him in the OSS, in Washington,
Pully made our small unit into a model of accuracy and efficiency
in analyzing the strength of the enemy. A clear-eyed, unwavering
realist, Pully was an implacable foe of fearmongering, scare tactics,
and hysteria, the policy of exaggeration and overreaction that he
considered a fig leaf for self-aggrandizers whose ultimate end,

though masked behind the invocation of "national security concerns," was the accumulation of power.

At war's end, he was transferred to the CIU and focused on providing the civilian and military leadership with the facts it needed to gain and maintain a sober, hardheaded appreciation of the economic and military capacities of the USSR and its satellites, as well as their strategic intentions.

Pully took me aside and asked if I'd help keep track of the out-of-control buccaneering and adventurism that was becoming routine behind the scenes and warping our intelligence operations. Specifically, given the personal relationships I still enjoyed within the Department, he asked if I'd provide him with details of the ever-widening programs to incorporate former members of the Nazi military, scientific, and intelligence establishment into U.S. operations.

I did as he asked not just out of friendship but also because I shared his concern. One project seemed to metastasize out of another. Operation Birchwood recruited members of Göring's planning office and the SS to forecast Soviet economic trends. Project Apple Pie authorized "taking functional advantage of"—in other words, hiring—key personnel from "the belly of the beast"—Amt. VI (Department 6) of the SS Reichssicherheitshauptamt (RSHA), the Reich Main Security Office under Reinhard Heydrich.

The capstone, so to speak, was Operation Bloodstone, which eventually became the basis for a whole series of ill-fated CIA-sponsored programs. Bloodstone skimmed off the cream of Nazi high-level intelligence experts and collaborators who had well-earned reputations for their ruthless and dedicated service to the Third Reich in the hopes of creating an armed resistance behind the Iron Curtain.

In many cases, the dossiers of these recruits were simply redacted to remove any hint of their involvement in war crimes. In others, their names were dropped from CROWCASS, as if they were deceased, and new identities were invented.

As far as the public knew, a handful of German and Eastern European refugees, with no connections to Nazi atrocities or mass murder, had been recruited to help fend off the Communist menace. The few journalists who made further inquiries were brushed off with the assurance that "no Nazi zealot or anyone connected to Nazi war crimes" had been recruited, hired, or brought to the U.S.

Although Pully never directly told me so, I realized he was building a case— from as many sources as he could—for sweeping reform of the country's intelligence operations. I'm unsure when and to whom he intended to make that case. Given the crisis over Berlin, Mao's victory in China, and the outbreak of the Korean conflict, Pully understood how easy it would be for Bartlett and his underlings to paint him as a fellow traveler or "pinko."

As the level of hysteria intensified, he held his fire. But he never lost his interest. Aided by a dozen agents and analysts who shared his concerns (a group he collectively referred to as the "Twelve Apostates"), Pully continued to compile his own chronicle of developments within our national security apparatus.

His career within government came to an end after he sent a guarded letter to the new head of the CIA, Allen Dulles, expressing his fear that, under the auspices of the Office of Policy Coordination, the agency was ballooning into a vast, undisciplined bureaucracy manned by those of doubtful competence and assisted in far too many cases by foreign recruits whose backgrounds disqualify them for any role in our national defense.

Dulles brushed off the criticism. Worse, he forwarded the letter to Carlton Bartlett, who was serving on the transition group Dulles had set up. Bartlett wasted no time in getting the word out that Pully was "an overcerebralized office-manager type" and a "pushy Jew obsessed with fighting the last war." A month into Dulles's reign, Pully was eased out and was hired at ISC.

(For the record, Louis Pohl's OSS file listed his religion as "NONE"—the same as mine. When I did a little digging of my own, I discovered Pully's father was a German-American Lutheran and his mother a Coptic Christian. They raised him as a Unitarian.)

I was summoned before a private session of the House Committee on Un-American Activities and questioned about innocuous involvements I had as a student. Soon after, at the direction of Allen Dulles's brother, Secretary of State John Foster Dulles, I was fired and a note attached to my file indicating my security clearance had been revoked.

My brother, a Jesuit at Georgetown, secured me a brief stint teaching. When that went away, I was for all practical purposes unemployable. Pully came to the rescue. He put me on retainer. He paid me out of his own pocket. Nobody else knew. I'm good at keeping secrets and so was he.

Mostly, I researched and reported on various business proposals. Once in a while, on the sly, he'd ask me to look into CIA-related matters, and I'd contact the sources we still had (the Twelve Apostates had been whittled down to two) and find out what I could.

After ISC acquired your agency, Pully asked if I'd like him to put me in touch with you. I demurred, and he let the matter drop. Deep down, I think, as well as knowing the deep regrets I harbored about the harm you suffered on that abortive mission to Prague, he knew we were birds of a feather who'd had our fill of the great world's problems and were content to tend our own nests.

In January of this year, he called my attention to a news item reporting that, after a hiatus of several years, Carlton Bartlett was returning to the CIA. I wasn't surprised. He'd cashed out of Bartlett & Partners for a bundle and, it seemed to me, returned to the Serengeti of intrigue and skulduggery—his natural habitat—where his skills placed him among the fittest and most likely to survive.

Pully was convinced there was a deeper significance. He proved to be right.

A few weeks later, he called me in an agitated state. He needed to talk. Could I meet him the next morning, at 6:30 a.m., at Grand Army Plaza? I reminded him that the temperature was in the teens. It would barely be light. Snow was predicted. As far as he was concerned, that was all for the better. Our solitariness would be protection. I kept the appointment. Right away, as soon as I saw him, I knew something important was up.

Remember that phlegmatic demeanor of his: how inside he could be erupting while outside he was always that same stolid stub of a man? Well, this time he was bouncing up and down on the balls of his feet—and it wasn't because of the cold. He took me by the arm and pulled me into the park. I couldn't tell from his red face whether he was happy or angry. What was unmistakable was his excitement.

As he talked, puffs of frozen air popped from his mouth like
bursts from a steam whistle:

—Turlough, you're not going to believe this.

—Try me.

—Karsten Heinz isn't dead.

For a moment, the name didn't register. Cold and fog of sleep
slowed my comprehension. Pully could see the confusion in my
face. He repeated what he'd said:

—Karsten Heinz isn't dead.

Even then, the name barely meant anything to me. It had been
so long. Then the light went on:

—SS-Hauptsturmführer Dr. Karsten Heinz? How could that be?

—It's a flesh-and-blood fact.

Pully led the way deeper into the park. A heavy, wet snow started to fall. On we trudged as he laid out the facts. He'd received a
letter from a Swiss couple interested in setting up an American
office for their medical supply business, which specialized in devel-
oping advanced diagnostic devices. They had patents they wanted
to protect as well as prototypes they wished to introduce to the
American market. They'd heard Wynne Billings speak at a business
seminar in London and were convinced ISC could help. They'd be
in New York the following week.

Pully wrote back and set up a breakfast meeting at the Savoy
Plaza, where they were staying. Only the man showed up. After he'd
spoken with Pully for some time, he confessed that he was there
under false pretenses: To wit, he wasn't Swiss, he didn't own a medical supply business, and he and the woman with whom he'd traveled to New York—his sister, as it turned out—were determined to
capture Dr. Karsten Heinz. Would he be interested in helping them?

Unsure with whom he was dealing, Pully posed questions of his
own. Who were they? Where did they get his name? What was their
interest in Heinz? Indeed, what made them believe Heinz was alive?
What evidence had they? For whom were they working?

Their answers satisfied Pully. They'd stumbled on the trail of an
Auschwitz physician, an SS officer, who'd been presumed dead. In
fact, he was alive but there seemed to be an impenetrably protective
wall set up around him. One source had told them if they were

interested in pursuing the matter, they should speak with Louis Pohl. They went to hear Wynne Billings speak only to provide a pretext for getting in touch.

They produced the dossier they had on Heinz. It spelled out the details of his postwar existence that they'd been able to piece together.

Before he could be returned to Nuremberg, Heinz contracted bron-chopneumonia and died. A month later, Oscar Hemmer, a refugee from East Prussia with no Nazi affiliations of any sort—a simple chemist who fled the invading forces of the Red Army—appeared at the offices of the International Refugee Organization in Rome.

His documentation in order, he was issued a Red Cross pass-port. He subsequently sailed from Genoa on the S.S. Garibaldi for Buenos Aires. He settled in that city for several years, working for an Argentinean subsidiary of IG Farben, the German chemical con-glomerate, in its research division.

Unlike most other German immigrants, he steered clear of reunions and social gatherings, preferring a quiet, comfortable, soli-tary life in the upscale suburb where he resided. In 1955, Hemmer returned to Europe and settled in Hamburg. He set up an import-export firm specializing in chemical fertilizers and pesticides.

The dossier pointed to the fact that Oscar Hemmer was the reinvented Karsten Heinz. It also traced his continuing connections to Reinhard Gehlen's intelligence operation—the Org—which con-ducted business under the aegis of the CIA. Hemmer/Heinz was consulted on his knowledge of the inner workings of Soviet intelli-gence. His import-export business was nothing more than a front for his reintegration into the Org.

In 1956, the Org became the Federal Republic of Germany's official intelligence service: the Bundesnachrichtendienst (BND). Gehlen was appointed director in chief. Out of genuine concern or a desire to play the ends against the middle—most likely a combina-tion of both—Hemmer/Heinz voiced to his contacts in the CIA his suspicion that the BND was hopelessly penetrated by Soviet moles.

His concerns were brought to Carlton Bartlett, whose brief included coordinating operations with the BND. It didn't take much to convince Bartlett of the worthiness of Hemmer/Heinz's suspicions.

They stoked his conviction that the Soviets had succeeded in riddling the intelligence agencies of our European allies with agents and satisfied his desire to keep a close eye on Gehlen's minions.

Bartlett made Hemmer/Heinz his mole in the BND. He authorized him to enlist a cadre of agents to spy on the spies and nose out possible double agents. Hemmer/Heinz wasted no time in forming a tight-knit unit made up of former SS colleagues.

Pully told me all this while the snow swirled around us. The buildings beyond were obscured behind it. I blurted out a condensed version of the conversation you and I had in the Drummond all those years ago. He'd heard it before but listened with rapt intensity.

We stood silently—I'm not sure for how long—until I broke the quiet with a question:

—Who are these pursuers of Heinz? On whose behalf are they acting?

—I'm going to meet with them again today. I'll fill you in tomorrow.

—Why not now?

—Because I need time to think.

We left the park where we had entered, at Grand Army Plaza. The white flakes stuck to us like paste. We must have appeared as two abominable snowmen who'd stumbled out of some mountain fastness into the middle of the metropolis.

I should have insisted on going with him. I had the distinct impression that this most reasonable and logical of men had fallen prey to his emotions and was about to do something he'd regret. Instead, I let him go.

As incredible as the story of Heinz's resurrection sounded, I knew it was true. Yet, though I appreciated Pully taking me into his confidence, I was unnerved—even resentful. I didn't want to get sucked back into this deadly vortex, especially when the stakes were so high. I was content with the life I had.

Alas, my fears about Pully's state of mind proved correct. This most logical and deliberate of men let feelings race ahead of reason. He contacted Bartlett directly and told him he knew all about Heinz. At first Bartlett pretended ignorance. The BND managed its own affairs, he protested. The story of Hemmer/Heinz struck him as a "*fairy tale probably spun from whole cloth in Moscow.*" Even if it did contain a kernel of truth, "*it's not the business of the CIA to hunt for war criminals.*"

Pully wouldn't be put off. He stayed on the attack, challenging Bartlett that "*this wasn't about hunting war criminals but harboring them.*" It so blatantly crossed the line between "*legitimate counterintelligence and soul-corrupting deceit and manipulation,*" it had to be exposed.

I knew Pully had made a dangerous error confronting Bartlett. I knew equally that his intent was not to discredit or subvert our entire intelligence operations but to purge them of the self-aggrandizing opportunists, fearmongers, and ideological zealots ("*the warocrats,*" he labeled them) who didn't care about the means—assassination, torture, employment of the worst sort of war criminal—so long as those means served the greater end of "*national security,*" however they chose to define it.

"*If we allow this to go on,*" Pully insisted to me, "*even if we win, we'll end up secondhand replicas of the very people we set out to defeat.*"

Bartlett appealed to Pully's sense of loyalty. He asked for the chance to discuss the case. It wasn't as simple as it first appeared, Bartlett said. "*Before the genie was let out of the bottle*" and the facts made public, he wanted a chance to give his side. After that, Pully could do as he pleased. They agreed to meet the following evening at the Commodore Hotel. I begged him not to go. But he wouldn't be dissuaded.

He still believed, despite all he knew, that some basic code of honor applied, that at worst Bartlett would try to bully or bribe him into silence. But Bartlett wouldn't succeed, he said. Heinz was the final and fracturing straw laid upon the camel's back.

Their meeting was scheduled for 6:00 p.m. At a quarter past the hour, I got a call at home. It was Pully. He sounded like a raving lunatic. The room was melting. The furniture was talking.

I immediately suspected what was afoot. One of the assignments I'd carried out for him was to delve into a secret program—code-named MKULTRA—set up at Allen Dulles's direction to test the ability of biological and chemical substances to affect the mind *and alter human behavior. Involving drug companies and universities around the country, it not only had succeeded in producing mind-altering substances but also had used them on unwitting subjects, including prisoners, soldiers, and civilians.*

The most intriguing—and, to my mind, dangerous—substance was lysergic acid diethylamide (LSD). Its use on uninformed human guinea pigs, in more than one case, led to suicide. Those dosed with it experienced a stream of hallucinations that varied from mellow insights to harrowing delusions. It could easily cause those unaware of what they'd ingested to believe they were going mad.

I tried to calm Pully over the phone, reminding him of the investigation I'd done into MKULTRA and warning him that the psychotic episode he was undergoing was almost certainly induced by a drug he'd been slipped. I implored him to lie down. I promised I'd be right over. I reached the hotel just as the police were cordoning off the sidewalk on which lay the broken form of a man who'd thrown himself out an eleventh-floor window.

I didn't know where to turn after that. The newspapers the next day reported Pully had called the front desk in a state of panic. A "colleague at ISC" was quoted as describing him as "seriously depressed for some time."

I was unsure how much—if anything—Bartlett knew of my association with Pully. Had he been listening when Pully phoned me? Was he aware of how Pully learned Heinz was alive? Despite Pully's beliefs to the contrary, it was clear that Bartlett would sink to whatever depths necessary to keep the truth from coming to light.

I hid as best I could. I gave up my apartment and rented rooms by the week in Brooklyn and on the Upper West Side. I lived off my savings until my funds were so low I had to go back to work. I took part-time positions as a proofreader and researcher, which is how I came across you.

On temporary assignment fact-checking a feature article on the growth of the private security business, I looked up a citation from an article in one of those silly, self-promoting industry-sponsored rags and, voilà, there you were: "Fintan Dunne: 'A Soldier's Soldier.'"

I immediately thought to myself, yes, if there's anyone I can turn to for help, it's Dunne. Still—both out of my own reluctance to risk any further involvement and the conviction that, in the final analysis, it wouldn't be fair—I hesitated. You'd moved on, put the war behind you. You'd had your last drop.

I wavered back and forth until one day I started following you. When I sensed you'd caught on, I stopped. Several months had passed since Pully's death. It seemed that no one was hunting for me, that our connection had gone undetected. I'd saved enough money that I could consider a move to the West Coast. Then I followed you again. Was I hoping—expecting—you'd sniff me out? I'm not sure.

I've no inclinations to become a hero or a martyr. I like to think I'm not a coward, yet I was never put to the test the way so many of you were. In the end, though I didn't have the stomach to tilt with windmills as powerful and relentless as Bartlett and crew, I couldn't walk away from Pully's memory without sharing the truth. When I spotted your reflection in the window of Rogers Peet, I felt a sense of relief.

You're free to do with this information what you wish. I offer no advice and make no judgments. I've come to admire the wisdom of those who relish their solitude and stick to caves and crevices where they can live undisturbed. Perhaps if I were braver, younger, and had greater faith in our human species—in our ability to learn from the past—I would think otherwise. But I'm not, and I don't.

Totiusque,
Turlough

August 1958

NEW YORK PUBLIC LIBRARY, MANHATTAN

"YOU HAVEN'T LOST THE KNACK FOR THE KNUCKLEBALL." DUNNE stood in the library hall beside the same backless marble bench on which he'd left Bassante the previous day.

"'Luck is fate's knuckleball. It has a will of its own.' So an OSS colleague once opined to me." Bassante dangled his hat between his knees.

Dunne studied the thinning weave of gray-black threads atop Bassante's head. "You have a good memory."

"You told me that once before. It's still good, I guess—just not as good as it used to be, like the rest of me." Bassante patted the empty space beside him. "Sit."

Dunne unpocketed the letter and offered it to Bassante. "Quite a story."

"Keep it. I don't want it back."

"Did the police investigation of Pully's suicide turn anything up?"

"There was no note."

"No sign anyone else was in the room?"

"Pros don't leave clues."

"Any idea what the autopsy showed?"

"Alcohol in the bloodstream. But he wasn't drunk."

"No drugs?" Dunne sat.

"No LSD, if that's what you mean." Bassante rested his hat on his knees. "But you have to know what to look for. The coroner hadn't a clue."

"Pully was acting kind of odd even before that, don't you think?"

"Odd?"

Dunne searched for a better word.

A group of tourists came up the stairs. The redhead librarian/guide from the day before was in the lead. Same curves but different package: pink blouse and tight black skirt replaced by blue dress with white polka dots. They stopped in the middle of the floor. She pointed at the ceiling. They raised their heads in unison.

It came to him: "'Agitated'—that's how you put it in the letter."

"He had his reasons. You read the whole letter, didn't you?"

"Yes. Did you see the dossier on Oscar Hemmer?"

"Pully told me what was in it."

"But you never saw it?"

"No."

"And the Swiss couple who weren't really Swiss?"

"What about them?"

"Who were they?"

"He didn't say."

"You never met them?"

"No."

"Or talked to them?"

"What are you getting at? That Pully made all this up? That he'd lost his mind?"

"I'm trying to figure out where to go with this." Dunne held up the letter.

Bassante snatched it out of his hand. "Well, if you think this is a lot of BS"—there was as much fury in his eyes as his voice—"I'll tell you where to go." He put on his hat and stood.

"Sit, please." Dunne tugged Bassante's sleeve. "I'm only following 'the simplest and most necessary rule of all,' the one Pully imparted to you, and you passed on to the rest of us: *Pay attention.*"

"Pully wasn't paranoid or deluded. He suffered from an excess of integrity, a handicap in most professions, a fatal one in the profession he chose."

"I'm not doubting the truth of what he told you. I'm trying to figure out what we should be paying attention to and aren't."

"I did what I could to help. I owed him that much. But he knew I didn't want to get sucked back in. He did his best to respect my wishes." Bassante sat down again and handed back the letter.

The tour group moved toward the Main Reading Room. Redhead guide/librarian turned with easy, unstudied Miss Ginny Thompson–esque sway, a resemblance he almost pointed out to Bassante but didn't. It couldn't be a happy association.

Dunne repocketed the letter. The marble bench had caused a throbbing at the bottom of his spine, old ache, old wound. His coccyx. "Who'd Pully trust besides you?"

"You."

"But I was in Florida for the winter." Dunne dug his thumbs into where the ache was.

"He kept to himself. You know that. We were two of a kind."

"He didn't have any friends?"

"That was his private business."

"What was?"

"He saw Dick Van Hull now and then."

"Van Hull?"

"They traveled some of the same . . . er . . . the same circuit."

"Which circuit?"

"The Bird Circuit. Pully knew I knew. But we never talked about it. I respected his privacy."

"Where's Van Hull?"

"I don't know where he lives. Pully used to meet him every once in a while at Red's Bar and Grill, corner of Fiftieth and Third. He teaches at a hoity-toity girls' academy on the East Side. He usually stops in for the cocktail hour. I was never inside. He had me drive his car and pick him up a few times. Van Hull was a regular. Pully worried about him."

"Why?"

"Booze. 'Van Hull's drinking too much,' Pully said."

"I'll do my best to keep you out of this, but at least give me a phone number where I can reach you."

"I don't have a phone. I live in a rooming house in Park Slope, on Union Street, off Seventh Avenue." Bassante salvaged pencil stub and paper scrap from his pocket, scribbled on it. "Here's my address. I move, I'll let you know."

They walked to the staircase. Bassante stared at the mural directly in front, on the north flank of the Reading Room. He swept his hand in an arc, indicating the companion murals in the hall, two on each wall, all four painted, he said, by the same artist who put Prometheus on the ceiling. "Standard-issue art of the didactic WPA sort."

Dunne stood back. He'd barely noticed them.

"They're meant to sum up the progress of the written word. This is my favorite." Bassante tipped his hat at the scene in front of them: Two white-robed monks in a scriptorium, one resting while the other labored at his desk over a sheet of parchment; in the distance, a building aflame and a barbarian on horseback thrusting his spear into a figure on the ground. He pointed at the mayhem in the background. "Something to be said for the cloister when the time comes around at last, as it always does, for our species to revert to its homicidal, bloodthirsty worst."

The sand in the hourglass on the monk's desk was running low.

"I was hopeful you'd be willing to take the lead on this."

Bassante extended his hand. "I'll give you what support I can. Just let me keep my distance."

They shook. Bassante went down the stairs and out of sight.

Red's Bar & Grill had been a speakeasy during Prohibition. Thanks to the local precinct captain—brother to the owner, Red McGinnis—it had enjoyed protection from the raids and shakedowns most speaks experienced at one time or another. When liquor became legal again, Red's privileged status allowed him to cater to a clientele more decorous and better behaved than the sullen, pugnacious crew found in many nearby gin mills.

Eventually, the joint became the anchor of the "Bird Circuit," the string of watering holes in the forties and fifties, on or right off Third Avenue—the Swan Club, White Gander, Blue Parrot, Yellow Cockatoo, et al. Red's heyday came at war's end and right after. "I'll meet you at Red's" became the unofficial motto of the men—soldiers, sailors, and civilians, birds of a feather—who frequented the Circuit.

The best time to find Van Hull was after five, Bassante emphasized, when cocktail hour arrived and the afternoon crowd of neighborhood widows, pensioners, and laborers ceded the premises to a white-collar, middle-age crowd made up exclusively of men, most of whom worked in the office towers on the other side of Lexington.

Dunne told the cabbie, "Red's, Fiftieth and Third."

"Yeah, sure, I know the place." The cabbie chuckled to himself.

They pulled up in front of Red's. Dunne paid the fare. The rearview mirror framed the driver's insinuating leer. "Want me to wait?'

He shook his head. The defensiveness he felt made him uncomfortable, as if he owed anyone in this city an explanation of his relationship with Dick Van Hull. He got out and slammed the door.

Unshackled from the shadows of Third Avenue's elevated railway that had rattled above for three-quarters of a century, the ravaged facade of Red's found its only consolation in the equally sad condition of the structures on either side. Marble pediments and sills had been torn away. Fumes from coal, oil, and gas formed a toxic mix with rain, ice, and snow, dripped down decade after decade, cracked and eroded limestone slabs, mottling them into morbid shades of black and gray.

At either end of the block, the much-ballyhooed redevelopment and construction boom promised in the wake of the El's demolition was under way. Modern high-rise, high-rent office buildings were replacing tenements and saloons. The recent recession had slowed but not stopped the inevitable changes. The Bird Circuit was fast becoming a flock of wild geese in flight, south and west. Red's impending fate seemed foreshadowed in the electrical malfunction in the neon sign that hung above the door: *RED'S BAR & ILL.*

A dozen men were at the bar in hushed conversations. No one took note of him as he entered. A row of high-backed booths ran along the back wall. The jukebox played Rosemary Clooney warbling "Come on-a My House."

He ordered a scotch, plenty of ice. He stuck a cigarette between his lips.

The bartender put down a glass, dropped in a handful of ice cubes, and poured the scotch directly in. A generous dose. He held out his lighter. Short, with a handsome, angular face, he had the thick forearms of a boxer.

Dunne inhaled. "Thanks."

The bartender stayed where he was. "Looking for somebody in particular?"

"What makes you ask?"

"That's the way it is around here." The bartender gripped the bottle by the neck and rested it on the bar. A blue anchor and "U.S.N." were tattooed on the back of his hand.

"What way is that?"

"Customers know each other or been recommended by somebody who does."

"Sounds like a private club."

"Not private. Just careful." His face was expressionless.

"My kind of place."

"You a cop?"

Dunne dragged on his cigarette, exhaled, sipped.

"Just so you know, the local precinct captain don't abide freelancers."

"I'm not a cop."

"I'd say you were once. I can tell."

"I've been a lot of things."

"What are you now?"

"A customer."

"I bet you're a private dick."

"I bet you're good at playing poker."

"Look, enjoy your drink. Red's has a reputation as a friendly place. A man can meet old friends, be introduced to new ones, and not worry about being harassed or bothered. My job is to keep it that way. So no prying. No interrogations."

"It's all right, Terry." The voice came from behind Dunne. "He's an old friend." A hand rested on his shoulder. "Give me the usual, only make it a double."

"Your usual *is* a double, TR."

Dunne didn't recognize the voice, didn't detect a trace of the upper-crust Hudson Valley accent it once had. Yet he was certain who'd spoken. Turning around, he thought he'd been mistaken. For an instant, he didn't recognize the wasted, hollow face, white hair atop—not gray, white as cotton. "Been a while, Dick."

"Come on, join me over here. Terry will bring our drinks."

Dunne followed him to a booth. The bartender delivered their drinks.

"Put them on my tab, Terry."

"Will do, TR."

"Sounds like you've got yourself a new handle."

"I ditched Richard, tossed Thornton, and vanquished Van. I'm TR Hull now."

"I guess that's why I couldn't find you in the phone book."

"It's more likely you couldn't find me because I don't have a phone. Here's to what?" Van Hull held up a highball glass, no ice, half filled with rye. "What's worth toasting these days, besides marshmallows?"

Dunne tapped glasses. Slight as it was, the sliding consonant in that last word—"mar*shhh*mallows"—gave away the jump Van Hull got on cocktail hour. "Here's to us."

"I'll drink to that!" Van Hull emptied half the glass in a single swallow. He shook his finger, reprovingly. "Look at you, Fin. You've hardly aged at all. You look as fit as the last time I saw you."

"The last time you saw me I was in the hospital."

"You know what I mean. Most of us have gone to seed since we left the service, but you—you're still trim, hardly a gray hair." He finished his drink and called over to the bar: "Terry-o, give us another round!"

Dunne waved his hand. "Not for me. I'm still working on this." He crushed his cigarette in the ashtray.

A steady tide of quietly stylish men in business suits—mix of young and middle-aged—filled the room. The bartender dimmed the lights. He went over to the jukebox and raised the volume a notch or two as Judy Garland sang "The Man That Got Away."

The bartender delivered a fresh drink. Van Hull twisted the glass in his hands. "You'd think I'd be shocked out of my pajamas to see you after all these years—and in Red's, no less—but I'm not. I've thought about you a lot. Pully often brought up your name. He said you were in New York a good part of the year."

"You hadn't changed your name, I'd have found you a lot sooner."

"What I always admired about you, Fin, was your honesty. For a minute I was afraid you were going to lie and say how good I look. In that case, I'd have thrown my drink in your face and told you to get out." Van Hull gazed into his glass, raised it, and took a long, slow draft.

"You're the one said we were a 'sad-ass version of the Bobbsey Twins.' Which was I, Rack or Ruin?"

"I don't remember." Van Hull smiled. "How'd you know where to find me?"

"Guess."

"Bassante?"

"None other. Our den mother from Bari."

"Poor Turlough, with that labyrinthine brain of his. It'd be funny he got labeled a Red if the outcome hadn't been so hard on him. Pully said Bassante had 'the most independent intellect' of anyone he'd ever met. I thought I'd see him at Pully's memorial service, but he was nowhere in sight. Thought I might see you there, too."

"My wife and I were in Havana."

"He was a sad man."

The bartender lowered the lights. A woman entered. She strolled passed Dunne to the far corner of the bar. Her face called to mind one of those "Mad Mugs/Silly Faces" fun books found at newsstands next to comics and puzzle digests: four horizontal slips each with a quarter of a face—hair and forehead, eyes and eyebrows, nose and lips, chin and neck—that could be combined and recombined to form mugs of all shapes and sizes, lovely, ugly, absurd. Except for the bottom quarter of her face, a chin more square than oval, the other three-quarters gave her an uncanny resemblance to Joan Crawford. None of the other patrons took notice.

"To be honest," Van Hull said, "I wasn't entirely surprised he took his own life."

Dunne focused his attention back on Van Hull. "Why?"

"Look around. You know what type of man hangs out here?"

"Yes."

"And it doesn't bother you?"

"Live and let live. It's a pretty simple proposition."

"Not really. Not for Pully. Not for all those threatened with public exposure, disgrace, blackmail, jail. Pully married once, briefly and unhappily. He went back and forth. I told him it happens. That's the way it is for some people. It just is. We are what we are. Accept it and get on with your life. He couldn't. He was tortured. Believe me, he has a lot of company."

"He ever talk business?"

"He didn't mix business with pleasure, so to speak. He knew if word got out, his career was kaput." Van Hull finished his drink and called to the bartender for another, which was promptly delivered.

"He mention anything about a Swiss couple?"

"In what context?"

"An investigation he was conducting."

"Why would he?"

"He trusted you."

"We trusted each other with the troubles of the heart. He never brought up that ISC crap and, well, I didn't bring up my job. Not that there's much to bring up."

Dunne caught the bartender's eye. He signaled for a check.

"Aren't you going to ask me what I do?"

"Not if you don't want me to."

"I teach English at St. Genevieve's, an all-girls academy run by French Ursulines. The girls' parents imagine the Gallic touch will help ease their daughters' entry into 'society.' I'm a kind of one-man English department. The head nun is thrilled to have a male teacher uninterested in seducing her charges. She leaves me alone in my quixotic quest to arouse the slumbering minds of my pubescent beauties to ecstatic enjoyment of Yeats and Frost and William Carlos Williams."

Dunne looked at his watch. "I just wanted to stop by and say hello. See how you were doing. Pully's death stirred a lot of memories."

"Death usually does."

The bartender came over and placed the tab facedown on the table.

Van Hull poised his almost-empty glass in the air. "A final toast before we go: *L'chaim.* Remember?"

"Dr. Niskolczi. Long ago and far away."

They clinked glasses. Dunne grabbed the check, hurried to the bar, and slapped a five-dollar bill on top. "Keep the change."

"Come back soon." The bartender extended his hand to Dunne. "Next time, I'll know who you are. Friends of TR's are always welcome at Red's."

"This should be my treat." Van Hull stood up, swayed, took hold of the back of the booth, and steadied himself.

"Next time."

"Let's not wait thirteen years." Van Hull tottered toward the door, taking the small, careful steps of a child learning to walk. Several men called out, "Good night, TR." He gave a generic wave.

Dunne held the door open. From the jukebox came Billie Holiday singing "God Bless the Child." The Joan Crawford lookalike dashed past, oblivious to Dunne.

"I noticed her earlier," Dunne said.

Van Hull laughed. "You mean *him.*"

"Him?"

"Michael Arlington Beresford, Wall Street banker, philanthropist, chairman of the mayor's Committee on Municipal Finances.

That's during the day. On nights like this, Mildred Pierce comes into Red's for some Dutch courage before heading off to join the other female impersonators at the Backstage Club on Charles Street."

Dunne stepped into the street. "I'll get you a cab."

"No need. I'm only a block away." Van Hull held on to a fire-alarm box. He twisted his head and gazed up at the neon sign. "Red's isn't long for this world. But none of us is. We learned that the hard way, Fin, didn't we—the *real* final lesson of war?"

"If you're not going to take a cab, I'll walk with you."

Van Hull stayed propped against the stout red alarm box. Instead of helping clear his head, the night air, humid and close, seemed to aggravate the effect of the booze. "Michael and I spent our last hours together right here. I'd received my orders. I took a cab from here to Penn Station. 'Life's handed us a rain check,' Michael said, 'that's all.' Trouble is, when the time came to use the check, *après le deluge*, the rain had washed him away."

"Come on, Dick. I'll see you home."

"And Pully—he was a good man, too."

Dunne gently peeled Van Hull from the alarm box.

He held Dunne's elbow for support. "I hope you're not spotted escorting a faggot home—and one who's blotto as well. Couldn't be good for a career at IBM."

"It's ISC."

"A weed by any other name is just as rank."

"It's nothing next to humping a buddy on your back up a cliff and bringing him home alive across several hundred miles of enemy territory."

Van Hull's apartment was on the fourth floor of a five-story walk-up. The marble steps were worn and veined with cracks. Dunne fished the key out of Van Hull's pants pocket, turned the lock, flicked on the light switch.

In the middle of the single room, atop a thin, worn rug, was a leather easy chair, a stack of books beside it, standing lamp behind. Two walls were lined with shelves sagging from the weight of the books crammed in them. In the right far corner was a sink, small refrigerator, cabinet, and two-burner stove; next to the single window, bed, unmade, and small desk. Above was a framed oil painting of a handsome, youthful, blond wavy-haired man. There were lieutenant's bars on the lapels of his uniform.

Shuffling his feet as he worked to keep his balance, Van Hull saluted the painting. "There was only one Lieutenant Michael Jahn in the whole world. *Only one.* That's the problem." He staggered toward the cabinet. "How about a nightcap?"

Dunne caught him before he fell. He guided him into the easy chair. "The night's already capped."

"That's why I quit and went home, Fin. Because of Michael. I didn't care about my reputation and less about my old man's. When he heard what I might be accused of, he sent a letter advising the honorable thing to do was to shoot myself. Nothing like a father's love, is there? What I cared about was Michael. I couldn't let them sink Michael's name in the slime and mire, so I resigned."

"How about you get into bed?"

"You know what George Orwell said about drunks like me?"

"What?"

"We drink because we failed and fail all the more because we drink."

"You didn't fail."

"You're kind, Fin. But look around. Your kindness is contradicted by these surroundings. I can't imagine what my father would say about them—and what they say about me."

"Come on, Dick. Bedtime."

"This is fine." Van Hull wiggled out of his jacket, unknotted his tie, leaned over and plucked at his shoelaces. "But at least I don't deny my failure or pretend my failure is success."

"Sit up," Dunne said. "Raise your legs." He quickly undid the laces and pulled off the shoes.

The rising banshee shriek of a siren flooded the room. It peaked and receded as a fire engine surged through the street below.

"That's the difference between Bartlett and his ilk and drunks like me. At bottom the Bartletts of this world are nothing more than word whores. They take fine phrases like 'free world' and 'liberty loving' and prostitute them into excuses for self-promotion. Whatever they touch they corrupt because truth to them is fungible, interchangeable with untruth, so long as it serves their purposes." Van Hull burped.

"You need to go to sleep."

"I need Pepto-Bismol. The bottle is in the medicine cabinet in the bathroom, if you wouldn't mind fetching it."

"Sure. Then lights out."

Dunne switched on the light in the closet-size bathroom. A roach scampered into a crack above the tub. He opened the cabinet and removed the pink Pepto-Bismol bottle. A metal vial was tucked into the corner. He unscrewed it. Inside was a plastic-coated lozenge. *Ecce Victor.* He dropped it into his pocket.

He went to the kitchen sink, rinsed out a glass, and half filled it with water. He delivered it along with the bottle and a tablespoon to Van Hull.

"No need for the spoon. I take my Pepto straight." Van Hull held up the bottle as if to toast the portrait in the corner. "I wouldn't have that portrait if it wasn't for you." He swigged from the bottle, then took a drink of water. "You saved the photo I had it painted from. Do you remember?"

"Sure." Dunne put the glass in the sink.

"And the inscription?"

"Yeats, right?"

"Your favorite poet." Van Hull wiped the pink traces of the Pepto-Bismol from his lips. He picked up the top book on the pile beside the chair. "*The Collected Poems.* Here, they're yours."

"That's all right. I'm still working on *The Oxford Book of Modern Verse*."

"Take it." Van Hull handed him the book. "Do you know how it ends?"

"The book?"

"The poem—'When You Are Old and Grey.'"

"No."

"Like this." Van Hull closed his eyes. "'And bending down beside the glowing bars, / Murmur, a little sadly, how Love fled / And paced upon the mountains overhead / And hid his face amid a crowd of stars.'"

"A lovely poem." Dunne took the sheet off the bed and draped it over Van Hull's stomach and legs. "Now get some sleep."

"And Pully was a good man, too." Opening his eyes halfway, Van Hull lifted up another book. "He sent me this."

"When?"

"It arrived the day after he died."

"Let me see."

"It's a Luther Bible, in German, a 1932 edition, the year before Hitler came to power." He handed the Bible to Dunne. "An odd choice—it's the thought that counts, I suppose—but Pully was an odd man. Eccentric, I mean. Odd in a good way. That was the problem with the OSS and what followed. The eccentrics were replaced by fanatics."

Dunne leafed through and stopped where a paper match bookmarked a page. There were pencil marks amid the lines. "Can I borrow this?"

"Be my guest. I haven't much interest in Holy Writ, particularly when it's in German." Van Hull's eyelids rolled down. He mumbled, "Some world we live in. Hunt queers, hide Nazis. Persecute lovers, protect murderers. A shit world, you ask me." His mouth fell open. He began to snore.

Dunne's eyes swept the room a final time. Lieutenant Michael

253

Jahn stared out from his portrait, lips parted as in the photo, as if about to speak, or sing, or ask a question:

What do you see, Fin?

A tired man who's had too much to drink.

It's become a habit, don't you think?

A bad habit, but it happens to good people all the time.

Do you think he's sick?

He's sick in his soul from missing you.

He's queer for sure, I know.

I know something else for sure.

What's that?

The queer heart beats the same as any other heart, loves the same, and breaks the same.

Dunne turned off the light. He slipped the volume of Yeats's *Collected Poems* and the German Bible beneath his arm and pulled the door shut.

Part VII
Thus Saith the Lord

Thus saith the Lord God unto these bones; Behold, I will cause breath to enter into you, and ye shall live:

And I will lay sinews upon you, and will bring up flesh upon you, and cover you with skin, and put breath in you, and ye shall live; and ye shall know that I am the Lord.

So I prophesied as I was commanded: and as I prophesied, there was a noise, and behold a shaking, and the bones came together, bone to his bone.

And when I beheld, lo, the sinews and the flesh came up upon them, and the skin covered them above: but there was no breath in them.

Then said he unto me, Prophesy unto the wind, prophesy, son of man, and say to the wind, Thus saith the Lord God; Come from the four winds, O breath, and breathe upon these slain, that they may live.

So I prophesied as he commanded me, and the breath came into them, and they lived, and stood up upon their feet, an exceeding great army.

Then he said unto me, Son of man, these bones are the whole house of Israel: behold, they say, Our bones are dried, and our hope is lost: we are cut off for our parts.

Therefore prophesy and say unto them, Thus saith the Lord God; Behold, O my people, I will open your graves, and cause you to come up out of your graves, and bring you into the land of Israel.

And ye shall know that I am the Lord, when I have opened your graves, O my people, and brought you up out of your graves . . .

The Book of Ezekiel

August 1958

Miss O'Keefe opened the door and entered Dunne's office. Hand to mouth, she muffled a yelp. "You startled me. I had no idea you were here."

Dunne looked up from the book that lay open on his desk. "I got in early."

"I see." She checked her wristwatch. "It's only eight thirty. Can I get you coffee?"

"I'm set." He nodded at the paper cup by his elbow.

"You saw the messages on your desk?" She raised the eyeglasses strung around her neck and put them on.

"Yes." He gulped lukewarm coffee.

"Mr. Billings called several times."

"I'll get back to him today."

"The last time it was Billings himself, not his assistant. He sounded annoyed."

Dunne went back to reading the book. "Can you get me a Bible?"

"A Bible?"

"There must be one somewhere in the office."

"Why on earth do you want a Bible?"

"I want to see how this translates into English."

"What translates?"

He pushed the book to the left side of the desk. "Have a look."

She came around the desk and leaned over. "It's in German."

"I know."

"I minored in German."

"Can you read it?"

"I can try. I was good at it."

Dunne got out of the chair. "Here, have a seat."

Perched on the front edge of the chair, she pressed the corners of her glasses between thumb and middle finger. She flipped back and forth through the pages. "It's Hesekiel—Ezekiel in English."

Dunne placed his finger on a verse bracketed by pencil marks. "Read here: Chapter thirty-seven, verse twelve."

Miss O'Keefe made a nervous adjustment to her glasses. "Some of these letters are underlined. Why?"

"I've no idea."

He watched over her shoulder as she read aloud, slowly: "*Darum weissage und sprich zu ihnen: So spricht der Herr.*" She cleared her throat. "'Therefore predict and speak to them, thus says the Lord.' . . . *Siehe, ich will eure Gräben auftun und will euch, mein Volk.* . . . 'Behold, my people I will open your . . .' *Gräben* . . . 'your graves . . .'"

She stopped and looked up. "What's with these underscored letters?"

"Go on translating. You're doing great."

"Where was I? Okay, here we are." She placed her finger on the text. ". . . *aus demselben herausholen* . . . 'and make you' . . . *herausholen* . . . 'get out— make you *leave* them' . . . *und euch ins Land Israel bringen* . . . 'and bring you into the land of Israel.'"

"I remember more than I thought I would." She removed her glasses and let them hang around her neck. "Amazing, don't you think, in light of the Jews' return to Israel?"

She ran her finger across the verse and stopped at the underscored letters. "But these—these underlined letters—do they mean something?"

"They must."

"What?"

"What's your guess?"

"You're the detective."

"I've no clue."

"Well, let's see if they spell something." She put her glasses back on, took a pencil, and printed the letters on the pad next to the phone: "*B-A-I-E-E-A-G*. No German word I'm familiar with."

"Could it be a word jumble? Maybe in English."

Miss O'Keefe printed *BEG A*. She shrugged. "That uses four letters but leaves *A-I-E*."

Dunne took the pencil and printed *BEIGE*.

"Nice try. But what do you do with *A-A*?"

"I'm sure the answer is staring us in the face. He wouldn't have made it impossible to decipher."

"Who's 'he'?"

"It's a long story."

"I don't see we're going to get anywhere with this unless . . ." She tapped the pad with the eraser.

"Unless what?"

"Unless it's among the oldest tricks in the code maker's book. We used it in the Girl Scouts." She printed the alphabet across the top of the page. "You substitute numbers for letters. *A* is 1, *B* is 2, and so on, right up to *Z*, 26." She wrote numbers beneath each letter. "Thus, 'LOVE' becomes 12, 15, 22, 5. Or we can do it the other way around, in which case 'BAIEEAG' becomes 2, 1, 9, 5, 5, 1, 7."

"A combination to a safe?"

She shook her head, touched each numeral with the pencil tip. "Seven numbers."

"So what?"

"What has seven numbers? Something we use every day."

"I'm no good at riddles."

She tapped the telephone with the eraser and rested it on the number printed in the middle of the dial. "Your number is SH-3-5264."

"You think 2, 1, 9, 5, 5, 1, 7 is a phone number?"

"Do you have a better idea?"

"Not really."

"Then let's give it a try. Start with the first two letters: B, 2; A, 1. That could be the exchange—BAltic, maybe—and go with the next five numbers: 95517. That gives us BA-9-5517."

"You're guessing."

"Only one way to be certain." She handed him the receiver and turned the dial seven times with the eraser end of the pencil.

"It's ringing." He put his hand over the speaker. "What should I say?"

"Try 'Hello.'"

Someone picked up. Dunne took his hand away. "Yes, hello."

He heard soft breathing on the other end. "Hello," he said again.

"Who is it you wish to speak with?" The voice was just above a whisper.

He pressed the receiver to his ear. "Ezekiel." Silence. He counted the seconds . . . eight . . . nine . . . "Hello? You still there?"

"Who is this?" The voice was so faint it was barely audible.

"A friend of Louis Pohl's."

He counted to six. The voice was distinct this time: "Louis Pohl is dead."

"He left me this number."

"And you waited all this time?" Feminine voice, a slight accent.

"He wanted it this way."

"What's your name?"

"Fintan Dunne."

"Where are you calling from?"

"My office."

"What's the number?"

He gave it to her. "Can we meet?"

"I'll call you back."

"When?"

"Shortly." She hung up.

He recradled the receiver.

Miss O'Keefe folded her arms. "Well?"

"You missed your calling. If you were head of U.S. cryptography operations, we'd have broken all the Russian codes by now. I'm going to see that you get a raise."

"Thanks. How about doing me another favor?"

"Shoot."

"Call Mr. Billings."

"Sure," Dunne said. "Right after the party I was just on with calls back."

"It could be hours."

"In that case, call the phone company. Get a name and address for BA-9-5517."

Miss O'Keefe stalked out of the room.

The phone rang. He snatched the receiver. "Hello."

"Is this Fintan Dunne?" It was the same voice from before.

"It is."

"Mr. Dunne, we spoke a moment ago."

"Sure."

"My name is Frieda. Frieda Schwimmer. Do you remember?"

Why remember one thing and not another? Van Hull and he work the cast-iron seesaw bolted to the floor, up and down, heigh-ho, it's off to Bratislava we go, green-eyed girl holds red-and-white kerchief above her head, ballerina-like, moves it up and down.

"In Slovakia."

Long ago and far away.
"With Doctor Niskolczi."
Oh dem bones.
"Yes, Frieda, I remember."

Noon at the seal pool in the Bronx Zoo: time and place Frieda Schwimmer stipulated on the phone. (The exchange turned out to be BAinbridge, not BAltic. Miss O'Keefe traced the number to an address on Marion Avenue, off Fordham Road.) Though the crowd at the seal pool wasn't as large as on weekends, feeding time always drew an audience.

The trainer appeared with a pail of pungent-smelling fish. The seals clapped, waddled, dived, barked, whatever it took to get fed. The audience (mostly kids and their mothers) cheered and laughed.

Except for the assertive way she stated where and when they should meet, Frieda spoke haltingly. But she was glad he had called. "We," she said—not "I" but "we"—"didn't know who to contact after Mr. Pohl left." She made it sound as if he'd taken a trip.

Dunne strolled the periphery of the crowd. Frieda hadn't said anything about what she'd be wearing. He didn't imagine he'd recognize her face. There was a better chance she'd recognize him. What he remembered most about her were her green eyes.

The one woman he picked out as a likely candidate had two small children in tow. He smiled and said hello. She smiled back. She had blue eyes.

Feeding time ended. The audience drifted away. He checked his watch: 12:45. He'd wait another fifteen minutes, then look for a phone booth. Maybe she got the time wrong. He recalled that tentative note in her voice. Maybe she was afraid of some sort of trap. Her address wasn't far away. If he couldn't reach her by phone, he'd pay a visit. He pulled a folded copy of the *Standard* from his jacket pocket and read.

A man who looked to be in his late thirties, early forties sat on the other end of the bench. Navy-blue suit. Gray hat. Black wing tips, highly polished. Crisp crease in his pants. Not the type to make a special trip to see seals being fed.

The odor of dead fish lingered in the air.

"Looks like feeding time is over." He stretched an arm across the back of the bench.

"Lions and tigers are next."

"I prefer the reptiles. They seem closest to humans." The man had an indifferent smile, hazel eyes. "I'm Stefan Schwimmer, Mr. Dunne. Frieda's brother. I apologize for being late. The bus was delayed. There were no cabs."

Dunne put down the paper. He was sure Stefan—if that was his real name—had been in the vicinity the whole time, observing him to make sure he was alone. "She never mentioned a brother."

"It never came up. I was in the room when you called."

"Where is she?"

"Home."

"I'll stop by and say hello."

"That wouldn't be wise."

"Let her decide."

"She's not well."

"If it's not contagious, it's not a problem."

"It's more emotional than physical. She's never completely recovered."

"She recovered enough to make an appointment to meet me."

"I don't blame you for being skeptical." Stefan Schwimmer got up from the bench. "Please, walk with me. I'll explain best I can. If you think I'm not telling the truth or you want no part of it, you're free to walk away. I understand."

"I don't have all day." Dunne tucked the paper back in his pocket.

"Neither do I."

They stood in front of the Lion House. Schwimmer took a cigarette from a silver case. He offered one to Dunne, lit both with a silver lighter.

Feeding time was imminent. The roars and snarls of the big cats reverberated across the courtyard.

"I'll try to make this concise." Schwimmer walked with his head down. "I'm the oldest of four children, thirteen years older than Frieda, the youngest. Our father was a piano manufacturer in Budapest. The business had been in the family for several generations. He thought I'd follow in his footsteps, but I took a different path. I graduated from university as a chemical engineer. That year, once again against my father's wishes, I joined the International Brigade in Paris and went to Spain to fight the Fascists.

"I was wounded. But I didn't return home. Few of us did. Admiral Horthy's regime made it clear we weren't welcome. I went to Prague and found work. Soon enough the Germans came to Prague. I fled to England. When the war broke out, I served with the RAF's Czechoslovak Squadron as a bombardier.

"At war's end, I returned to Budapest. Strangers lived in our house. They said they knew nothing of my family. The family business had been expropriated by the Nazis and then seized by the Communists. I soon learned that my parents and three siblings had all been deported to Auschwitz. Although I was told in so many words that it was a waste of time to look for them, I set out in search of any survivors.

"After several months, I located Frieda—the only survivor from my family—weak and emaciated, in a displaced persons camp in the British zone in occupied Germany. The wounds to her body gradually healed. Her soul continues to bleed. Once she was a master cellist. People spoke of the great career she had in front of her. Now she has no interest."

Schwimmer tossed his cigarette on the asphalt path and crushed it with his heel. "I was hired by a Swiss chemical company and sent to head up their offices in Toronto. I tried to limit my traveling. Frieda hates to be alone. Despite my reluctance, since I was fluent in English, German, and Spanish, the company had me on the road a good deal.

"About two years ago, in the lounge of the Alvear Hotel in Buenos Aires, a garrulous gentleman sat next to me. He introduced himself as Hans Bleier, proprietor of a photography supply business. When he heard my name, he asked if I was related to 'the piano people.' I said yes, but we were Jews and the company had been taken by the Nazis.

"Bleier drew close. It was obvious he didn't want to be overheard. He said he was half-Jewish and had left Germany for Buenos Aires the year Hitler came to power. 'I smelled disaster,' he said, 'from the very first time I heard that Austrian shit speak. Some of my Jewish friends and relatives stayed. They were convinced Hitler would soon fail and Germans would come to their senses. They paid for that mistake with their lives.'

"He didn't bother mentioning this to the other German émigrés with whom he sometimes spent a social evening dining and drinking. Their numbers had exploded after the war, and though his presence was tolerated, his lack of military experience and absence from Germany during the existence of the Third Reich meant he was treated by most with a certain degree of distance, if not distrust.

"One evening, after a good deal to drink, a tablemate mentioned the name of Oscar Hemmer. The word was Hemmer was returning to West Germany. Well in his cups, the man went on about that 'stuck-up little ass-wipe *der Blaue Engel*,' who never deigned to share a drink with his fellow exiles: 'He's lucky he isn't going back to be hanged. But I guess they can't hang Hemmer since Heinz is already dead.'

"There were a few snickers. The topic was changed. Bleier didn't ask any questions. The next day, he undertook his own quiet inquiry into who Oscar Hemmer was and what relation he had to 'der Blaue Engel' and 'Heinz.' It didn't take long to find out the story of SS-Hauptsturmführer Dr. Karsten Heinz, who'd worked at Auschwitz and died of natural causes while being interrogated in London in 1946. But what to make of the remark 'they can't hang Hemmer since Heinz is already dead'?

"Bleier had no success in making an appointment under some business pretext to meet Hemmer face-to-face. When he learned Hemmer had put his villa up for sale in preparation for his return to Europe, he pretended he was interested in buying it. The house was in the process of being emptied of its contents when he visited. He managed to make an impression of the key used by the real estate agent who showed him around."

The day was warm. Dunne had started to perspire. "Let's sit." He indicated a shaded bench directly ahead. The Reptile House was directly behind them. Schwimmer reopened his cigarette case and offered another to Dunne, who declined. Schwimmer took one for himself, pounded the tip on silver cover, and lit it.

"Bleier returned that night and had a look around. Most of the furnishings had been removed. He opened the drawer of a battered desk left behind. There were scraps stuck in the back that looked to be pieces of a torn-up photo. He slipped them in his pocket.

"When he got home, though a few pieces were missing, he was able to reconstruct a photo of five German officers in a wooded glade. On their collars were the distinctive SS runes. The one in the middle, who appeared to be in charge, was laughing. On the back, in faded ink, was printed: AUSCHWITZ, APRIL 1944.

"Bleier called the real estate agent and made a large bid for the villa—so large he was able to wrangle a short meeting with Hemmer. He attached enough conditions to the bid to guarantee it would be rejected. Yet, seeing Hemmer, Bleier was convinced he was the same person as the laughing SS officer in the photograph.

He wrote a letter to the Mossad and included a touched-up copy of the photo, one of several he made.

"Months went by before Bleier got a letter back, short—far from sweet—thanking him for the information he'd sent and reminding him that the service's current priorities centered on the threats posed by Israel's hostile neighbors.

"The Mossad stated it had neither the time nor the resources to track down every sighting of alleged war criminals. Hitler's secretary, Martin Bormann, for example, had been sighted in South Africa, Argentina, and Saudi Arabia—all in the same week. They had no record of an SS officer named Oscar Hemmer. Karsten Heinz was already dead.

"In the future, Bleier was advised, all inquiries, information and/or photos should be sent directly to the West German BND, which had formal responsibility for apprehending and prosecuting alleged war criminals.

"Hemmer, as far as Bleier knew, had gone home and opened an import-export firm specializing in chemical fertilizers. Whatever the truth about Hemmer, the war was over. Nobody seemed interested in revisiting the particulars of what had taken place. Bleier gave me his copy of the photo. 'I don't need any souvenirs of those bastards,' he said.

"I stuck it in my suitcase and forgot about it. One morning, several months later, I heard Frieda screaming. I ran to her. She was yelling over and over, '*Heinz, der Blaue Teufel! Der Blaue Teufel!*' Before her on the table was the picture Bleier had given me. Frieda had gone to use the suitcase and had found it.

"I had no idea she'd had any personal acquaintance with Heinz at Auschwitz. I never questioned her about her experiences. I decided to do some investigating of my own. I traveled to Hamburg. Oscar Hemmer was indeed in the import-export business. Yet he rarely came to his firm's offices. I found his home address. It was a substantial house on the outskirts of the city surrounded by a high wall. It was clear that the chauffeur who drove him around also acted as a bodyguard.

"I contacted the BND and made a formal inquiry about SS-Hauptsturmführer Dr. Karsten Heinz. The officials with whom I spoke seemed nonplussed by my interest. The file they had on him was thin. I was told that British intelligence in London, where Heinz died, probably held the bulk of the records.

"In Bonn, I asked to speak with someone at the American embassy about a possible war criminal. Nobody seemed to know what to make of my request. After I persisted, an official from the 'special interest section' came to speak with me. I presume he was CIA. He told me to consult with the West German government. I said I had.

"There was really nothing he could do, he said. The primary war criminals had been dealt with at Nuremberg. If I was serious about pursuing the issue further, I should contact Louis Pohl, who worked with a consulting firm in New York and still seemed interested in the subject: 'An old colleague—nice guy—he's off the wall on this one, like those paranoid types on the lookout for UFOs.'

"I stayed a while in Bonn. I met a former colleague of mine from the Czech Squadron. He'd defected from the People's Republic of Czechoslovakia. He'd been attached to the Warsaw Pact intelligence office in East Berlin. I told him about my interest in Hemmer. He said that the Soviets were convinced that the CIA had set up a special section within the BND to keep an eye on Gehlen and hunt for moles.

"Rumor had it, he said, that the unit was run by an ex-SS officer who reported directly to Washington. So far, even the ex-SS agents the Soviets had recruited and slipped into the BND had been unable either to confirm the rumor or penetrate the unit.

"I tracked down Pohl and discovered he was with ISC in New York. Not wishing to get entangled with a devotee of UFOs, I approached him cautiously. I represented myself as the owner of a

Swiss medical supply business interested in entering the American market and endured an hour of his generalities and banalities.

"I had Frieda stay with an aunt of ours in the Bronx. I met with Pohl at the Savoy Plaza and told him that I'd heard of his work in keeping track of Nazi war criminals. He was put off at first. He was there, he said, to discuss my interest in protecting my firm's patents and pursuing opportunities in the American market, not hunting for Nazis.

"I revealed we were Hungarian Jews and that, except for my sister, my family had been wiped out at Auschwitz. I told him about my pursuit of Hemmer/Heinz. He remembered hearing about Heinz's interrogation in London and his death. It was quickly apparent he was no deluded pursuer of UFOs. He understood what I was talking about.

"He added more details to what I already knew about Heinz's stint in Mauthausen. He mentioned your name and someone named Van Hull. I recall that because I wrote your names down in the notes I took. I showed him the dossier I'd compiled.

"That night, I read Frieda the notes I'd taken in my discussion with Pohl. When she heard your name and that of Van Hull, she was sure you were the Americans she'd encountered in Slovakia."

Schwimmer finished his cigarette. They resumed walking. Dunne bought two orangeades and a bag of peanuts at a refreshment stand. Schwimmer peeled back the tin-foil cap and took a long drink. "We met again the next day. Pohl filled me in about Carlton Bartlett at the CIA. He told me he intended to confront Bartlett with Heinz's existence. I thought perhaps he was having sport with me. 'You can't be serious,' I said.

"'What other course is there?' he answered.

"'That's the reason my sister and I sought you out.' I said. 'The intelligence I've gathered on Hemmer/Heinz is convincing. But we must make it airtight. When we have, we'll go to the proper authorities.'

"Pohl grew angry. '*The proper authorities!* By the time you get the BND to pay attention, which in itself is doubtful, Bartlett will have resubmerged Heinz so deep Captain Nemo couldn't find him. You couldn't get the Mossad interested in pursuing the case. What do you think it will take to get the BND off its rear?'

"'What if we took Heinz into custody ourselves,' I said, 'and held him until the authorities were ready to act?'

"'Kidnap him?' Pohl said. 'And hold him for ten years? Where? Under what authority?' He accused me of not having thought the whole matter through. Heinz had a bodyguard—probably several charged with making sure he wasn't snatched.

"I understood what he was saying. I was frustrated as well. 'We should kill him then. Assassinate him and be done with it.'

"'That's the worst course of all,' Pohl said. 'This isn't about bringing one criminal, however monstrous, to justice. Think about it: When the Jews of Hungary were deported to Auschwitz, they were murdered up to three thousand per gassing. By my tally, about five thousand people have been formally convicted of war crimes and under a thousand—a relative handful—condemned to death, and five hundred or so actually executed. That's the equivalent of a sixth of the men, women, and children slaughtered in the space of twenty minutes and incinerated in the crematoria.

"'When it comes to the larger picture—the mass shootings carried out by the Einsatzgruppen, the gassings at the other *vernichtungslager*—Treblinka, Belzec, Sobibor—the *konzentrationslager* network and its slaves, the millions of Russian prisoners starved to death, the untold numbers of civilians murdered in Poland, the Ukraine, Belarus—what will the killing of Karsten Heinz do to bring some measure of justice to those victims?'

"I suspected Pohl was right. Still, I was confused. How, I asked, would confronting Bartlett make any difference?

"Bartlett and his associates, he said, would have to face that they'd no choice but to own up to an epic miscarriage of justice and begin dismantling the framework of deceit and denial that stood in contradiction to the very values they claimed to be defending.

"'This is about more than retribution for a single criminal,' Pohl insisted. 'Heinz is the key to unlocking the dirty secret of those who've been allowed to escape justice, who've reestablished lives of comfort and security behind reinvented identities and expurgated biographies, confident that the world no longer cares about their crimes, that history has moved on.

"'Bartlett must be made to see that the moment of truth has arrived. It can't be evaded any longer. He can either join the process or stand aside. But he can't stop it.'"

Schwimmer tossed the orangeade container in a trash can. "I continued to argue against going directly to Bartlett. I thought I'd convinced Pohl to wait at least a few days. I let him take the dossier. I thought we'd have time to deliberate the alternatives. Two days later, I read in the papers about his 'suicide.'"

"He had help getting out that window." Dunne shelled a peanut, flipped the contents in his mouth, and swigged the orangeade.

"I've no doubt. I was afraid for Frieda and myself. I was concerned Pohl might have mentioned us to Bartlett. But it didn't seem so. We were left alone. I tried to contact Van Hull but couldn't find a trace of him. I was told you were semiretired and spent most of the year in Florida. I worried about contacting anyone at all lest I draw attention. Then you called. How you got the number, I have no idea."

"From Pohl. He did a good job of hiding it. Almost too good." Dunne offered the bag of peanuts to Schwimmer.

Schwimmer broke a peanut shell with his teeth. "And the dossier on Heinz? Did he hide that, too?"

"Knowing Pohl, I'm sure he did."

"Too bad he didn't leave a clue where that might be."

"Maybe he thought we'd be smart enough to figure it out."

"It appears he was mistaken."

Dunne tossed the container of orangeade into the same over-flowing trash can Schwimmer had tossed his. "Maybe we're not paying attention where we should."

"Even if we could find the dossier, it won't be of use unless we can locate Heinz. By now Bartlett must have hidden him in some remote corner of South America."

"The confrontation with Pohl has to have rattled Bartlett. He's got to figure Pohl had help. We've got to keep him rattled. Nervous men are prone to make mistakes."

"And to commit murder, it seems."

A directional post indicated that to the right were the polar bears, to the left, the Elephant House. "I think it's inhumane to take creatures from the Arctic and display them in a climate like this. Let's go this way." Schwimmer bore left.

At the entrance to the Elephant House was a large sign: PLEASE DO <u>NOT</u> FEED THE ANIMALS. Dunne put the peanut bag in his pocket. "For now, you resume your business travels. Go back to Hamburg. I'll see what I can stir up on this end."

They paused in front of a stall in which an elephant was munching hay. The smell of elephant dung was overpowering. Schwimmer held a handkerchief to his nose. "I'm grateful for your help, Mr. Dunne. I truly am. But this is hardly a plan."

"Call me Fintan, and you're right. This is an aspiration, not a plan. But maybe that's where all plans begin." Startled by a sudden tug on his pocket, Dunne swung around, half crouched, poised to throw or avoid a punch.

The elephant's trunk curled back inside the bars of the stall and whipped the peanut bag in its mouth.

Someone was paying attention where he should.

GRAYBAR BUILDING, MANHATTAN

AFTER HE LEFT SCHWIMMER, DUNNE TREKKED WEST, ACROSS FORDHAM Road, to Jerome Avenue. He rode the IRT to Grand Central and stopped at his office. Miss O'Keefe was at lunch. He sat at his desk. Pohl was a loner. He didn't socialize much, but he'd trusted Bassante and Van Hull. Who else did he trust? Dunne opened the top desk drawer and shuffled through the papers until he found the note he'd received from Pohl's mother. He put it in his pocket.

He took a cab to Penn Station. He descended onto the capacious main concourse, with its vaulted, steel-trussed glass ceiling. He turned left, past the shoe-shine stand. It was manned by the same handsome Negro who'd been there since the war and was known as much for the glossy shine he delivered as for the flair he delivered it with, tossing the brush in the air, spinning around, and catching it before it hit the floor.

Dunne went downstairs and bought a ticket to Forest Hills. Several times more expensive than the subway but three times as fast, the trip on the Long Island Rail Road took barely twenty minutes. He asked a ticket clerk about the return address on the envelope. The clerk said the location was an apartment building only a short walk from the station.

The faux-Tudor neighborhood was leafy and quiet. Absent rain, warm beer, rumpled clothes, wilted presence of a place worn down by war, it aped rather than replicated an English town. He stopped in a florist shop to buy a modest bouquet.

He entered the apartment building and examined the names on the brass mailboxes. "Mrs. G.M. Pohl" was in M4. He proceeded through a sunny main-floor lobby decorated with framed prints of English squires and ladies hunting, dancing, and feasting. M4 was two doors down the corridor on the left.

He pressed the button on the door frame. Nothing. He pressed again. The peephole opened. A gray eyebrow and a pupil the color of an olive pit rose into the round space.

"Mrs. Pohl?" Suddenly self-conscious about the bouquet he was carrying, he moved it behind his back.

"Yes, what can I do for you?"

"My name is Fintan Dunne. I was a friend of your son's."

The eye sank away for an instant, returned. "My son?"

"Yes, Louis."

"He's deceased."

"That's why I've come."

"Why?"

"Because I was out of town when he died and never got a chance to pay my respects in person." He held the bouquet in front of his chest.

"What did you say your name is?"

"Fintan Dunne."

"You sent me a note after Louis passed, didn't you?"

"Yes, I did." Dunne hesitated to invite himself in but feared their entire conversation would be conducted garden-wall style. "And you wrote back."

"Louis spoke highly of you." The door slowly opened. "Come in, please."

An old woman, tiny in stature and badly stooped, Mrs. Pohl steadied herself on a rubber-tipped cane, shuffling in mop-size slippers across rug-less floors. She must have had to stand tiptoe to see out the peephole. At the end of the hallway was a cluttered living room. Directly ahead was an artificial fireplace. On the mantel, amid a company of porcelain figurines of dancers and musicians, was a copper urn—the final resting place, Dunne presumed, of Louis Pohl's ashes.

He handed her the flowers.

"How sweet of you, Mr. Dunne. I must put them in water immediately." She went into the kitchen, slippers gliding noiselessly across the linoleum, and put water and the bouquet in a ceramic vase. "Would you join me for a cup of tea?"

He stood near the kitchen door. "I don't want to put you to any trouble."

"No trouble. I was about to make one for myself." She held

the kettle under the faucet, half filled it with water, and settled it atop a burner on the stove. "Louis was a wonderful boy."

"We met in the service."

She came out of the kitchen, put the vase on the dining table, and went over to a hutch. She picked up a thick album, laid it on the table. She sat and put on her glasses. He stood next to her. She turned the thick, cardboard pages with bent, arthritic fingers.

"This was Louis when he was a little boy, Mr. Dunne." She touched a gnarled finger to the faded photo of a chubby, thumb-sucking child propped up in a baby carriage. A petite woman in a flower-bedecked hat gripped the handlebars. In the background was a lawn dotted with picnickers. "My husband, George, took this in Prospect Park. 'Fresh air is the best medicine' was a favorite saying of his. We went to the park every Sunday in those days, rain or shine, no matter the season. George was like that. Everything regular and on schedule. That was the German in him."

She turned the pages slowly. Some of the photos had become unglued. She asked Dunne to fetch a small jar of glue on the hutch. She reattached the photos, delicately pressing them onto the pages. She talked continuously, an uninterrupted commentary on the life and career of her only child, a quiet, cooperative boy whose intellect and academic prowess was a source of great pride to his parents.

"Here's Louis when he graduated from high school. First in his class, with a scholarship to Columbia."

Short and broad, unsmiling face topped by a mortarboard, Louis stood between beaming mother, expressionless father.

The kettle began to whistle. "Stay where you are," Dunne said. "I'll get the tea."

"That's kind of you, Mr. Dunne. The tea bags are in the canister next to the sink. The cups and saucers are in the cabinet above. The sugar is here on the table. There's milk in the icebox. I prefer my tea plain."

"I do, too." He dropped the tea bags in the cups, poured in

the hot water. He opened the cabinet drawer between the refrigerator and stove and put spoons on the saucers. He used a tray he found in the dish rack to carry the cups to the table.

Mrs. Pohl was hunched over the album. She turned a page. Speaking in a voice so soft it was barely audible, she reminded Dunne of an old priest reading from the altar missal as he said Mass, a ritual that required no audience.

Dunne pulled up a chair and sat next to her. They sipped their tea. He retrieved two more albums from the hutch. She continued her narrative, pictures and words, the liturgy of Louis Pohl.

Next-to-last picture: unsmiling Louis standing in front of the Christmas tree in Rockefeller Center, his ancient mother leaning on his arm, her hat trimmed with fur instead of flowers. Last picture: high school student in cap and gown. "This is my nephew, the only son of my husband's brother. His name is Louis Pohl. He's in college at Brown. It brings me some comfort to know that my Louis's name is being carried on."

She closed the album. "My son was lonely, Mr. Dunne. I hoped he'd find the right girl, but he never did."

"He had friends, Mrs. Pohl. We all admired him."

"I'm afraid he was more comfortable with books than people. He could read when he was only three. Books were his lifelong companions."

"We all respected his learning."

"'Better to have love than learning.' That's a saying among us Copts." She removed her glasses. "But learning was what he had. The last thing he left me was a book. A book he loved. It was the day . . . the day . . . before he . . ." She shook her head.

"What book?"

"Do you like books, Mr. Dunne?"

"Some."

Resting her palms on the table, she pushed herself up. She took her cane, went into the bedroom, and returned with a book under her left arm. She hooked the cane over the chair and handed the book to Dunne. "I want you to have this."

"Are you sure?" It was an old book, leather-bound. The gold-lettered title engraved on the cover was in a Gothic script he couldn't decipher.

"It's an early edition of Goethe's *Die Leiden des jungen Werthers*. It was a favorite of Louis's. Do you read German, Mr. Dunne?"

"No, I don't."

"No matter. *The Sorrows of Young Werther* is the title in English. The important thing is that you have one of Louis's prized possessions. I'm sure he'd be pleased."

As he opened the cover, the stiff, brittle spine creaked softly. Tucked into the frontispiece was what looked like a red ticket stub. He shut the cover.

"I don't know why he took his own life. I've tried to understand. He was lonely but not unhappy. Can you understand that?"

"I can."

"There's a line in Goethe's book that's brought me some comfort. It's where he writes that it's just as silly to call a man a coward who dies by his own hand as it is to call a man a coward who dies from a malignant fever."

"Your son was no coward." He wrote his address and phone number in Florida on the back of his business card. "Let's stay in touch, Mrs. Pohl. I don't know if you travel much, but my wife and I would love to have you visit us in Florida."

"How tempting. More likely, it will be a phone call. I enjoy talking on the phone."

PENN STATION, MANHATTAN

DUNNE WAITED UNTIL HE WAS ON THE TRAIN BACK TO MANHATTAN to examine the red ticket stub. It turned out to be baggage-claim receipt, number 100936, issued by the Pennsylvania Railroad, Pennsylvania Station, New York City.

When the train reached Penn Station, the evening's flood tide of rush-hour commuters was ebbing away, giving the concourse the air of a beach just after a violent squall. He went upstairs to where he remembered the baggage checkroom was located.

A hot dog joint now occupied the space. A railroad porter came by pushing a dolly stacked with luggage. Dunne went over to him. "Where's baggage claim?"

The porter stopped. "Hasn't been here for a few years."

"Last time I was here it was."

"Lots of things aren't where they used to be."

"Where's it now?"

The porter removed his cap and ran his finger around the sweat-stained inner band. A thin, meticulously tended pencil mustache crossed his cocoa-colored face. "Used to be that everybody traveled everywhere by train, here to New Orleans, points west and south. More and more, it's the cheap-ticket crowd commuting next door to Jersey and Long Island." He nodded in the direction of a nearby staircase. "That's why they got hot dogs up here and baggage below."

The baggage room was at the end of a corridor that had a subway smell—sweat, urine, and stale gum. Dunne handed the ticket stub to a clerk in a frayed, soiled beige smock. The clerk held the ticket by both ends. He frowned. "Christ, this is a nine-oh."

"A what?"

"It's been here over ninety days. Going to cost you an extra, let's see"—he pulled the pen stuck behind his ear and did some quick calculations on a pad—"four dollars and seventy-five cents, which brings it to six bucks and fifteen cents."

"Fine." Dunne put a five and two singles on the counter. "Keep the change."

"Thanks." The clerk opened a receipt book.

"That's not necessary."

"Maybe not for you, but the railroad requires it."

"Excuse me, but I'm in a hurry."

A stylish, twentyish-looking woman behind Dunne held up a round blue traveling case. "I need to check this."

The clerk continued filling out the receipt. He detached it from the book and gave it to Dunne. "Have to wait your turn, Miss."

"I'm going to miss my train!"

"Everybody's got to wait his turn, no exceptions." The clerk sauntered down an aisle lined with metal shelves stuffed with suit-cases and bags.

"Oh God, you're hopeless!" the girl yelled at the empty counter and hurried away.

The clerk returned in a minute or so—less time than Dunne anticipated—with a brass-latched canvas satchel. "I appreciate your patience. Nobody wants to wait their turn no more. Not like the old days." He put the pen back behind his ear and lifted the satchel onto the counter. "Here you go."

"Thanks." Dunne unfastened the latch, took a glimpse inside. There was a thick manila folder. On the cover in block letters was a single name: *KARSTEN HEINZ*. He tossed in the book Mrs. Pohl had given him and closed the satchel.

He walked to the staircase, removed a ten-dollar bill from his wallet, and folded it in his hand. At the top of the stairs, he veered right and mounted one of the three empty chairs on the shoe-shine platform.

"How you this evening, sir?" The shoe-shine attendant wore a smock similar to the baggage clerk's, but his was clean and belted. "What will it be? Regular or deluxe?"

Dunne rested the canvas satchel in his lap. He slipped the ten-dollar bill into the attendant's breast pocket. "Super deluxe."

The attendant peeked into the pocket. "Man alive, super-duper deluxe it is!"

Dunne picked up a copy of the evening paper from the chair beside him, unfolded it, and pretended to read. "How long you been at this stand?"

"Since Adam met Eve." The attendant laid a thick layer of brown paste on Dunne's shoes and rubbed it in so hard it felt like a foot massage. The pomade in the attendant's black, marcelled hair glistened in the artificial light from above. "You're a worried man."

"Ever meet a man who wasn't?"

He looked Dunne in the eyes. "I met plenty wasn't as worried as you."

"Bet you know this room better than Adam knew the Garden of Eden."

"What got you worried?" The attendant picked up a brush and pushed it hard across the front and sides of Dunne's shoes.

"I'm not sure yet."

"Worst trouble of all is the trouble you don't know you got." He threw the brush from hand to hand, buffing the shoes all the while. "Cop trouble?"

"You know about cop trouble?"

The attendant paused his brushing. "Every colored person in this city knows about cop trouble. Don't have to look for it. Sooner or later, one way or other, it'll come your way. Think you got a tail?"

"What do you think?"

The attendant threw the brush in the air, swirled in a circle, caught it, and worked on Dunne's right shoe; he repeated the same routine on the left. "Every Eden got its snake." He removed a felt cloth from his belt, laid it across the toe caps, pulled down on the ends. "You got two: snake number one by the newsstand, snake number two by the stairs to your left." He snapped the cloth as he moved it to the sides, working away until the shine seemed to lift off the leather. "They ain't railroad dicks, I'll tell you that. Them I could pick out with my eyes closed."

Dunne dismounted the stand. He took his wallet out.

The attendant shook his head. "You're all paid up."

"Not yet." Dunne stuck a five in the same pocket as before. "What's your guess?"

"About what?"

"My best way out."

"Way you came, downstairs, hop the subway."

"Thanks for the shine." Dunne shook the attendant's hand. "And the advice."

"Get home safe."

"I'll have the best shine on the A train."

"Be sure to tell everybody where you got it."

Retracing his steps, Dunne went past the baggage room, made a left to the Eighth Avenue subway entrance. He bought two tokens at the ticket booth, pushed through the turnstile, and leisurely made his way down one flight of stairs, up another, and emerged on the express platform.

He sat on a bench midplatform. Without removing the book from the satchel, he opened it and randomly underlined letters with his pen. A downtown express arrived. Passengers exited and entered. He closed the satchel. About a dozen people still waited on the platform. Snake number one was reading a newspaper at the southern end; snake number two loitered with arms folded several yards to the other side of Dunne.

The approach of the uptown express was heralded by steel-on-steel grind and screech. The train came to a halt. Snake number one entered a rear car. Snake number two lingered one door away. He waited until Dunne got in the car and took a seat before he did the same.

The doors closed. Dunne held the satchel in his lap. The train idled in the station. Snake number two was on the same side of the car as Dunne but at the north end. The doors opened once more, then closed. The train still didn't move. Suddenly, it jerked into motion. People swayed in their seats. It stopped, jerked again.

Dunne bolted to his feet and toward the door that led to the car behind. Snake number one had already made his way into it.

Framed in the door's glass panel, he had his hands around the white enamel pole in the middle of the car.

Dunne pulled on the door handle. It didn't budge. He pulled twice more. It turned down. The heavy metal door slid open. He stood between the cars. Snake number one, in the car behind, let go of the pole and moved toward him.

Dunne pulled the dossier from the satchel and shoved it down the front of his trousers. He dropped the satchel on the car's metal ledge, scaled the trio of iron chains linking the cars, perched for an instant on top, hands on opposite walls. The train started to gather speed.

He jumped onto the platform, skidded, tumbled, caromed off a bench and into the wall. The train disappeared into the tunnel. He lay sprawled on the floor. His hat rolled on the tracks. A woman screamed in a high, panicked voice, "Oh my God! Oh my God!"

A man in blue overalls loomed over him. "You trying to get yourself killed or what?"

Dunne sat up. His knuckles were badly scraped and bleeding. His right trouser leg was ripped. A bloody knee protruded.

The man continued to hover. "Stay where you are, pal. Somebody went to alert the token clerk to call the cops and get an ambulance."

"Help me up, will you?" Dunne extended his hand.

"You might've broken something or have a concussion. Don't move."

"I didn't break anything. Please, help me up."

"It's your funeral." He gave Dunne his hand.

Dunne walked a few steps. His knee throbbed. "Thanks, I'll be okay."

"What the hell were you thinking?" The man scratched his neck.

"I realized it was an express. I wanted the local."

"It don't matter. The next stop for both is Forty-second Street. You could've switched there."

"Now I know."

"You risked your life for *that?*"

"I didn't want to keep my wife waiting."

"You must have some wife."

Dunne hobbled away. He ignored the staring people who kept their distance as he passed. Slowly mounting the stairs, he noticed his shoes were badly scuffed. A great shine gone to waste. He hopped into a cab on Eighth Avenue. He imagined that by now snakes one and two were paging through *The Sorrows of Young Werther*, pondering the underlined letters, and the code they might contain.

He rolled down the window. Traffic was light. They sped up the avenue. The wind hit his face. Fresh air: The best medicine.

September 1958

ST. GENEVIEVE'S ACADEMY, MANHATTAN

THE SUDDEN MIDDLE-OF-THE-NIGHT RING JOLTED DUNNE AWAKE. HE rolled over. The luminous hands on the clock beside the phone pointed to 2:47. He switched on the light. At this hour, you could be sure you weren't being notified you'd won the Irish Sweepstakes. The best to hope for was a drunk who'd dialed the wrong number. Otherwise, someone had died, or another war had started, or some equivalent misfortune. He held the receiver slightly farther from his ear than usual. "Hello."

"Fin, is that you?"

"Who's this?"

"Bassante."

"What's up?"

"Bad news."

"How bad?"

"Really bad."

"Shoot." Dunne reached over and grabbed an open pack of cigarettes.

"Dick Van Hull is dead."

"When did it happen?" He lit the cigarette.

"Five days ago."

"And you're just calling me now?"

"I just found out a little while ago. I stopped into Red's to see how he was doing. Terry, the bartender, gave me the news. Dick died right there, in the bar, massive heart attack as he got out of a booth."

"What about funeral arrangements?"

"There were none. He had no next of kin, but he had a proper will that directed he be cremated and his ashes thrown in the harbor. Terry's already seen to it."

"Nice of him to let us know."

"That's the way Dick wanted it, quick and quiet. But Terry said there'll be a memorial ceremony at St. Genevieve's, where Dick taught."

"When?"

"Tomorrow, noon."

"You have the address?"

"Not with me. But it's in the phone book."

"I'll see you there."

It was drizzling on and off. Dunne had trouble finding a cab. The crosstown traffic crawled. He arrived twenty minutes late. The turreted, three-story gray stone Gothic facade was two parts imposing, one part oppressive, like an old-style penitentiary. He rushed up the stairs. The chapel was next to the entrance. It was empty. The shimmering, spotless linoleum hallways were deserted and silent. Maybe Bassante had got the time wrong.

He stepped back outside. Bassante signaled from the corner. "Over here!" He led the way into the building's side entrance. "It's in the auditorium. The sisters couldn't have it in the chapel. Fond as they were of Dick, he was a Protestant. The head nun said it was all right for us to attend. They're already well into it. It seems like it's going to be short."

They slipped into the last row of seats. Faced framed by drapery of auburn hair, the teenage girl at the podium in the center of the stage read from a sheet of paper held in an awkward way as she tried to speak into the microphone. Her voice quavered slightly.

In front, beneath the stage, was a motionless curtain of nuns in black wimples; behind, several rows of lay faculty, overwhelmingly female, a sprinkling of men. The rest of the auditorium was filled with the girls of St. Genevieve's Academy, homely and lovely, most yet to bud out of girlhood, a few in full flower, all dressed in identical uniforms of knee socks, plaid skirts, white blouses, and blue vests.

The girl put aside the paper and left the stage. A tall nun rose from the aisle seat in the front row. Railing gripped in right hand, robe raised an inch or two above old-fashioned high-buttoned shoes with the left, she mounted the stairs to the stage and went to the podium.

"Mr. Hull was a godsend to this school." She leaned close to the microphone. "He might not have been the best organized person who ever walked these halls . . ."

A murmur of muffled laughter rippled through the room.

She swept the room with a stony, cursory stare, a reminder that her interest was in brevity, not levity: Say what should be said; don't dillydally, or indulge in frivolity, or violate the truth.

The laughter stopped.

"But he was a dedicated, talented teacher. Let him be remembered by us all as a man of true allegiances—to his country, to this school, and, above all, to his students. Let us pray he has found eternal happiness in the presence of God." She left it at that.

The girls stood, their clapping tentative at first, then louder and more confident. When they were done, the tall nun led the girls up the aisle, out of the auditorium.

Dunne stood with Bassante on the steps of the school. A light drizzle fell. Bassante pulled down the brim of his hat. "Didn't sound to me like that nun knew Dick very well."

"Dick was a private guy." Dunne glanced to see if a taxi might be coming down the street. They hadn't seen each other in almost a decade and a half, and even during their time in Slovakia, they hadn't talked much about the lives they'd lived up until then, childhoods, careers, stuff that might have mattered in some other time, some other place, although neither was much for sharing revelations or reminiscences whatever the circumstances. "That's something we had in common."

"I know that—so am I. But Dick was a hero. He deserved something more."

"I suppose." *Dick deserved a full military funeral, honor guard, the salute of bugles and rifles, flag folded in farewell and placed in the hands of his beloved. Except he's left all that behind when he'd resigned from the service rather than let Michael Jahn's name be besmirched.* "But I think maybe that's all he would've wanted."

"Still, that nun barely said anything at all."

Dunne kept on the lookout for a cab. *Either Dick was in a place where there was nothing, no sadness, no joy, only oblivion, or he was happy in a place where happiness was forever. Believe what you want or need to believe. Who can say for sure? The only thing that could be said with certainty was what that nun, whether she'd realized it or not, had got exactly right: Thornton Richard Van Hull IV was a man of true allegiances.*

The drizzle stopped. After scouting the street one last and futile time, Dunne took hold of Bassante's elbow. "Come on, let's go find a bar and get a drink."

"Now there's something we can agree on. The last time we had a drink together was in London, just before you left for Prague. And that awful weather—remember?"

"Hard as I try, I can't forget."

Under pretext of attending to company business, Stefan Schwimmer left for Europe to use the dossier to scare up what interest he could in Hemmer/Heinz. "What's important," Dunne told him, "is the perception that the hunt is still on. Even if you don't get close, odds are he'll be moved somewhere. The more he moves, better our chance of getting a bead on his whereabouts. Meantime, I'll do my best to rattle Bartlett."

"That could be dangerous, don't you think?"

"He doesn't know what or how much I know. Far as he's concerned, I'm a small-time operator, a onetime favorite of Bill Donovan's who, at worst, can't be much more than a minor headache. Any time he spends on me is, as he sees it, wasted time. Still, I might be able to put a dent or two in that iron-sided self-confidence of his."

A note arrived from Bassante. He'd found a permanent job as a translator at an import-export firm in lower Manhattan and rented a room in a boarding house in Brooklyn Heights. He provided the address. *You can reach me here,* he wrote, *if you have to.*

Dunne endured a painful lunch with Wynne Billings. He half listened as Billings did his diplomatic best to convey the corporation's dissatisfaction with the performance of PISS in general and the level of Dunne's interest in particular. "You're a real pro, Fin, and your service to our country is recognized and appreciated . . ." Blah, blah, blah . . . But that was then and this is now, "and, well, in this critical time when we're redefining our priorities . . ." Blah, blah, blah.

After Dunne apologized for creating the misimpression that he wasn't focused on his work and reaffirmed his commitment to "implementing the changes necessitated by our SEA strategy," Billings was mollified enough to grant what was in effect a temporary reprieve. "We'll see how things work out over the next several months."

Dunne then set in motion the process that he knew would result in his immediate and final termination. He called Ken Moss at Bartlett & Partners and congratulated him on his new job. Moss was delighted to hear from him. "This place is better than I hoped. It's plugged into everything. At last week's executive lunch, Roy Larsen from Time Inc. was the guest."

"I'm happy for you, Ken. I also have a favor to ask."

"Shoot. You know I'll do whatever I can."

"It's as much for Wynne and ISC as it is for me."

"All the better."

Well aware that Moss knew of his relationship with Bartlett going back to the OSS, Dunne bluffed. "Wynne thinks I might drop by the next time Bartlett's in New York for a casual conversation about our desire to deepen the relationship between ISC and Bartlett and Partners. Wynne said Bartlett uses his office there when he's in the city."

"He's formally severed his ties."

"Sure, except we know how it works. Informally, his advice still matters."

"Did you contact his office in D.C. about setting up a meeting there?"

"There's no getting through to him in D.C. It'd be easier to get an appointment with Ike. Wynne thinks if we knew the next time Bartlett is going to be in New York, we could arrange a casual chat."

"He's not here on any regular schedule. It's hit or miss."

"All we need is a heads-up."

"A heads-up?"

"A call. Nobody'll know."

"I'll see what I can do."

Moss called a week later. "Tomorrow. Nine a.m. Flies back to D.C. at four." He hung up before Dunne could blurt out a thank-you.

Dunne arrived in the lobby at 8:30. He parked himself in the phone booth closest to the elevator bank. Promptly at nine, a plain-clothes type scouted the lobby and spoke to the elevator dispatcher, who directed one of the operators to hook a red cord across the entrance to his car, indicating it was reserved.

A moment later, Carlton Bartlett's escort preceded him though the revolving doors. Plump (but no plumper than he'd been the last time Dunne saw him), wearing a gray homburg and a well-tailored double-breasted suit, he waddled/strutted with duck-like gait to the elevator.

Dunne folded open the booth door, popped out, and blocked the way. "Carl!"

Bartlett took a step back.

"Funny, Carl, isn't it, running into you like this after all these years?"

Bartlett's escort scurried to his side.

"Dunne. OSS." Dunne stretched out his arms as if expecting to be frisked.

Bartlett stared at him blankly. "I'm sorry but . . ."

"Prague, remember?"

"Yes, of course. Prague." Bartlett attempted a smile. "You look fit."

"You haven't changed a bit."

"Nice to see you again, but I'm late for an important meeting."

Dunne stayed where he was. "Too bad about Louie Pohl, don't you think?"

"Who?"

"Louis Pohl. He went out a window at the Commodore."

"Pohl, yes. I read about that. Tragic."

"What made him do it?"

"Tell me, Frank, have you returned to your position as a patrolman?"

"*Fin*, as in Fintan."

"Sorry. It's been a long time."

"I was a homicide detective, Carl, back before the war."

"I knew you were some kind of policeman. I just wasn't sure what kind."

"For the last few years, I was an associate of Pohl's at ISC."

The elevator operator unhooked the cord. The escort guarded

Bartlett as he stepped into the car and turned to the front. "Take care, Fred."

Left hand on hip, right on the elevator frame, Dunne moved forward. "It's Fin. I can tell suicide from murder."

The escort pushed his palm with gentle firmness against Dunne's chest. "This is reserved, sir. You'll have to take another car." He tapped the operator on the shoulder. "What are you waiting for?"

The operator shrugged. "I thought you gentlemen was having a conversation."

"Let's go," the escort snarled. "*Now.*"

The elevator dispatcher came over. "What's the problem?"

"No problem." Dunne pointed at Bartlett. "Carl and I were in the same outfit in the war. We bumped into each other and were having a chat."

"See?" The operator looked back at Bartlett. "That's why I didn't shut the door."

"I was telling Carl I'd been a homicide detective."

"My brother's a cop," the dispatcher said. "He on the burglary squad."

"I was saying that the thing about detectives is the good ones follow their instincts. They don't need a pathologist to tell the difference between suicide and murder." Dunne rested his forefinger on the side of his nose. "They smell it."

"If I had the time, I'd stay and chat. But I don't." The artery in Bartlett's neck was prominent and throbbing. He turned to his escort: "Are we going to spend all day here?"

The escort shouldered the operator aside, grabbed the door handle, and shoved the lever to the right. The door closed.

The dispatcher followed the arrow on the floor register as it tracked the car's nonstop ascent. "Big shots are always in a hurry. That's why they're big shots, I guess." The arrow came to rest on the top floor. "God is in His Heaven. Maybe he'll relax now."

The dispatcher accompanied Dunne through the lobby to the revolving door. "What you said before about instinct—I've heard Angelo, my brother, say the same thing a couple of hundred times: 'You got the nose or don't.'"

Miss O'Keefe was packing the contents of her desk when Dunne arrived. He apologized for being unable to salvage her job. "Billings wasn't in the mood to extend any measure of clemency."

"You certainly succeeded in teeing him off."

"Wasn't hard." On the phone the night before, Billings hadn't held back: *What the hell were you thinking? . . . Intercepting C. B. Bartlett in the lobby? . . . Have you lost your goddamn mind? . . . Unpardonable, unprofessional, un-everything . . .* blah, blah, blah.

She placed a half-dozen marble-covered notebooks on her desk.

"What are those?" He nodded at the notebooks.

She peered over the top of her glasses, a skeptical stare. "Take a guess."

"You're writing a book?"

"A novel."

"You're finished?"

"First draft. Now comes the hard part, editing, rewriting, cutting out the crap and clichés, making the characters believable. What'd you think of the parts you read?"

"The parts I read?'

"I can tell when someone's been poking around in my desk drawers. Comes from working for a first-class detective."

"I only read a few lines."

"How come? Didn't you like it?"

"I did."

"You're a bad liar. I didn't like it either. For starters, it needs a new title. *Springtime of Our Love*—ugh. I hate it. I got the story down. Now comes the hard part—turning it into a real piece of writing."

He opened his briefcase and handed her a book. "This is for you."

"Oh my, *The Collected Poems of W. B. Yeats*. I love Yeats." She caressed the gold-embossed lettering and opened the cover: "What a lovely inscription: *To D., May love never flee or hide his face, M.* You sure you want to give it away?"

"An old friend gave it to me. He'd be pleased I'd passed it on to someone who'll put it to good use."

He went into his office. A message in all caps was printed on the pad next to the phone: *9:30 A.M. CALL FROM THE OFFICE OF WILLIAM DONOVAN (DONOVAN, LEISURE & IRVINE). PLEASE RETURN ASAP.* He dialed the number and asked for the general's extension.

The general's assistant thanked him for returning the call. "He's working from home today," she said. "He hoped you could stop by at his residence, at Four Sutton Place, at two. He has a matter he wishes to discuss."

South Sutton Place, Manhattan

Donovan's apartment, the maid took Dunne's hat and led him into the living room. He sat on an elegantly uncomfortable couch. There was a shuffling sound in the hallway. A white-haired figure wandered around the corner. Powder-blue bathrobe hung halfway down hairless, ghostly pale calves. One of his terrycloth slippers was brown, the other plaid.

"Nice of you to come." Donovan shuffled back down the hallway. Dunne trailed behind. It was five years since he'd last seen Donovan. They'd met accidentally outside the Waldorf Towers. Donovan had recently been appointed ambassador to Thailand. They had a brief, affable chat. He seemed healthy and fit, still recognizable as Wild Bill.

At the end of the hallway was a small office. Except for a large map of China and Southeast Asia, the walls were bare. An antique cherry writing desk and chair were placed before French doors that led to a small balcony. The view was of the East River and Welfare—formerly Blackwell's—Island.

"Please, have a seat." Donovan indicated the green leather wing chair angled toward the desk.

Dunne was sure he knew why Donovan had summoned him. He expected to be taken to task for allowing use of the picture in *Modern Detection*. He'd already decided not to offer excuses or finger Ken Moss. He'd accept blame, apologize, be done with it.

"Personally, I think he's got a hell of a nerve." Donovan opened the drawer and removed a typed, note-size letter. He put on his glasses. "I've barely heard a word from him since the day I was fired. Now he wants me to"—he read from the letter—"'to talk some sense into Fintan Dunne.' Do you know who I'm speaking about?"

"I can guess."

"He claims that"—he read from the letter again—"'however worthy the wartime service Dunne rendered to the OSS, he is attempting to make a nuisance of himself by meddling in matters of national security way beyond his concern or comprehension.'" He dropped the letter on the desk. "He says you appear to have 'a mental impairment,' and that while he hates to involve me in such a trivial affair, I'm the one person who can perhaps reason with you."

"You're one of them."

"I'm not going to ask what this is about because I don't give a damn, and if it involves 'matters of national security,' I prefer to put my faith in you over— What was the nickname Mulholland gave Bartlett that everybody used behind his back?"

"The Pear."

"Yes, the Pear. To think a second-rater like that rose to where he is, and so many good men never made it home. Lieutenant Osbourne—remember him? A fine, intelligent officer. Brave. Blown to bits. I saw it happen."

"Private Mullen was killed with him. Lots of others. That was the first war."

"Our own artillery got Osbourne."

"And Mullen. Same shell."

Swaying slightly, Donovan steadied himself on the back of the chair. "The first war. So many good men. In both wars."

"You okay?" Dunne rose from the chair.

"Fine, fine, stay where you are."

Dunne sat back down. *So many good men.* Quartet of three-man teams he'd helped train in preparation for D-Day, a dozen men up in smoke on a training field in Sussex. He struggled to recall their names. Some he remembered: Hale, Miller, Mortone.

Donovan laid his glasses on the desk. "Arteriosclerotic atrophy—that's the diagnosis. The doctors won't put a time on how long I have. They're either too kind or afraid I'll do what Jim Forrestal did and jump out the window. They needn't worry. Jim lost his faith. I still have mine."

He maneuvered his chair so he had a view out the French doors: river, island, sky.

No Wild Bill or Black Will anywhere in sight.

Only William Joseph Donovan. Old, sick, dying, remembering.

"Truman fired Forrestal, too. Truman, that nonentity, a cog in a corrupt political machine, a crook for a boss, and he's elevated to the presidency. In his dismissal letter, he thanked me for my 'capable leadership.' *Capable.* One notch above incompetent.

"Ike was supposed to be a big improvement. Sure, I worked hard to get him elected. But I never shared the great expectations. Luckiest SOB who ever lived. Spent the first war drilling recruits. Never made it overseas. Never commanded anything above a battalion until FDR somersaulted him into Supreme Allied Commander in Europe.

"Then he goes and has an affair with that pretty driver—

what was her name?—lovely Irish girl originally from Cork. How could I forget her name? We joked together about us both being 'black Irish.' I liked her very much. Ike told General Marshall he was going to divorce Mamie and marry her. Marshall wouldn't permit it."

He sat, fiddled with his glasses, tapped them on the desk, rapidly, like a telegrapher. "Key . . . no, Kay . . . Kay Summersby . . . that's it. Stevenson was too much the gentleman to use it against him in the '52 campaign. Can you imagine if Ike had been up against Truman or a bastard like Joe Kennedy? They'd have smeared him every which way but Thursday."

He continued to reminisce: J. Edgar Hoover, weasel; Tom Dewey, wooden; the Dulles brothers, Tweedledum and Tweedledee. Secretary of State John Foster: self-righteousness incarnate. Who says God doesn't have a sense of humor? The old Presbyterian prig winds up with a son who not only turns papist but, to add injury to apostasy, becomes a Jesuit. Ha, ha. And CIA director Allen: pipe-smoking, philandering, two-faced manipulator, pretending he was working to make Bill Donovan head of the CIA when he was working all the while with his brother to take the job for himself. It wasn't surprising a schemer like Bartlett would prosper as one of his protégés.

"I'm going on, aren't I?" Donovan stood.

"I'm grateful for your time."

Donovan picked up the letter. A bit of color had returned to his face. "Take it. I don't want it. Pay attention to the last paragraph. He sounds a little unhinged."

He led the way to the door, stooped, hands in pockets. "The best men are left on the battlefield. That's the trouble with war. The real heroes never make it home."

The quick moved on. The dead stayed behind.

"I belonged with those men." The blue in Donovan's eyes was faded and watery, reflection of his melancholy, a space in the soul neither time nor medicine could fix or fill. Maybe atop that trench was the moment he was most alive, vertical updraft of history intersecting with horizontal line of biography, fate fulfilled, right place, right time, flashbulb of revelation: *This is the moment I was born for. The moment I'm destined to die.* Everything else—fame, success, money—would be a footnote. "I've always felt guilty about the fuss they made about me, when the honor belonged to them."

They shook hands. A last time.

Dunne crossed Sutton Place to the eastern terminus of 57th Street. He sat on a bench above the river, pulled out Bartlett's typed letter and read the last paragraph:

> I'm afraid to say that the Reds had the right idea with their *zagradotryady*, the special details charged with shooting down any soldier whose behavior might create panic in the front line. Typical Red callousness, yes. But there was a kernel of wisdom in it. When your back is against the wall, there can't be any option for retreat, and there's where we are now—all of us. Our backs against the wall. The final showdown will occur within the next decade. We all know it. Those in the front line shouldn't be made to worry about being pestered by irresponsible imbeciles whose one overriding interest is drawing attention to themselves.

Bartlett was rattled. It remained to be seen how rattled, and what—if anything—he'd do. And when.

Forum of the Twelve Caesar's, Manhattan

DUNNE TOOK TERESA DOLORES O'KEEFE TO DINNER AT THE FORUM of the Twelve Caesars as a way of thanking her. "Do me a favor," she said when he phoned to invite her. "Call me Tess. That's the name I'm going by now."

"I'll pick you up at seven, Tess."

Accustomed to seeing her in the understated outfits of an ISC executive assistant—fashionable, never flashy—he was surprised by her low-cut black dress and the way she filled it. He helped her into a cab. "You look lovely."

"You sound surprised."

"Disappointed."

"By what?"

"By being old enough to be your father and happily married."

"I like that about you."

"What's that?"

"I've met men who wouldn't be deterred by either."

The maître d' kept them waiting several minutes before handing them off to an assistant to be seated. Dressed in modified togas, the waiters presented them with elaborately designed, oversized menus. Tess put her hand over her mouth when she saw the prices.

"Order what you want," Dunne told her.

"You don't have an ISC expense account anymore."

"My severance package will cover a lot of meals like this."

"That's the difference between you and me. When you cry yourself to sleep at night, you have a severance package under your pillow."

"I don't cry myself to sleep and neither should you. You've got your novel under your pillow. That'll be your ticket."

They had champagne and oysters to start. The tableside preparation and service of the Caesar salad were somewhere between Hollywood and High Mass. There was a sudden stir when Joan Crawford and her CEO husband arrived. The maître d' cleared the way for them. Chin held high, pretending not to notice the attention that the patrons pretended not to pay, she allowed herself to be led to the Forum's premier roost, a corner booth at the back.

"I can't say I'd like to work for her. But still, I admire her. A woman doesn't get what's she got without fighting twice as hard as a man. Not that men have it easy." Tess shook her head. "Those idiots can't know what they're doing if they let someone with your experience and integrity go."

"They know what they're doing. So do I."

"Really? You're not just saying that?" Her black hair was swept back from her face; pearl earrings accented long neck, curvature below.

"Really, Tess."

Along with the clatter of cutlery and plates, the room was filled with the chatter of the Forum's wealthy, powerful, and famous patrons, all lacquered with the same sleek, manicured gloss that advertised their success, that said they belonged. There was no indication of the secrets and insecurities swirling beneath, addictions, deceptions, adulteries, peculations, betrayals, hidden catalogue of the seven deadly sins and all their infinite permutations, illicit desires, forbidden inclinations, fear of exposure they engendered.

The moose-size lamb chops they ordered were capped with miniature chef's hats. As she ate, Tess kept gazing around. "I hope I'm not embarrassing you by gawking like a farm girl. But I've never been in such star-studded company."

"Go ahead, gawk. They could get the same food at cheaper prices plenty of places. They're here to be noticed."

After they'd shared a flaming desert of cherries jubilee, she excused herself to go to the powder room. Dunne looked for the waiter so he could get the check. In a booth on the opposite side of the room from Joan Crawford's—another prime roost, though not a corner as prestigious as hers—a thin, well-groomed, square-chinned gent in a gray suit, lobster bib around his neck, gestured vehemently with a silver claw cracker at his companion, who sat at an angle that made it impossible to see his face.

That square chin. He'd seen it before. Where? Maybe on television. Maybe on a campaign poster. It wasn't until Tess returned and he stood to leave that he glimpsed the real Joan Crawford and made the connection to Red's Bar & Grill—the Joan Crawford three-quarters look-alike hurrying to get a cab—that he was positive it was him: Michael Arlington Beresford, fat-cat chairman of the mayor's Committee on Municipal Finances.

"Now you're the one doing the gawking." Tess pivoted slowly on the balls of her feet. "I might as well take it all in since I'll never be back."

"You'll be back, but on your own terms. Next time they'll all be pretending not to stare at you."

On the way out, the profile of Beresford's tablemate was visible. Carlton Bartlett swiped his fingers on his lobster bib and lifted a glass flute of champagne.

The doorman hailed a cab. Tess O'Keefe got in. Dunne went to the driver's window. He peeled off several bills from the roll in his pocket. "This is an off-the-meter job. Jersey City, okay."

The driver counted the bills. "Sure thing. Jersey City, it is."

Tess rolled down her window. "This is unnecessary, Fin. I can take the tubes. Be home in no time."

He leaned in, touched the pearl dangling from her ear, kissed her cheek, scent of perfume and champagne. A man can dream. And if age brings wisdom, that's all he does. "Better hurry. Come midnight, this cab turns into a pumpkin."

"We love pumpkin in Jersey City. I'll drop you off on the way."

"I left something inside." He stood back. The cab pulled into the traffic; brake lights blinked good-bye.

Breezing past the maître d', who was poring over his reservation book, he beelined to the booth where he'd spotted Michael Arlington Beresford.

"Mr. Beresford?"

Beresford didn't look up. He seemed to presume a waiter was addressing him.

"I believe we've met before." Dunne put out his hand.

Beresford raised his eyes. Indifference molted into confusion. "We have?"

"Yes, I'm Fintan Dunne."

"Fintan Dunne?" He took Dunne's hand with soft, uncertain grip.

"At Red's."

He released Dunne's hand. "Red's?"

"Third Avenue. I didn't recognize you at first."

Face as red as the lobster carcass on his plate, Beresford opened his mouth. No words came out.

"I'm a friend of TR Hull. We served together in the war. Those days, he went by Dick Van Hull."

"Sorry, you're mistaken." Beresford's fleeting attempt at a smile turned into a grimace. "I don't know you or Hall."

"*Hull.* Carlton here knew him, too."

Bartlett ripped off his lobster bib and threw it on the table. He drained the champagne from his glass. "You don't know when to stop, do you?"

Dunne picked up Beresford's full glass of champagne.

"Really, I've no idea what he's talking about." Beresford looked pleadingly at Bartlett. "Do you?"

"He's trying to make a nuisance of himself. He's becoming expert at it."

"I propose a toast." Dunne raised the glass. "To the memory of the late Richard Thornton Van Hull: *Suscipiat Dominus sacrificium.*" He poured the contents on Bartlett's head, turned, and ambled confidently past the waiters in their faux togas, and the tony dinners, and the maître d' who was doing his practiced best to ignore the guests waiting to be seated.

Outside a line had formed of people waiting for taxis. The doorman stood in the street. The traffic was backed up. A frustrated driver sounded a triple honk. Others joined in. The horns blared a discordant chorus of bugle-like blasts.

In the morning, when Dunne left his apartment to get breakfast at the corner coffee shop, there were two men in the lobby surveying the mailboxes. They homed in on him immediately. No need to flash their shields. The combination of polished shoes, worn-down heels, off-the-rack suits, and the bored resignation on their faces was as good as any badge.

The shorter, thinner of the two stepped into the middle of the hall. "Fintan Dunne?"

"Who wants to know?"

"Detective Daniel Hanlon." He pulled a weathered black leather fold from his breast pocket, flipped it open, and nodded at his sidekick. "This is Detective Steve Spiro."

Dunne didn't bother eyeballing the shields. "What can I do for you?"

Hanlon repocketed the fold. "We need to talk."

"About what?"

"Last night."

"What about it?"

Hanlon smiled a detective's smile, sly, mechanical, mildly threatening. "Suppose we go someplace more private for a quiet chat?"

"I'd ask you up to my place, but my wife's been away. It's a mess. Let's go outside." He stepped around Hanlon and pushed open the door.

"Wait for me here, Steve." Hanlon turned his back on his partner and followed Dunne out the door. They stood under the canopy that led to the curb. A mild autumn breeze cooled the morning air.

Dunne took out a cigarette and offered one to Hanlon.

"Thanks." Hanlon parked it between his lips. He patted his pockets in search of matches. "This isn't exactly private."

"Private enough." Dunne struck a match. "I don't see any eavesdroppers." He raised it in the cup of his two hands so Hanlon didn't have to lean down. "How'd you know who I am?"

"Instinct. Cop's gut. And your picture's on file. You've managed to compile a fair-size sheet, which brings me to last night . . ."

"Save your breath. I'll give you a full confession: I had dinner with a woman who's not my wife, and I had too much champagne. Which am I being charged with?"

"You're not being charged with anything. Not yet." Hands in his pockets, Hanlon worked the cigarette to the corner of his mouth and puffed. "You remember a cop named Bill Hanlon?"

"Chief of Homicide?

"Yeah."

"Decent guy," Dunne said. "Good cop. We helped each other out a few times."

"He died three years ago. Lung cancer. Only been retired six months."

"Sorry to hear it."

Hanlon nodded. "He was my old man. I remember hearing a few stories about you from him. He didn't respect many people. He respected you."

"It was mutual. But what's this got to do with last night?"

"This morning I got summoned to Headquarters by Deputy Inspector Moriarty. He's young and full of himself the way all the ones with college degrees are. He says there was an 'incident' last night at a swank midtown eatery. Didn't go into a lot of details. Some high-ranking official from D.C. got a drink thrown in his face."

"Poured on his head."

"Whichever." Hanlon kept puffing on the cigarette. The arc of dead ash at its tip curved toward the sidewalk. "Point is, this guy has a top-level position that's all hush-hush, and he calls the commissioner complaining he's being harassed by some crank—an ex-cop with a grudge—and while he appreciates the commish keeping the incident out of the papers, what he needs now is, quote, 'for it to be taken care of at the local level.'"

The ash broke away and spilled on Hanlon's lapel. He brushed it off. "Moriarty is one of these out-with-the-old, in-with-the-new, everything-by-the-book types until the new runs dry and the book don't serve his purposes. He tells me the situation and says the commish wants it handled 'discreetly.'

"'You know what to do when a fly keeps bothering you?' he says to me. 'You give it a good swat, enough of a warning to send it on its way.'" Hanlon flicked the reminder of the cigarette into the gutter.

"So you're here to swat me?"

"If I was, you'd already be swatted. I got better things to do than serve as messenger boy for Joe College and the *federales*. I'm here to discover you're nowhere to be found. The super says you left this morning with a suitcase. You told him you were headed out of town and didn't plan on returning. You didn't mention any destination."

"What if I decide to stick around?"

Hanlon held up one finger and signaled to his partner inside the lobby he needed a minute more. "I think you're smarter than that, but if you're not, then Moriarty will find out soon enough, I'll look like a liar, and some other dick, whose father didn't know you, will come up and see you get swatted."

"What about your partner?"

"Spiro? He feels the same way about Moriarty as me." Hanlon waved, and Spiro exited the lobby. As they started toward the corner, Hanlon turned. "Lots of people head to Florida this time of year."

"Sounds like good advice."

"It is. Take it."

Part VIII

Only Then Can the Dead Rest in Peace

File 6704-A: *Document Declassified and Released by Central Intelligence Agency, Sources/Methods Exemption 3B2B, Nazi War Crimes Disclosure Act, Date: 12/06/2000*

***CLASSIFIED: SECRET. Folder 6704-A: DR. KARSTEN HEINZ IS HEREBY SEVERED FROM U.S. v. DR. KARL BRANDT et al. Custody is transferred to Central Intelligence Group, Division Headquarters, Berlin. Information herein not to be shared with unauthorized persons. 2/4/46.

Military Tribunal, Case No. 1, United States v. Dr. Karl Brandt et al., Folder 6704-A: Document No. 2, Précis of Witness Statement (12/14/45): Dr. László Niskolczi, Supplementary Documents, pp. 105–210.

[p. 105] Witness's oath: I, the undersigned, Dr. László Niskolczi (LN), swear to God almighty and omniscient that this is a true accounting of events to which I was witness and that nothing has been added or withheld. (29 December 1945)

EXCERPT:

[pp. 311–315] "It is several days before the partisans find us." Those alive suffer from the "gamut of afflictions visited on inmates: typhus, dysentery, malnutrition, pneumonia, dementia, etc." They are transported to a Soviet field hospital and receive full medical attention. LN: "Bereft of my family and lost to my former homeland, I am barely able to walk when the Russians greet us. But driven by the desire to put on the record what I saw and endured, I have survived. All those who have participated in these crimes, perpetrators and collaborators alike, from the highest echelons to the lowest functionaries, must be judged. Only then can the dead rest in peace."

December 1958

DUNNE KNEW BARTLETT WOULD FIND HIS FLYSWATTER ONE WAY OR another. To stick around any longer wouldn't serve much purpose. The chances of getting anywhere near him another time were close to zero. But the point had been made. There were pests out there—tiny in number, crackpots for sure, but they were there—who didn't accept the official version of Louis Pohl's death.

Maybe when Bartlett woke up in the middle of the night with indigestion and went into the bathroom for a bicarbonate of soda, maybe he'd wonder if he'd tied up the Hemmer/Heinz business as tightly as he could, maybe it was time to move him again . . .

Maybe.

Immediately after the visit from Detective Hanlon, Dunne sent a telegram to Schwimmer in Europe providing the address in Florida to which all future correspondence should be addressed. He telegrammed Roberta. Her cruise ship was due back in San Diego the following day. He told her to go directly to their home in Florida. He'd left his job at ISC. Their belongings in New York were being packed and shipped.

Two days later, he spoke with her on the phone, did his best to keep it short.

"What happened?"

"I'll explain when I get home."

"Did you leave on good terms?"

"Good enough."

"We can rent a place in New York for ourselves, and if you want to keep busy, you can always go out on your own. For now, you can sit back and take it easy."

"Sounds good."

"I missed you."

"I missed you, too."

He stayed a couple of nights at the Hotel Pennsylvania under a phony name. He wrote to Bassante. He let him know he was going back to Florida and the PO Box to which all correspondence should be sent. He included Schwimmer's address and the fact he was looking for help in continuing the search for Heinz—help for which he'd be willing to pay.

A letter postmarked Bonn arrived in Florida soon after Dunne had settled in. It was from Schwimmer. Bassante had contacted him. Perhaps he could be useful. More important, Schwimmer was in touch with a German prosecutor who'd recently been appointed to office. A Social Democrat who spent the war in exile in Sweden, he made known his dissatisfaction with the studied inaction of his colleagues in identifying and indicting war criminals: "He believes it's time the Federal Republic make clear that, far from being a closed book, the investigation of Nazi war crimes is a story still to be written."

Schwimmer gave the prosecutor a copy of the Heinz dossier that he'd received from Dunne. He delivered another to an official with the Israeli Reparations Mission in West Germany. As well as passing it to Tel Aviv, the official asked the same question as the prosecutor: Where was Hemmer/Heinz now?

Schwimmer confessed that he had no idea. The house in Hamburg was empty, the import-export business shut down. He contacted Hans Bleier in Buenos Aires. No sign of Hemmer/Heinz there.

"Till we crack this nut," Schwimmer concluded, "there's little more we can do."

Several weeks went by without any more letters from Schwimmer. Dunne called Alvin Capshaw (byline: Mr. Grapevine) at the *New York Standard*, who'd worked under Bartlett at the OSS churning out articles and press releases. Mr. Grapevine rented his name for freelance pieces, like the one in *Modern Detection*, and ran items in his widely read gossip column that press agents regularly fed him and that he printed in exchange for meals, drinks, theater tickets, ringside seats, and the occasional hooker.

Pleasantly surprised to hear from Dunne, Mr. Grapevine chuckled when Dunne told him that the favor he was calling to ask for was a two-line item in his column: *Longtime bloodhound and OSS vet Fintan Dunne hot on the trail of WWII bad guy. "Stay tuned for the caper's finale," sez Fin.*

"Sounds like you're working on a novel," Capshaw said.

"Trying to stay busy, that's all."

"I thought all you guys did down in Florida was play golf and take naps."

"No golf but plenty of naps. In between, I'm working on tying up some loose ends from the war."

"Well, I'm always glad to help out a buddy from the old outfit." Capshaw ran the item at the head of his column.

Thanksgiving came and went. Still nothing from Schwimmer. On the day before Christmas, Roberta left the house early to do some last-minute shopping. Dunne made a pot of coffee, went out on the patio, sat by the pool, and read the paper.

The lead stories all focused on the mounting success of the rebels in Cuba. There was heavy fighting around Santiago de Cuba in the east. The rebellion seemed to be gathering strength. Yet it was hard to tell what was really happening. Fulgencio Batista, onetime army sergeant and former president who'd seized power in 1952, claimed his forces were killing and capturing mounting numbers of rebels. The impressive toll, however, never seemed to add up to anything decisive.

A former American general was quoted as believing that Batista was trying to lure his opponents out of their guerilla strongholds for "a pitched battle in which his 40,000-strong army and American-equipped air force will crush the rebellion once and for all." He noted "this strategy echoed what the French, with infamous result, had unsuccessfully attempted against the Viet Minh at Dien Bien Phu."

The press reports contained plenty of indications that the sand in Batista's hourglass was running out. The Eisenhower administration had cut off new arms shipments. There were rumors in Washington the CIA had advised the president that, although it enjoyed overwhelming numerical superiority, Batista's combination of thugs, mercenaries, and hapless, unmotivated recruits would eventually fall apart.

The main American aim at this point, one columnist posited, was "to grease the skids" for Batista's departure. Power would be handed over to military professionals. The *barbudos*—the ragtag company of "bearded ones" who spearheaded the rebellion under Fidel Castro—would be admitted to a secondary role in the transition government.

Elections would be held. A new government, though more democratic than the old, would "respect and protect the substantial American business on the island." Left unsaid—but clearly understood—was that this included the casinos run by the American mob.

Despite the turmoil, it was obvious that the lure of Cuba remained strong. There were splashy ads for all the big Havana hotels and casinos: Capri, Riviera, Sevilla Biltmore, Plaza, Deauville, Habana Hilton, etc. Though the swanky Nacional didn't have any rooms left, "a limited number of reservations were available for the New Year's Eve Midnight Supper & Show."

Dunne finished his coffee and put aside the paper. If Bartlett even saw that item in Capshaw's column, he'd probably chuckled. He had more important matters to attend to than the deluded pretensions of a two-bit ex-flatfoot. No need to react. The fly had proved easy enough to chase away. That was the thing about flies. They could be a nuisance. But unlike Pohl, who represented a real threat, you needn't call in the artillery to deal with them. In the end, they were nothing more than a short-term bother, a fleeting buzz, easy enough to shoo. Or swat. Dunne swam a couple of laps in the pool. The Christmas tree, hung with ornaments and silver tinsel, was visible behind the palm ferns and the sliding glass doors.

Christmas Eve, they ate dinner by the pool. Roberta went inside to finish wrapping presents. He went off to Midnight Mass.

Peace on earth to men of good will.

It didn't look likely anytime soon.

They exchanged presents when he got back. They went to bed and made love. He woke before dawn. He turned on the Christmas-tree lights. He went onto the patio and lay on the chaise longue. He put Bing Crosby's Christmas album on the record player. The lights' festive glow faded with sunrise. A warm breeze fussed with the treetops.

Christmas in Florida. Every bit as out of place as a polar bear in the Bronx.

Time had its own momentum. The days after Christmas dragged by. After his swim, Dunne lay on the chaise longue. Sun, warm and gentle, rested on cheeks and eyelids.

Ring, ring, ring.

Dunne sat up with a start. He reached over to turn off the

alarm. There was none. The ringing was from the phone inside the house. He lay where he was, expecting it to stop. It didn't. He threw on his robe and went inside. A longtime peeve: What kind of idiot didn't understand that if the phone rang thirty times and nobody answered, either nobody was home or the somebody who was home didn't feel like answering.

He picked up the receiver. "Who the hell is this?"

"Fin?"

"Yes."

"Stefan."

"Where are you?"

"Havana."

"Cuba?"

"I've found him."

"Who?"

"*Him.*"

"In Havana?"

"Can you come?"

"When?"

"Now."

"Now?"

"Fin, it's *him.*"

"I'll see what I can do."

"I need you."

"You're sure it's him?"

"Beyond any doubt."

"Where in Havana are you?"

"The Barcelona. I need you *now.*"

Roberta laughed. "Havana? Why not see if Mount Vesuvius is about to explode? You could book a room at the Pompeii Hilton."

It took a while to tell her the whole story, the detailed narrative he'd never shared before. Van Hull, Bartlett, Dr. Niskolczi, the Schwimmers. He tried to leave nothing out.

"I'm coming with you," she said.

"That doesn't make sense. This isn't a vacation."

"I won't get in your way. But I'm coming." A simple statement of fact that he knew from experience not to argue with.

In the afternoon she booked their flight. The Barcelona still had a room available. She booked that, too.

Barcelona Hotel, Havana

They shared a taxi from the airport at Rancho Boyeros to downtown Havana with a couple from the Midwest. The wife was blonde, attractive but bulky. The husband owned a Ford dealership in Minneapolis. They'd made a spur-of-the-moment decision to come to Havana. It had nothing to do with the weather. Neither of them minded the cold. Some years they went to New York for New Year's.

Havana, however, offered a triple play. He wanted to look into the opportunities in Cuba. In the decades ahead, this was going to be one of the fastest-growing car markets in the Americas. Along with business, there was the nightlife. "We're going to take in some of those live sex shows."

His wife slapped his hand good-naturedly. "Jack, please, they'll think you're serious. We have reservations for tonight at the Flamingo, and Jack used his connections to finagle seats for the New Year's Eve extravaganza at the Tropicana."

"And who knows?" the husband added. "Maybe we'll have ringside seats on a revolution? From what I read in the papers, it looks like this might be the next banana republic to give *el presidente* the boot. Could be exciting to watch—though not as exciting as a sex show."

"Oh, Jack, stop. This nice couple will think you've only one thing on your mind."

"They'll be right."

She slapped his hand again. "Jack says we've got nothing to worry about. It happens all the time down here—revolutions, I mean. They only shoot one another. Nobody wants to drive away the Americans and ruin the tourist trade. Still, I'd have preferred New York."

They passed an army roadblock. The soldiers, looking bored and leaning against their truck, waved them through. The cab dropped the other couple at the Plaza, then proceeded to the west side of the Prado, to the Barcelona. Roberta went ahead to the bar. Dunne stopped at the front desk.

The English-speaking desk clerk had the formal but friendly manner of a true Habanero. He frowned when Dunne asked what room Señor Schwimmer was in.

"Señor Schwimmer? I don't believe we have a guest by that name. But let me check." He turned the guest register sideways so that Dunne could follow his finger as he traced the columns of guests' names and signatures. "See for yourself, Señor Dunne, nobody here by that name. Is there another hotel you wish me to check with?"

"That's all right. Must be a mix-up. Are there any messages for me?"

"No, señor. No message at all."

He joined Roberta in the hotel bar. She was sipping a daiquiri. He ordered one for himself. He lit a cigarette, rested it on the ashtray rim. "I've already made my New Year's resolution. I'm giving up cigarettes."

"You're lucky there's no statute of limitations on making New Year's resolutions. This is the tenth year in a row you've made the same one."

The bartender delivered his drink.

"*Cuándo es el próximo tren para Habana?*" Roberta raised her glass.

Dunne touched his to hers. "*No comprendo.*"

"It's a colloquialism Wilfredo Grillo liked to use. Literally: 'When's the next train to Havana?' It means, What do we do next?"

"We wait for Schwimmer to contact us."

"How long's that?"

"We won't know until he contacts us."

At dusk, they walked to the Malecón. A steady wind from the north sent wave after wave crashing into the concrete wall. The sun sank into the clouds and spread a crimson-tinged, mushroom-shaped light.

The Prado was more crowded on the way back. Nighttime Havana was coming alive. They stopped at Pigalle, a French-style bistro on Calle Trocadero. The mostly Cuban clientele filled the dimly lit room with festive chatter. Two men got into a political argument. When they seemed ready to come to blows, the manager summoned the police.

The men were gone by the time two plainclothesmen arrived. They ordered the manager to turn up the lights. The room went silent, whether with relief or dread was hard to tell.

On the way back to the Barcelona, Fin and Roberta bumped into the couple from Minneapolis. They'd just left the bar at the Plaza. It was abuzz with the news President Batista had sent his children to New York "on vacation." There were also reports of a battle between the rebels and Batista's forces at Santa Clara in the center of the island.

"It's reported that Dr. Guevara, one of Castro's top lieutenants, has been killed," the wife said. "Maybe we really will get to see a revolution!"

Warm air swirled in from the Gulf, collided with cool air from the north: a recipe for stormy weather. But it stayed still and close. They slept with the ceiling fan on, unusual for December. Dunne woke at seven. Roberta had her back to him. He dressed in the bathroom. He rotated the doorknob slowly. Roberta rolled over. "Give me my handbag, will you, please?"

"I wanted to let you sleep." He handed her the bag. "No need to get up now."

"It's all right. I've been awake a while. I was having terrible nightmares."

"What about?"

"I don't remember." She fumbled among the contents of the bag, lifted out a palm-size, snub-nosed, silver-plated pistol. "Here, take this."

"You took *that* on the plane?"

"Customs officers haven't sunk so low they'd search a lady's handbag."

He slipped the pistol in his pocket. "Loaded?"

"Would I give it to you if it wasn't?"

The clerk who'd checked them in was back at the front desk. He approached Dunne as he came down the stairs. "*Un momento, Señor Dunne, por favor.*"

"*Sí, qué pasa?*"

"In the dining room is a man who asked for you. I offer to call your room. He says his wish is not to disturb you so early. He waits until you came down to breakfast."

"Did he give his name?"

"No. Perhaps the señor of whom you inquired yesterday, yes?"

"*Quizá. Gracias.*"

In a banquette in the rear corner of the dining room, beneath a huge antique mirror, sat the sole patron, his distinctive, sharp-beaked face poised above a half-eaten grapefruit. Turlough Bassante beckoned Dunne, "Come, have a seat."

Dunne sat across from him. Out the glass doors to his right, where he remembered there used to be a patio and a small garden, a pool glimmered in the morning sun. *Habana vieja* genuflected to *Habana nova*, even the old hotels compelled to offer some version of the amenities routinely available in glass boxes like the Hilton and Flamingo.

"Why don't you have some breakfast?" Bassante signaled for the waiter.

Dunne ordered a *café con leche*. "You're with Schwimmer?"

"He asked me along."

"He didn't mention you'd be with him."

"Would that have altered your decision?"

"No, but I'd prefer not to have any more surprises."

"I didn't contact him. He contacted me."

The waiter took away Bassante's grapefruit and delivered Dunne's *café con leche*. "Where is he?"

"In the Vedado. You know where that is?"

"The rich folks' neighborhood."

"Nouveau riche, mostly."

"Let's not play *Twenty Questions*. Tell me straight."

Bassante rested his elbows on the table. He refolded his hands, put them together as if to pray, tips of index fingers touched tip of nose, briefer's pose, same as in Bari, gestures as distinctive as eye color or fingerprints.

He'd written Schwimmer, who contacted him when he came to New York. Schwimmer made clear he understood the power and resources possessed by those determined to thwart his search for Heinz. Louis Pohl's demise left no doubt about the ends they'd go to. Yet the criminals and their accomplices—and their protectors—couldn't be left in peace; and if he didn't succeed, someone somewhere would. Justice would be done. Not perfect justice. But enough that the world could never again deny or hide or ignore what happened.

Bassante caught the waiter's attention. He asked for half a cup of *café americano* and a double shot of rum. "What about you, Fin?"

"A little early for rum, don't you think?"

"My first and last of the penultimate day of 1958."

Though impressed by Schwimmer, Bassante said, he didn't have a "road to Damascus" moment in which he suddenly decided to put aside his resolve "to stick to caves and crevices." Yet he wasn't surprised to hear himself say he wanted to help—that he'd do all he could—and wouldn't accept anything beyond reimbursement for expenses.

"Why the change?" Bassante shrugged at his own question, as if unsure of the answer. "In the end, I suppose, I did it for selfish motives. Years ago, I sent a request to General Donovan to be transferred from my role as a briefer and sent on a mission. I didn't want that transfer. I'd briefed enough agents who never came back or were physical or psychological wrecks when they did.

"I couldn't admit it to myself at the time, but I phrased the request in such a way I was certain it would be rejected. It's never stopped haunting me. I knew this would be my last chance to get that transfer, so I took it."

Bassante traveled to Bonn with Schwimmer, who'd cultivated a contact within the BND. A former member of the Abwehr, the military intelligence operation run by Admiral Canaris, Schwimmer's contact avoided the fate of Canaris and his circle, who were executed by the SS for plotting to overthrow Hitler. He harbored a deep loathing for the former SS members now working within the BND and described to Schwimmer the rivalries rife within the organization. This included the existence of a top-secret unit that was said to report directly to the CIA.

Schwimmer's source confided that the unit was being reorganized. Its chief had been whisked out of the country. The reason was unclear. Rather than send him back to his former hideout, there was an unconfirmed report that he'd been temporarily parked in Cuba.

"That struck me as an odd choice," Bassante said, "till I gave it more thought. In fact, it's perfect: A country in turmoil, consumed by conflicts that concentrate the attention of participants and spectators alike; the dictator in power unlikely to do anything to aggravate or complicate relations with the U.S.; the insurgents too absorbed in taking power and setting up a new government to care about much else.

"I came to Havana to see what I could find out. A buddy from Counterintelligence who retired here put me in touch with a local private investigator. I didn't get too specific. I gave him a general description of the person I was looking for. Turns out that Havana is a very small big city. Everybody knows everybody else's business, and when a foreigner takes up residence—especially when he rents a mansion and is accompanied by bodyguards—interest is high.

"The investigator got back to me within a few days. He was sure he'd located the person I was looking for. Rumor was that the foreigner was a Swiss or German, a doctor who was planning to operate as an abortionist for an exclusively wealthy clientele. I went out and scouted the place. I caught a fleeting glimpse of him in the backseat of his car as it left the driveway. He was leaning forward to say something to the chauffeur. It was Heinz. No doubt about it. He apparently feels supremely secure in Havana—and why not? Chaos has always been his friend. Amid the current turmoil, he's no doubt aware of how little anyone cares about his presence."

The waiter brought the coffee and rum. Bassante poured the rum into the cup, raised it to his lips with both hands. "We have a plan."

"That's what Schwimmer said on the phone. What is it?"

"Heinz resides in a comfortable villa off Calle G in the Vedado. He has two bodyguards, who are probably Cuban policemen hired by his protectors to provide personal security. He goes to the Hotel Nacional several times a week for either lunch or dinner but follows no set schedule—with one exception.

"Wednesday and Saturday nights he visits a brothel on Calle Consulado, in the shadow of the Capitolio, where the national assembly sat until Batista seized power. Heinz travels with one bodyguard, who stays in the car. In true SS style, Heinz carries out his mission with efficiency and punctuality—arrives at midnight and leaves at one."

Bassante placed a leather cigar holder on the table. He flipped it open. Inside was a hypodermic needle. "This is for the driver, in the neck. The one who administers the needle hides on the car floor. Heinz will be annoyed to find him asleep but not surprised. The other two pounce, cover his face with a chloroform-soaked sponge, shove him in.

"What do you think, Fin?" Bassante finished his coffee and rum.

"Then what?"

"We drive to the harbor." Bassante put the cigar holder back in his pocket. "We've hired a boat, small but seaworthy. We sail to the Yucatán."

"And what if you're stopped by the Mexican authorities?'

"We've acquired the proper papers."

"To authorize a kidnapping across international borders?"

"To assure we won't be interfered with. They didn't come cheap."

"And after the Yucatán?"

"Mexico City."

"What's in Mexico City?"

"The Israeli embassy."

"They're expecting you?"

Stefan Schwimmer slipped in from the barroom to the left. He put his hand on Dunne's shoulder. "I'm glad you've come, Fin."

"I'm explaining the plan." Bassante fiddled with his empty cup.

"I heard." Schwimmer sat beside Bassante on the banquette. "You have doubts?"

"Questions."

"For instance?"

"You're going to take Heinz to the Israeli embassy in Mexico City, but they're not expecting you?

"I met with the Mossad station chief. He said they've more

'pressing priorities than chasing phantoms.' I persisted in presenting the case that Hemmer is Heinz—that he's alive and well. He suggested I'm 'too emotionally involved' to make a rational judgment. 'Is there any Jew devoid of emotional involvement in bringing these Nazis to justice?' I asked. He claimed they had 'more concrete prospects.' We'll see what they think when SS-Hauptsturmführer Karsten Heinz is delivered to their doorstep."

"*If* you deliver him."

"You don't think it'll work?" Bassante continued tapping his cup.

"I think you're way ahead of yourselves."

"We're about a decade and a half behind," Schwimmer said.

"Let's hear Fin out."

"Are you sure you're not being followed?"

"By whom?" Schwimmer wiped perspiration from his palms with a napkin.

"By anyone."

"I'm sure."

"What makes you sure?"

"I've never noticed even a hint of being followed."

"All that might mean is you're being followed by a pro."

"We're *not* being followed."

"Suppose you are . . . suppose the driver only pretends to be asleep . . . suppose he isn't alone . . . suppose you turn out to be the hunted, not the hunters—what then?"

"I've no idea how long Heinz will be in Havana. For all I know, he'll be gone tomorrow, God knows where. Tomorrow night—Wednesday—is perfect."

"Tomorrow night?"

"New Year's Eve, streets filled with revelers, nobody paying attention."

"Don't you see what you're doing? You're making the same mistake Louie Pohl made. You're jumping the gun."

Schwimmer threw the napkin on the table. "The only gun Pohl jumped was when he trusted Bartlett. This is the best—perhaps last—chance we'll have to get Heinz. I'm not letting it slip through my fingers."

"I don't want to hurt your feelings, but look, you're amateurs. You don't have the slightest notion of what it takes to make sure a mission like this goes right—or what to do when it goes wrong."

"You forget. I served in the RAF."

"As a bombardier, if I remember correctly."

"You're a professional, aren't you? A veteran of clandestine operations?"

"Long ago and far away."

"I asked you here because I thought you'd ensure our success. If it turns out to be only the three of us, so be it."

"Three?"

"Yes."

"Bassante, you, and who else?"

"Her."

Dunne looked up. *Mirror, mirror on the wall.* The lean, honey-haired woman reflected in the glass above Schwimmer's head approached with quick, determined stride. He didn't recognize her face but remembered her eyes: green and as purposeful as her step.

Dunne lingered in the lobby with Frieda after her brother and Bassante left. If she were the damaged, fragile creature her brother had made out, she gave no sign.

"Stefan didn't want me to come. He thinks people who give expression to their emotions are weak. I think the opposite."

"There's no room for mistakes."

"He thinks he knows what I endured. He doesn't. Not all of it." She stared down at the carpet.

"Your brother is trying to look out for your best interests."

"How is it possible for anyone who wasn't there to truly know?" She looked up. Her green pupils seemed to intensify into fiery emerald. "I was one of the girls Heinz sterilized. It was an 'experiment.' There were a dozen of us, Jewish teenagers. He did it without any anesthetics. Four of the girls died from infections. I was the one who labeled him *der Blaue Teufel*."

"You survived."

"Yes, thanks to Dr. Niskolczi, I was among the few. Did you know he took his own life?"

"I didn't."

"When he reached Budapest, he confirmed that his wife and daughters had perished at Auschwitz. He came to Nuremberg and gave a lengthy deposition for use against Heinz. After he learned of Heinz's transfer to London, where he 'died,' Niskolczi bit down on a lethal pill. He suspected the truth, I'm sure."

"I admired him."

"And he admired you . . . and your companion, Major . . ."

"Van Hull."

"Yes."

"He survived the war, yes?"

"Yes. He died only a short while ago."

"Stefan says you're not alone."

"I brought my wife."

"Though he won't tell you so, my brother was displeased. He thinks she'll be an impediment."

"Roberta, my wife?" He laughed. There was no way to share her story—their story—in a few sentences, saga of the last twenty years, how they'd met, her strength and courage, how their marriage came about, what it survived, crests, plateaus, troughs, distances imposed and incurred, all they'd come to mean to one another. Why even try? It would all come out garbled and sentimental. "If anything, she'll be an asset."

"You sounded so dubious about being part of this." The

intensity in her eyes had subsided. Her face was expressionless. "Yet you've agreed."

"I'm still dubious. What I'm certain of is what will happen if I *don't* go along."

"You're brave."

"I'm just too far down the road to turn back."

She took his hand, gently squeezed. "A great philosopher once said: 'That which does not kill me makes me stronger.' I'm stronger all the time now. Stronger than my brother. Hearing your voice on the phone, I remembered the assurance Niskolczi gave us. Providence, he said, would see to it some measure of justice is done."

Dunne had a vague memory of the exchange: *Providence.* A third-rate city in a third-rate state. Or something more. It remained to be seen.

The plan they agreed on took advantage of the presence of Roberta and Frieda. They'd rendezvous on New Year's Eve at nine p.m. in the Barcelona's second-floor ballroom—tourists enjoying a festive supper with good food and a Latin band, and none of the overpriced excesses associated with the high rollers at the splashy nightclubs and casinos.

After the midnight revel, the women would retire to their rooms. The three men would go for a stroll, mixing with the crowds who filled the streets, rich and poor mingling in a raucous but good-natured melee of drinking, singing, and dancing. They'd gradually make their way west to Calle Consulado, where the presence of several well-known but discreetly run brothels added to the celebratory mix.

Once they'd taken care of the bodyguard and chloroformed Heinz, they'd drive to a prearranged spot on the Prado, where Frieda and Roberta would be waiting in a car hired by Schwimmer. (He'd dropped a wad of dollars on the driver to get him to take the night off and, after a stormy disagreement with his sister, consented to let her act as driver.) They'd transfer Heinz and proceed to the pier where the boat to Mexico was moored.

In the morning, they did a dry run, visiting each location and going over every detail. A bottle of champagne with compliments of the management was delivered to Fin and Roberta's room in the late afternoon. They left it untouched. When they were on the boat to Mexico, they'd have a real celebration.

The ballroom at the Barcelona was filled to capacity. They did their best to look as if they were enjoying the New Year's festivities, taking turns on the dance floor with Roberta and Frieda, who, unlike the men, genuinely seemed to be having fun. They bantered with two other American couples at nearby tables, toasting with champagne-filled glasses they conveniently misplaced or spilled.

By half past twelve, the reserve exhibited earlier in the evening had fallen away. The band was playing louder. Everybody was up dancing. A conga line formed. Roberta and Frieda made an inconspicuous exit. Dunne led Schwimmer and Bassante out among the tide of swaying dancers, strolling guitarists, bongo players, and sloshed *yanqui* tourists surging through the streets.

They turned onto Calle Consulado. Roused by a burst of fireworks, a squadron of bats swooped around the dome of the Capitolio. Heinz's car was where they expected it to be. The driver puffed on a cigarette, ignoring the antics of giddy, inebriated pedestrians.

They huddled in a darkened doorway across from the brothel. Schwimmer pushed back his sleeve and nervously eyed his wristwatch. "Heinz will be out any minute. Let's take our positions." He turned to Bassante. "Ready?"

Bassante carefully removed the syringe from its case. "Ready."

"Soon as Fin and I get to the other side, make your move."

Dunne surveyed the street. Perfect setup for an easy snatch. Too perfect. Too easy.

"Let's go." Schwimmer stepped out of the doorway.

Dunne grabbed his arm. "Wait."

"For what?" Schwimmer spit out the words in a tight, angry whisper.

"For Heinz to come out."

"For Christ's sake, that's not what we agreed to." He shoved Dunne's hand away.

"Heinz may not be in there."

"If you're backing out, fine. Bassante and I will take care of this."

Dunne stepped close to Schwimmer. "Are you sure that's Heinz's regular driver?"

"What are you getting at?"

"Maybe this is a diversion."

"If it isn't, we're blowing our best—and probably last—chance to grab him."

"What's the harm in waiting until Heinz comes out? We'll still have the advantage of surprise."

"Fin is right. If we go ahead and he isn't in there, we'll be exposed."

"It's already ten after one." Schwimmer glowered at Bassante "This is a hell of a time to change plans."

"It's better to make sure before we move." Bassante repocketed the syringe.

"I guess you two have made up your minds." Schwimmer stalked away. Dunne followed him to the other side of the street. They loitered silently in the gloomy space beneath the portico of shuttered building beside the brothel. A few tipsy patrons emerged and went their way. Heinz wasn't among them. His car and driver stayed where they were. Bassante peeked out of the doorway once or twice. One thirty came and went.

Schwimmer began to pace. "I think we should go in and see if he's there."

"I doubt the madam will give us a guided tour."

The crowd in the street thinned until all that was left was a woman in a long gown and her escort in a bedraggled tuxedo. They fell asleep on a doorstep.

At two o'clock, a portly, cigar-smoking man in a guayabera and paper party hat stepped out of the brothel. He pulled a string of firecrackers from his pocket, lit the fuse with his cigar, and tossed them into the street. He stopped in front of the portico and smiled at Schwimmer. "*¡Feliz año nuevo!*"

Schwimmer smiled back, unprepared for the left hook that crashed into the side of his head and sent him reeling toward the street. Brass knuckles flashed in the light of the street lamp as a second blow hit. Schwimmer swayed but didn't fall.

Dunne pivoted. His neck was noosed by a thick forearm that jerked him back. The choking pressure made him feel as if he might pass out. He rammed his elbow backward, swung around, grabbed his attacker's hair, pulled his head down, and shot a knee into his face. A geyser of blood spurted from his nose.

Schwimmer lay in a ball on the ground—knees drawn up, hands covering his face—trying to protect himself from a ceaseless succession of kicks. Dunne pulled his gun from his pocket and slammed Schwimmer's attacker at the base of his skull, knocking off his party hat and sending him to his knees.

"Fin!" Bassante wobbled toward him from across the street. He stopped and collapsed face first. His head hit the curb with an ugly, hollow thud. Whoever he'd been struggling with hopped into the car supposedly waiting for Heinz. The driver stomped on the gas pedal and the car roared away.

Dunne knelt beside Bassante and rolled him on his back. The syringe he'd held at the ready was stuck in his wrist. Dunne dragged him under the portico. Schwimmer lay moaning in the shadows.

Their attackers had fled. Dunne pounded on the door of the brothel. It stayed closed. A car turned the corner from the direction of the Capitolio. Dunne stuck the gun in his belt, planted himself in the middle of the street, and waved his arms back and forth as the headlights approached.

The car stopped. The passenger door opened. Roberta ran toward him. "Fin, we waited on the Prado. Finally, Frieda insisted we look for you. Where are the others?"

"Help me get them into the car." He led her to the portico. They lifted Bassante and Schwimmer, who were both unconscious, into the back. She gasped when she saw their battered faces.

Dunne got in the front seat. At his feet was a small ice-filled bucket with a bottle inserted upside down. "What's this?"

Roberta popped her head up from the back. She pressed a handkerchief to Bassante's bloodied face. "It's the bottle that was sent to our room. Frieda and I thought we'd celebrate once we got to the boat." She held out her hands. "Pass me the ice."

Dunne plucked a chilled bottle of champagne from the bucket. "You got a little ahead of yourself, don't you think?" He lifted the bucket and shifted it to her over his shoulder. "'The best-laid schemes o' mice an' men gang aft agley.'"

He read her eyes in the rearview mirror: more irritation than fear. She scooped out a handful of ice, wrapped it in her handkerchief, and held it to Bassante's face.

As Frieda drove down Calle Consulado, he gave them both an abbreviated version of what had happened. Frieda banged the dashboard with the heel of her hand. "Heinz fooled us."

People were streaming toward the Malecón. The celebration seemed to be spontaneously reviving. "Do you know where he lives, Frieda?"

"I rode past with Stefan. It's off La Rampa. I'm sure I can find my way."

"We have to get these two to a hospital." Roberta leaned into the front seat. "Heinz must be gone by now."

Frieda veered onto the Malecón and sped toward the Vedado. "We won't know for sure until we see for ourselves." They turned left when they reached La Rampa. The car in front braked to a sudden stop. She had to swerve to avoid hitting it. Lights were coming on everywhere. Cuban flags sprouted from windows.

"Pull over." Dunne stopped a crowd of teenagers. "*¿Qué pasa?*"

They danced around him. "*¡Batista se fue! ¡El Presidente ha huido!*"

A band of men wearing red-and-black armbands—the colors of Castro's Twenty-sixth of July Movement—marched down the middle of the street. They surrounded the car. Several waved revolvers. A twentyish-looking youth lowered his revolver, stuck his brown, handsome, smile-creased face into the car. He glanced around and yelled, "*¡La revolución está aquí!*"

Frieda looked at Dunne. "What should I do?"

"For starters, put the car in park." Dunne reached down, grabbed the bottle of champagne, opened the door, and got out. He ripped off the gold foil, untwisted the wire around the top, and levered the cork with his thumb until it shot into the air with a loud, celebratory *pop*. Fizzing, bubbling liquid gushed out. A cheer went up

Dunne raised the bottle to his mouth, gulped. The contents spilled across his chin. He wiped his mouth with the back of his hand and passed the bottle to the revolver-wielding youth, who took a generous swig as he simultaneously pointed his revolver into the air and fired a shot. There was more cheering. "*¡Acompáñenos!*" The youth put his arm through Dunne's. The crowd moved off with Dunne in tow.

"Oh God." Frieda sounded close to tears. She rested her forehead on the steering wheel. "What else can go wrong?"

Roberta climbed out of the rear seat. Dunne was stopped at the corner. Several men were around him. He had one hand on the shoulder of the young man with the revolver; with the other, he gestured toward the car. The young man nodded. He raised the champagne bottle, as if making a toast. Dunne turned and walked back.

"I was afraid they wouldn't let you go." Roberta took his hand. "What did you tell them?"

"The truth." He opened the rear door. "I explained my two friends in the back had a run-in with the police, and I had to get them to a hospital. The champagne helped. They were sympathetic. They're headed to the casinos to show that the Cuban people are taking back their country. Batista has already fled"—he snapped his fingers—"just like that. It's the gangsters and the American government they blame. They bear no grudge against the American people. At least for now." He gave her a gentle shove. "Get in."

Frieda drove slowly. The swelling mobs parted reluctantly to let the car proceed. In the distance, there was a telltale percussive rattle, either Batista's loyalists making a last stand or, as seemed more likely from the growing numbers in the streets, the rebels celebrating their triumph. Maybe both.

Stefan Schwimmer lay still. Bassante let out a moan. His eyes were closed. The ice-laden handkerchief Roberta held against his mouth was soaked with blood. "Let's get these two to a doctor. We've had enough bad luck for tonight. We can try again in the morning."

"We're getting close." Frieda looked around intently. "I know it."

"Roberta's right," Dunne said. "There's just no sense trying to make our way through this chaos."

Frieda pulled onto a side street and parked. "The house is right around here." She grabbed her shoulder bag, hopped out of the car, and started down the street.

"You've got to stop her!" Roberta said. "I'll stay here with these two."

He stared at the dashboard. He ran his hand back and forth over the surface. It looked like metal but felt like water, cold and liquid. Which was it? He pushed on it with the tip of his index finger.

She poked him hard. "What are you waiting for?"

"The dashboard."

"What about it?"

He felt it again. The water turned back to metal. How could that be?

"Fin, are you all right?"

"Fine." He stepped out of the car into the street. The outlines of the large, impressive houses that lined both sides of the street loomed in the darkness behind a wall of protective shrubbery. Frieda passed beneath the watery light of the street's lone lamp-post. He followed her. The light grew brighter as he approached until it was so intense he had to shield his eyes. When he was directly below, he looked up. The moon and lamp had melded into an eye the size of a giant grapefruit. Surrounded by a green iris, the pupil was translucent. Yellow light streamed through it.

"This is it, Fin. I'm sure of it." Frieda was calling to him in a low voice from a few yards away. She stepped around the shrubbery into a driveway. The carpet of finely ground coral crunched beneath her feet. Ahead was a gracefully arched porte cochere. She mounted three stone steps onto the veranda of the house

As Dunne walked onto the doorway, the bits of coral scurried away. He heard them cry. They were alive. He tiptoed as lightly as could, trying not to crush them. He joined Frieda on the veranda as she peered through a locked set of French doors into a room that was empty except for some scattered pieces of sheet-covered furniture. She shook her head. "I'm afraid we're too late. He's already gone."

He put his face to the glass. The sheets rotated around one another in a dance-like motion. As they circled, they fell to the floor, revealing not chairs or sofas, but piles of bones. The bones stirred, snapped together, toes to feet to ankle bones, pelvis and ribs, self-constructing skeletons, each crowned by a smiling skull. They joined hand to bony hand.

"Christ almighty!" Dunne twisted and jiggled the unyielding doorknob.

Frieda seized his arm. "What are you doing?"

"Look in there!"

"Lower your voice, Fin. We don't know who might still be around."

"Look at them!" The skeletons had formed a slow-moving conga line.

"Look at what?"

"At them. The way they're dancing."

"Who?"

"*Them.*" He pulled his arm loose. "Look! Look before they're gone!"

She cradled his face in her hands. "Your pupils—they're dilated."

He pushed her hands away. "Look!" The line of dancing skeletons snaked into an adjoining room.

"Fin, you're seeing things."

"They're real, I'm telling you."

"Come with me." She took firm grip of his hand and led him off the veranda, through the porte cochere, onto the lawn at the rear of the house. She helped him lie down, stroked his head, and took his pistol from his belt.

The blades of grass tingled against his neck, individual and distinct, hundreds of them but no two alike, the same as with snowflakes and those bits of coral that were all different, all alive.

"Do you hear me, Fin?"

"Yes."

"I don't know how it was done, but you've been drugged. Do you understand?"

The blades of grass tickled his hands and neck. He laughed.

"Close your eyes and relax. Don't move until I get back, promise?"

"Promise."

He opened his eyes. She was gone. The stars were faded and half-drowsy. The sound of the tumult that had enveloped the city echoed ever more faintly in the distance.

The blades spoke with chirping voices:

Is this the happiest you've ever been?

No, I've been happier.

When?

I can't remember exactly. But this is fine. I'm happy enough.

We're happy when you're happy.

It doesn't bother you that I'm lying on top of you?

That's what we're here for, and when you're doing what you were put here for, you're happy. That's true for everybody, every-thing.

I have to think about that.

Go ahead and think all you like.

The bits of coral chimed in, murmuring a steady protest against the tires rolling over them. Dunne sat up. Just short of the porte cochere, a car came to a stop. The headlights flashed on and off. A set of cellar doors angled into the foundation of the house swung open. Bag in hand, a figure emerged and hurried toward the car. The driver leaped out and trotted in front of the headlights to greet him.

Dunne recognized the lights, their harsh brightness. He lifted his hand to shield his eyes from the glare. They'd taken Dick Van Hull prisoner. He had no doubt about it. "Hey!" he shouted as he got to his feet. "Stay where you are!"

The driver turned and crouched. A sharp crack and spit of fire was instantly followed by a metallic whine so close to his ear that Dunne sensed its sting. He held up his hand. He'd catch the next one.

A hard thrust from behind, directly below his knees, cut him down and sent him sprawling face first onto the grass. He turned and craned his neck to see who was on top of him. Roberta's face was only a few inches from his. She pressed his shoulders to the ground and spoke directly in his ear: "Stay down."

The driver fired again. The bullet whizzed overhead.

As he squirmed to get free, Frieda stepped out of the shadows. She aimed a gun at the car, her right wrist held steady in the grip of her left hand. "Heinz!" she screamed.

The figure behind the driver, half shielded by the open car door, looked toward her. She fired, once, twice. The first bullet shattered the window shield; the second hit him square in the middle of the forehead. He crumpled onto the driveway.

Wisps of smoke hovered in front of her face.

The driver fired a rapid succession of shots as he dragged the body into the car, ran around the rear, and hurled himself into the driver's seat.

Frieda fired another shot. The rear window shield exploded.

The car reached the street, screeched into forward, and raced away.

"*Der Blaue Teufel*, I killed him! I saw it! I killed him! She repeated herself several times, her voice growing louder with each repetition.

Roberta stood. "Give me a hand with Fin," she said. They helped him to his feet. He looked up.

The weary, bloodshot moon winked at him.

Fin, wake up, you're having a bad dream. Whirr and wheel of time. Seesaw up and down. Drip, drip, going, gone. Maybe time makes no sense. Maybe we make sense of it because if it makes no sense, we make no sense.

Leftover thoughts from the night before.

Asleep, her back to him, Roberta purred. Her thick auburn hair spread across the pillow. He lifted the sheet. Her body curved like two hills, a shallow rift between.

The motionless mahogany blades on the fan suspended from the stucco ceiling: Dunne tried to make sense of them. They were no longer shaped like coccyxes, giant cuckoo beaks, opening and closing ravenously. The blades were just blades.

He stretched his left arm to the nightstand beside the bed, groped past radio, phone, champagne bottle. His fingers closed around cigarettes and matches. He lit one.

Inhale, exhale, repeat, inhale, exhale, repeat.

A rim of sunlight, square and thin, framed the curtains in front of the door leading to the balcony.

The curtain was just a curtain. No longer a giant movie screen featuring Technicolor newsreels with Gene Kelly and Rita Hayworth dancing up the steps to the podium at Nuremberg's Zeppelin Field as Peter Bunde and Harry Mundy descended by parachute, landing on each side of the chorus of altar boys intoning the Suscipiat.

Fan was just a fan; curtain just a curtain.

He sat on the side of the bed, naked, and smoked.

Inhale, exhale, repeat.

He ran his fingers through his hair, clasped the cigarette in his teeth, poked the small pile of clothes on the floor with his toes. Under Roberta's nylons and garter belt were his shorts. He pulled them on and stood. He staggered, grabbed hold of the bed's headboard, and steadied himself. He gazed down at Roberta's face, placid, intact.

He went into the bathroom. He tossed the cigarette into the toilet and took a leak. The leak was just a leak, ordinary. He aimed the yellow stream directly at the butt, an old habit, blasting those Jap aircraft carriers, *Remember Pearl Harbor.* He gripped the cold-water tap, held a glass beneath, filled it till it spilled, emptied it without pausing.

He filled the basin halfway, splashed face. Repeat, splash, repeat.

The face in the mirror above the sink: his. He touched nose, cheeks, chin.

Last night, the melting face in the mirror above the bureau in the bedroom—whose was that? Roberta's. Her hair was green.

Roberta's hair was auburn, not green. Her face hadn't melted.

He noticed red marks on his shoulders. Roberta clasped them in an iron grip. Her nails dug into his flesh. There were lifeless heaps of rags lying about. She wouldn't let go, and then he didn't want her to. He exploded inside her, out through himself into her, and through her, into the sky, soared, swooped, wings spread, and landed on the wine-dark sea, only it wasn't winedark. It was azure. Her body rippled beneath him, steady rhythm of waves meeting shore, repeat, repeat, repeat, until they subsided and stopped.

—Ah, she said.

—Ahh, he said.

A jumble of dreams, illusions, illuminations impossible to untangle. Nothing made sense. Everything did. It all fit together. It all fell apart.

A thought rushed through his head: *¿Cuándo es el próximo tren para Habana?*

He stepped across the bathroom floor. The black tiles were tiles, not spiders. He went into the bedroom. The rug was just a rug, soft and dry, not a puddle of water.

He put on his pants and shirt, pushed aside the curtain, and went out onto the balcony. The Havana air was gentle, cool; sky, bright blue. In the distance, Morro Castle, solid, sturdy, stood guard over the entrance to the harbor.

Torn paper, broken bottles, smashed slot machines, and the

tops of decapitated parking meters littered the street below. The remnants of a New Year's celebration as well as a revolution. Pedestrians waved Cuban flags. The celebration continued. A truck went by, horn blaring, voice on the loudspeaker cackling, *¡Viva la revolución!*

Dunne returned inside, closed doors, curtain. Roberta continued to purr. There was a soft knock on the door. He hesitated. Maybe whoever it was would go away.

Knock, repeat, knock repeat.

A dream?

—Who is it?

—It's Frieda.

He put his shoulder to the door. He enjoyed its solidity. The door was just a door, neither dream nor hallucination. His lips almost kissed the panel.

Roberta woke as soon as he opened it. She wrapped the sheet around herself and dashed into the bathroom.

Frieda sat at the desk. "Are you all right?'

"I'm not sure what I remember, what was real, what wasn't." Dunne dropped on the bed. Fragments began to form patterns, like pieces in a kaleidoscope. Turn the brass cylinder, pieces fall in place; turn again, they fall apart.

Roberta came out of the bathroom wrapped in one of the plush white robes the hotel provided. She took a cigarette from the pack and lit it. "You said something strange about the dashboard before you got out of the car. I got worried. I decided to follow you."

"Give me one, will you?" Dunne turned the brass cylinder again. "I saw Heinz get it right here." He tapped the middle of his forehead. "I'm sure it wasn't a hallucination."

She tossed him the pack. He flubbed the catch, bent over, and picked it up.

"It wasn't," Frieda said. "Your gun but my aim. I'm an expert shot."

Dunne lit a match. The flame wobbled as he held it to his cigarette.

"I didn't know what to think at first. I was afraid you'd cracked and lost your mind. But when I saw your eyes, I was certain you'd been drugged." Frieda gazed into the street. "That champagne that was sent to your room—it must have been laced with the same stuff they gave Louis Pohl. Those Cubans who drank it—they must have had an interesting night as well."

Roberta stood next to her. "What about your brother and Bassante?"

"I saw them this morning in the hospital. Bassante has a fractured jaw and a concussion. Stefan has several broken ribs. The place is crowded and chaotic. But they'll be all right."

"And you, Frieda? How are you?"

"Me? I'm better than I've been in a very long time."

Dunne lay back, head on pillow, forearm over his eyes.

Maybe he slipped back into the dream. Maybe he listened to the conversation between Roberta and Frieda. Maybe it was the kaleidoscope talking, Dick Van Hull, Michael Jahn, Dr. Niskolczi, nameless, numberless others:

Heinz is dead.

At last.

Case closed, no?

They'll destroy every trace of him. As far as historians will know, SS-Hauptsturmführer Dr. Karsten Heinz died of bronchopneumonia in London in 1946.

Hasn't some measure of justice been done?

Some. One murderer made to pay. A legion of others to be pursued, exposed, judged. The dead can't rest until they are.

When?

We'll see.

* * *

Dunne and Roberta flew out of Cuba on the day Fidel Castro made his triumphal entry into Havana. Bassante had left the day before. Frieda and Stefan Schwimmer drove with them to the airport. The crowds were immense and enthusiastic. They were delayed at one intersection for almost a half hour.

Stefan watched intently as bearded rebels in green fatigues paraded by. "A truly stirring sight," he said. "It reminds me of when I was in Barcelona, during the Spanish Civil War, and young idealists like these marched off against the Fascists. Unfortunately, I was also there when the NKVD purged their ranks, and the revolution gave way to the secret police, and the pursuit of human freedom was replaced by enforcement of ideological orthodoxy.

"I wish them the best. Maybe it will be different this time. For my part, I'm a charter member of the International Brigade of ex-Idealists. I don't believe in a perfect world. What I seek is a workable one where torturers and murderers of every stripe are brought to justice, the memory of their victims both honored and remembered as a warning against what must never be allowed to happen again."

Dunne shook hands with the Schwimmers at the bottom of the boarding stairs. Roberta hugged Frieda. The Schwimmers were leaving the next day for Mexico City and, after that, Tel Aviv.

"Stay safe," Dunne said. "Look us up when you're in Florida."

"We will. Meanwhile, stay out of trouble. You've seen more than your fair share." Stefan walked away.

Departure was delayed by a brief squall. Rain splattered against the window, droplets sliding into one another, plump, plumper, streaming down the glass, vanishing.

Frieda Schwimmer stayed at the gate until the plane took off. Though he knew she couldn't see him, Dunne waved.

Though he knew she couldn't hear, he whispered, "*L'chaim,* Frieda. *Totiusque.*"

Part IX
Addenda

OUR HIDDEN HEROES
by Alvin Capshaw

(Special to *The New York Standard*, Sunday Supplement, September 9, 1945)

The war formally concluded last week on the deck of the USS *Missouri* is now history. Though various heroic exploits are already well known, time alone will allow a fuller, if never complete, account of our fighting men. Certainlly, each branch of the Armed Services takes pride in highlighting the valor of its members and celebrating their contributions to victory—that is, every branch but one: the Office of Strategic Services (OSS). Rather than seek the spotlight, the OSS hugs the shadows.

The reason for this reticence isn't self-doubt or an instinct for self-effacement on the part of OSS founder General "Wild Bill" Donovan. It reflects the outfit's founding mission to undermine the enemy through the "dark arts" of psychological warfare, clandestine operations, and counterintelligence. How many OSS operatives gave their lives as part of this secret war may never be known.

In some instances, as with Operation Dawson, the outcome is a matter of public record. The twelve OSS agents involved were captured in Slovakia while on a mission to rescue Allied fliers, shipped to the Mauthausen concentration camp, brutally interrogated by the SS commandant Franz Ziereis, and shot. It's alleged that their bodies were given for dissection and "racial analysis" to an SS doctor.

The end of the Dawson team has drawn much attention. But the dramatic events that followed have gone unheralded. While honoring the commitment to anonymity and confidentiality, it's worth recalling a few of those whose insistence on going above and beyond the call of duty is at the heart of the OSS.

In January 1945, in the wake of the Nazis' success in crushing the revolt in Slovakia and capturing the Dawson operatives and the Allied fliers they were sent to rescue, the OSS considered how best to turn the tables. A new mission, Operation Maxwell, made up of three of the OSS's most experienced veterans, was soon under way. Unbeknown to the trio of OSS agents, not only had the Dawson operatives already been dispatched to Mauthausen but the SS had intercepted a squad of partisans and extracted details of the rescue mission.

The agents were barely on the ground when the SS arrived on the site. A firefight ensued in which the youngest of the team, a lieutenant of Slovak ancestry, was killed. Over the next several days, the two surviving operatives moved so rapidly and skillfully the Germans thought they were dealing with a far larger contingent.

At one point, their only way out was to jump from a precipice. One of the agents broke his ankle. Undeterred, they succeeded in hijacking a high-performance car and blew up an ammo dump as they made their getaway. When the odds of being stopped on the road became too great, they borrowed a handcar and pumped their way west. On learning that a trainload of Panzer tanks was on its way from Slovakia to East Prussia, where a Russian breakthrough was imminent, they sacrificed the handcar and improvised a blockage that derailed the German train, thus stopping the tanks from reaching their destination.

Back on foot, they did their best to hide in plain sight amid the swelling hordes of refugees and displaced persons crowding the roads. Dressed in worn, ragged civilian clothes, they moved steadily west, north of Vienna and south of Prague, where they guessed the American army would eventually push through into Czechoslovakia.

Their luck seemed to run out when one of them came down with typhus, which was raging among the uprooted, lice-ridden population. Sick, feverish, in a half-stupor, the afflicted agent encouraged his companion to leave him and flee unencumbered toward the American lines. Instead, he made his way to the nearest village to seek out a physician. When a German sentry stopped him, he resisted, killing the German and drawing the attention of local partisans who took him and his companion under their care, hiding them in a brewery, where they were given rest and medical care.

Had the story ended there, it would still reverberate with the resourcefulness and endurance that distinguished the wartime operations of the OSS.

But there's a final chapter that adds a heightened degree of drama and derring-do.

In one of those devil-take-the-hindmost moments that has earned Wild Bill and his organization their reputation, the general summoned one of his most trusted operatives, a man who in civilian life had been a prominent player in the public relations industry and was among the first to put his talents at the disposal of the OSS.

Donovan charged him with a special mission—the kind only the OSS would be bold enough to undertake. Using a captured German staff car, he and two assistants were to take $30,000 in gold coins and drive hell-bent for Prague, where they'd make contact with the Czech resistance.

With their help, he was to head to Theresienstadt, the so-called model concentration camp, where the prominent Czechoslovak chemist and leading layman of the Jewish community in Brno (Brünn during the German occupation) Dr. Herschel Cernak was among the remnant of prisoners being held.

Seizing on the uncertainty of when the Soviets might arrive and the newborn, eleventh-hour desire of elements of the Nazi apparatus to distance themselves from the regime's worst crimes, Donovan gambled that Dr. Cernak could be brought to safety.

Against all odds, the mission succeeded. The agent reached Prague, made contact with the resistance and proceeded to Theresienstadt. The rear guard of SS left in charge, devoid of its former swaggering omnipotence and amenable to bribery, turned a blind eye. Frail and thin, close to death, Dr. Cernak was brought to Prague and hidden.

Before he figured out the not-inconsequential matter of how to make the return trip, the agent made inquiries about the missing trio who had been dropped in hopes of rescuing the Dawson team. Headquarters presumed them dead, but he wanted to make sure. To his surprise and delight, he learned that the resistance was sheltering two surviving members. He arranged for them to be smuggled into Prague and stowed away safely.

On May 5 the resistance launched its uprising against the Germans. There was heavy fighting, but the Red Army entered the city on V-E Day and the game was up. After seven years of German occupation the first city to fall under the Nazi heel was free.

Happy as they were to witness the war's end in liberated Prague, the OSS agents unanimously agreed to complete their journey under their own steam. They were determined not to rely on the Soviets, whose mixture of hospitality and suspicion made it hard to spend time out of their sight, and to bring Dr. Cernak to the West.

Once word reached Donovan of the agents' situation, he sprang into action. Aware of the need for medical supplies in the Czech capital, he arranged a flight to deliver an emergency shipment. The plane landed on the very night that the city was set to celebrate the grand gala reopening of the Prague Opera House. The new government, the diplomatic corps, and the Soviet military command would all be in attendance.

Dr. Cernak and his American rescuer were also among the invited guests. Pretending to set out for the opera, they picked up the two OSS agents and made a beeline to the airport. They boarded the Lockheed Electra, which had just finished unloading its gift of medical supplies, and immediately took off for Paris.

The adventures of these OSS agents are small dots on the grand canvas of the war. Yet in their particularity—in the agents' consistent dedication and determination—is a unique reminder of that band of men, those hidden heroes, who have made the Office of Strategic Services, well, oh so special.

The New York Standard, August 26, 1973

CARLTON BAXTER BARTLETT, FORMER PUBLIC RELATIONS EXECUTIVE
AND GOVERNMENT OFFICIAL DIES; ILLUSTRIOUS CAREER ENDED
BY INVOLVEMENT IN BAY OF PIGS FIASCO

Carlton Baxter Bartlett, a former senior government official who was assigned much of the responsibility for the Central Intelligence Agency's failed attempt to topple the Castro government at the Bay of Pigs in Cuba, in April 1961, died suddenly yesterday at his apartment on Beekman Place, in Manhattan. He was 75.

Mr. Bartlett had heart problems, said Kenneth Moss, president of Bartlett & Partners, the international public relations firm Bartlett founded in 1930, which is now a subsidiary of ISC.

While his role as a principal architect of what became a disaster for the newly installed Kennedy administration is widely remembered, Mr. Bartlett had already made great, though largely unsung, contributions during and after World War II.

As director of the Department of Information, Communication & Policy Analysis for the Office of Strategic Services (OSS), he served as a highly regarded aide to its legendary founder, General "Wild Bill" Donovan. "Where some agents of the OSS were content to fight the war from behind a desk," commented Mr. Moss, "Carl Bartlett could usually be found in the field."

As deputy director of planning for the CIA, he helped guide the clandestine operations that toppled the left-leaning government of Iranian Prime Minister Mohammad Mosaddegh in 1953 and installed Mohammad-Reza Shah Pahlavi. He is also credited with playing a pivotal role in bringing about the 1954 coup d'état that ousted President Jacobo Árbenz Guzmán's administration in Guatemala, which was seen by many as the spearhead of Communist subversion throughout the Western Hemisphere.

Recalling that Mr. Bartlett "helped design and implement efforts to counter Soviet spy efforts throughout the world, and especially in Western Europe," Mr. Moss said that Bartlett would "be particularly

347

remembered for his role in rebuilding the intelligence capabilities of the Federal Republic of Germany."

Mr. Bartlett submitted his resignation shortly after the Bay of Pigs operation. In 1971, on the tenth anniversary of that failed invasion, President Nixon awarded him the National Security Medal, calling his contributions to American intelligence operations "unique."

Little in his previous life appeared to point him toward intelligence work, much less clandestine activity.

Carlton Baxter Bartlett was the son of Waldo Bartlett, an executive at the Equitable Life Insurance Company, and Marigold Alden Fiske, a descendant of Mayflower Pilgrims. He attended Yale but did not graduate, choosing instead to join the firm of Ivy Lee & Associates, which managed press relations for some of the country's most prestigious corporations.

Bartlett helped pioneer the firm's involvement in the business of subtlety by aggressively protecting and burnishing the reputations of corporations and their executives. Today a multimillion-dollar industry and mainstay of corporate activity that has grown to include celebrities as well as politicians, "public relations" was still in its infancy when Bartlett began.

After his service in the OSS and his postwar involvement in creating what eventually became the CIA, Bartlett returned to the leadership of Bartlett & Partners. He was subsequently recalled by both Democratic and Republican administrations to serve in various high-ranking positions within the national intelligence community.

Though remembered by friends as "modest and shy," Mr. Bartlett has been a mainstay of New York City's social circuit and art scene. The acquisition of Bartlett & Partners by ISC in 1957 left him an extremely wealthy man. He enjoyed a reputation as an astute collector of modern art, and his perspicacity in buying some early works by leading Abstract Expressionist painters allowed him to amass a collection now valued at several million dollars.

All three of his marriages ended in divorce. He leaves no survivors.

"Carlton Baxter's successes far outweigh his failures," said Mr. Moss. "For now, many of those achievements remain classified information. We can only hope that the day is not far off when a full accounting of this man's remarkable life can be entered into the public record."

THE NATIONAL SECURITY ARCHIVE
THE CIA AND NAZI WAR CRIMINALS:
National Security Archive Posts Secret CIA History

Released Under War Crimes Disclosure Act

Washington, D.C., February 4, 2005. The National Security Archive today posted the CIA's secret documentary history of the U.S. government's relationship with General Reinhard Gehlen, the German Army's intelligence chief for the Eastern Front during World War II. At the end of the war, Gehlen established a close relationship with the U.S. and successfully maintained his intelligence network (it ultimately became the West German BND) even though he employed numerous former Nazis and known war criminals. The use of Gehlen's group, according to the CIA history *Forging an Intelligence Partnership: CIA and the Origins of the BND*, was a "double-edged sword" that "boosted the Warsaw pact's propaganda efforts" and "suffered devastating penetrations by the KGB."

The declassified two-volume history was compiled by CIA historian Kevin Ruffner and presented in 1999 by CIA Deputy Director for Operations Jack Downing to the German Intelligence service (Bundesnachrichtendienst) in remembrance of "the new and close ties" formed in postwar Germany and to mark the fiftieth year of CIA–West German cooperation. Declassified in 2002, it contains 97 key documents from various agencies.

This posting comes in the wake of public grievances lodged by members of the Interagency Working Group (IWG) that the CIA has not fully complied with the mandate of the Nazi War Crimes Disclosure Act and is continuing to withhold hundreds of thousands of pages of documentation related to their work. (Established in 1999, the IWG has overseen the declassification of about eight million pages of documents from multiple government agencies. Its mandate expires in March of this year.)

Several members of the IWG went on record with their criticisms. Former congresswoman Elizabeth Holtzman stated that "the CIA has defied the law, and in so doing has also trivialized the Holocaust, thumbed its nose at the survivors and also at the Americans who gave their lives in the effort to defeat the Nazis." According to Washington attorney Richard Ben-Veniste, "the posture the CIA has taken differs from all the other agencies that have been involved, and that's not a position we can accept."

Louis Pohl, a lawyer and activist with the Human Rights Foundation who has written extensively on alleged CIA abuses and whose uncle was a member of the Agency's founding generation, stated: "The time is long past for the CIA to come clean about its extensive involvement with former members of Hitler's terror apparatus." Pohl wrote the foreword to Turlough Bassante's 1981 book, *Let the Murderers Be Judged*, an exposé of the U.S.'s recruitment and use of Nazi intelligence agents, which was dismissed by many at the time as "sensationalist" and "unfounded."

The documentation unearthed by the IWG leaves no doubt that the relationship between Nazi war criminals and American intelligence organizations—including the CIA—was far deeper and more intimate than formerly thought. For example, current records show that associates of Adolf Eichmann worked for the CIA; a score of other Nazis, including former SS concentration camp personnel, were actively recruited; and at least 100 officers within the Gehlen organization were former SD or Gestapo officers.

The IWG enlisted the help of distinguished scholars and historians to consult during the declassification process. Last May, they released their own interpretation of the declassified material, *U.S. Intelligence and the Nazis*, in which they concluded: "The notion that they [the CIA, Army Counterintelligence Corps, and the BND] employed only a few bad apples will not stand up to the new documentation . . . Hindsight allows us to see that American use of actual or alleged war criminals was a blunder in several respects . . . there was no compelling reason to begin the postwar era with the assistance of some of those associated with the worst crimes of the war.

"Lack of sufficient attention to history—and, on a personal level, to character and morality—established a bad precedent, especially for new intelligence agencies. It also brought into intelligence organizations men and women previously incapable of distinguishing between their political/ideological beliefs and reality. As a result, such individuals could not and did not deliver good intelligence. Finally, because their new, professed 'democratic convictions' were at best insecure and their pasts could be used against them, these recruits represented a potential security problem."

In answer to the question "Can we learn from history?" the IWG's consulting historians quoted from the conclusion of Turlough Bassante's *Let the Murderers Be Judged*: "The real question is not whether we can make use of our past to deal with the present and shape the future, but whether we have the courage, vision, and resolve to do so."

◆

Eat the Moon *by Thornton Van Hull. (Forensic Manor Press)* Before his death in 1958, OSS veteran Van Hull deposited his manuscript on a library shelf in the girls' academy in which he taught. It lay there unread until the school closed and a local bookseller was invited to cart off what he wished. "The dusty binder that tumbled into his hands," writes military historian John Murray in his introduction, "contained a firsthand account of a botched rescue mission in near war's end. It's a small, elegantly told tale filled with the larger truths of what war really involves." Van Hull's ground-level view is of ordinary men who do extraordinary things not in service to patriotic abstractions but out of loyalty to one another. Among the memoir's many notable aspects is Van Hull's frank description of his homosexuality, in particular his love affair with a fellow OSS agent (identified only as M.), who was captured and killed by the SS. The title is taken from Yeats's poem, "Brown Penny": "O love is the crooked thing / There is nobody wise enough / To find out all that is in it / For he would be thinking of love / Till the stars had run away / And the shadows eaten the moon." Amid the unending torrent of WWII narratives, Van Hull's is a reminder of the millions of untold stories and tragedies hidden forever beneath the shadows of the last "good war." (www.bookblitz.com)

◆

Cutchogue, New York, 12/30/13: With a dozen bestsellers behind her—several made into movies—writer Tess O'Keefe might seem ready to sit back and smell the roses. (Or, as part owner of a vineyard on the North Fork, sip chardonnay.) But at age 76, she's just signed a contract for a series of detective novels featuring private eye Fintan Dunne. "I took the name from real life," says O'Keefe. "Fintan Dunne was a mentor of mine. He had a wonderful edge about him, a blend of cynicism and humanism, sharpened by a decade on the NYPD and service in both world wars. But my Fintan won't be a duplicate of the original. He'll be cyber hip and post-modern, with a Peruvian partner/girlfriend who shares an apartment in Williamsburg." Dunne makes his debut in November 2014. (www.newyorkpressgang.org)

◆